Land Without Laughter

THE AUTHOR, WHOSHER AKHUN, AND ABDUL AKHUN

LAND

WITHOUT

LAUGHTER

By

AHMAD KAMAL

AUTHOR OF
The Seven Questions of Timur

toExcel
San Jose New York Lincoln Shanghai

Land Without Laughter

Published by toExcel
an imprint of iUniverse.com, Inc.

For information address:
iUniverse.com, Inc.
620 North 48th Street
Suite 201
Lincoln, NE 68504-3467
www.iuniverse.com

ISBN: 0-595-01005-9

Printed in the United States of America

To

MY MOTHER

Who by her unflagging confidence
inspired this work

And to

NURBEBE JAN

Where she walked there was light
And in her touch was proof of her perfection,
for she was also mortal

Book One

"My religion," said Lao Tze, "is to think the unthinkable thought, to speak the ineffable word, to do the impossible deed and to walk the impassable way."

1

CAREFULLY, or carelessly, filed away in the archives of the Soviet Military Intelligence is the original of what this book started out to be. Should a Soviet official read this and desire to investigate further, let him look in the index of incompleted cases. There, under the name of Ahmad Kamal—American—charged with espionage, sabotage, and conspiracy against the Soviet, will be found all that pertains to a misadventure.

There, classified, will be voluminous scientific reports on the customs and culture of Central Asiatic peoples, including several hundred photographs of interesting anthropological types, also reams of somatological and philological data.

Concerning myself?

"Physical description of prisoner: Age 24. Height 5 feet, 11 inches. Weight 163. Head shaven, beard red-blond. Eyes gray-green. Scars on left cheek, right forearm, base of skull and center of forehead.

"Details: Speaks the Uighur (Tatar) tongue too dangerously well to be disinterested in Central Asiatic politics. Entered Turkistan via India, Tibet and the Himalayan Karakoram. Arrested at Aksu: Sov-kiang (Chinese-Soviet Turkistan). His companions: Nesserdin Hadji, Kichik Akhun, Muhammad Imin Ibn Azizoff, and Hashim Akhun executed while held with American in Urumchi prison.

"Released for lack of evidence and because of external pressure, the prisoner was taken to Kumul for deportation. Order for re-arrest issued on discovery of his having served as an officer with the rebel Tungan army. Eluding Sart Commandant of Public Safety Bureau, the American fled into Mongolia and Gobi before mistake discovered and rectified.

"Standing order for the apprehension of this enemy of the Soviet."

What this report leaves untold is that the American prisoner was turned out of prison weighing forty-three pounds less than when arrested. Too, that he was released minus all possessions —with the exception of two blanket-filled saddlebags, a teapot, a wooden eating bowl, less than one hundred and twenty-five Chinese dollars, a gangrenous right arm, and dysentery.

However, I feel that there is a definite plot to all things. In losing, I gained. Doubtless a far more capable Soviet scientist will measure Tatar heads and compare their verbs. My academic dissertations will be eclipsed by his more able works. And, having lost my files, I shall be unable to contest a word he publishes. Nevertheless, I begrudge him not an iota of success—even hope my papers assist him in the winning of laurels.

Let me explain: seating myself before the desk on which the ensuing chapters were written, I put from my mind any attempt to recollect lost technical data. Instead of Tatar skull measurements, I have endeavored to preserve for all peoples, and time, their souls.

The manner in which the journey to Tataristan was brought about—minus its chaotic sequence of events—bears out my contention that all things are with purpose. The venture's immediate groundwork was laid when as a little chap I was too sickly to attend public school, instead travelling about the southwestern part of America. My mother and I—Father having died during my infancy—went from Indian reservation to Indian reservation while she wrote a history of each: Yaqui on the Mexican border, to Sioux in North Dakota.

4

LAND WITHOUT LAUGHTER

Time came when it was decided that I must have a tutor. The first of these was Lothar von Richter, the distinguished, disinherited son of a Prussian nobleman. He had heard of my mother's search for an appropriate mentor and one day in Houston, Texas, a lean sharp-jawed Heidelberg-graduate cowboy presented himself: Lothar von Richter.

Being of such ancestry he was expected to teach me German; he didn't. When, after several years, he went away--last heard from he was in the New Hebrides, *recruiting* "blackbirds"—I knew little of subjects included in the curriculum of sane educational institutions. I was, however, in possession of a more or less sound knowledge of military organization, battle tactics, and archaic Turkish. In his youth trained for a military career, Lothar had seen to it that I was likewise educated. A student of archaic Turkish, he had insisted I learn that tongue.

The next of my tutors was Musa Jan, a little gray-eyed man—one-time Fellow of the Imperial Institute for Asiatic Research, Moscow—who left his puttering in Papago and Apache ruins near Tucson, Arizona, to perpetuate my education. The first day of our association was devoted to a résumé of my past training, and I shall never forget the look on his face when he learned of my knowledge of the Turkish tongue. It was his native language, for his birthplace had been Kazan—once seat of the great Muslim Khanate, now a part of Russia. The climax was reached when he learned of my ancestry: which might well be mentioned here.

In the year A.D. 1794 a group of Muslim refugees settled in Pest, across the River Danube from Buda. This is attested by Austrian, Hungarian, and German military records of that date. These files tersely mention the arrival of one merchant family, minor chieftains of the Black Sheep clan, from Bokhara, Turkistan. But why had they departed from their homeland? The answer is to be found in old Russian military records. A clique of Muslims had banded together to re-establish, by force, the crumbled Khanate of Kazan! The Imperial Russian forces moved before those of the revolutionaries. The cause was lost ere the first mile was won. So came my great-great-grandparent to Buda-Pest! His children's children were to emigrate to America in 1874, eighty years later.

With such a heritage, and never for an instant was I permitted to forget it, was I brought up; and the traditions, too, were perpetuated. A Muslim by precedent and choice, being formally accepted into the faith by Mir Waiz Muhammad Yusuf of Kashmir, North India, I came to know a great deal of Islamic countries—their peoples and histories.

It must, however, be admitted that under Musa Jan's tutelage I did acquire a more general education than had been possible with the previous Lothar von Richter. But, in comparison, all else was eclipsed by the Asiatic lore which was drilled into me. I was taught the meanings and practices of ethnology, anthropology, and somatology. I doubt that there ever breathed a man more completely devoted to scientific ancestor worship than old Musa.

Time emancipated me from these tutors. Relieved of such domination, suddenly I realized—not without some dismay—that the studies I had so long been compelled to withstand had become a part of me. No race, no subject, could I approach without comparing it with the Muslim Tatars. I had become a specialist, one of these men of whom some one aptly said: "They know more and more of less and less, until they know positively everything about nothing!" Then, in the year 1935 —unexpectedly having come into sufficient funds, and wholly recovered from my childhood frailty—I planned a pilgrimage to the land of my forefathers. There are many shrines at which mortals are prone to worship. Many of these are dedicated to the faiths of men, others to the arts of men, but all are in truth more consecrated to the past than to intrinsic values or holiness. I know not why we gather before ancient things and not the new. Perhaps it is because the old have proven themselves and because the new, like ourselves, have not. I know only this, there is a shrine on a mountain peak in Ceylon. There, impressed in the rock, is the alleged footprint of Adam. On coming away from this place of pilgrimage one has a great belief in the ultimate destiny of man. If thousands of years have failed to erase a thoughtless footmark in the earth, may not immortality be conceivable? Whatever the scheme, it is the ancient things, the crypts of saints, the fine steel blade which once hung at the belt of a Mongol prince and now reposes upon my desk, beside it the illuminated Arabic lexicon—for which manuscript Tamerlane five and one half centuries ago bestowed 5000 ducats upon the author—these are the things that give me pride in my very existence. Having knelt at the throne of antiquity, I find the future inconstant and vulnerable. Am I not of the same substance and manufacture as those who have made glorious the past? But, irrespective of this present vanity and conceit, constant obedience to yesterday led me to purchase passage to India, first port of call en route to Turkistan.

Sailing from San Pedro harbor, California, on board the Japanese liner *Taiyo Maru*, I trans-shipped at Hong Kong, China. There I took the coal-burning freighter *Ginyo Maru*, and set forth on the last sea-lap to India.

Now, returned to America, *I am he who realized his dream and was not disillusioned.* However terrible were some of the months I spent in Tatary, I lived them all. Every moment of the day and night—I *lived.* I found a land wherein reason and method were relinquished, wherein everything was vivid: thought, action, joy, anguish, death, and agony. And the last was so wholly alive that it became an entity in itself, a living thing, to be respected and at times enjoyed in preference to colorless neutrality.

7

LAND WITHOUT LAUGHTER

A violin's music, if maintaining a certain pitch, can shatter a crystal goblet. Inaudible and transparent, this musical pitch has in its trilling self the capacity to excite sympathetic response the instant it finds any object's fatigue-frequency. Turkistan has found my fatigue-frequency; Kuen, Kadir, Ali, Syim, Nurbebe, Ma Hsi Jung, Ughlug Beg, Song Soldier—all have become fiddlers. And all play a melody that forever haunts my memory. I am returning to their Tataristan; *Inshullah*, to be once more with them. . . .

You will find that many of my acquaintances speak with surprising fluency. Illiterate, dark, these sons of Tamerlane pride themselves on a perspicuous speech. One of my Tatar friends defended his people's illiteracy, saying:

"Why should men be literate? Educate a man and you confine him, for his knowledge is another's, and vainly will he long for greater wisdom. And confinement, to the great mind, is sorrow; to the mediocre, vexation; to the dark, fury.

"The margined page is a trail bound on both sides by un-scalable heights. And at its end is what? Nothing more than the repetition of another's thoughts."

Let not such wisdom prevent your reading of the *Land Without Laughter*. Herein you will find no narrow doctrine, but a man realizing his lifelong dream, and the tale of a people you should know—for they are of the blood of your fathers.

2

Pitch bubbling from every seam, the dirty little *Ginyo Maru* phlegmatically propelled her rust-streaked bulk through the Arabian Sea. Tropic, consequently too intense, the superabundance of color rimmed the eyes with red.

The sea was leaden and lifeless, except for the horizon; there rhinestone waves told of a vagrant breeze. Off the starboard quarter, where drifted the greasy black smoke from the *Maru's* stacks, lay the riotous green of the Indian coast, shimmering in the heat. Above, the arching electric-blue incandescence of the equatorial sky and an overzealous sun withered all beneath them.

Dozing, shirtless, his unbuttoned trousers revealing a two-quart navel and a belly that gave his soul plenty of room, the Japanese captain lay flat on his back under a listless and sooty canopy.

First class had retired to its respective cabins to doze stickily until tea-time. Endowed with God-given vigor and perennial youth, an ancient missionary maiden argued a game of shuffleboard with her apathetic and wilting protégé. Lounging in the baggage-cluttered companionway (Bombay in the morning), two Japanese stewards played a disinterested game of Go-Mo-Ku. From time to time a choleric English army officer fulminated against the bar-boy because of the heat, threatening to make that unfortunate one drink all of his "bloody tepid beer!"

Revelling in the heat of their homeland, the deck pas-

sengers lay on top of the gray hatch covers. A couple of huge
Sikhs, well on their way towards drunkenness, sprawled in an
open doorway. Amused at the inconvenience they caused the
little Japanese seamen, they roared with laughter. Mad—a
little Afridi hunched over a white-hot charcoal brazier. None
spoke to him—nor he to them; forty years in China had taken
his native tongue as well as his mind.

Not content with lying in my bunk, not wanting to be converted by the ever-crusading missionaries, I spent most of my
time in the bow with the natives. Forty-three days out of San
Francisco, one day from Bombay, I went once again to the
bow, having found the most interesting of my shipboard acquaintances were in third, not first, class. Perhaps because he
spoke the best, and most amusing, English of all the Indians,
Wali Ahmad Khan was my closest companion. Ours was a
natural brotherhood; he knew the Himalayas—I wanted to
know them.

The ex-colonial officer came out from the bar, impatient at
the boat's sluggish progress; angry at the world in general
and looking with jaundiced eye at me in particular.

"God damn," he ejaculated. "Fool Yankee! Fraternizing
with these stinking natives." Still louder, anxious that I should
hear, he repeated himself. I ignored him. Thwarted, he vented
his spleen on the bar-boy. "Hey, there—you—you—you little
bastard, bring me some of that hot bilge you call beer." Pursuing the little Japanese, he left us in peace.

While the aged engines shivered the deck beneath us, Wali
Ahmad Khan and I lay prone under an ovenlike canopy. Heads
overhanging the bow, we watched the sea-snakes and sharks
that, according to their respective natures, darted away or lazily
dodged the turbulent water about the prow. At intervals shaken
by a hacking cough, my companion cautioned as to how I
would best succeed in taking a caravan to Tibet, then to Turkis-

tan. Wali's words were an amusing, if weird, selection of vulgar barrack jargon interspersed with classic afterthought.

"Ah, Sahib," he began, "if only I were as strong as I once was I would go with you. First to Kashmir, then Tibet, then Tataristan, Mongolistan, then out to China. Aiii, Ullah! I should like to go!

"But I must spend the last days of my lungs at the home of my family." For a moment he fell silent. "However, I can tell you how to succeed."

A third came up on the forepeak to join us and, like us, fixed his eyes on the water.

"Pretty soon I get home—get plenty girls—pretty damn fine nice." The newcomer continued, first cocking his turban to one side, "I pretty big damn fool—I married." Abruptly he turned to me, questioning:

"You married, Sahib—huh?"

I replied in the negative.

"No—huh? You pretty wise fella, Sahib. You pretty good head." Still gazing down into the water he revealed: "I am got wife since I am fifteen. By Ullah and by Ullah, it is a terrible thing this wife; she make hell—sure thing—when I catch other woman—damn! When I am young fella, I no got head."

Abruptly the speaker broke into his native Hindustani. I asked Wali Ahmad Khan to translate.

"He recites a poem of his people, of a man who have got big aim in his life," Wali explained. "This fella got a big mountain he want to climb. He go up and up. Pretty soon comes down raining—all same rivers dump out of sky. This fella come by nice shelter and some one inside him say, 'Stop! We go on tomorrow. Tonight we get hot and dry,' but this fella say to the man inside of him, 'No! I must go on. I got to get my aim.' So he climb on. Pretty soon it snow. Golly, it snow deep, and cold. The fella what got the aim find it too damn tough climb, by this mountain. Pretty soon it snow some more and then, all like the sudden, this fella comes by another house and in this house burns a bright fire. A beautiful woman stands by the door, all naked, and calls to this fella in the storm: 'Come in—stay the night with me. Share my hot bed, my body, tomorrow you climb mountain.' 'No!' this hero fella say, and he go up the mountain."

He who had been reciting paused a moment to comment, "Pretty damn big fool that fella—eh!

"After many hardships he reaches top side this place—the peak. He is conquer himself and the mountain. This hero, he die there; he fall off slab of snow; but he die happy because he is conquer his life."

The narrator picked himself up. "I no conquer myself and climb the mountain of my destiny like hero fella," he confessed. "I find naked woman and I stop long time, catch maybe two—three little baby. What use my be hero? Die some day anyhow."

Our entertainer gone, Wali Ahmad Khan turned to me.

"That man in story not too smart. Smart fella stop one night, eat lots, have woman, and go on next day. When you go to Tataristan you will be the same as that man with his aim—only you listen now to me, and I will tell you how best you make your aim.

"You take bride—Tatar bride. She will teach you the custom of her people and teach you all that you do not already know of her language. She will be what the *Englis* army men call 'sleeping dictionary.'"

I laughed aloud.

"No-o-o—not funny," Wali admonished. "Without a wife you will have trouble—too much. After you get aim, then you can dispose of wife."

LAND WITHOUT LAUGHTER

Pausing a moment at my pretense of horror, Wali Ahmad Khan hastily reassured me:

"Yah, Ullah! I do'n' mean kill; I mean you run away from her. You already know her people's custom, her bed no longer make you silly with thrill; what more you want with woman? That fella in story—if he had live with mountain woman a little time he get his aim much easier. A man can pick up a big load, but with a long stick, a lever, he can pick up *too* big a load. No?"

"Yes," I agreed.

"You will know how Tatar women love, how they cook, how they live. Mebbe you know best how they love—No?"

Again I agreed, mildly amused.

"Enough, then you easy get your aim. You think one day that it is time you go on up the mountain of your desires to get your aim, then you say to your wife—first giving her for two weeks mebbe *too* much love—'Ah, my wife, I must do for you something. Aha—aha—this for you I will do, I will give you money!'

"Not too much money," Wali cautioned, then continued.

" 'With that money you will, my wife, go visit your papa and mamma. You will be much too happy and I shall be glad for you.' Then you say, 'When I call for you, my wife, you must hurry home to me.' "

Slyly winking at me, Wali Ahmad Khan elaborated:

"You will bury her suspicions by saying, 'I, my wife, cannot be too long without you at my side, to share my bed, to conceive my children.'

"Then she will say inside of her," the worldly Wali explained, "she will say inside of her, 'He is a good man. He loves me too much. I will go visit my people, but return to him with too much haste; I will try and fill my womb with a son for him.' That is what she will say!" swore my adviser.

"Then you wait till she go one way to the home of her mamma and papa—then you go other way, to your aim, much too fast; like hell, so fast."

"Like hell!" I affirmed.

The next morning we docked in Bombay. My last glimpse of Wali Ahmad Khan was as he descended the gangplank. Bedecked in his policeman's uniform and a brand new turban, his sundry belongings in a sack over his shoulder, he passed out of my orbit.

3

My introduction to Bombay was portentous. A deluge of coolies in exaggerated diapers attacked my luggage so savagely I had literally to beat them off. While I was buying rupees from a hawking money merchant, a little untouchable dashed away with two of my suitcases. Catching him, I turned to find the money changer had absconded with all funds. By the time I had located the rascal, who professed not to know me, another made off with my bags. It was evening when at last I passed through the customs.

After Bombay came Agra, Delhi, Lahore, Peshawar, Rawal Pindi, and at last the Switzerland of Asia—Kashmir. The previous months' equatorial temperatures were forgotten; it was December, in Kashmir.

Above and about the winter-whitened city of Srinagar towered the bleak Himalayas; my journey had begun. To the north and east lay the mountain-lost village of Leh-Ladakh, Western Tibet; the last outpost of man on the southern slope of the Himalayas. It was my immediate objective. Still farther to the north, beyond the Himalayan heights, lay Turkistan—the land of the Tatar peoples.

Permission to journey onward proved more difficult to obtain than I had anticipated. The British Raj did not encourage foreign penetration into Ladakh, and absolutely forbade any one crossing into Turkistan. First there was the British Resident in Kashmir to convince; he did not encourage the venture nor, apparently, seem entirely convinced of my harmlessness. My proposed journey was, according to him, impossible, dangerous, fatal, and suicidal. The passes, he said, defied all who attempted to cross them in the winter-time. Ice-sheathed, swept by winter gales of hurricane velocity, they were supposedly impossible to cross.

The city of Srinagar, built on the banks of the Jhelum River, has canals for streets and consequently has need for many bridges. From a boat, as we passed under one of these multitudinous spans, I saw for the first time the strange people from beyond the Himalayas, Central Asians, Tibetans, Turki-Tatars, Mongols. All were clad in furs.

The Tatars most interested me. All wore heavy coats of a skirl-skirted Cossack cut, lined with red fox and with sleeves so long as to hang four inches and more beyond the tips of their fingers. Fox and Astrakhan caps were cocked jauntily on the sides of their heads; legs were shapeless under a mass of felt wrappings, feet encased in moccasins. Once we paused beneath a bridge that was literally jammed with Tatars. They hung over the hand-rails and watched all that passed with interested, twinkling eyes. I asked one of my boatmen what these men did besides stare.

"Nothing, Sahib," he replied. "They stay here and stare at every one until the snow on the high passes melts. Then they return to their country to get more gold, and furs, and rugs, and then come back to stare some more—they are very strange men from strange country!"

The Khan Sahib—attaché to the Resident's office—a stalwart and white-bearded Afghan, was in charge of all Ladakhi and Tibetan affairs. He accepted my application for a northward journey. Warning that it was very hazardous, and futilely attempting to discourage me, he argued:

LAND WITHOUT LAUGHTER

"You do not know what the Himalayas are in midwinter; even the Turki people stay here until spring. It is too cold now, and you," he assured me, "will find yourself dead if you, who know nothing of the mountains, try to cross into Ladakh!"

I laid plans for an immediate departure.

I purchased all manner of equipment for the proposed journey, most of which I was to throw away before I had travelled two hundred miles. Showing the list of purchased paraphernalia to the Khan Sahib, I insisted that he personally recommend the feasibility of the venture to the British Resident. The Khan Sahib bargained. I was requested to go to the Sapaka-Dal *serai* (compound and stables, the Central Asiatic version of a "hotel") where stayed the Turkis from beyond the passes. There I was to speak with those men most recently come down from Ladakh. And if I could then return to him still wishing to go, he would do as I asked.

The *serai* was found close by and the Muhammadin in charge sent for such a man as I sought. Eventually a furred counterpart of those who hung over the bridge rails came before me; he listened quietly to my questions and then answered with one word: "*Kismet.*" (That which has been, what is, and that which is to be—is written.)

To my query, "Is there any real danger on the passes?" he replied: "Only God knows; for one man, there is nothing to fear, for another—" A shrug of the shoulders completed the interview.

When I returned, the Khan Sahib listened attentively and seemed satisfied with the Tatar's philosophy.

Morning of the following day brought an invitation to the Resident's home for a discussion of the particulars, during which time we spoke of God, the price of gasoline in the States, dogs, the stock market, automobiles, and the condition of Ger-

17

man highways. At last we parted; my application having received no mention.

The second day the Khan Sahib sent one of his chaprasis to my residence with a chit:

"My dear Ahmad Kamal; the credentials necessary to your journey are at my office and awaiting your disposition."

I rushed over, determined to get possession of the papers before some one changed his mind.

In snowbound Sonemarg, four days out of Srinagar, I cooked my Christmas dinner. The chimney of the little *serai* room, clogged with ice, refused to draw. Groping my way about the smoke-filled room, I cursed the fact that none in Srinagar had been willing to accompany me as servant. All had asked the same question, "Do you intend to cross the Zoji La?" and when I answered in the affirmative all had backed down. Ten times their accustomed salary would not induce them to come. The Zoji La—a mountain pass—was, according to them and the rest of Kashmir, the worst pass in all Asia; I was destined to learn the truth of their convictions.

My Christmas Feast consisted of pebbly, unwashed, gummy rice. The tea was unaccountably seasoned with onions. I ate from the cooking pots, sitting cross-legged on top of the lone table to escape the floor-cold (my thermometer read seven degrees below zero—in the room). That was a memorable Christmas night. After the repast, while I speculated as to whether or not the blackened and crusted pots were worth salvaging, the voices of strangers intruded upon the winter silence.

Opening the door, I saw a band of furred Turki men come in through the deep snow about the *serai* gates. Two of them slid from their horses and approached.

"Art thou *Englis*?" One spoke from behind an icicle-festooned beard.

LAND WITHOUT LAUGHTER

India had prepared me for direct questioning and I assured him that I was not *"Englis."*

"Art thou a Mussulman?" he further queried.

That was affirmed, but the Turki demanded proof.

"Testify."

"La illaha il Ullah Muhammad rasool Ullah!" (God is God and one, and Muhammad is his Prophet.) Satisfied, the bearded one greeted me as one of his kind:

"A-Salaam Ali Qum." (Peace abide with thee.)

"Wali Qum A-Salaam." (And with thee may peace abide.)

We were one. The whole group, by this time having taken the packs from their mounts, salaamed and at my invitation shared the smoky warmth of my hearth, shedding layers of furs.

The eldest, who spoke *Englis,* was a grizzled old fellow with all-compassing eyes. To his right crouched another, a Mongol type; broad of face, slit-eyed, and boasting a wirelike moustache that hung well below his chin in two thin strands.

As we hunched over the fire he who had first addressed me introduced himself as Abdul Kadir, Effendi. Pausing a moment painfully to pull ice from his beard, he introduced his fire-hugging companion as Muhammad Hadji Palta Hadji.

Their party, he explained, was headed for Mekka on a pilgrimage. They had departed from home, Kashgar, in Sin-kiang (Turkistan), forty-seven days before.

With the thermometer registering thirty-two degrees below zero, the Turkis spent the night in my room, huddled together for warmth. The inconvenience had its reward, for I learned much of what lay before me.

Abdul Kadir examined my equipment and discarded fully two thirds. He laughed when I told him what footgear I intended to wear over the Zoji La. Tossing the heavy hiking boots into the same corner where lay most of my cast-off goods, he pulled off his own moccasins and a pair of heavy felt stockings. Giving them to me he warned against close-fitting footgear; even feet encased in soft felt and light moccasins froze in the cold of the passes. At his sacrifice, and my protest, he scoffed:

"Hah—I no longer have need of them; the cold is before thee, behind me."

Stealing a glance at the thermometer, I wondered just what I was going into.

At dawning, as we both prepared to go our respective ways, Abdul Kadir ventured further advice. Leading me to a window, he pointed to the jagged granite spires towering thousands of feet above.

"Behold!" He pointed out the long streamers of ice particles that ribboned straight out from the peaks. Dyed silver and red by the rising sun, they looked to be great flames searing the sky. The ice-floored valley in which we stood, no more than a great crevasse, still enshrouded in the purple dawn-dark, caught the reflection and seemed on fire; an inferno of ice.

"Beautiful!" I confirmed.

"Beautiful? Does one call the flame that burns one *beautiful?* It will not be 'beautiful' if ever it touches thee. That *is* a flame. Such cold is so intense it chars the flesh. If, when the time comes to cross the Zoji La, the fires of winter burn in the skies, then wait. Only when the snow on the peaks lies quiet, dare thou cross."

At our parting Abdul Kadir took my hand.

"My people have a proverb," he said in farewell. " 'Mountains meet only once, men may meet again.' Ullah willing, we may prove it true."

LAND WITHOUT LAUGHTER

Eighteen days from Srinagar I looked upon the little fortress-bazar of Leh-Ladakh. On the crags above it clung lamaseries and their ruins and still higher soared the huge Tibetan eagle, the raucous-voiced *lamagyre*. A great and ancient castle towered above the city, it in turn dwarfed by the ice-mantled Kardoong Pass that rose more than six thousand feet above the eleven-thousand-foot Leh.

People came from their homes as the stranger limped into the bazar, as strange to him as he to them. Tibetan women wore huge bat-winged head-dresses studded with turquoise and silver. Both men and women were clad in homespun. Turkis, Tatars, Mongols, Tibetans, and Ladkhis lined the street to stare open-mouthed. Among them were red and yellow-skirted Lamas down from their monastic heights. But not even the sight of a *Sahib* from beyond the passes was sufficient to make them whirl their prayer wheels one whit slower or to stop their lips from repeatedly mumbling the sacred formula:

"*Om Mani Padmi Hum.*" (The jewel in the heart of the lotus.)

Combined with the roll of prayers in the rapidly rotating wheel, it might win them Nirvana!

Half blind from the glare of the snowfields, frostbitten in the toes of both feet, lungs on fire from breathing too much cold air, I knew only regrets. Among them, the greatest, that I had ignored Abdul Kadir's warning and crossed the Zoji La when the ice flames blew. There was small solace in the doubtful distinction of being one of the two known occidentals to cross the pass in midwinter.

4

THE VIBRANT moan of the Buddhist Lamasery horns filled the valley; pitched very low they were as much felt as heard, a quivering in the solar plexus.

Snowbound in mid-Himalayan Leh, I had listened to those horns for two frigid months. The one consoling thought was that with the dawn I would begin the trans-Himalayan journey to *Tataristan:* farthermost land from the seas—and from the ken of men. Even now my caravan awaited me fifteen miles farther up the granite-walled valley.

Two sputtering candles contrived, with the faint glow of the hearth fire, to illuminate my tiny dwelling. Tomec Tojilak, my Kulmuk Mongol servant, just returned from the bazar, crouched over the fire. From time to time he was seized with paroxysms of coughing. Blowing on the smoldering embers, he would stir up the ashes of the horse-dung fuel and, inhaling, choke on them.

On the floor, hunched in his furs, sewing a torn saddlebag and apparently immune to the intense cold, sat my newest acquisition in servants, Abdul Akhun. The swarthy little Turki,[1] a native of that country to which I was about to journey, cocked his head to one side, listening. The vast sobbing of the winter gales came down to us from the roof of the world.

"That is a good sign, Effendi," the Turki chuckled. "When the wind so blows everything freezes solid and the rivers become broad highways for a caravan such as ours. Two weeks

[1]See Glossary: Races of Turkistan.

22

and, God willing, we shall be on top of the world; the Karakoram."

Tomec listened to the shriek of the winds. A gust blew down the chimney and tossed ashes into his face. He spat disgustedly.

"I have crossed the Karakoram and I know this is not the time to go!" He nodded toward the bundles he had brought from the bazar, the last of the requisites for my coming journey. "There is food that thou shalt have no need for, unless the gods indeed love thee. Thou, instead, wilt be food—for wolves!"

Abdul, pulling the last stitch through the bags he mended, replied in a low monotone intended for my ears only:

"Yah! 'The gods,' he says, the Kaffir (unbeliever). God is God and *One*, not as he says, the Budd, 'ten thousand.'" Frowning at Mongol Tomec's back he railed, "Aiii—Tomec! Thou hast crossed the Himalayas how many times? Once! What knowest thou of them? Nothing!"

The Mongol drew his furs a bit closer and gave a last despairing puff at the embers of the now extinct fire.

"This is the best time of the year," Abdul persisted. "If we were to wait for the spring we should be caught in the avalanches, and the ice on the rivers would break, drowning us in the floods. Now, Ullah willing, we may cross with only the cold to hinder us."

Tomec laughed wryly:

"Only the cold, eh? Frozen feet, frozen hands, horses' hooves breaking off with the cold. Thou dost not think rightly saying '*Only* the cold.'"

Abdul was about to reply when Tomec, determined to prove his superiority, bid the Turki return to his abode, the caravanserai. Seeing that I was of the same mind, Abdul promised an early return and was gone into the night.

LAND WITHOUT LAUGHTER

Before we could secure the door the chill wind found entrance. A stream of ice particles lashed across the threshold. Tomec grimaced as he licked away the snow clinging to his moustache. Lighting first the extinguished candles and then his long Mongol pipe, he dourly remarked,

"Think! There shall be no shelter for thee once thou foreswearest this."

Outside the dry snow crunched and squeaked beneath the weight of Abdul's retreating footsteps.

Late in the night, the saddlebags filled except for one large package that I did not recognize, I asked Tomec what it contained. He replied bashfully,

"My gift to a departing friend."

"And in it, Tomec?" I questioned.

"Thirty pounds of roasted barley flour; *Talkun* the Turkis call it. When Genghis Khan and my ancestors made war, it was this food and nothing more they carried. When thou art hungry, a handful of Talkun and enough liquid to moisten it will sustain thee.

"If one of thy horses is about to die, as many will, take a bowl and, slitting the animal's throat, catch its blood. *Talkun* mixed with blood will give a man the strength of a *djinn!*"

The bags packed, Tomec rekindled the fire and together we drank the tea he brewed. The Mongol told me of his home in Turkistan, and how he had once served a Mongol Governor of Sinkiang, since murdered. He warned that a war, the like of which I had never seen, raged in the land. Countering, I told of the wars of the Occident. He scoffed; as had I. Even as he argued against my going, I tried to win him to my side, promising him wages greater than any he had ever before earned if only he would accompany me. We both failed. He would not come; I would not stay.

LAND WITHOUT LAUGHTER

Before he left for his home on the other side of the valley, Tomec took from its sheath his long Mongol knife.

"Thou art going into a country at war and wilt travel among the Bolsheviki; it is best thou hast something with which to wage a war of thine own." He toyed with the beautiful blade. "This has not the bark of a gun, but its bite is as deadly."

Wrapped in the fur robes of my bed, I sat gazing out the window. A moonlit blanket of snow spread over the world within my vision. The heavy drone of the demon-frightening horns again rolled down from the Lamasery. With the horns' mournful sound came the fine shrill of pipes; Lamas were preparing for a festival in honor of one of their idols—and I was prepared for the trek to begin on the morrow.

Tomec woke me early to hand me a heavy cotton-padded coat and breeches, the garb I was to wear for the next month. In addition to those garments I donned two pairs of felt stockings and the woolen binding that encased them; my feet I bound in curl-toed Himalayan moccasins, the like of which I had laughed at in Kashmir. Tomec looked on with evident distaste; the trip was, to his mind, suicidal.

Abdul—who was to be my man from this point on, in Tomec's stead—thumped on the door and was let in. Through the frosted window could be seen two big Turkistani horses, backs humped against the icy wind. Abdul hurried the saddlebags out and onto the animals.

The roughness with which he handled the two small cases of scientific apparatus gave me qualms as to the future of my precision instruments: skull-measuring calipers, the exquisitely fragile transit, sextant, and artificial horizon. Much expense and worry might have been avoided had I, at the time of their purchase, anticipated the ultimate fate of these delicate toys.

LAND WITHOUT LAUGHTER

Tomec and I followed the little Turki out into the bitter cold. Shivering, Tomec kicked at the frozen snow.

"Thou art going in this, the worst time of the year, as I have told thee a thousand times already, and thou dost not fear because thou knowest not what lies ahead."

It was no use; we shook hands and, at Abdul's urging, I turned to the outward trail, Tomec to his home.

I had warned Abdul of my intention to avoid meeting any one before I departed. But ours was a tardy start, and it seemed there were as many in the bazar, to see me off, as had seen me come. A Hindu telegraphist walked beside me for a moment and asked where I was bound.

"North," I replied, and devoutly thanked Him who had sent avalanches to down all the wires on the Zoji La. The local authorities could not get in touch with the British Resident in Kashmir until I had passed over the Chang La, the 18,000-foot pass that lay five days' journey from Leh. The British absolutely forbade any one crossing from Leh into Turkistan. Should the Resident learn of my departure, a detachment of Gurkha soldiery would be sent to bring me back.

A few Turkis salaamed as we passed through the city gates. For the most part the bazar's inhabitants were too surprised to do other than stare.

As we rode up to the caravan camp that Tomec had established a month before, Abdul ran ahead to quirt several energetic animals. Threshing about on the ground, they were trying to roll out from under their packs. The caravan was ready to travel.

We rode into a milling mass of horses, forty-four animals, of which only twenty-nine were destined to survive the rigors of what lay ahead. Each was an individualist, from the high-headed sorrel stallion that, because of his great size, immediately took my eye, to the mean little mule that caught my attention as I dismounted. Setting her teeth into the shoulder of my coat, she lifted out a piece of cloth the size of my hand. That time I fared lucky. She was later to make me painfully aware of her presence, innumerable times, while she kicked, bit and squealed her way across the Himalayas. That little devil who all but crippled three men, myself included, crossed the mountains and down to the fertile blossoming valley of her Turkistan without a saddle-sore, a fall, or a human friend.

The day over, I was for the first time able to size up my outfit. The animals' packs were piled into three substantial but far from windproof walls, a sheet of homespun stuff stretched over all. We sat within the shelter and in a circle about the big black pot. From beneath its cover rumbled forth delicious promises of the meal to come.

My men were all handsome in a swashbuckling sort of way. To the last man they boasted profiles that would have been the pride of aristocrats. These were the Mughals of Indian history. I had expected to find at least one or two who measured up to the poet Yamin-ud-din Muhammad Hasan's (A.D. 1325) description of the Mughal:

"*Their eyes were so narrow and piercing that they might have bored a hole in a brazen vessel. Their stench was more horrible than their color. Their heads were set on their bodies as if they were without necks. Their jowls were like unto leather: full of wrinkles and knots. Their noses extended from cheek-bone to cheek-bone and their mouths from cheek to cheek. Their nostrils resembled rotten graves, and from them the hairs descended as far as the lips. Their moustaches were of extravagant length, but the beards about their chins were very scanty. Their breasts, in hue half black, half white, were*

*covered with lice which looked like sesame growing on bad
soil. Their whole bodies, indeed, were covered with these insects, and their skins were as rough grained as shagreen leather,
fit only to be converted into shoes. They devoured dogs and
pigs with their nasty teeth. Their origin is derived from dogs,
but they have larger bones. The king marvelled at their beastly
countenances and said that God had created them out of hell
fire."*[1]

The only way in which my men approximated the above
description was in the length of their moustaches. Yamin-ud-din
Muhammad Hasan was, I fear, a bit biased.

Kuen Akhun, caravan *bashi* (head), a son of the Turkoman
chieftain, Ughlug Beg, of whom more will be said anon, sat
beside me. Tea sipping, he belied the Kuen I had seen a while
before when the shelter was being erected. One of the men had
angered him and his now heavy-lidded eyes had flashed quite
as if they might bore holes in brass; the miscreant had suffered
a thorough quirting.

Then came Kadir Akhun, whose tremendous winglike moustache held hirsute supremacy over all the caravan men. Though
forever grumbling, he was, I later learned, after Kuen, my most
valuable man; nothing could daunt him. Throughout the
journey he was to spend every evening, as now, so close to the
fire that he was forced eternally to be on the watch for sparks.
His clothes were charred in a hundred places, proof of the
futility of his careful watching.

As he sat there in the smoke, the lint of his clothing going
up in sparks made quite a novel lighting effect. He cursed the
smoke while tears rolled over the bridge of his aquiline nose to
its hooked point. There they hung an instant, scintillating in the
firelight, then on to lose themselves in the jungle of hair that
adorned his upper lip. Between oaths, he would lick them out

[1]Translator unknown.

of his moustache to spit in the fire and, not infrequently, into whatever cooked upon it.

The others: Tokhta Akhun, another son of Ughlug Beg, but by a different wife; Muhammad Akhun, still another son, by still another wife of the Turkoman chief; Imin Akhun, Ali Muhammad Khan, Rose Akhun, Abdul Akhun, Whosher Akhun, Zenib and Ogre Akhun, a conglomerate of countenances and characters of which I already knew considerable from the talkative Abdul. They were, according to *angel* Abdul, a pack of rascals.

Of Tokhta Akhun, Abdul told this story:

"Understand me, Effendi," the wiry little Abdul had begun, with deprecating tone, "I do not say that I am the best of all these men—I leave that for thee to decide.

"Now this Tokhta—dost thou suppose he is a caravan man far from his native home.—No!" Abdul earnestly assured me, "He is a very terrible man. He was a very great thief in our home land. It is like this:

"All habitations in Tataristan are constructed of earth. Hamlet and home alike, no matter how humble, are surrounded by high walls. In time of war these walls make admirable barricades; pierced, they become perfect battlements. In every Tatar army there are a few men that do nothing but pierce walls—loopholes for riflemen. In time they become uncommonly adept at the practice. Proof of this is the fact that a veteran, such as Tokhta, can drive twenty holes through a three-quezz[1]-thick wall in one hour. Oh, but Tokhta is a very terrible man," Abdul again assured me.

"Disbanded soldiers, such as he was, are conspicuously poor citizens. Not suited to peacetime pursuits, the morally weak—such as Tokhta—often turn their doubtful talent to lucrative, if unlawful, advantage. Often wealthy merchants woke in the

[1]Approximately three feet.

29

morning to find their homes rifled of all movable, salable belongings. A neat hole in the wall, large enough for a man to crawl through, was the only clue as to that rascal's entrance and exit. Usually it was Tokhta's work. Is he not a terrible person, Effendi?"

I urged Abdul to continue with his tale. Tch-tching at the impression he supposed he was making, the little scoundrel rambled on.

"This terrible fellow also considers himself superior to the rest of us. In Tataristan he harangued the people in the bazar with his revolutionary thoughts, and every day he was forced to flee the soldiers sent to fetch his head. Nights, necessarily, were spent procuring a livelihood—a thieving livelihood."

"What is it this 'Tokhta' desires of the world?" I questioned.

"Did I not say he was a very vicious person?" Abdul replied. "He has fought and pierced walls in three wars, and never did it matter what the war was about just so that he fought against an existing government."

Tokhta was a radical. I assumed that his were interests sympathetic with the Bolsheviki, but Abdul dispelled those thoughts.

"Twice he fought against the Russ, and once he was the unforgivable"; Abdul shook his head dolefully. "He was a bandit! Terrible . . . unforgivable . . . Tokhta."

Peering across the smoke-filled shelter, I discerned him of whom Abdul had spoken. The firelight playing on his sullen face revealed Tokhta to be without a nose: syphilis. A black inverted-v-hole replacing his vanished nose and nostrils, the man carried a remarkable likeness to the popular conception of a ghoul. Possibly the disease had also eaten away other more indispensable portions of his anatomy. Reason enough for his eccentricities.

30

LAND WITHOUT LAUGHTER

"That bad fellow has no other place to go. Every city in Turkistan has a price on his head—a great price." Once more under way, the irrepressible Abdul continued: "All of these men except Kuen, Kadir, half-mad Zenib, and myself, have prices on their heads. See Imin there."

A tall gray-eyed man with diamond-cut features poked among the glowing coals; finding one to his liking he picked it up with nimble fingers, pressing it to the bowl of his pipe. Inhaling deeply of the aromatic tobacco smoke, he squatted back on his hunkers, hungrily contemplating the simmering evening meal. Abdul rambled on.

"He is wanted by the *Englis;* five thousand rupees do they offer for his head. Ten thousand for the head of his uncle, the Wazir of Alingar. Together they have killed many hundreds of *Englis* on the Northwestern Frontier of the Hindustan.

"Muhammad, that one sleeping among the felts," Abdul pointed him out, "is wanted in Sibir. Once he served with the Bolsheviki army; now that army would like to catch him. Muhammad's commandant one day got drunk and beat him. Muhammad did not like this so he cut the Russ's throat, s-s-kh-h-h!" Abdul drew a dirty finger across his throat.

"When the soldiers learned of what Muhammad had done they came to arrest him, so he killed them—six of them—and ran away. He went first to Urga in Mongolistan and again he proved what a wicked fellow he was by sleeping with the Russ commandant's wife—and killing the commandant when he caught them together. Today this bad man must hide in the mountains.

"Rose Akhun—the one-eyed one—" Abdul pointed to where the man crouched in the shadows. "He is of a Tatar father and a Pathan mother. The *Englisi* want him too; for castrating a soldier that smiled at his—Rose Akhun's—wife.

"Ali Muhammad Khan—he is very bad. His blood is as bad

as his temper and that—Oh-h!" In mock horror Abdul threw both hands in the air. "He has been a soldier since the day he leaped from the womb! Not even he can remember how many armies he has served with. A murderer he is—an eater of babies, a drinker of life's blood—a wicked fellow that has sword-steel for a heart. The bastard son of a Kabli prostitute, and how many fathers—his mother knew not."

Looking at Muhammad I saw not an ugly behemoth but a midgetlike fellow. Not more than five feet tall, though very heavily built, the "bad" man was conceitedly preening his moustache before a round pocket-mirror. Plucking, patting, the little warrior-peacock twisted the heavy growth with unconcealed approbation.

"Whosher," Abdul explained, "is the cook. It is not that he was born a cook, it is just that he is too lazy to be otherwise." In a stage whisper I was warned, "Always be on the watch for evil when he is about; only Ullah knows how many men he has poisoned!"

A pleasant prospect! However, Whosher was to come no nearer poisoning me than by suggestion. He was given to carrying the remnants of past meals under his fingernails. Whenever he baked his own brand of indigestible bread, after kneading the dough those nails of his would become clean.

Then there was Zenib Akhun. The youngest, feeble-minded and hard-working, he was probably the strongest, though the most abused, of all.

Ogre Akhun was the caravan kleptomaniac. It was he whom I had seen Kuen beating. His name, *Ogre*, meant *bandit* in Turki. His was an unhappy lot; no matter what was missing the caravan men would go to his bags and find it, and, of course, beat him. Should he be innocent, a beating was given him anyway.

I was, in the course of the ensuing journey, to learn about

a race, a nation: the Tatar! And a summation of their souls might read thus:

Preposterously chivalrous; loyal, intense, but divorced from sincerity or insincerity. Subtle to the extreme of rank intrigue. At once sly, and indiscreet. Impulsive, emotional, unsympathetic, turbulent; intimate with piety, capable of barbarity. They were to be conspicuous for their lack of toleration; and for a prodigious memory for suffered injustices and no recollection of transgressions against others. Ardent. A nation of virgins who walk alone in the night: Tatar. In short: not so very different from you and me.

5

A THREE days' march up the ice-floored valley saw our caravan camped in the little Buddhist village of Tagar at the foot of the Chang La. Kuen bargained with the "Budd" people for hay, grain, sheep, and even wood, for from Tagar on there would be very little fuel. Kuen had his own efficient system of purchasing. First, he would get all the "Budds" so drunk on *chung*, a sort of Tibetan beer, they would sell anything, even their wives and daughters; which was hardly ever necessary. My men merely pursued any of the opposite sex above ten years of age that they caught abroad after dark; seized, roped, and raped.

"These women are only 'Budds,' worshippers of a thousand gods. Are they not deserving of a raping?"

Kuen approved the men's actions.

"See how these women go about with their faces uncovered, the *kaffirs!* What else can they expect! And," laughing, he added, "they don't run very fast!"

Two days in Tagar fitted us for the journey that lay ahead. The horses were loaded, half the animals carrying sacks of provisions for the others that bore freight.

It was at cold-gray dawn that we began the ascent of the Chang La, the trail no more than a corrugated writhing ribbon over the snow and so narrow that the men and beasts dared not step off it, struggling upward one behind the other.

At 12,000 feet we crossed a glacier, a huge blue-green ser-

34

pent, which writhed in a gorge as though held an unwilling captive by the granite walls. At 14,000 feet the trail disappeared before a welter of snow and ice and a strong icy wind blew at our backs. Kuen took five or six of the men and went ahead to break a way through the waist-deep snow. The animals were already beginning to feel the altitude.

Another thousand feet and several of the horses began to stagger under their burdens and fall off the broken trail. Plunging madly in the soft snow, they would often lose their packs, which were then carried by the men to a point easier for reloading. In the rarefied atmosphere every one was panting for breath. It was amazing the way the men kept the horses moving. Floundering through the deep snow, they picked up and bore, not only packs but horses as well. Kuen set an example by cutting the tip of one horse's ear and sticking his knife through the septum of another's nose. Either the pain or the letting of blood seemed to straighten the animals out. Many that had, previous to his cutting them, staggered alarmingly, became more sure-footed. The trail was flecked with blood and tiny puddles of it formed at twenty-foot intervals. It seemed that twenty feet was about as far as the horses could go without coming to a heavy halt. There they would rest despite any amount of whipping.

Finally, in the midst of a fierce wind that hurled chunks of ice the size of a fist as though they were marbles, we attained the summit. Beneath, all was obscured by the wind-driven snow, but about us in the glaring sunlight towered the Himalayas. Shining upon the thicker driven snow beneath us, the sun turned it into a blinding silver sea, above whose broad expanse we seemed to occupy a different dimension. At 18,000 feet we looked up, as well as down, at a vast waste of winter-blasted granite peaks. It was not beautiful, but on so vast a scale as to dumbfound and depress one. Kuen looked out over the roof of the world.

"There was anger when this place was created!" he voiced my thoughts.

That night we camped in a filthy caravanserai halfway down the pass.

One week on our journey found us at Chong Jangal, in Turki, "Great Jungle." Which does not mean that there was a miasmic swamp, lush with vines and dark from the sun-screening tree growth. A "jungle" is not necessarily a forest—that is an occidental misconception. The word means, literally, a wild place, and anything more fearsomely wild than Chong Jangal would be hard to imagine.

Fourteen times we had forded the twisting Shyok in a single day. The last crossing had been disastrous. The river was high and swift and there had been no way to circumvent it. We had travelled up the river canyon for days and the rock walls, rising sheer, confined us to the boulder-strewn depths.

At the last fording Kuen crossed the rushing river ahead of the caravan, perched high on his horse's back. The water had been shoulder-deep to his mount; satisfied that the place was fordable, the caravan-*bashi* called for the rest to follow. Three of us made it. Then, with all the horses in the stream, one lost footing and was swept into the others by the swift current. Every horse and man, with the exception of us on the bank, was thrust deep into the ice-filled water. The fording became a bedlam of panic-stricken horses and near-drowning men.

We on the bank discarded our coats and plunged into the stream to salvage as much as possible. The shock of immersion in the cold water took our breaths and in an instant our joints were stiffened. One of the men was seized with a cramp in the groin and disappeared beneath the water, a moment later to be fished up by noseless Tokhta. In half an hour all the horses were standing, shivering and ice-coated, on the bank, but the

36

drenching had caused serious harm to the poor beasts. Worst of all, five large bags of grain had been lost.

That night a miserable caravan, horses and men, rested beside the river at the very foot of the world's most formidable mountains. The range looked to be the petrified jaw of a gigantic shark, turned teeth to the sky. Hundreds of feet up the side of a neighboring cliff hung a solid, blue-and-white waterfall, frozen into still motion. An avalanche started down from the heights. First came a hairline of snow and ice trickling over the canyon wall. As it gained in volume a tremendous slab of rock detached itself and roared down to the valley floor, exploding like a bomb, first drenching the canyon with bits of flying rock and then with eerie echoes. The horses were so miserable from the cold, that the avalanche passed unnoticed except for a few shuddering snorts. Normally such a noise would have sent them in forty-four directions.

Two hard marches up the river course we came to where the trail turned through a break in the Shyok's echoing walls. Leaving the comparative smoothness of the river bed we crossed into a maze of rock and ice, each vying with the other in grotesque form and jagged cutting edge. Henceforth the journey would be difficult; just, in truth, as if it had only begun!

Trembling with fatigue, my belly growling with hunger, I at last cast pride aside and sought Kuen out, asking him when we could camp. This took place approximately fourteen hours after the march's start. Taking a piece of bread from the bosom of his shirt, kept next his skin to prevent its freezing, Kuen handed it to me.

"Eat this, Ahmad Kamal, for this night there will be no rest."

He pointed to the water underfoot. About two inches deep,

it flowed over the ice, coming straight towards us from the dark heights ahead. Earlier in the evening—it was now dark—miles behind, the flow had been much shallower and easily avoided. Now, in weariness, and because of its increased volume, we dumbly slogged through it; the chill water freezing over our moccasins, dangling in tinkling pendants from our woolen leggings, and squishing between numbed toes.

"That water will be waist deep before morning!" Kuen warned. His face set grimly. "And after that, who knows? A great wave will course down this canyon to empty in the Shyok. Somewhere ahead of us a glacier has dammed a stream and now the water has gathered behind the ice until it can no longer be held. It will break the dam and come down over this same trail we now tread. I think thou hast strength enough to go on now, eh? We, with the help of God, will not be here when the water comes."

We tramped on and ever upward throughout the moonless night. Often we had to lift fallen horses to their feet, the deepening water having robbed them of an always precarious footing. Again, we assisted them when the trail's steepness became too great.

Despite the night's darkness a strange luminosity exuded from beneath the streaming ice. It was as though the winter lighted the way for an extinguished moon. And when, an apt pupil, a crescent moon at last showed itself, each man paused to stroke his ice-coated beard and voice the traditional: "*Al hamdu Lillah:* Praise unto God." Then, like so many clumsy beasts, we drew our bearded chins down upon our breasts, shrunk deeply into frosted furs, and, tugging the animals along, clumped onward.

Again, within the night's journey, we halted. Once to watch, terror-stricken and mute, as a leaden snowfield detached itself from a dominating slope. Aware of it as much by the thunder in our ears and the unholy trembling under foot, we beheld through the frozen vapor of our breath the avalanche pleat itself into great ridges over the trail ahead.

Then again we halted as Tokhta took the lead, tugging after him the big red stallion; the two disappearing into a glacier crevasse like phantoms drifting through an unbroken wall. The other animals dumbly followed, melting one by one into the icy labyrinth. After them, each looking long at the bleak heavens before vanishing into the ice wall, came the men. Pouring from the cleft into which we entered was half a foot of swift water!

Far below the surface of the ice monster, threading through its sullen crevices, speaking to God when not cursing the splashing animals, we were abruptly hushed by a sudden light. Flooding down through the opening far above, forcing a way through the ancient ice, came an increasing glare and with it a great shriek. Somewhere ahead a man shouted, unintelligibly. The caravan animals plunged madly. Less imaginative, we humans stared upward, waiting. The crystal lips of the opening above, framing a ragged strip of sky and stars, seemed to ignite. Flickering light flamelike leapt over them, snapping from one wall to the other; it crept down to us in the depths and with its coming the sound increased. Its very intensity chipped fragments of ice from the walls and these fell sharp but unfelt upon wide-eyed staring faces. Without warning a fiery star screamed angrily out of nowhere, flashed across the ice-framed ribbon of sky, and, an instant later, burst against a distant mountainside. Then, as halfwit Zenib later said:

"In the new dark silence Ullah heard his name many times repeated with various pious appellations attached."

It was saying things like that that often made me wonder if Zenib were really mad or just too worldly wise to be as the rest of us. But in that awful moment when the dawn darkness

39

came crashing down upon us, we *did* call upon the Unknown. One, invisible in the dark, cried out in an agony of relief; brandishing a drawn knife:

"May Ullah transfix the infidel djinn with that arrow of flame!" And others echoed his words, saying:

"God is great. Verily, he hath transfixed the *kaffir* djinn!"

Then we went on, driving the bewildered horses before us, sometimes quirting the jaded creatures; sometimes hurling after them bits of granite plucked from the moraine rubble which lay in broken layers throughout the glacial caverns. Just before daybreak we came to a fork in the canyon. From one branch poured an ever-increasing stream of ice-filled water. The other was dry.

Safe; we quickly looted our saddlebags for dry felt *pipok* (felt stockings), pulled them on, and resumed our journey.

We soon passed out of the ice jungle and, as a dull sun broke over the mountain heights, came into a dry rock-floored bowl hemmed round by seemingly unbroken cliffs. The three step-brothers, Kuen, Tokhta, and Muhammad (the only three of all the caravan men who knew where they were), led the way. We crossed the bowl and, just as the sun pierced the haze, looked into a dark shadowed gorge. This was to be our exit; by name it was the Kazakh *Ishk*, or Kazakh Door.

With this before us, the night's journey behind, a camp was made and a fire kindled. All of us were so weary that we could not sleep and after feeding the dead-beat animals, sat about the fire. I cannot remember having ever laughed so heartily as that chill morning. We held our sides in pure pleasure as we recollected fears of the night just finished. It was not healthy pleasure that made us outwardly so happy, but a narcotic distilled out of deathly tiredness. It was easily enough dissipated. Imin, who had gone back over the trail to search for a lost teapot and rope, returned with a new and strange face.

LAND WITHOUT LAUGHTER

"The glacier opened, the canyon is full!"
Zenib laughed alone.

Later, I turned to Kuen.
"The worst is behind, eh, Kuen?"
Speaking as much to the others as to myself he replied:
"The worst is not yet within vision; that lies ahead."
"But home, too, lies beyond it." It was Zenib who spoke.
And Kuen clapped him on the cheek in gentle jest.

"Yes, home too. But this night, when cold again unites
mountain and ice—when the avalanches still—then will we go
into the Kazakh *Ishk*. Then, God willing, the morning's sun
will see us nearer home: where you will behold grass and trees,
growing things and women, and sheep on the mountain slopes."

With these words pictured in our minds we gazed again at
the trail behind, before, and at the cold gray walls about. Some
went forward to examine the dark Kazakh Door; some cared
for their animals, then all sought out a secret place to say nearly
forgotten prayers; each man ashamed of this sudden weakness
after many years of deliberate forgetfulness.

Three days farther on our way found us camped at Kizil Yah,
which was a known camping place. (We were once more on
the trade route earlier forsaken at the threat of being engulfed.)
The following day would take us over the Depsang Pass and
on to the 17,000-foot Depsang Plateau. For the moment we
huddled miserably in the frigid Red Canyon 'mid the bones
and carcasses of animals and men that other caravans had sacri-
ficed to the cold. Full five days we had travelled a trail that was
literally paved with the bones of animals fallen on the march.
Some were but chalky reminders of the time when Timur
Padishah (Tamerlane) had come over this same trail to wage
war on the Tibetans. Other animals lay just where they had

fallen, perhaps a month before; their frozen rock-solid carcasses as yet spurned by the wolves.

Men there were, too. *Hadjis* (pilgrims) fallen on their way to Mekka. Others had succumbed in pursuit of their profession, leading caravans over the highest trade route in the world. Two had died at the hand of an assassin. We found them lying in the shadow of a great boulder, heads smashed by blows from a rock which itself, blood-stained and frost-cracked, lay nearby. Both bodies were perfectly preserved; it was as though they slept for an hour instead of forever.

My men were forced to drag a dead horse out of the way to make sufficient clearing amid the dead to pitch the tent. When in half an hour our shelter was blown down we moved our belongings closer to the lee of a big smoke-blackened rock. It had sheltered many caravans since the time when some pioneer of the Himalayas had found this heroic way from Turkistan to Tibet and the Hindustan.

About twenty feet from the tent lay five Hadjis, just where they had died, huddled together for what warmth they could, in their last moments, draw from one another's freezing bodies. Over them we laid an old felt with boulders on top to keep the wolves away. Farther up the red-walled canyon were three others tucked under an overhanging rock ledge. Their fur coats spread over them, rocks piled on the coats' edges, only the feet grotesquely protruding told of what we could not see. Kuen said a prayer over them, and then hurried back to crouch beside me in a snow-filled, wind-sheltered crevice in the canyon wall.

"May our caravan no more than look upon such things throughout the journey which, Ullah protect us, hath only begun."

It was at that freezing camp, the thermometer registering

sixty-four degrees below zero, that Kuen first revealed himself to me. Late in the evening, the others already asleep, Kuen and I lay side by side under a chest-crushing, but warming, weight of felts and furs. Attempts to raise the tent having been futile, such was the force of the wind, we huddled in the lee of our pack barricade. Eyes fixed on the twinkling celestial chandelier, I lay quietly, wondering at the expression I had seen on Kuen's face when we had looked upon the dead in the canyon.

Suddenly, a shooting-star cut a brilliant path across the heavens; looming close in the rarefied air it seemed as though I might have reached out and caught it. The swift intake of Kuen's breath told that he too had seen. Deliberately, softly, as to the night itself, Kuen spoke; his words rich with that resonant poetry characteristic of the remote peoples of the world.

"Glistening slabs of blue-white ice, torn from mountain glaciers by flooding freshets, now lie in brown fields. Farmers go around those boulders of rock-water with the plough, turning the earth that it may thaw more quickly.

"The trumpeting of the mating stallion fills the air. Cows conceive calves; mares—foals.

"Muslim maidens wear the red that bespeaks a virgin, and the transparency of their veils reveals a desire to change their raiment's hue.

"Men bring forth the remainder of last year's melons, cut away the cellar rot, and, seeds in their beards, exclaim at the flavor.

"The camel's wool falls away from his hide in matted, ragged patches.

"It is spring in my home, Ahmad Kamal! It is spring and yet the One who rules my destiny says I must walk the path of eternal winter!"

I had listened to what I thought to be a monologue, but

43

Kuen had been addressing me. As though conscious of my surprise, and abashed by it, he fell silent.

"Tell me, Ahmad Kamal," at last he spoke again, "what is it that afflicts me? Thou art from a country of light. Surely thou must know."

As I made no reply he spoke again, answering himself.

"Not even thou knowest. I feared it! It is a very strange thing, this life. I think and think and yet I can never solve it; never have I found what I look for!"

He paused a moment.

"No man knows what he seeks, Kuen," I counselled. "Many times I have asked myself *why?* To what end?"

"*Thou* hast wondered." Kuen again addressed the black bowl of night. "*Thou* hast thought as I. And has thought made thee as unhappy as it has made me?"

Before I could reply he continued:

"Intelligence and thought are brothers—of one womb, but by different fathers. The intelligent do think, but the thinker is not always intelligent. When a man is as I, the stepson of intelligence, cursed with a measure of intellect and a mountain of thought, he is a strange fellow—to himself. But, if thou, an enlightened one, can'st not solve the mystery that haunts me— and perhaps all men—what can I hope to accomplish with my dark brain?

"Ullah frowned on Adam the day he gave unto him the faculty of thought, of that one thing out of all this world, am I sure. If only He had given us the lone faculty of instinct, and the blessing of stupidity, how much happier we should be. I would not try to solve my destiny, fool that I am, but would be a happy, reasonless creature. Instinct would serve me, however stupid. It is the opposite of all these things—it is knowledge, and its pursuit, that is the curse of man, the evil of all the world. Without knowledge there would be no war, no

44

avarice, no hate, no love; are not all to be detested—and feared?
All will, if fondled, with the flick of a scorpionlike tail, fill the
veins with the venom of sorrow. If only I were like the beasts,
I would not be forever searching for my destiny. I would live,
and beget my kind, and die; and no more."

These words from the mouth of a Tatar caravan-*bashi*, from
one who had never been, and never would be, anything else!
I turned my eyes upon the frost-whitened fold in the furs where
Kuen's head lay. A halo of breath-vapor, freezing and thick-
ening on the fur robes about his face, told of his every breath.
A dense cloud of vapor preceded his next words.

"We—all of us, thou, and I—are fools. Knowest thou why
I lead caravans over this God-forgotten land? Knowest thou
why thou art here? It is because we seek what I think those
dead men up the canyon have found!"

A tower of condensed breath rose in a frosty cloud and was
whipped away by the tearing wind.

"Once—only once in many years—am I able to speak what is
in my heart, and tonight it is so," Kuen again spoke. "I am
smiled upon, for this time I speak to one who can understand
me. Before, I had only the moon with which to speak and he
gives very belated replies."

In the past whenever I spoke of philosophy or religion, the
Tatar had replied:

"Forgive me, Effendi, but I know not of what thou speak-
est. That there is *one God*—that I know; nothing more. I am
a dark man. Mine are a dark people; we cannot read, nor write,
nor comprehend such things."

The man who had so spoken had put into words the eternal
quest of mankind; too profound, too bewildering, for me. Customs and morals, I concluded, might be geographical, but minds
and men, the world over, were one.

45

6

WITH the dawn began a Herculean struggle upward. Forty-one of our original forty-four animals remained. Three we left in Kizil Yah, victims of the cold. It was that omnipresent cold that tortured all of us. Despite our voluminous furs the piercing wind bit to the bone. Noseless Tokhta wrapped a scarf about his head in an effort to keep out some of the cold that poured through the great aperture in his face. I, too, suffered with the toes frostbitten on the Zoji La; once more the flesh had begun to blacken and peel.

As we neared the summit of the Depsang Pass the wind increased in velocity and it seemed we would be swept from the mountainside. Luckily, the snow had a hard crust and bore us easily. In time that same crust became pure glistening ice, and stumbling, falling and slipping, we were compelled to stop and wrap our moccasined feet with hair rope. Like the hair between a polar bear's toes, it clung to the ice and bore us handily.

Another curse of the ice fields beset us. The dead white of the terrain lost all form in the sun-glare, becoming but a blob of blinding light before our eyes.

Muhammad walked beside me. Just as the day began to wane and the snow to change from glaring white to a soft blue, he pointed to a great peak that towered thousands of feet above the 17,000-foot Depsang Plateau over which we tramped. It was a mountain of solid blue ice, that, as we watched, caught the rays of the setting sun. Like a prism it converted the light into a thousand flashing colors and with prodigious extravagance

46

hurled them out over the winter waste. A spectrum-prism, it towered more than twenty-four thousand feet into the skies.

We held the march well into the night, not daring to halt because of the cold. So exhausted was I that each time I fell I thought it was the last. I asked Kuen when he intended stopping.

"We will soon reach the place I seek," he promised. "To rest here in the open would be fatal if a bad wind came."

Twenty-two hours from our start, we camped. Abdul spread my sleeping-bag and I crawled into it, boots and all; for that matter I never took them off unless I fell through the ice or got them wet as on that terrible march up the flooding canyon. Hardly was I asleep before Kuen woke me. Angry, I turned upon him with a volley of abuse. Taking no offense, he insisted I rise, then, thrusting into my hand a bowl of soup and meat, demanded I eat. Pushing it from me, I insisted that all desire for food had fled before fatigue.

"And that is what most of the dead on this trail said twenty hours before they died!" commented Kuen. "Tomorrow we cross the Karakoram *Dawan* (Pass) and a man must have food in him for strength. If the wind blows again, as it has today, we all shall want strength."

I ate.

By the flickering firelight the horses could be seen standing among the dead left by other caravans, and nibbling at the snow. The exhausted beasts had had no water in five days except what they derived by mouthing snow and ice. There was absolutely no water on the heights except that in solid form. The water we used for cooking was melted snow, and the fuel was wood carried on the backs of horses from the distant Shyok valley. Nor was there enough fuel to serve our needs unless we crossed the Karakoram on the next march. At lower altitudes the gnarled *burtze* root could be found; on Depsang nothing grew; this altitude was as sterile as the moon.

LAND WITHOUT LAUGHTER

No more than two hours did we rest at that camp. It was still dark and bitter cold when we arose, struck the shelter, and moved on up the rocky gorges. There was no trail, just the deceiving smooth surface of the snow, which one moment bore us and the next let us sink in up to the shoulders.

We crept along ice-walled gorges. Every one of us held his breath for fear that an avalanche might descend upon us. Twice the roar of toppling mountains chilled our hearts, but none came down upon us.

"Ullah, Emperor of Destiny, smiles upon us." Kuen voiced our thankfulness.

Ali Muhammad Khan, he who had "sword-steel for a heart," once passed and the words formed by his lips were prayers, not oaths.

Midday saw the pass itself before us, a broad trough in the mountains, so long it seemed to reach to infinity. Abdul and I went ahead of the slow caravan and thanked *Him* who controlled the winds for the breathless sunlit quiet of the pass. Such was the effect of the altitude that both Abdul and I were compelled to stop every ten or twelve yards, then, our lungs once more replenished with oxygen, continue on, ever upward.

The summit attained, we stood upon a monument at its highest point, to look to the east and see the spires of Tibet; to the south and west, those of Ladakh and India; to the north, the country to which we journeyed, Turkistan—*Tataristan!*

Waiting until the caravan once more caught up with us, we plunged down the Turkistani slope. A quarter of a kilometer to our left, running parallel with us, gliding over the snow and then halting abruptly to sit and watch our progress, ran several silver-pelted Karakoram wolves. At last, tiring of the sport, they vanished over a hill.

It was at Balti Barangsa that we found seven dead Hadjis: two men, two women, a young girl, and two infant boys—all

48

frozen. Kuen came up behind us and stood looking at the
corpses. Hunched where they had died, the men lay in the lee
of a tremendous boulder. One sprawled, face down, on the
ice. The other hunched over on his knees, chin touching them
and hands drawn under to the warmth his body had afforded.
Both women and the girl had been torn by wolves, as had the
infants. The men were untouched except, like all the others, for
the eyeless sockets. The ravens had visited death. Kuen, trail-
wise, commented:

"They have no bags or blankets!"

For a moment his eyes scoured the surrounding territory.

"They have no saddlebags, no belongings, no horses, and
yet their coats are made of silk!"

Again looking upon the corpses, he pointed out:

"The lobes of the girl's ears are torn; she is naked. Wolves
rip clothes to shreds—not remove them! Both of the women
are naked; the coats of the men are split along the seams; what
does that mean to thee?"

Himalayan tragedy! Some caravan had been hired by these
Hadjis! Once they were well into the mountains the caravan
men, really bandits, had robbed their charges and left them
to die. The richness of their dress and the fact that they had
not a single piece of goods, other than the clothes that clad
them, indicated their fate. The girl's ears had been torn when
the ear-rings were snatched from them. We left these, like those
we had previously passed, with rugs and rocks piled over them,
safe from further molestation by wolves or, worse, men.

Days passed before we came out of the mountains onto a
great plain. The almost unendurable cold of the altitudes gave
way to a more comfortable temperature, but never above zero.
We were now in the relative lowlands of 14,000 feet. Tibetan
gazelle fled like wraiths before us in swift effortless bounds.

LAND WITHOUT LAUGHTER

Ravens became the greatest curse while in camp. They would light on the horses' pack-galled backs and viciously tear off strips of living flesh. Zenib was given the task of keeping the huge devils away, but despite the way he would lash out with a club, the ugly creatures would boldly land on the suffering horses' backs.

The plateau crossed, we again plunged into a riot of mountains. However, travelling was much easier, for we passed over the broad surface of the Yarkand *Deria* (River). Day after day we trudged over the highway of ice, twisting from one side of the river to the other, avoiding, if we could, the hundreds of domed ice hummocks which too often threw our exhausted animals' feet from under them.

The men, gathering earth in the skirts of their coats, would precede the animals and spread it on the trail ahead so that the horses' hooves might have a purchase on the slippery ice. One day, as we wormed our way in just this fashion, I felt a strange shuddering underfoot. A noise, such as a giant tree makes when falling and crushing its branches beneath it, reverberated through the canyon. Like cannon-fire a series of dull booming reports emanated from the ice underfoot. Some one shouted that it was sinking, and we all made for the canyon wall at a dead run.

All forty-one of the horses were in the center of the river—at this point about two hundred and fifty yards wide—when the ice first began to sink from beneath us. Not unlike miniature geysers, water spurted through newly formed crevices in the ice, and before Imin and I could reach the head of the caravan we were in water up to our hips.

Kuen's angry voice, echoing and re-echoing through the canyon corridors, called down the wrath of Ullah. The horses, panic-stricken at feeling themselves being slowly let into the river, made for the same side as we, or none would have been saved. Even as it was, all but two lost footing and lay on the ice, frantically trying to regain their feet and escape the rising waters.

Our first fright over, we rushed to their aid, working waist-deep in the blood-chilling river. Some of the horses were completely submerged except for their upstretched heads that showed white-rolling frightened eyes. We worked frantically, first taking the loads from their backs, then lifting the animals to their feet, after which one of us would lead the fear-maddened beasts to safety. Kuen and Kadir were farther out in the water than any of the rest of us, both floundering about a fallen horse, trying to drag him back from the sinking ice. Time and again they fell, to disappear beneath the rising water. At last Kuen drew his knife across the animal's throat and, dragging the pack, he and Kadir returned to the firmer ice next to the canyon wall.

"His leg is caught in a crevice," Kuen explained. "I would rather some one cut my throat than be left to breathe ice water instead of air."

But the dark look Kuen interpreted as censure had not been born of his merciful act. Instead, my glance had fallen upon the salvaged pack cases, now lying smashed and soggy at our feet. Even before I cut the packs' bonds I knew what would meet my eyes—and so it was—sextant, transit and aneroid, all smashed beyond repair. His foot caught in the ice, the horse had tried to escape, breaking his leg instead. Falling, he had crushed the instrument boxes.

During the night the ice returned to its former level. On the following morning the dead horse, like a beetle caught in amber, was encased in a crystal sarcophagus. Another horse collapsed as we attempted to load him; he, too, was put out of his misery. Another such catastrophe and not a single animal would survive.

LAND WITHOUT LAUGHTER

That same day we came to a great cleft in the mountain, where three rivers met and became one. The men knew the place as *Hoppaluk*. It meant, and was, a place of despair. Mountains rose straight up on every side, sheer rock walls climbing from the ice-river to the jagged, frozen spires a mile above.

While we searched in the mountain gloom for a suitable camping site, a faint cry reached our ears. Ali Muhammad Khan with the cry, "Bandits!" dashed to the horse that carried his saddlebags, and returned with a huge wickedly curving knife. The horses, having halted in their tracks, now turned to stare across the ice, ears forward and eyes questioning. While Ali rushed up and down, wickedly slashing at the air, working himself into a fighting frenzy, Kuen pointed out a tiny white shelter far across the ice.

Coming towards us, we could see a lone man feebly crossing the ice. A dog trailed behind him. Whosher Akhun, caravan-cook, recognized the figure on the ice.

"It is the boy that Teriff Shah Hadji [I had contracted with his Ladakhi agent for the use of the caravan animals] left here to watch the freight! He has piled it into a house."

He pointed toward the distant dwelling:

"It is made of baled felts."

Kuen voiced the obvious:

"He is not well, nor his dog. They run, yet they move slowly."

Ali despondently put down his blade.

We stood in our tracks until the two, man and dog, reached us. The boy was a scarecrow of a fellow; his furs were ragged, wind-whipped tatters; his face gaunt, and his body emaciated. Tears rolled down his cheeks at the sight of us and he was so overcome as to be unable to speak.

The dog, half wolf, gaunt as his master, slunk rheumatically away to sit hunched against a bit of pressure ice and from there stare at us out of one white and one blue eye. Pitching camp beneath the threatening but wind-screening snout of a glacier, we turned our attention to the visitor. The sobbing boy was invited to come in and sit by the fire; his dog, however, contented himself with crouching against the tent's outer wall and viciously snarling at all who passed.

The stranger told his story, and a wild one it was. He had been living in the shelter three full months, waiting for another caravan to come and take the freight he guarded. Twenty-one days before our arrival, a band of bandits, perhaps the one that had murdered the seven Hadjis, had ridden up to his shelter and demanded food. When they had eaten, they picked up his store of meat, the bags of flour and *talkun*, and lashed them to their horses' backs. The boy begged them to leave him sufficient food on which to live but, instead, they had beaten him with their rifles, then stripped him of the clothes he wore, even to his felt stockings. Leaving their victim naked upon the midwinter ice, they had ridden away. Reviving, he had found a coat, discarded, no doubt, by the bandit who had taken his.

With his dog, the boy had existed for twenty-one days without a fire, the bandits having stolen his matches. The little food he had had was a mixture of flour and ice that was melted by the heat of his body, a paste that had sustained life. Fireless, the two, dog and boy, had huddled together, a few felts over them for warmth, until our coming.

Next morning as we broke camp, the boy trudged back to his watch. A good meal in his stomach, ten boxes of matches in his pockets, meat, tea, and rice (that we could ill afford to part with) slung over his shoulder, life for him again seemed worth living. Either that boy was blessed with an utter lack of imagination, or he was endowed with a heart that knew no fear. The brigands might return. The winter had almost claimed him. Boy, you're a better man than I.

53

LAND WITHOUT LAUGHTER

Yanga Dawan was crossed with a loss of two animals. By that time the feed was getting low and the horses were making double marches on half rations. We marched against time. Kuen swore that unless the gaunt animals had more to eat, and soon, we would lose the lot.

Even our own food was exhausted. Between dark and dawn at one camp, the horses had torn open the provision bags and devoured the flour, the rice, and even the tea. Eleven pounds of *talkun*, roasted barley flour, Tomec's contribution, was all that remained. Eleven pounds of food to sustain twelve men on a nine-day journey to Kargalik, the first bazar of consequence. It was a five-day journey to the nearest habitation. To make the prospects no brighter Kuen said that the Topa Dawan, still to be crossed, might take, weakened as they were, the lives of the remaining animals.

Resolving to leave the slowly dying caravan (the fewer mouths to feed the greater their chance of surviving), I asked that the two best animals be brought before me. One was a little sorrel horse from Zanskar; the other, the she-demon, the black mule. She, who had by lavish use of heels and teeth removed all my corners and protuberances. Kuen gave to both a full ration of feed.

It was over the evening fire that I voiced my intention of leaving the caravan in the morning. All of the men fell silent and stared into the flames. Kuen was first to break the silence.

"All men must part; some to die, some to walk a different path. I sometimes think," he soberly added, "it would be easier to die than say farewell to one of a chosen brotherhood. Any man may be born a brother, many men may come forth from the same womb, but I have chosen my brother from all those I have walked and talked with on the road of my destiny. It is thou."

Deeply moved, I knew not how to express myself. Kuen took

54

up his wooden bowl, still half full with the evening meal. Presenting it to me, he asked that I forever keep it, repeating the Tatar proverb:

"Parting friends exchange both clothes and bowls and meet again, for a bowl forever seeks the mouth it first fed, and clothes the back they first covered."

I passed him my bowl, then, with a jest I did not feel, tossed him my Astrakhan cap and caught his. (*Kuen's bowl and hat, one scuffed, the other moth-eaten, lie on my desk as I write.*) Half-wit Zenib, unimpressed, broke into laughter at the solemnities. Sitting before the fire, Ali Muhammad Khan deliberately unravelled his crossed legs and, standing, gave the still laughing Zenib a resounding kick in the ribs. We all followed Ali out into the moon-drenched night.

A few hundred yards from the camp, standing on the brink of the canyon wall, staring down into the abyss below, I was startled by a sound behind me.

"It is I, fear not." Out of the shadows came the reassuring voice of Kuen. Approaching me, he paused a moment, trying, it seemed, to find words for what was in his heart. The sound of rushing water and grinding ice floes came to us from the river a mile below. Drawing his knife—a long, beautifully curved Turkish blade—he presented it to me, hilt first.

"Kadir Akhun could take the caravan on to Kargalik bazar, and I would be a better man for thee than any other!"

The answer came hard, but Kuen was no man's servant, and honest conviction was in my reply.

"Kuen Akhun," I said, "thou could'st not take Abdul's place!"

The man took affront at the words and thrust his knife back into its sheath with an angry, hurt expression.

"Abdul is a servant," I explained. "Thou could'st never be that. As a companion I would choose thee first; as one to black my boots, never. Thou sayest, 'We are brothers.' Could I let my brother, a caravan *bashi,* become a servant—a man with women's work?"

His feelings were assuaged. Taking my hand in his, he pressed it; then held the hand to his heart, voicing two words: "Amerikaluk akasi." (American brother.)

The sun rises late in the mountains; it was still dark when Abdul and I prepared to travel. Only three saddlebags did we load on each animal, yet I wondered if the wobbly beasts could bear that meager burden. The little horse had a bad spot just over his shoulder, a septic hole about the size of a quarter. For that matter the entire back was covered with galls of a lesser or greater degree of infection; at every step yellow matter pumped through several wounds. It was a criminal act, the loading of that suffering beast, but there was no alternative; he was in better condition than any other horse of the caravan!

The mule was in good shape, but for the fact that she was unbelievably thin. Abdul joked about the animal's condition as he punched new holes in the cinch straps and then pulled them tight.

"These horses are strong. Nothing soft here."

He drew the cinch a bit tighter and tied it. Then, thumping the hollow flanks and jutting hip-bones, he said:

"Horses like wood; certainly no one else was ever so fortunate as to have such *hard* animals."

The caravan men were cleaning the backs of the other animals. All had horrible septic pack-sores. Gangrenous, they had given off such a stench that for the past week the men had avoided walking on the lee side of the caravan.

Kuen had insisted I take Ali Muhammad Khan along; with his long knife, the little fellow, Kuen had assured me, was

56

invincible. The three of us, Ali, Abdul, and I, made our departure after bidding farewell to each of those we left. Our good-byes having been said the evening before, Kuen and I added nothing. As we turned away Kuen bowed, hand over heart, as did every man in the caravan. Wind tearing at their clothing, whipping the shaggy fur of their hats into their eyes, they stood quietly until we turned into a canyon and were lost to view.

I shall always remember them, standing there beside the sick horses amid the debris of the forlorn camp. Kuen was apart from the rest, atop a great table-rock. His lips, I have always been certain, formed the words:

"And now who is to understand me? Again I shall speak what is in my heart, with only the moon to listen. And he gives a very belated reply."

7

MARCHING down the rocky defile, I alone regretted leaving the caravan. Both Abdul and Ali seemed relieved.

Our foodstuffs consisted of two eight-ounce cans of potted beef and one and one-half pounds of *talkun*. For the animals we had only sufficient feed to last two days. Ours was truly a race—five days' caravan journey to any habitation, with one day's supplies. The animals were our only real concern; we knew we could hold out. Surviving the winter-wrath of the Depsang and the Karakoram, we had come to think of ourselves as almost immortal.

Eighteen hours after leaving the caravan we camped amid a jungle of tremendous boulders, the wreckage of a fallen mountain. In the day's journey we had crossed one river thirty-four times. Compelled to cross the maddened serpent of ice, imprisoned in the dark gorge-depths by sheer walls, we, by the grace of Ullah, escaped a hundred avalanches. The river ice was rotten and incapable of bearing our weight and at each crossing, while the avalanches thundered down from the heights, we cursed the mild temperatures. It was the thaw, the time most dreaded by all caravan men, that persecuted us. A dozen times the ice had collapsed and let us into the river; the *talkun* got wet and turned into an unappetizing muddy mess. Spring is *Hell* in the Himalayas. Our little sorrel took two bad falls and Satan's mistress—the mule—had given up kicking, content to use her feet solely to stand upon.

Food eaten, we sat about a meager fire. Ali fed the animals

and we decided to continue throughout the night. Nothing remained of our rations. We had to reach a habitation; or starve.

Less than a mile was covered before we began the ascent of Topa Dawan, picking our way through the maze of glacial boulders that were strewn in magnificent confusion about the mouth of the gorge. Somewhere, far ahead of us, some one began to sing a yodelling sort of melody—in a starlit mountain pass in Tataristan!

As we worked our way higher the trail gave way to patches of snow. When thirst gripped us we scooped up handfuls and from it sucked a gritty moisture. The animals had to suffer along as best they might, and suffer they did. The trail called for the energy and nimbleness of mountain goats. Our pack-animals had neither.

Ali, for all his pigmy stature, held the horse up and boosted him along whenever the trail got too steep. Our labors became purely automatic. We picked up the animals so many times that it no longer was an effort to do it again. Fresh strength, in our exhaustion, came to us; pulling, pushing, lifting, cursing, we struggled up the mountainside. The sorrel's head was a death's-head; lips thin and drawn back from the teeth, deep hollows just over the eyes, skeletonlike. And yet we couldn't even leave the poor beasts to die in peace. Finally, we unburdened the horse and the three of us each chose one pair of saddlebags and threw them over our shoulders. The pack-saddle was thrown away.

Worn out, we at last sank down upon a shelf of rock, determined to take a breather. Then the voice, which we had heard hours before, once more broke into song, quite near this time. Rounding the ledge on which we rested, three men came face to face with us.

They salaamed, but we were too tired to acknowledge the salutation. We only eyed them sullenly. The thought that any one could sing while we so labored filled our minds with strange anger. Nor were the strangers oblivious to our black thoughts. They wasted no time leaving. First whispering, then carolling, they passed down the midnight mountain trail.

How we managed is still a matter of conjecture, but we did at last reach the summit of Topa Dawan. The trail went almost straight up the last three hundred yards and we three tugged and carried the two beasts that distance, over the skeletons of animals that had previously chosen that particular place to give up the ghost. Ali barked his shins on the skeletal neck of a deceased camel and angrily kicked its head a hundred bumping feet down the slope. When at last we had attained the top and had lain down beside the trail to rest or die, he spoke:

"Ullah in heaven drop a star on us before we must rise to walk again."

As though we feared Ullah would take Ali at his word, we rose and stumbled down the mountain until, at the end of an hour, we found that we had wandered off the trail into a natural culvert that some glacier had maliciously carved. Our predicament was not realized until we walked far into the bottle-necked trail that wasn't a trail. It was so narrow that we couldn't turn the animals about and return. We three held a conference in that deep, dark ditch.

"Where do we go now?" I foolishly questioned.

We were about twenty feet below the surface of the ground and the crevice was getting tighter at every step.

"*Shaitan* take it! We will go ahead and hope that the over-hanging ledge will fall on us and relieve us of all our cares," answered the disgusted Ali.

Five minutes farther down the defile found us at the end of the trail so far as we were concerned; the canyon had narrowed to a mere slit. So constricted were the walls that they touched both sides of the animals' heaving flanks. Ali crawled between the legs of the horse and mule, that for some reason let him escape with his life, and, standing beside me, fumed at the blank wall ahead. Abdul broke the *impasse* by climbing out of the crevice. Bracing his feet against one wall, back against the other, he wriggled his way to the surface of the world. Prowling back and forth above, he would occasionally call down to us in the bowels of the earth to ask what he should do. The question infuriated little Ali and he danced with anger. I was beyond such emotion.

At last Abdul solved his own problem, and ours too. The ledge, soft from the melting snow, collapsed under his weight and came down with a rush, the fright-whooping Abdul with it. After extricating first ourselves, then the near-smothered Abdul, we found the way out lay before us. The ledge, in falling, had caused a fill that formed a passageway upward.

Thirty-seven hours after leaving the caravan, three men, a horse, and a mule came wearily to a halt before a low, earthen-walled *zemindar's* (farmer's) cottage. After kicking at the door until it was opened, we tramped in, told the *zemindar* to care for our animals, and lay down to sleep. We minded not in the least that we occupied blankets that had been, at our arrival, vacated by the feminine members of the household. A forty-eight-mile forced march is, to say the least, fatiguing.

Awakening, I lay quiet a moment, wondering where I was. As I attempted to sit up a cramp tied the muscles of one leg into little knots. In sympathy, the other leg followed suit. I remembered. Turning my head, I could see Abdul; he too was awake. Finding my eyes on him he dolefully assured me he was dying—most assuredly dying.

"My heart," he whispered, "has fallen apart. My bowels are shredded. Surely thou can'st see I die? Listen!" he demanded, "hear!"

61

LAND WITHOUT LAUGHTER

Not in any mood for his foolishness, and a bit in need of sympathy myself, I angrily demanded what he meant me to listen for.

"The muscles of my back. Surely thou can'st hear the muscles of my back. I not only feel them tearing away from my spine, I hear them too. Hear!" he again demanded. "They sound like the string of a warrior's bow as the arrow speeds forth."

"Muscle by parting muscle I die," he wailed, and then broke into uproarious laughter at the ludicrous sight we made.

Runt Ali of the "sword-steel heart" slumbered on as one dead. I, with grave doubts as to whether I should ever straighten again, stood up and took stock of the surroundings.

Some one had kindled a fire on the hearth. A *chogun* was simmering. Crossing the room, I peered into a bundle of quilts that, judging from the noise emanating from them, held life. It was our host, a good-looking young Turki. From him I turned to Ali. Sprawled on the floor, flat on his back, arms at right angles to his body, legs as close to right angles as they could be without being disjointed, he looked like a rape case or a broken doll.

From where I stood over Ali, I could see into the next room. Three very young maidens were saying their morning prayers; rising, kneeling, and touching their brows to the prayer rug. The grace with which they performed the adoration was, to me, divine in itself. Tiny red and gold embroidered caps perched on the backs of their heads, and from under them cascaded heavy blue-black braids. All were clothed in flaming-red gowns that achieved the impossible; at once both accentuating and concealing the femininity of those within.

When the three completed their devotions, they turned to find me staring at them. They were in no measure as disconcerted as I. This was attested by the matter-of-fact way they went about their chores, ignoring me, except for a few self-conscious smiles they could not contain. All were unbelievably attractive (romance had not lighted my life for months) and definitely Aryan in type.

"M-m-m, beautiful, eh!" Abdul evinced his interest by remarking from where he crouched by the fire.

The remark aroused me, and, being at a lack as to what to do with myself, I kicked at Ali until he protestingly awoke and sat up. Abdul duplicated my methods and woke our host, who immediately arose and greeted me. That done, the sensible fellow sent one of the girls for tea, another for bread, and then, humanely waiting until we had eaten and drunk our fill, besieged us with the many questions that had been in his mouth since our moonlight arrival.

"Whence came you? How long has it taken? How many horses did you lose? And men?"

He politely marvelled at the distance we had travelled the day before; *tsk-tsk'd* at the condition of our animals, and told us that only two *potai*, four miles, remained to reach the nearest outpost of soldiery at Kukiar.

While our loquacious host rattled on, Ali put aside his teacup and, going out of the room, returned a moment later with his hand full of little white bars. Winking, he beckoned me to him; it was then that I saw he carried bars of soap, Lux, to be exact. The soap, manufactured in Bombay, seemed more highly perfumed than our American variety.

Pushing three bars into my hands, Ali explained:

"Whenever I go to Ladakh, I buy many pieces of this *sobun*; it is of great value here in Turkistan."

I asked him why he gave it to me. Speaking from the corner of his mouth and in a very low tone, he explained: "The women, the beautiful women, all of them love to smell like a flower. This *sobun* smells like flowers. They will do anything," he corrected, "almost anything, to get possession of a piece.

63

For thee," Ali stepped back and eyed me, "for thee, with thy beautiful red face and yellow hair, they would do anything!"

I tried to look shocked.

"Yah," Ali snorted, "I have watched thee—as thou hast watched those three females; it has been a long time since thou——"

"Enough, Ali!" I warned.

"They would be willing, I am sure of it!" he insisted. "This man is their master, but if thou wert to leave by the front door, and, walking around the valley, accidentally arrive at the back, I am sure thou would'st find one of them waiting for thee. With thy yellow hair—and red face—and a piece of *sobun*—ah-h—Effendi!"

Taking the bars, I went back to where I had sat the minute before. One of the girls passed with a pot of tea, and, as I proffered the bar, she snatched it, not greedily, but as if she could not believe her good fortune. In an instant the other two besieged me and, receiving their soap, retired in happy embarrassed haste, all the while voicing flattering appreciation.

"*Rakhmet*, thank thee, beautiful one. Thank thee, Tatar of the golden hair and the fine red face."

It was worth it even if Ali did sulk in the corner, cursing the waste of good *sobun*.

A moment later the three girls returned and, sitting before the fire, each sewed her own bar of Lux into a little silken bag. That done, they affixed a cord and, by it, suspended the whole around their necks, tucking the bags between their breasts. Ali snarled from the corner:

"See! See! *Aiii!* Such waste. They will carry those bars of soap until they are old women. Tatar women don't use it to wash with—they like its scent of flowers. Pah!"

When I am a very old man those three girls, by that time grandmothers, will tell of the beautiful red-faced man with the

64

golden hair. And, as they dandle grandchildren on their knees, might jealously suffer the babes a sniff of the precious *sobun*. When those aged ones die, their descendants will come into possession of the heirlooms and they will perpetuate the legend of the beautiful stranger. Long after this book is forgotten that legend *shall* go on, and on. I am immortal—all because of a bar of soap!

Meanwhile, Ali lamented.

"*Aiii!* Such waste. . . ."

Of that, however, provident Ali never could be entirely sure.

Departing, we filled our sashes with proffered cornbreads. Our twenty-one-year-old-host-with-the-three-beautiful wives got a four-penny knife for a night's lodging, a wealth of cornbread, and feed for our animals. Soap with the perfume of flowers! Two-bladed knives! I am known all over Tataristan for my generosity.

Muscles aching, we went plodding up the warm valley. By the time the sun found its zenith our lack of stamina was painfully evident. A supreme effort was required to put one foot before the other. Twice we had to pick up the little sorrel, so weak that he would collapse in a sort of stumbling side-slip when the mule brushed against him. Three times we halted to rest and feed the animals, doing our best to save the valiant little horse from Zanskar, now reduced to a bony, shaky wreck.

At the day's end we surmounted the sand dunes and there before us lay Kukiar. The houses were concealed by a rise in the ground, but on the horizon were the waving tops of poplars, sure distinguishing sign of an oasis in Turkestan's deserts.

Halting, I scanned the countryside. Before me spread a new world, a region over which towered the Father of the Ice Mountains, the Golden Mountains, Star Plateau, and the mountains of both Paradise and the Sun. Coursing from glacier to desolation and oblivion were rivers—White Water, Bitter, and Black Jade. And roaming over this their land, or abiding in one place, doing as their fathers did before them, were many and various peoples: remnants of the Golden, the Black—the great—hordes that once ruled Asia and terrorized Europe. Tataristan was no longer an aim—it was an accomplishment!

Book Two

"Oh ye who Believe:

"When ye meet the Marshalled legions of the infidels, turn not your backs to them:

"Whosoever shall turn his back to them on that day, unless he turn aside to fight or to rally some other force, shall incur the wrath of God; Hell shall be his abode and wretched the journey thither."

(KORAN)

1

PERHAPS it is appropriate, at this point, to set down a few words about myself. In justification, if you will.

Re-reading what you are about to read, I find instances in plenty where the uninitiate, perhaps logically, might say: "What colossal ego! What arrogance! This fellow Ahmad Kamal seems to fancy himself the chosen one of Ullah! He ignores both warning and counsel. He contests the rights of authorities through whose dominions he journeys. He—Hell, he seems to think all others must kowtow when he goes riding by; irrespective of their position and his intrusion."

As regards warning, and counsel: Swarming about the Asiatic frontiers there are two distinct species of men. These are the *negative* and the *positive*. The *negative* are those who know. They do not voluntee. information, or advice. For they also *know* that whatever they say to the amateur will be not only ignored but resented. Anyhow, these wily few are usually too weary, from the toil of past experience, to care what happens to the novice.

The *positive* are usually those who *do not know*. They are very determined to advise, contest, and veto. Too, they are very often officials. Many of those who opposed my entering Turkistan—British and British-Indian authorities—had never visited that country. Others considered it beneath their dignity to so much as understand, much less speak, the languages of their wards. (This is not only a British, but also a French failing. In French Morocco one finds multitudes of officials who, despite their years in colonial service, speak not one word of any native dialect.) Such men I will not listen to!

As concerns the chieftains one contacts in the Central Asian wilderness, they are exponents of the law: "Blessed are the arrogant and well-armed, for theirs is the Kingdom!" One must meet such men as a superior, an equal, or better not meet them at all.

So, in vindication:

I *do* speak several Muslim-Asiatic languages. Some better than others, the Turkic-Tatar (Uighur) so fluently as to have been able to pass as a Tatar among Tatars.

I *am* of the same faith as those whose trails I travelled.

I *did* succeed in crossing the most formidable frontier in the world.

I *had* a great-grandfather, himself a Tatar, who blessed his descendants by bequeathing them this crest:

> "With courage,
> With constancy,
> With capability
> We conquer."

I'm satisfied.

Walled cities, scimitars, armored warriors, mounted hordes—all have been relegated with King Arthur and his Knights, to the realm of fable and mythology. They have become more of *legend* than of history. This is very wrong; Tataristan (Sinkiang) holds all of these *today!*

Tataristan, almost three times the size of France, is a desert land with verdant oases rising amid the dunes. Each city is, on the average, about eight days' hard ride from the other. Almost all are surrounded by high fortress walls and battlements above which rise only the heads and shoulders of sentinels, and wind-whipped poplars. The sentinels are as necessary as the walls, for today, as in past centuries, hostile armies are on the march. It has been thus for thousands of years, and probably shall so persist throughout the ages.

Tataristan is the most isolated country in the world: to the west are the impenetrable Pamir Mountains; north, are the Siberian wastes; south, the Himalayas—truly the abode of snow. Wrapped in the blizzards and glaciers of eternal winter, they bar the way to Tibet and the Hindustan. To the east is the Great Shamo—the Gobi desert—and for those able to survive months of camel caravan across its desolation of waterless waste and creeping dunes (whose eternally whispering sands, the Mongols swear, are the powdered bones of the dragons that once ruled the world) far beyond, there lies Cathay.

It is a strange and feudal land peopled with the descendants of the great armies of the past; legendary armies that made conquest of Asia. In the veins of the men of Tataristan courses the blood of Mongol, Hun, Macedonian, and Chinese. In their hearts are the tenacity of Genghis Khan and the ferocity and boldness of Atilla's and Alexander's armies. In them is the fanaticism of Saladin's and Tamerlane's *Islam*, and a rich heritage of Chinese wile.

It may be said that the heroes of the past bequeathed to these, their descendants, great hearts and left in their veins not alone the pulse of blood, but the throb of charging legions' battle drums. These men are Tatars.

The year 1930 saw the beginning of the bloodiest rebellion ever to escape the press. A revolt that has to date snuffed out more than three quarters of a million lives and, by way of notice, earned perhaps five hundred words of highly inaccurate newsprint. The happenings, being delineated as they were released by *Tass*—the official news organ of the Soviet Union—

have by reason of their origin been aborted and bled dry of all facts that make for good news copy. Russia was, and still is, deeply involved in the strife. Without her participation it would long ago have come to an end.

War is one activity that cannot be condoned by civilized peoples, but in this instance it can, at least, be understood. The corrupt Sovietized Chinese rulers of Sinkiang imposed so vicious a tax system that the people could no longer bear up under it. Landowners were in some instances compelled to pay taxes for two hundred and forty-seven years in advance—to the year 2177. The edict was enforced with torture and imprisonment. Tatars could no longer, would no longer, stand by to see their life's work go into Bolshevik money chests. In several instances the avaricious tax collectors took Tatar virgins when the peasant farmers had naught else to surrender. There was *War!* As by spontaneous combustion the whole of the lost dominion, almost three times the size of France, burst into flame. Muslim pitted himself against the Soviet-Chinese infidel.

For months the conflagration raged throughout all of Sinkiang; from the Siberian steppes to the Himalayan foothills. At last came what seemed at the time the turning-point of the war—the Chinese, in defeat, called upon the Kremlin for aid. Thereby hangs this tale.

Even before the day of Ivan the Terrible the Tatar people hated the Russian with heart and soul. Tales are still told around Muslim hearths—of the glory of Tatary when their cavalry twice swept over Russia to pillage and burn Moscowa. Such legend dies hard in the hearts of a subjugated, once-ruling people.

Within five weeks after the Chinese call to Russia, every corner of the vast desert dominion felt the pounding hooves of a mounted Tatar horde; and "in the name of Ullah—the Just, the Merciful, Protector of the faithful," men rode to war. Blades were whetted and rust cleansed from ancient muzzle-loading rifles. Some even delved into the chests of their ancestors and brought out ancient helmets, shirts of woven chain, emblazoned with the crest of *Islam* and Tamerlane. And soon, somehow, out of the south—across the glacier-clad Himalayas—came *Lewis guns* and modern *British* rifles!

Two powers were coming to the aid of these fighting factions of a forgotten people. *Soviet Russia* to the Chinese, *British* to the Muslim. Both had long desired to make the Dominion their own: Britain, not because she liked the Muslim, for she didn't, but because she urgently felt the need of a buffer state between Sovietized Sinkiang and her India. And Russia because Sinkiang was her most convenient route if she was to make conquest of India or to send munitions to China! That Sinkiang is fabulously rich in mineral, petroleum, and agricultural resources was an added incentive to both powers. Ever watchful, avaricious as the Soviet, endowed with an uncanny proficiency acquired by many years of meddling in Asiatic affairs, the British were first to strike. A few thousand rifles and machine guns were a cheap enough price to pay for protection and a new sphere of influence in Asia.

Pitted against the Soviet Government and Chinese Communists, the entire Tatar nation, aided by the British, took the offensive. Not since the time of Tamerlane, more than five hundred years before, had such a horde taken the field.

City walls proved not bulwarks against them, but targets for their hate. Towards and over the towering battlements swept the horde and at their passing there were left only the fire-gutted ruins of once great cities. Gobi sands began to finger over the blackened thresholds of what had been Chinese homes in the midst of oasis gardens. Gardens built with the suffering and nourished with the blood of enslaved Muslims were now ravished by the white fury of Muslim vengeance.

73

LAND WITHOUT LAUGHTER

Vengeance soon wears itself out by its very intensity and at length came the time when the Tatars began to feel the ravages of exhaustion—of men as well as resources. Then went forth the call for aid in the Holy cause—to two boys in Kansu Province, China, that territory stretching along the eastern borders of Sinkiang.

Both boys had yet to see their twenty-first year and yet they had achieved, at the head of their armies, a reign of outlawry second to none. It was not alone that they were Muslims that decided them to aid the Sinkiang Muslims; they were too much a part of the sword to be very close to the Mosque. It is more likely they had their fill of Kansu. Every hand in the province was turned against them for their indiscriminate depredations.

Their city, Suchow, was bled dry; there were no more revenues to be had from the populace. The two bandit generals had captured and ruled the city for a year and their troops at last had become fractious from inactivity, and hungry for loot. In fact, so many deserted that if the people in the bazar had but known they could have by their very numbers overthrown the garrison. The boys seemed to have agreed it was best to seek new pastures—and quickly. News from the east had it, and by good authority, that a force greater than theirs was on the march to attack them; that force—the Chinese Central Government!

It was at this psychologically perfect moment that they were invited to war in Sinkiang. The invitation was accepted. On their arrival the war took on new life. The Tatars of two provinces, now allied, by their very fierceness defeated armies twelve and fifteen times their number—and they numbered thousands. Battles were fought with artillery, machine guns and gas. In a very frenzy of hate the forces resorted to hand-to-hand warfare.

74

LAND WITHOUT LAUGHTER

Three years passed and the war persisted with ever diminishing intensity. No longer were there the thousands that began the war. Many cities knew as populace only women; their men never to return. Those that remained in the field were tiring of war and one by one they deserted to take up the tilling of their long-neglected acres.

It was because of this lapse in fortitude that those still bearing arms met defeat. Three times were they smashed. Twice they rose again. The third defeat was more than defeat—it was annihilation. The Russian aircraft and gas spared, unknowingly, only a handful of beaten men under the two bandit generals. One of them even went over to the Russians at their promise to spare his life: he died of *acute indigestion*.

Out of all this chaos there came a man, barely having attained man's estate, twenty-two-year-old Ma Hsi Jung, the remaining one of the Kansu bandit chieftains. More than six feet of slim, battle-scarred, finely featured Tatar with the bearing of a conqueror and the eyes of a hungry Himalayan wolf. That man began the reorganization of his beaten and scattered rebel cavalry. How, none but he shall ever know, but it was accomplished, and, at the head of an army stronger than those surrendered to the Bolsheviki, Ma Hsi Jung once again waged war. This time not for the forgotten cause—but for himself.

Then began not only a war but the ascension of a new satellite in the blood-dripping sky of conquests and conquerors. A human satellite that rode at the head of the finest and fiercest cavalry since the time of Genghis Khan. A satellite that had, to ride at his side as aides-de-camp, four dark stars and bosom friends—*the four horsemen of the Apocalypse.*

From Urumchi, the city of his defeat, the young general led his army southward, besieging and taking every city in his path. Ma Hsi Jung was taking his force to some distant region, far from where the Bolsheviki could attack him, there to re-mold his armies. Every city in his path was hostile—until they learned who it was that besieged them; then they became panic-stricken.

Some, the wise, acceded to his demands: unconditional sur-render, arms to be delivered into his hands, all wealth to be surrendered, sustenance to be given his armies until they chose once more to take the march. Those not so wise lived to see an apparently invulnerable Tatar lead his men over their walls; then died to regret their folly eternally. All that was left of the opposing cities were their blackened walls; perhaps a few women, those not beautiful enough to be taken with the other treasures. Every man and beast, even to the dogs in the bazar, died.

Ma Hsi Jung massacred, raped, and burned, not in reason-less rage, but for effect; the end justified the means. He cal-culated, and succeeded, in making his name one to strike terror into the heart of all Turkistan. His adversaries had numbers, *he* created terror: it, with his few, conquered. The sharp scimitars of his men were formidable in combat, but more terrifying to the enemy were the tales of his barbarities in victory—or defeat. Such was the alarm preceding his coming that often his troops rode into cities deserted by their inhabitants —all having fled into the mountains!

In the fall of 1934, barely four years from the date of the first shot of the revolution, Ma Hsi Jung, older, stooped with wounds, led what was left of his armies through the ancient gates of Khotan. Not three thousand men rode into the walled city nestled close to the Tibetan border; graves and battlefields had claimed the bulk of the once great force.

76

2

As we struggled out of the desert and into Kukiar natives gathering about us voiced the Turki greetings:

"Salaamet, Yokshi Keldi Ma?" (Greetings, hast thou had a good journey?)

One pressed forward and took Ali's hands between his.

"Asalaam Ali Qum," he greeted, stroking his beard.

He questioned Ali as to whether the one with the golden hair and the red beard was a Muslim. At Ali's affirmative reply he turned to me:

"Peace abide with thee."

"And with thee may peace abide."

We stroked our beards. The natives stared at us. One woman, seated on a donkey, picked up the corner of her veil that she might better see the strange trio. And a ludicrous sight it was, for we were all clad in the same clothing we had donned in Leh a month before. Appropriate for the frigid Himalayan altitudes, the padded clothing now absorbed the rivulets of sweat that trickled down my spine as we steamed in the blazing sunlight. Kuen's wild fur cap was cocked on the back of my head, broken moccasins adorned my feet, and a torn, faded coat my back. Not one of the curious Turkis looked as ragged as did I, leaning against the sorrel that he might in some way take strength from me.

Then came the first Tungan I was to see in Turkistan, a surly Turki[1] who rode up on a great white stallion with rifle

[1] All of the Tungani cavalry are designated as "Tungan" irrespective of their race.

across knees and scimitar slung over his shoulders. So monstrous
was the beast he rode that the stirrup, and the broken boot it
held, were on a level with my eyes. Long before he spoke he
was in my bad graces. The effrontery of it, his riding up on
such a creature, while I, who had trudged across the Himalayas,
stood in the dusty road holding up a sorrel horse that was fit
only for a fertilizer factory! Bringing his nervous mount to a
standstill after all but riding us down, the ragged Tungan
soldier demanded in a stentorian voice who we were and
whence we came. I disliked the fellow's attitude and forbade
my men to answer him. Abdul, however, was frightened.

"Tibet," he answered the Tungan.

The fellow rode closer and, pointing to me with the muzzle
of his rifle, asked who I was. This time Abdul had sense enough
to hold his silence. Pushing the muzzle away, I told the fellow
to dismount if he wished to question me. Instead, he became
ever more menacing.

"Who and what art thou?"

I ignored him and turned to Ali to ask him to direct me to
the *Yamen*. The soldier wheeled his mount and dashed off,
presumably to call out the reserves. I made a mental note that
in the future I would ride into bazars. Being accosted by a
mounted belligerent, while on foot, gives one an inferiority
complex!

Ali and I went double time to the *Yamen*, leaving Abdul
to support the two animals. We found the *Yamen* to be nothing
more than a glorified caravan-*serai*, the rooms occupied by
officials instead of wayfarers. Two tattered sentries stood at the
gates and followed us as we entered. Ali was in his heyday,
immensely pleased with the attitude I had taken with the
soldier. He expectantly fingered his weapons when, irascible
and disgusted with waiting in the hot sun-drenched compound,

LAND WITHOUT LAUGHTER

I stalked through one of the cloth-hung doorways and seated myself in the cooler officers' quarters.

The room, to all appearances, was that of the commanding officer. The doorway was draped with a length of red cloth on which were sewn two lines of white Chinese characters. A bowl of raisins tempted me and a handful was being consumed when I heard some one question Ali.

"Where is the foreigner?"

"Inside," he replied curtly.

Three Tungan officers entered the room and I, recalling the discourtesy accorded me by the soldiers, retained my seat, acknowledging their bows with a nod of the head. The high and mighty air of all three rapidly changed to confused deference at my superior and nonchalant manner. One, a tall, sharp-featured fellow, minus an ear and with his head cocked over on his right shoulder, stepped forward and addressed me in Chinese. I did not understand him. Another spoke in Turki:

"He says thou art welcome, and that he is sorry that he was not here to greet thee."

It was obvious that we were going through the general routine of the East. When at last all of the hypocritical niceties were dispensed with, I explained who I was and my mission, all in the proper flowery manner.

"I am an Amerikaluk. My name, Ahmad Kamal. I have come from my country, a seven-months' journey from Sinkiang and across the great waters that lie to the east. My mission is to speak with thy first-in-command—Ma Hsi Jung." (While in Ladakh I had heard of the man. Tomec Tojilak, my Mongol servant, had once served under him. Tomec had warned that I would best become a friend of the general, whose conduct was molded on the Biblical precept: "He who is not with

79

me is against me." The general's enemies were notoriously short-lived.)

The three at once placed themselves at my service. My bluff had worked. They asked that I honor their abode by there abiding. On the morrow they would furnish me with horses and an escort to Kargalik. They swore that their dwelling was no longer theirs, but the Amerikaluk's, to do with as he pleased —to burn to the ground if he so desired.

Abdul had arrived and now stood outside the door with Ali, their heads together, peeping in. Surprise was written across their leathern faces, at my whole-hearted acceptance by the Tungan officers. My stock had gone up; I had "much face."

One of the Tungans asked if I had any objections to his examining my luggage and, at my reply that he should go right ahead if he felt it necessary, he belittled its need and stamped my bags as inspected.

The evening was passed without event but for the arrival of the Aksakal effusively to extend his greetings to "the *Musaphir*, the *Mehman*, the Pasha, the Amerikaluk!" Turkis spent the evening walking past the *serai* trying to get a glimpse of me. When I went out of the compound better to see the people I had come so far to know, they greeted me with the eternal "Peace abide with thee" of all Muhammadin peoples. Several of the younger Turkis approached and, squatting in a circle, asked all manner of naïve questions, characteristic of the East:

"How wealthy art thou? How many wives hast thou? How long has it taken to come from America? And how much has it cost? Is Stalin thy Padishah? How far is the city *America* from Moscowa? Are there many Muslims in thy country and art thou Tungan? Hast thou ever seen a *Howai Jehaz*—that which makes war in the air? Do Amerikaluk women wear veils, like those of Turkistan? How often dost thou sleep with thy wife? Once?—Twice?—Three times a night?—More?"

LAND WITHOUT LAUGHTER

At my reply that Amerikaluk women wore no veil whatever and that they bathed in public with just *this* and that part of the body covered, all agreed that Amerikaluk females were as the Russ—to the last one, *Jilops* (whores)!

I had answered most of their queries and was about to invite my new-found friends to tea—incidentally being hopeful that they would be willing to submit to some somatological measurements—when one of my Tungan hosts urgently called me back into the *serai*. He was obviously agitated and explained that there was great danger that I might be robbed or knifed by the bandit Turkis. Laughing at the fellow, I made as though to return to those who awaited me outside, but such was his insistence that I stay off the streets, that I succumbed and kept within the *serai*.

So vanished my first opportunity to conduct any sort of research. Justifiably nettled, I was sensitive to the tension in the atmosphere. Cornering Ali, I asked him what had brought about this change of demeanor on the part of our hosts. Ali knew no more than did I, so we sought out Abdul, who assumed an expression supposed to be innocent. No, he knew nothing, except that he had told the arrogant Tungan officers that the "Effendi" was a great man, a great *Russ!*

I asked Ali if it was true that bandits were in the neighborhood.

"No!"

So . . . the Tungans thought I was a Russ, perhaps a spy. (Abdul had never heard of America, and he thought that because I spoke his language, I was a Tatar from the Volga or the Caucasus.) From that minute on I was under suspicion. The fool, Abdul, had boasted that I, his master, was a Russian Tatar! The Tungans were at *war* with Russia!

Night saw soldiers guarding all the doors, and at breakfast my host was a little less congenial. Tea and bread consumed, we prepared to leave, Abdul and I. Ali was to be left behind to bring the animals on to Kargalik at leisure. The two of us were very courteously escorted to Beshterek,[1] a little bazar about four miles from Kukiar, and it was there that my Tungan host of the night before took leave of us.

We were delayed in that bazar about three hours, during which time I foolishly made matters even worse by speaking with an old Turki, showing off my pidgin Russian which he extolled, because of his ignorance of the language, as being perfect. To the Tungans this was substantiation of Abdul's tale. I had, the previous evening, before Abdul had *hexed* me, been told by the Tungans how they hated the Russ, especially their general, Ma Hsi Jung. Now I was believed to be one. Certainly I was getting a fine start towards a firing squad!

The soldier who was to act as my escort eventually came, and, with him, two beautiful big animals. We mounted; Abdul was promptly thrown on his head, which saved him serious hurt. Any idiot, I told him, who, in hostile country, falsely boasts of his master's affiliations with rival powers, could land on his head without injury.

Our companion was a scar-faced Turki of anything but gentle mien, armed with both scimitar and rifle. From appearances the only thing the soldier and I had in common was the delight in seeing Abdul do his damnedest, with the help of the horse, to bash his brains out. He managed to get thrown every five miles or so, and his every fall further cemented the ripening friendship between Sho-Sho Phugen[2] Aziz and myself.

A few hours out of Besh Terek we were surrounded on every side by desert, rolling sand-dunes to the very horizon. Aziz

[1]Beshterek: Five poplars.
[2]Sho-Sho Phugen: The first ranking position over that of the common Tungani Soldier.

82

suggested we give the bit-rolling, prancing horses their heads. We both forgot the hapless Abdul in the exhilaration of speed. The big brutes took the bits in their teeth and raced over the desert, great muscles coiling and recoiling with every bounding stride. The horses were wonderful animals, of a size greater than any I had ever seen used as mounts. They were like the chargers which one sees in old prints and, like them, none of the three we rode weighed less than fifteen hundred pounds. Most amazing was the fact they would run like the wind. They were as heavy in the barrel as a Percheron, but unlike that breed they had long, gangly coltlike legs.

I recalled a tale Ali had told of the Kichik-Emir (a prince killed by the Tungans). Whenever overcome with despondency the Emir would order his fleetest horse saddled. Mounting, he would go racing out over the wasteland with no object but the outdistancing of his cares. Returning hours later, his horse blowing and lathered, the young chap would say:

"My cares have flown with the wind that sang in my ears, and the shattered rocks that flew from my horse's hooves."

Ali had sworn that the youthful Emir was mad, but as Pegasus, my bearer, that seemed a part of me, rocketed through the gathering desert dusk, I understood a bit of the Emir's feelings.

Tungan Aziz and I raced the setting sun for half an hour, drawing up at last by main strength as the embers of the dying day burned lower beyond the purple horizon. Our iron-jawed animals were blowing not at all and still fighting the bit. Aziz turned to me and put into words his buoyant feelings.

"If only a night wind would fall before my horse when he so runs, straight to *Beisht* (paradise) we would go—up—so!" He swept his arm to the lone star that had put in premature appearance.

Abdul Akhun's whoop cut short whatever else Aziz might

have said, and we turned to find him far behind and, at once, spurring and curbing his mount. The animal was frantic at being left behind, so it handily threw Abdul and came galloping up to us with Abdul chasing behind, cursing the animal heartily.

The chill in the night made comfortable the heavy cotton-filled *chapans* (coats) that had been a damnation in the heat of the day. A breeze sprang up. Aziz turned and addressed me.

"Ahmad Kamal, Effendi, it is not good, this *shamal*. It will blow the trail away and without a trail this desert is difficult to travel."

The wind continued to rise, and with it came a fine cold sand that drove persistently into our squinting eyes. The horses coughed and snorted. Then came a wall of sand, freezing-cold, driving into our eyes and faces. Weird at the moment was its strange wrenching quality, besieging one from every angle at once, tearing with tremendous force. Then, suddenly as it had come, the wind was gone.

"A whirling wind and a great one! There are many on this desert but few so great," Tungan Aziz spat.

We watched the ugly shadow depart, a tremendous black cone so high it seemed to have origin in the moon itself.

"And where is the trail?" cursed the Tungan.

After a brief angry argument it was decided to give the horses their heads.

Hours later we rode up to a *zemindar's* home. With kicks at the door we roused the whole lot, men, women, and children. Three little boys were given our horses to care for. Entering the farmer's dwelling we called for a fire and tea, generally disrupting the family and their night.

Aziz and I, hunched over the fire, finished countless corn-breads and inhaled quarts of tea. Abdul had deserted us an hour before. A single *chini* of tea, and he had disappeared into some other part of the cottage. Our host had done likewise after directing one of his daughters, Jennett Han, to tend our wants. Aziz and I had comfortably settled ourselves, one on each side of the fire with backs against the wall, absorbing warmth and debating the respective virtues of American and Tatar females, when suddenly sounds of tumult and angry altercation reached us.

"*Chattok!* (Trouble)," Aziz groaned, rising disgustedly.

Our beautiful young hostess[1] dashed off. We followed. The racket was rapidly rising to a crescendo as other female voices joined. Aziz grabbed his scimitar as we ran out of the room and I my quirt. We found the riot well in progress and Abdul its center. He was backed against a wall and just above his head, in its niche, was the lone sputtering oil *chirak* that lit the closetlike room. On the raised mud *kang* huddled a woman, a felt ineffectually concealing her nudity. It was she we had first heard and her shrieks still filled the dwelling.

Jammed into the room were a number of women and our host himself, elaborately cursing both Abdul and his companion.

Abdul, he declaimed, was "a dog's baby, a pimp, and a thief of women." The woman, a bovine creature with bulbous breasts and vast buttocks, was "a whore, a bitch, and a faithless wife." Abdul, surprisingly enough, was not in the least daunted by a situation that threatened to end in mayhem. He warded off the angered husband by the simple expedient of holding before him threateningly a steaming *chogun* of tea. Aziz brought the scene to an end by using the flat of his sword on the posteriors of male and female alike. The room was cleared of all but Abdul, Aziz, our host, the woman, and myself. Our host continued his tirade, but now that there were reinforcements, Abdul ignored him and appealed to us for aid.

[1]The farmer folk indulge in no such vanities as the veil which obscures the faces of all wealthy city women. Nor do these pastoral women appear at such a disadvantage as their city sisters. Certainly they have a voice, however obscure, in most family matters.

LAND WITHOUT LAUGHTER

Meanwhile the woman shrieked to Abdul that he must save her. And our host kept asking if we had any objections to his castrating Abdul.

"No," Aziz grunted.

However, I objected. Abdul was in my service and I would need him a while longer. Aziz suggested that I give the outraged husband some money. With this, the Tungan grabbed Abdul by the arm and pushed him through the door, jostling the women massed in it to watch the massacre. I paid the *zemindar* two hundred *seer* (about $1.60) and while he counted it, Aziz got the miscreant out of the house and to the horses.

A few minutes later we were once more ambling across the desert, Abdul surly and silently sweltering under the barrage of jibes Aziz and I threw at him. The three of us rode straight towards the waning moon, our laughter resounding over the silent desert.

The night was dark, the trail obliterated by a swift cold wind, but despite the distance they had borne us the horses were in fine fettle. Catching me unaware, my mount, an iron-jawed beast, took his head and almost flew from under me, joined at once by the other animals. Suddenly the trail dipped down to a little arroyo carved by some extinct stream. The stallion saw it at the same instant as I, and gave a great bound that cleared the chasm, and pulled up. Before I could call, the Tungan was on and over the place. He, too, reined in and we both shouted to the approaching Abdul, whose animal, sensing something amiss, had slowed in its stride. It reached the brink, gathered itself and jerkily leapt to the farther bank, throwing Abdul in the sudden lunge.

The trail changed from sand to rock; stones ranging from the size of an egg to that of a man's head paved the desert.

LAND WITHOUT LAUGHTER

Aziz rode ahead, hunched in the saddle. Like him, I crouched low trying to escape the biting wind that heralded the approaching dawn. Eyes heavy for want of sleep, I dozed, rousing at intervals to seek signs of habitation, or watch the sparks fly from the rocks beneath the iron-shod heels of the Tungan's bearer. As the dawn lighted the eastern skies, Aziz roused me with a shout.

"Not much farther, Effendi! Only two *potai!*"[1]

He gave another whoop and, kicking his horse in the belly, went clattering off in the graying darkness. I followed and came up beside him, both of us fanning our mounts to greater speed.

My animal was in a dead run when he stumbled and stood on his head. I had a swift vision of Mother Earth extending her bosom to me—followed by stars, very real ones. Throwing myself to one side to avoid being pinned to the ground by the saddle's high cantle, I struck, first on ear and shoulder, followed by the rest of me. For a moment I lay quiet, afraid to move lest the grating edge of some fractured bone knife its way through my flesh. Next I saw the Tungan's face over mine.

"Yah, Ullah," he muttered, sure I was dead, and with real concern in his voice.

Abdul came running to lift the horse from my leg. Aziz kept asking if I were all right. Carefully I tested each limb; nothing was broken.

"*Hodia Shukrea!* Thanks unto God! If thou wert injured Ma would have my head as forfeit."

It was only the responsibility for my safe conduct from Kukiar to Kargalik that troubled the rascal.

The fallen horse at last stumbled to his feet much the worse for wear, a patch of hide the size of my hand hanging over one eye. Taking Abdul's horse, I left him what was left of mine. The remainder of the ride was sober and slow.

[1]Approximately four miles.

87

3

AT THE break of day we reached Kargalik. We rode
past mud houses, through spring-green fields in which men and
women crouched, answering the demands of nature, fertilizing
the earth and likewise sowing the seeds of dysentery, plague,
and death to come, in the fall. The narrow bazar streets were
lined with *nun* shops, the buns piled high before them, giving
forth an aroma that was, as Abdul said, "so good as to make
one's belly sing."

Sho-Sho Phugen Aziz changed in demeanor at first sight of
the city. His jesting abruptly ended. He was once more the
soldier. Banners flew all about, and we were halted for ten
minutes while hundreds of soldiers marched past, all singing
a battle chant. Eventually, we drew rein before the *Yamen* and
were at once surrounded by a mob of soldiers, who escorted
the three of us to the inner sanctum; a place festooned with
banners and with sentries posted every four yards. There
another Tungan took me in tow. I was at length delivered into
the presence of one who, I was later to learn, was second in
command in Kargalik: the Aksakal, "Whitebeard" (Village
Elder) or Amban (Mayor, Chinese), Keeper of the Keys, and
even more. The old, white-bearded Turki greeted me, looking
down from lanky heights. Over his rose-hued silk robe were
generously distributed remnants of past banquets.

Then the eternal, "Who art thou? What art thou, and
whence comest thou? And why?"

Of all the questions I answered only two and, using the same technique as in Kukiar, I accentuated two points—the length of time it had taken me to reach Kargalik, and the fact that I had as destination Khotan and *his* General Ma Hsi Jung. Realizing that nothing could be accomplished in my present status, I asked for immediate transportation to Khotan.

My attitude was not lost on the old Turki nor upon his subordinates, who knelt in a semicircle behind and about him. His imperious manner was replaced by one of disgruntled courtesy and respect. Tea was brought and he plied me with raisins and walnuts. A water-pipe was offered, and polite routine questions were asked as we sat in the chairless, rug-walled room.

Ma See Ling, as he termed himself, was evidently ill at ease and one could detect his passing thoughts by their play on his face, "Who is this foreigner and is he as mighty as his airs?" The old fellow did not want to make the mistake of entertaining one beneath his rank, thus losing face. At last he excused himself and went out. I knew that he went to seek advice.

His retinue followed him while I, left alone, betook myself to the door, to find it blocked by a young Turki soldier. As I pretended to pass, he extended the rifle's barrel. At my angry query as to what he was about, he started lamely to speak, then, thinking better of it, with a determined set to his jaw, once more blocked my way. It was evident that he had been given definite orders that I was not to be permitted out of the room. Though he seemed discomfited by my anger, he was more in fear of those under whose orders he acted. I sat down.

An hour passed, and just when I was about to make another assault at the door, in came two officers with shoulder straps, condescending airs and choleric, overstuffed countenances. Explaining that I was to come with them, they started off. Disgusted, I followed.

We went through dusty streets to what I later learned was

the home of the Zeho, a fat, oily fellow with little piglike eyes and a bull neck that ran with little rivulets of sweat. With him I took the offensive and adopted the condescending manner. The stratagem was not lost on the fat little general, and immediately caused a narrowing of his eyes. He offered me a chair and the eternal tea and raisins, then asked the stock questions, which I ignored except to show my passport and to demand that I be taken to General Ma. General Zeho was as disgruntled with the situation as I was. He couldn't get me to part with my credentials or to answer any of his questions.

"My business is with Ma Hsi Jung," was all I would say.

At a loss, the swine gave a bellow that brought half the garrison on the run. An officer was instructed what to do with me, while I listened trying to appear undisturbed. Instructions complete, my new guardian told me to follow him. Instead, I reseated myself, feeling that I had been ordered about enough for one day. At which Zeho urged me with gestures to follow the supercilious Tungan. Nettled, I told him and the rest to go to hell, that I had come a long way and wasn't going to be ordered about now that I had nearly reached my destination.

Zeho bounded to his feet and, wagging a fat finger at me, declared:

"Thou art a Russ!"

Again my passport was displayed and I swore that I was an American.

"American. Amerikaluk. Amerikansky."

He rolled the words about on his tongue, then came to the conclusion that the region was a part of Soviet Siberia. Waving his arms, he demanded I follow the officer. Having accomplished nothing by passive resistance, I changed tactics.

"Thou wilt in the future regret this discourtesy, once I speak with General Ma."

He continued to bluster, without, however, the previous ardor. Finally he looked me straight in the eye.

"Perhaps thou wilt come with me, eh?" he asked.

We went to his own private residence where I was given rooms adjoining his. The place was spotless and furnished in the best Russian fashion with tables, chair, and bed. A large, cylindrical, Russian-type oven stood in one corner, and in the wall was the economical, narrow, acutely arched Turki fireplace. On either side were the set-in wall-shelves of the Turki home. Over the fireplace was a niche for an oil lamp. Opening out of the outer wall was a large shuttered window. Luxury of luxuries in this land of earthen floors were the brilliantly colored Khotan rugs.

"Abide thou here until my runner carries word of thy arrival to Ma Hsi Jung, in Khotan. When his reply is in my hands thou shalt be disposed of. If thou art no Russ," he spoke as if this were an extremely doubtful possibility, "it is best thou art a guest of the Zeho. If thou art Russ, thou art also finished and it is just as well these last few days are so spent."

A nod and he pompously strutted from the room. At the threshold he paused, tapped his chest with a pudgy index finger:

"I have spoken!"

Sometime later Abdul was brought to me, cursing at the way in which he had been ordered about. We were prisoners. As the sentries were changed before the door, Abdul began to sniffle.

"Art thou truly a spy, sahib?" he questioned me, his voice quavering.

Shortly I was aroused by a flock of small boys, all in uniform, each bearing something—bowls of raisins, candies, sweetmeats, and a sliced melon. After placing their burdens on the table, they vanished. At worst, we could eat, drink and be merry; on the morrow we should see.

91

LAND WITHOUT LAUGHTER

Deep inroads were being made on the confections when a barber appeared. Perhaps, we thought, the Zeho was realizing his mistake. I gave myself over to the luxury of having my face scraped and beard trimmed. The barber was a thorough fellow, if nothing else, making up in vigor what he lacked in skill. The flesh of my face, forehead, ears, and neck was thoroughly lacerated. Abdul *tsk-tsk'd* as I writhed under the ministrations of this high priest of torture. I submitted to having my ears explored, and shed tears of exquisite agony when the monster removed my moustache without the use of either soap or anesthetic; but bounded to my feet when the fiend, taking advantage of my post-moustache weakness, viciously thrust a long spoon-capped needle up a nostril with the evident intention of seeing the color of my brains.

Another child soldier put in his appearance. The *Hummmum* was ready. I survived the ordeal of having a brawny athlete scrub me until the flesh came off in little needlelike rolls, and the shock of stepping into a pot of boiling water, and then having a bucket of ice water dumped over my quaking frame. At length I was taken back to my domicile under guard. The precaution, considering my post-shave, post-bath condition, was hardly necessary.

That moonlight midnight, roused by the demands of nature, I wandered out of the house and prowled about in the compound, anxiously searching, and appreciating in retrospect the advantages of the open desert. One of the sentries bugled an alarm that brought many soldiers running. Half-clad, the Zeho himself arrived. I was released by the dozen hands that held me. Zeho eyed me narrowly.

"Thou art not a Russ, eh? Then why dost thou attempt to escape?"

I was returned to my room and a Tungan guard was placed

over me. Not knowing the one Tungani word needed in my case, I resorted to pantomime. The guard got the idea and called in his dialect to the sentry outside. The sentry repeated the message to some one else; voices in the darkness could be heard appraising the situation. Twenty minutes later an officer, rubbing the sleep from his eyes, presented himself with a smart clicking of heels.

"The Zeho's apologies. He misunderstood, but it will be impossible to find a woman for the guest until the morrow. If only the guest will content himself for this night, the following nights spent in Kargalik shall not be so lonely." He saluted, bowed, and left.

Stumbling back to bed, I pulled the covers over my head and fervently prayed that my intelligent guard would accidentally trip the trigger of the rifle he dozed on, chin over muzzle.

The next dawn two men were placed in my room. The idiots took to staring at me until I drove them out. Disgruntled, and mumbling to themselves, they went to the far side of the compound on which my lone door and window faced, to lounge under some budding mulberry trees.

A soldier who was sent to act as my personal servant filled an hour telling me his life story: about his father (he was also a son of Ughlug Beg—father of three of my caravan companions—just as each of them had been by a different mother, so was this fellow!), of his services in the Shah Mansur's[1] army, of his two wives, Tuda and Tara Han, and how often he cohabited with each. He told how he was conscripted into the Tungan forces from the position of shopkeeper and explained the difference between Turki, Uzbeg, Kazakh, and Turkoman[2] soldiers like himself, and the true *Tungan* who were bandits

[1]A Pre-Tungan king of Khotan.
[2]See Glossary: Races of Turkistan.

and came from Kansu Province, on the eastern border of Sinkiang.

Of all the Tungan forces, less than a tenth were the original Tungans that captured the country two years before. The others had been conscripted from home or the bazar, and beaten into submission if need be. The country was devoid of youth. Every last boy above the age of twelve had been drafted into the army. Only wild tribesmen, cripples, women, and aged were left to till the fields, of which more than half the fruits were paid to the Tungan overlords. For everything bought, sold, or grown, a heavy tax was levied. Whatever the Tungan chiefs wanted, they took, be it soldiers, grain for their horses, meat and flour for their armies or women for their beds. The soldiers, that we heard drilling night and day, were paid twenty-five *seer* (18 cents) a month. There were no leaves; enlistment was permanent.

Punishment for desertion was decapitation. For stealing, the hand would be chopped off and the stump plunged into boiling grease, after which the culprit would be chained by the neck to the Yamen door, while his severed hand was nailed to the gate behind him as a warning to the citizenry.

For espionage there was a very specific torture. A long pole was lashed across the suspect's back, with the arms spread against it, at right angles and tied securely for their full length, forming a sort of human cross. Then each of the feet would be tied to a length of rope, the slack in the rope pulled up behind the bound one and then passed over his head. At last, his feet suspended in a kneeling position by the neck rope, and his arms pinioned against the pole, he would be carried before a red-hot plate of iron, under which roared a fire. Here the accused would be given his choice; he could speak and be beheaded without more ado; or he could remain silent and be barbecued. If he refused to speak, he was picked up—by two men at each end of the long pole against which he was bound—and held over the fire. Knelt on the red-hot iron, he would be rocked from one knee to the other; when they lost all feeling the man would be laid on his back; then on his stomach.

I asked my narrator if these men did not prefer to confess and be beheaded.

"No-o-o, Effendi," he assured me, almost as if surprised. "No—they rarely confess."

"And why not—surely the knife is a more merciful death?"

"Death is the least of destiny, Effendi," he replied. "What is death—a transition. . . . 'A more merciful death?' What does it matter how a man dies? All this we call life is very contemptible. Hast thou ever seen thy face when a woman lay in thine arms? Hast thou never seen a flower by the roadside, stained and broken where some man made water on it? Hast thou never seen the Jews' eyes, self-love and self-pity in one, avarice and deceit in the other? That is life. What matters it, how a man dies—if only he dies!"

"But do these tortured ones never confess?"

"Rarely—perhaps three in fifty."

"And why not more?"

"Because every man has a companion—within. A companion with whom he makes a pact; once that pact is made there is no breaking it; there cannot be. That companion is the thing men call a soul; and that companion seeks paradise; to betray one's soul is to seek Hell. The Hell of remorse has a cold flame that burns not the body, but the brain, and never ceases burning. Not even madness can still that agony. Hast thou never seen an idiot that sat staring into his past? To betray the soul is to betray God and," he finished, "I should rather dare the fury of wood-flames than those of God's anger!"

Other punishment for crimes of a lesser nature consisted of cutting the muscles in the back of the neck; forever after a man would find his chin on his chest and his eyes upon the ground. Or the great muscle above the heel might be severed, after which a man never ran again. For one that cheated, the bones of the hand were broken, then the fingers and palm split with a knife. The hand was then bunched into a fist and bound in a bit of wet cowhide. If it did not rot off, the hand would remain a fist to its possessor's dying day. Never would he cheat with it again.

I asked Syim if the people had never heard of chains and prisons.

"Yes," he admitted, "they have, but it costs too much to feed a man who lies in a prison and, besides, it would not be good to separate a man from his family for too long a time."

The human note in his voice made me ashamed to have suggested so brutal an alternative!

Syim took me up to the flat roof whence we could see, over the roofs of other dwellings, the soldiers drilling on a great parade ground near the edge of the city. The drill step was a cross between the goosestep and the swagger of a sailor—arms swinging violently to and fro before the body, not at its sides. Every man had the crisp precision of a West Pointer and the appearance of a beggar, with patched and repatched uniforms.

We watched them throughout the entire day, and still they drilled—marching, running, and climbing a great wooden wall that stood at one end of the parade ground. Even calisthenics were performed. The parade ground was sufficiently large for four regiments to maneuver at the same time, and every foot of that field was being pounded by the feet of the thousands that occupied it. Never before, or since, have I witnessed such intensive training as that to which those soldiers were being subjected.

Syim swore that it had been so for every day of the past two years; ever since the Tungani had captured this southern fraction of Sinkiang.

The day at an end, tired of breathing the clouds of dust that rolled off the parade ground to hang a yellow halo over the bazar, I was about to return to my quarters when Syim touched my arm.

"Look," he said. "Over here in the direction of my home."

He tried to pick the roof of his home from the multitude of other housetops. Despairing of the task, he pointed at a distant flickering light that had suddenly appeared out of nowhere. As the evening purple grew heavier, the light grew correspondingly brighter.

"This is the best time of the day," Syim assured me. "This is the *Aksham,* the candle-lighting time. The sun, already below the desert horizon, has left only the lengthening shadows to mourn its passing."

As we watched, the Masjid cast a black tongue of shadow across the bazar; other candle flames sprang into being. From the Masjid came the tremulous melodic call of the *muzzin.* Below us, in the bazar street, merchants boarded up the fronts of their shops to hurry off and perform their ablutions and then the evening prayer.

An *ishek,* ugly little donkey, filled the night with his raucous braying, whereupon a midwife rushed from a near-by dwelling to give him a resounding kick in the belly. Unaware of us, who stood not forty feet from her, she paused a moment to make certain he kept silence. Then, wagging a fat finger at the dejected little beast, she scolded, quoting from the *Book of Wisdom and Logic:*

"Prayer, and no greater sound, is to be heard at the birth of a son of Adam. What would a man, or beast, to fill the air with mountain-splitting din as a child, like a sword, comes forth from its sheath to do battle for life!"

97

LAND WITHOUT LAUGHTER

She waddled back to her duties in a low-roofed dwelling from which came the whimper of a woman in labor. I had a strange sensation of guilt, as though I had heard what was not intended for man's ears. A night wind became a part of me and, as I looked up towards the skies, the woman again whimpered—this time a more urgent sound.

Syim, caught in the meshes of the same nostalgia that held me, encompassed the whole city with outstretched arms.

"Ah—I love my land and my people," he whispered. "Young tribesmen," he continued, pointing to a group of men slowly moving through the darkening streets, "still clad in the furs of the turned season, stroll through the bazar streets. Too young to be devout, they leave the evening *nemaz* to their elders; time enough for prayer when they are aged. Quietly they stride along, each taken up with his own thoughts, anticipations, and the avoidance of mud holes. It is their custom to spend this hour in search of forbidden sights, of unveiled faces."

The suddenly eloquent poet-soldier continued, pointing towards the Masjid that now began to give up its worshippers:

"In the Masjid the devout have begun the completion of their prayers. Already some, the younger, go quickly through the darkening streets to their homes. The aged, feeling in stiffening joints a nearness to the shroud, pause awhile before the final '*Ah . . meen, Ullah hu Akbar.*' (The end, God is great.) Aged minds more fully realize the terrors of many hells, and delights of seven paradises."

Syim spoke to me and yet it seemed my presence had been forgotten. His words were directed to the night, to another dimension.

"Turkistani streets are always empty of humans after sunset. The hours between dawn and dark are precious: the very young sleep. . . . The adolescent dreams of the pleasures of his elder brother, the nuptial bed. . . . Virgins artfully woo

98

sleep that they may once more dream the dream of the night before. . . . All Turki women consult the *Book of Wisdom and Logic.* To brides it counsels: 'All thou wives of one hour, virgins, forget artfulness. Within thee is a barrier to be broken by thy master.' "

I watched Syim as he spoke and his physical reaction to the words that flowed from his mouth was amazing. When he first began, his face had been that of a celibate. Sexless, celestial, serene, he had seemed. But now, as he spoke of women, his face beaded with sweat. Here was a strange fellow, capable of ethereal and poetic thoughts and at the same time bound to, and preferring, lust and flesh. I wondered what motivated his thoughts; whether his words excited his soul, or if a knavish, wandering soul gave voice, like a bloodhound, as it tracked down an emotion.

Caught in the throes of his self-created word-aphrodisiac, Syim turned glistening eyes upon me. He was a vain fellow and my interest seemed to throw him into a very frenzy of eloquence.

"Abiding by the tenets of the *Book,* women go to their masters and for the night fulfill their destiny. 'Life's lamplight hours populate the future' is another quotation found in the *Book of Wisdom and Logic.*"

For a moment Syim fell quiet and looked at me. I smiled, which was all the vain man needed to replenish the fire of his Tatar eloquence.

"The aged, man and woman, alike, are secure in realization that their knowledge surpasses that of all books. In a very ecstasy of remorse for having done the things that made youth livable, loins aching with rheumatism instead of passion, they silently pass the night in prayer, kneeling by a window, eyes fixed on some far-off star, swaying in rhythm to the poetry of the Koran."

There was a note of finality in his next words:

"All this is my country, are my people. Centuries pass as days in Turkistan. The symptoms of the plague have not altered in ten centuries, nor has anything else. All this is the land of my people." Syim spread his arms wide. "And even when the Gobi blooms again, and it never will, my people shall be the same."

Abruptly he halted, deflated. There was nothing more he could say. That realization suddenly saddened him.

4

WITH Syim homeward bound to, as he said, "make my wives realize that I, their husband, am a male," I attempted to bluff my way past the sentries guarding the compound gate. But bluster and threats were of no avail. Much as they might fear me, the soldiers feared more the wrath of General Ma Hsi Jung. Heads fell when his wrath was incurred.

"It is forbidden," they said simply. "We are unhappy. We sorrow. But speech is forbidden. All is forbidden."

As I prepared to retire, my fingers already reaching to snuff the candle, there came a knock upon the door.

"Enter," I called, pulling a robe about me.

First came the same idiot who, the evening before, had tendered the Zeho's apologies for being "unable to find one beautiful enough to grace the *Mehman's* bed." Behind him stood a veiled girl.

Foolishly embarrassed, I suggested that he take *"it"* away. Instead, pushing the girl forward, he sought to reassure me.

"Have no fear, Effendi, she is beautiful, and a virgin as well."

Though hidden by the veil, the girl turned her face to the floor and, bending by the fire, her back to us, seemed to tremble with fright. Both of her hands she held under her veil, attempting, it seemed, to hide all parts of her that might betray emotion. She sank to her knees, still facing the fire.

Again I asked that she be taken away but the Tungan ignored my words. It seemed he thought them merely born of embarrassment; perhaps he was right. At any rate he called into the dark beyond the threshold; a wizened old Turki with a nicotine-stained beard came into the room. Without more ado, he broke into a quavering Arabic chant,[1] then, suddenly as he had begun, he stopped. Following the Tungan out of the room, he paused for a moment in the half light of the doorway to mouth a lengthy, sighing, "Ah-meen."

I was left alone with my wife: a great-granddaughter of Ughlug Beg!

The words the rascally old Emam (priest) had recited were the equivalent of the marriage ceremony. The Turki peoples, Muslims, forbidden by the Koran to commit adultery, have developed a "marriage of convenience." The bonds are easily tied; practically all formalities such as the marriage contract have been dispensed with. Easily made, such a marriage is even easier to dissolve. The husband need only pronounce two words, "Eutch Talak," and divorce is complete. Only the male may speak those words. Such marriages are forbidden in the Koran and are not to be confused with the really sincere contract. But they may be binding providing the male so desires.

I turned to see my wife, who still knelt before the fire. As I approached, her head sank a bit lower. Her hands fluttered like two frightened birds in her lap. As I knelt beside her and put out my hand to brush aside the veil, she stiffened and gasped audibly. Her tension transmitted itself to me, and I, too, could feel the weird agony of expectation that must have held her in its grip.

Unable to command my hand to lift the veil, I took up a heavy auburn braid instead. Metallic, glistening like burnished copper in the firelight, it seemed as unreal as she who breathlessly knelt beside me, her head turned away. The wood fire hissed and crackled; the braid between my fingers made tiny

[1]The Fatihat—or First Sura of the Koran, being a part thereof.

audible sounds that I heard through the tips of my fingers; and I could not be sure whether it was the rush of blood or the sound of her breath that was in my ears.

She was the first to throw off the spell, and, with a quick movement, tossed her veil up and away from her face. A sensation strange but not unpleasant seized me in the area known as the solar plexus. The Asiatics say that a man's emotions begin in his stomach, not his heart. Nura Han was beautiful, a dream personified. Her face was oval, a cameo set in the red gold of her hair. Her complexion milk white, her eyes almond-shaped, oriental, and green as those of the leopard.

Each time I took her chin in my hand, lifting her face until her eyes looked into mine, she, with a flirt of her head, and a blush, escaped to stare again at the fire. I suppose in the egotistic masculine scheme of things there are few more satisfying experiences than for an abashed woman to turn her eyes away from those of a man. After a dozen such victories at last she put her hand in mine, and whispered an endearing *"Khodjüm"* (master).

With the passing of the hours, I learned a bit more about my acquisition. She was fourteen years old; at least she thought she was fourteen! (No one in Turkistan really knows his or her age. "What does it matter?" they say. "While I am young I shall feel young. When I am too old, I shall die. Enough! What more can man ask!")

Nura Han assured me that she did not in the least mind being allied with the Amerikaluk, whatever sort of Tatar that might be. My face was, she said, "beautifully red," and my beard "golden." Boldly she proclaimed, "Our children will have fine red faces and beards." What more could we hope for!

It developed that the selection of the girl had been left to Syim, the officer who had been my companion throughout the day. Just that morning he had gone to Nura Han's father, paid him five hundred *seer*, and promised to give the girl—as is the custom of the country—a complete new wardrobe. From the tips of her tiny silk-stitched boots to the otter-brimmed cap, it had been done. Lying before the fire, no longer frightened, Nura Han proudly held up first a dainty booted foot, then a slim white wrist on which softly clinked four silver bracelets. Her long braids, coiled about her head in magnificent disarray, vivid against the dark colors of the soft Khotan rug, revealed a pink ear-lobe from which dangled a tremendous silver-filigree ear-ring.

"But," she prettily pouted as she spoke, "five hundred *seer* is so little for one such as thee, *Turam* (my champion), to pay for a bride."

The endearing *"Turam"* recalled the fact that she who lay before me was my wife, legally if informally. The swell of her breasts, budding from the low-cut bosom of her green dress, all was mine. Silken, her garment clung to the flesh beneath, revealing every contour, depression and shadow of her body.

And then a black cloud swept between us: I remembered what Kuen had once said as I looked at noseless Tokhta:

"The conquering hordes of the past left good blood in the veins of their descendants. It had to be good or we would never survive the disease that came with it. Many of my people are born with syphilis."

At my call into the darkness, a sentry appeared. Grinning like an ape, he listened as I asked for Syim. Pretending not to understand, he attempted to look over my shoulder. Nura Han, as befitted a married woman, turned her back. Again I asked for Syim. The Tungan rascal, not speaking a word of Turki, jabbered back at me in his native dialect. By dint of saying repeatedly, "Phugen Syim," I got the idea over. He stole one last look over my shoulder and departed.

LAND WITHOUT LAUGHTER

Shortly there was a rattling of Chinese in the garden and, hoping that the fellow would bring Syim, I shut the door and turned to Nura Han. Standing before the fire, her firm little figure cast into relief by the flames, the lamp wreathing her head in a circle of light, she seemed of another world. Her breasts, irrepressibly bubbling over the edge of her bodice, added a mortal touch.

With this goddess of a mate all mine I hung back, checked by the cautious brakes of civilization and a knowledge of hygiene. My medicine kit held only iodine, oil of cloves, and adhesive plaster. Any sensible Tatar would have said: "Here now! This creature of musk, ivory, and spun gold chances as much as I do. For all she knows, I might have how many American diseases she never heard of!" But each time her breast found its way into my hand, of all things, noseless Tokhta's face would frame itself in my mind's eye. Only that the face was mine and not Tokhta's.

Putting her from me, I handed her the discarded veil and the otter cap to hold it in place. Helping her into her coat I ignored the questioning eyes.

"What have I done, Khodjiìm? What art thou doing with me?" she whispered.

Behind us the door cautiously opened and Syim peeked in. Seeing me beside the girl, he hurriedly withdrew. My call brought him back. He stood just within the door, smiling perplexedly.

Nura Han, veiled, knelt in the shadows. Her eyes, visible through the veil, glistened with reflected firelight.

"It is a mistake," I began lamely. "I want no woman. Take her back to her father."

Syim, leaping to a conclusion, cursed:

"D-dongesiki! She is not a virgin? Her father swore it!"

He raved on before I could speak.

"Yah, Ullah! He shall return every *seer*."

Seizing one of his arms I quieted him.

"Ah, Syim, but she is." I gave the girl the benefit of the doubt. "She is, and she will remain a virgin insofar as I am concerned."

Misunderstanding, Syim was off at once on a new tack.

"Then she has resisted thee!"

"Art thou mad, Nura Han? Thou knowest such as these," with a sweeping gesture he compassed her entire person, fingering the silk of the violently green dress. "All of this. And a man such as he." I was pointed out. "And yet thou wilt not lie with him! Art thou truly mad!"

Closing the paper-covered windows I gestured that Syim be silent, praying meanwhile that the racket would not reach the sentry.

Nura Han was by this time sobbing noisily, and, between each fresh rush of tears, voicing a plaintive:

"*Whi Jan! Whi-i Ja-a-an!*"

As I returned to the fire, she threw herself into my arms. Raising my hands to put her away, I touched the soft flesh of her throat.

"It is the way of these accursed women," Syim ranted on angrily. "But by Ullah and by Ullah, can'st thou not take her? Can'st thou not possess that which is thine? Thou art a man and an Amerikaluk; first of all, a *man! She* is thy wife!"

For a moment he watched her, still clinging to me.

"I think she will be thine now," he said.

"Nura Han must be returned to her father," I insisted. Suddenly outraged, the girl pushed away from me and began to cry again.

"She will be thine," Syim repeated, sagely.

"The five hundred *seer* are her father's to keep, and the clothing jewels hers," I said.

Nura brightened visibly at this.

"She will be returned to her father at once."

"No-o, Effendi. It cannot be done," Syim contradicted. With a long face he shook his head. "It is impossible! Her father would drive her out. Never would he believe his daughter had been married, and few would want the risk of having an unmarriageable woman on their hands permanently; much less a poor farmer such as he. Not one suitor would be willing to take as wife a female who has spent a night in another's arms."

With a wave of the hand he silenced my unspoken protest.

"It is the same. But," he slyly continued, looking at me from the corner of his eye, "it could be arranged in another way if—if the Effendi is quite sure the girl is still a virgin. After all," he shrugged his shoulders noncommittally, "thou hast spent three and more hours with her. Alone and undisturbed with a beautiful female for such a long time"; he pursed his lips, "how many flowers could I pluck in that time! But—if thou art quite sure she is a virgin, I have a solution."

Angry, I awaited the diplomatic scoundrel's proposal. Nura Han had quieted at the turn of the conversation, content now with an occasional whine, hushing even that when we spoke.

"If thou swearest thou hast not taken her——"

I swore, with impatience and vexation.

"Then give her to me!" he said, grinning.

Somehow I was not surprised. Both of us turned to the girl, who seemed bewildered. Syim was, I had to admit, a good-looking fellow withal his cruel eyes. Not even his patched homespun uniform could take the edge from his dashing figure. Too, he had a fine red beard and fierce moustaches that were the very essence of Turkistani manhood. True, they were not as red as mine, but their magnificent spread outdid me.

Abruptly I remembered the relationship between Syim and

the girl. Upset at my reminding him of something he would rather forget, Syim sat back on his heels, cursed, then told me that there was no way I could dispose of Nura. It was at that moment she spoke, addressing me with infinite scorn:

"Truly, thou art a strange *Adam* (man). Not without sounding it would my father cast away a coin as false. Never, before riding it, would my father curse a horse as lame. Nor would my father pass a rose without smelling it; a pomegranate without tasting it. But thou art different. Thy tongue is not unlike mine own, but thou art truly a foreigner; foreign to the ways of men!"

There was both fury and caress in her voice. I knew which to heed.

5

ON THE following day I tried a dozen times to get out of the compound. At last I was promised freedom, but only after I threatened to force my way out. The Zeho put in his appearance and asked me what in *Ullah's* name I wanted. He had procured a woman for me; had given me decent lodging; food such as General Ma himself ate, and still I made trouble. He swore by *Ullah* in *Beisht* (Paradise) and *Shaitan* (Satan) in *Davsakh* (Hades) that a man so ungrateful had certainly lost face, at which I countered that he had lost his as well as mine by having me confined. We wrangled a while longer when he, at last, capitulated and gave me his word that I would be permitted to enter the bazar.

"The soldiers will not know who thou art and will undoubtedly make thee regret having acted so rashly," he added ominously.

I assured him that he, too, would have cause for regret, once *General Ma* knew of the circumstances.

As the Zeho had promised, I was permitted to go into the bazar, but with an escort of five soldiers, evidently with orders to stay close by my side. Every time I spoke with any one, one of the soldiers managed to break the conversation. Officers, these men were. The least in rank was Sho-Sho Phugen Syim; the others were real Tungans, not Turkis, and ranged as high in rank as Sho-E Ju Yi. As our little parade marched through the bazar, all the shopkeepers came respectfully to attention and, as we passed, bowed, the right hand over the heart, a Turki *salaam*.

109

LAND WITHOUT LAUGHTER

In the bazar, shops stacked with Russian goods—candies, confections, matches, and cheap cloth—lined the narrow street, mere holes in the wall. Many were less than eight feet long and only deep enough to hold a few bales of goods, the ever-present water-pipe, and the Turki *docandar* (shopkeeper). Overhead, spanning the entire bazar street from one end to the other, were poles covered with reed matting. Sunlight, beating down on the canopy, streamed through the broken matting to drown the street in mottled flecks of light.

The *ishek*, tiny dog-sized donkeys, were forever trying to make themselves heard. Their squeaky braying drowned the cries of the vendors, and even the booming of the cotton bows: bows that in the hands of men shredded the thick matted wool to fluffy fibres that were kneaded into the felt of the country.

Women walked and rode through the streets, tiny velvet-crowned, otter-brimmed caps holding in place the eternal veil that makes of Turkistan a land of beautiful women. Now and again some exceptional beauty raised the corner of her veil, coarse or gossamer according to the modesty, vanity, or daring of the wearer. I would be given a delightful stolen glimpse of alabaster cheek, red lips, a heavy ear-ring, and dark eyebrow before my prying eyes would be noticed. Then the veil would swiftly drop and its wearer turn away, head in air, her tiny cap tilted so far forward that it rested on the very eyebrows that she had so heavily blackened to excite the admiration of the opposite sex.

Another rode past after her husband—riding, as do Turki women, astride. Her tiny booted foot searched vainly for an elusive too long stirrup. Vexed, she drew up her horse; voiced a smothered *Shorwicha* (pimp), and tossed her veil over the top of her cap to disclose a pretty face and a frown. A length of red-trousered leg was displayed as she jerked her skirt out of the way. Stirrup leather found, she hauled it into place, inserted her foot, and, flipping the veil back into place, once more settled herself in the saddle to ride on after her lord and master.

Fifty feet down the street she again lost the stirrup, and erupted in a stream of profanity such as would make a mule-driver's ears burn.

The Turki is the most profane race in the world. I heard a mother call her little naked son by the endearing *"Harram-zada"* (bastard). Hers was the mother's right. A pack of children, caught and cuffed for stealing a melon, cursed their captor, once they had regained liberty, fervently, vehemently, and distinctly before they went off to bedevil some other shop-keeper.

A leper beggar displayed his deformities to the best-worst advantage and moaned piteously when any passed near. When left to himself, he sat back in the dust to count, with stumps of fingers, the already filthy notes he had collected. The beggars hold the theory that predominates throughout the East: that they, by extending to others the opportunity of doing good, themselves gain merit.

Shops were amazing for the diversity of goods they stocked, and the countries from whence they came: flowered silks from Japan, Russia, and the Hindustan lay beside plainer native cloths. Shoes, sandals, and gold-embroidered, curl-toed slippers from Japan, France, and Badakshan were piled beside a silver-mounted Mongolian saddle. Next to it was a box of cheap knives and little round mirrors from Germany and Belgium.

A lank, studious furrier sat in his tiny shop alternately sewing on a *Kara Kul* (caracul) hat, and puffing on his water pipe. Deftly tying the last stitch, he held the velvet-crowned *telpek* at arm's length, surveying it with undeniable approval. Taking up a slender switch, he briskly thumped the fur to fluff it. Dipping his hand into a bowl of water, he crushed a dried *Kara Gul* (Black Rose) in his dampened palm. Immediately a heavy blue-black dye oozed from between his fingers. Carefully brushing the fur with the dye-stained hand, he paused only when his handiwork shone jet and handsome. Hanging the finished hat upon a wooden peg, he announced to those laymen who watched:

"*Pfti!* (Finished)." Haggling over its cost began. Before a price was arrived at the furrier had a piece of red fox fur in his hand, and with the other pawed over his velvet scraps, looking for a suitable crown.

The staccato beat of the copperworker's hammer caught my attention. A sooty fellow with a singed beard and eyes bloodshot from looking too long at the forge flame took turns at a bellows and at beating a bit of copper that would one day be a chogun and for which he, the *usta* (master), would realize, if he were shrewd, seventy *seer* (sixty cents) and consider himself well paid. His house cost him, unless he owned it, about fifteen *seer* a month. His food, including that of his wife, or wives, and children, eighty *seer* a month. Living is cheap and life is good in Tataristan.

The fat-tailed sheep provide the finest mutton. Rice he grows himself, flooding his fields after the crops are harvested. Women he has, thus avoiding the expense—unless he prefers variety—of visiting a *jilop* in the bazar. Contentedly he pounded away, fashioning things of metal. When old, he would have, Ullah willing, sufficient sons to care for him. Daily, providing his sons are liberal, he shall purchase a drug from the *kaffir* Keti (Infidel Chinese) to spur on his flagging manhood. Possibly, as did the Aksakal Ma See Ling, he will take unto himself, the desire for the fairer sex having waned, a boy or two.

Syim no longer accompanied me to the roof, nor did he utter a single unnecessary word; I was in coventry. Respectful but morose, he sulked in silence after one short-lived outburst of righteous indignation: it was about the girl.

On the morning of my ninth day of detention the Zeho visited me. At his heels came Ma See Ling. After him a travel-worn Turki; eyes bloodshot and red-rimmed for want of sleep; face haggard and beard gray with desert dust. The courier back from Khotan! With the Zeho on one arm and Ma See Ling on the other, I was subjected to a vigorous arm pumping. With great enthusiasm they assured me that all was as they had suspected. I was, it appeared, "a very *modest* and very great man!"

Uncertain what manner of villainy was in the wind, I called the dispatch carrier to me, asking that he read aloud the message from Khotan. Looking first to the Zeho for approval, then to the sweat-stained paper, he laboriously translated from the Chinese script into his Turki tongue. Squinting his eyes, cocking his head to one side, intermittently chewing on his tongue and uttering strenuous Oh-h's and Ah-h's, he began:

"The welcome and salaams of Ma Hsi Jung, Commander in Chief of the Newly Organized Army, to the Megwi.

"With this letter in his possession, and by my authorization, he will be equipped with a fitting escort and come at once to Khotan. He is my guest. This letter is to open all doors and clear all roads leading to Khotan. All are to accord him the utmost respect. He is to be permitted no expense and is to be given all that he may desire or need. His mounts are to be from my stables.

"This is the word, the wish, the command and the seal of Ma Hsi Jung, Sovereign. Obey!"

Within ten minutes two Tungans, my escort, had arrived. Swinging their rifles to a place beside the scimitars on their backs, they dismounted and presented themselves with a clicking of heels and a salute. The largest, more than six and a half feet tall, was appointed my man by the Zeho. Every one saluted every one else, and, mounting a fine black stallion, I led our little cavalcade out of the compound. The two soldiers rode like centaurs, but Abdul, as usual, met his horse only on alternate jumps. We stormed through the bazar, not reining in until Kargalik lay miles behind. The two Tungans came up beside me and for the first time I took a good look at them.

The big fellow, a giant-with-an-ogre's-face, had an infectious bloodthirsty grin. By name he was Ma Ki Fu. The other was squat and heavily built, not unlike a wrestler, but his voice was that of the Angel Israfel, which, according to the Koran, is the most exquisite of those of all God's creatures, celestial or mortal, and who on the day of reckoning shall sound the trumpet. Ma Ki Fu's perpetual song, which wavered an octave higher than any I had ever before heard, had earned for its singer the title "Gazell Eskare" (Song Soldier). Both Song Soldier and Ma Ki Fu possessed the bodies of Titans and the visages of Medusas; and their hilarious behavior promised to make the journey interesting.

My man, Ma Ki Fu, named seventy battles in which he had fought since coming to Sinkiang with his general, Ma Hsi Jung. He opened his tunic that I might count eighteen mementos of them on his tremendous muscle-corrugated chest and stomach.

"That isn't all. Tonight I will show thee as many more," he promised.

Shortly after dark we rode up to Cholok, a lonesome fort built beside a spring in the midst of a sea of dunes.

LAND WITHOUT LAUGHTER

Resting before the fire, my stomach comfortably full of mutton and tea, I was given no peace by the enthusiastic soldiers. Each tried to outdo the other with his display of scars. I found out why the musical one leaned so far to the left when in the saddle. Rising from his hearthside seat, he dropped his trousers to display only half a rump. One buttock had been sheared away. He explained that while fighting in the saddle with another mounted soldier, he, Song Soldier, had suddenly seen an opening and lunged forward to deliver the deathblow. What he had not seen was another mounted enemy who spurred out of the battle's mêlée to strike at him from the side. Song Soldier patted where his missing rump cheek had been, then, scimitar in hand, trousers around his ankles, demonstrated how it had been lost.

"I struck forward, thus! Just then the other bastard I had not seen struck at where I had been—and slashed so much . . ." with thumb and forefinger he showed that "so much" meant about three inches, "off that which was still beneath his sword!" I agreed that it had been a royal T-bone of a wound.

Ma Ki Fu showed where an erratic machine gun had cut little scallops in his ear, shoulder, hip, and calf. Then I, not to be outdone, displayed the scar of an appendectomy. Both regarded me with new respect and asked if a bayonet had "done that."

"Not a bayonet, but a knife," I explained. The two wanted to know if I had killed my assailant. I admitted he had escaped. They commented that the wound was in a bad place and that I should have killed him for it.

Four days' hard ride over a desolate desert found us in Zanguy and with but two days' travel separating us from Khotan. Song Soldier rounded up five Turki musicians. Two drums, two *dutars* (two-stringed guitars), and a flute comprised the orchestra. After the musicians, came three dancing girls who favored us with professional smiles. We three—Song Soldier, Ma Ki Fu, and I—lay close to the fire. Abdul no longer stayed near me, having become even more careless in his duties than before. My questions he would answer in surly monosyllabic phrases. He hated the Tungans and considered me gone over to them; our parting of the ways was imminent.

As the music wavered in its minor key and the three girls danced, we drank tea and nibbled at raisins, walnuts, and Soviet lump sugar. Graceful as tree-moss in a breeze, the girls lost themselves in a dance that was more of the arms, wrists, and hands than of the lower limbs. The feet performed tiny deft toe and heel steps, but were no more than accompaniment to the liquid torso and flowing arms. Two hours of this and the music began to gain in tempo, attained a crescendo, and abruptly ceased. The whirling dancers cast themselves down beside us and lavishly bestowed perspiry kisses and lascivious caresses.

The music-makers rewarded for their efforts and gone, we turned our attention to the unveiled painted ladies. The one part of the anatomy that the Turki female delights in painting is the eyebrows. All of our entertainers had a black smear half an inch wide, covering each eyebrow and extending in an unbroken line across the breadth of the forehead. They hoped to earn the supreme flattery of being called *"Kara Kash"*–(Black Eyebrows). Boldly they lavished their affections on us.

"These Turki women are not unlike cattle in the spring!" Song Soldier commented.

She who had attached herself to me admitted her age to be fourteen and her price fifteen *seer*. Both Tungans were outraged; the figure was exorbitant. They pointed out that in Kargalik five *seer* (approximately four cents, U. S.) was considered a top price unless for a virgin.

LAND WITHOUT LAUGHTER

Toward the end of the next day, we emerged from the dunes to ride through a great salt marsh from which protruded long naked poles, hung with bits of rag and hair. Hundreds of the ugly things jutted at every angle from the swamp. I asked Song Soldier what all the grave markers—for that is just what they were—were doing in the swamp? He laughed and patted his rump.

"The place where I lost this," he indicated a square mud tower that stood on the top of a hill that rose like a wave in the center of the swamp. "That is where the Turki army hid," then pointing back towards the desert whence we came, "and there is where we lay in the dunes and reeds."

We drew nearer the hill. Dividing the swamp it was about fifteen hundred feet long, pierced in the very center by a roadway. A series of breastworks ran the entire length of the hill in four graduated rows, their mud fronts and many loopholes facing us and the road which we travelled. At the top of the hill, the big Tungan drew up his horse. Looking down into the graduated breastworks, I appreciated what a superb strategist he had been who first conceived them. This was the road to Khotan and the only road from Kargalik. To go around the salt marsh would be a several days' journey and unfeasible because of the lack of water. The water of the marsh itself had such a high salt content it encased the grass and reeds in long needle-sharp crystals, and coated the ground with a foot or more of the white stuff.

Song Soldier began to tell the story of the battle fought on the hill where we stood, its slopes covered with jungles of ugly poles from whose tops fluttered shreds of wind-whipped uniforms. Thousands were dead here.

A soft wind shushed over the land and fluttered the drooping grave markers. In the inverted caldron of peacock-blue sky boiled cumulus clouds of angry countenance, black bellies and myriad silver heads, looking for all the world like the demon-gods in the Tibetan lamaseries. A brittle sound like a beetle marching across a drumhead came from the marsh: salt crystals splintering and complaining as wind-blown reeds disturbed them.

"Look there," Song Soldier pointed to a brown thing that lay half covered by the grasses, the sunburned salt-cured torso of a human. Healthy green grass grew out of the abdominal cavity; near-by a jawless skull gazed with infinite melancholy at the horizon.

"There are more than five thousand like him beneath this hill," commented Ma Ki Fu.

While the big fellow rolled a cigarette, Song Soldier continued the narrative:

"We Tungans fought a fierce battle on this hill and in that marsh. It was when we first came into this part of Sinkiang, two years ago. Until this place, we had taken every southern city without a single shot fired, or a man killed; all had fled at the word of our approach. Only Khotan's Padishah was foolish. He sent an army against us, thinking he could drive us back, and that a puny barricade such as this could halt us."

I looked back over the marsh to the sand dunes a thousand yards away, then to the formidable, seemingly invulnerable walls that the Tungan contemptuously called a "puny barricade."

"We were there," he pointed towards the distant dunes; "they here. For days we sniped at one another. We Tungans had no water; our horses began to die; we suffered terribly, for many of us had open wounds earned in the north. The sun would rise and set but we could do nothing but hide from their snipers, pick the maggots from our gangrenous wounds, and wait."

"But why?" I queried.

"They had five thousand men behind these walls, and all were armed. We numbered less than one thousand six hundred; our weapons were worn and clogged with the sand of the desert winds. It was, we feared, the end of our once great army.

"One gray dawn, when the agony of our bodies and the sorrow in our hearts cast a mist over the marsh, the bugles woke us. At first we thought it was our second army caught up with us, but it was not so. Ma Hsi Jung had commanded the reveille. As the bugles sounded a second time our alarmed enemy emptied their cannon at us."

Song Soldier chuckled as he recollected that rude awakening.

"Cannon balls fell all about us, but none of our force was injured. Only a single horse—and a sick one—was killed. Our Ma Hsi Jung laughed at the surprise that we had given them, and they us. Then he commanded us to saddle our horses and mount, our weapons unsheathed. We were to attack. It was a great relief."

I remembered the Tatar proverb, "A hundred who want to live will fall beneath the blade of him who beholds no terror in death." Song Soldier whipped his scimitar from its place behind his shoulders; spitting on it, he polished the gleaming steel with a ragged sleeve.

"In parade formation, we lined up before him, then, rising in his stirrups, he spoke to us." The Tungan's eyes shone as he repeated the words of his sovereign hero.

"He said, 'Their cannon are full and angry, ours are behind us. We are equal!

" 'They are five to our one, and behind walls. We are equal.

" 'They have for our single rifle—five! We are equal.

" 'They are mere men, we are *Tungans. I say we are truly equal!* I say we shall be victorious! Ullah shall fight on our side!' "

LAND WITHOUT LAUGHTER

Imbued with the spirit of that fateful dawn, Song Soldier flourished his scimitar. So vividly did he paint the picture that, though we sat our mounts on a silent hill that was but a mantle for the bones of those that had once fought on it, I could hear the noise of that battle fought and finished two years before.

"Then he told us to charge across the swamp and over the puny walls. He told us to forget our rifles and to use our swords. He swore that the man that lived to retreat would slowly die to regret it. Then he told the boys with the bugles to blow them, and we started—Ma Hsi Jung first. We hurtled across that swamp as thunder across the heavens, as lightning across the night sky, as *Tungans!* The enemy's cannon and rifles killed six hundred of us, but still we advanced. Our enemy became frightened when we did not turn back. Does not the Koran say that the man who turns his back on the battlefield is damned? Did not Ma Hsi Jung ride at our head? Retreat for us was impossible.

"Ma Hsi Jung was the first to reach the walls and go over them. At his coming our enemy rose from behind their bulwarks and every last man of them fled for the back of the hill, where they had stabled their horses. Not more than fifty of the five thousand were mounted when the other horses broke away in fright. The soldiers threw down their weapons so that they could run faster. *All* five thousand tried to flee over that little road."

He pointed down the road on which we stood. It was about twenty feet wide and had been constructed about two feet above the marsh level. The hill descended on all sides into marshland. I could visualize the panic-stricken mob, that had been an army, rushing for that road. Never could a man hope to escape through the waist-deep mud and reeds of the swamp itself.

120

"Ma went down that road first and all of us after him, through those *Chan'tu* (Turbaned-heads) and back and through again. So."

The scimitar in his right hand swung in full sweeps, first to his right and then to his left, as he described the slaughter.

"Six hours saw the battle over and every last one on the road, dead. Then we went on towards Khotan where we caught all those that escaped the battle, and killed them."

Song Soldier put up his sword and, self-satisfied, sat back lopsidedly in the saddle.

As we continued on our way, Abdul, who had been unusually silent throughout the trip, spoke another race's thoughts of the battle.

"My people did that which is forbidden in the Koran: they turned their backs on an enemy. To disobey the Koran is to lose a battle before it is begun! You Tungans did not kill every man in one hour. You left wounded men to die slowly in the salt marsh. It was twelve days before the last man died —twelve days lying in salt water, with the salt in your wounds and the sun baking a man as he dies of wounds that would not kill a child if cared for.

"You Tungans left men to die slowly in that marsh because they were less trouble dead than alive and because you had not the bullets to waste on shooting them or the stomach for going out into those stinking reeds and finishing the task you began!"

I was as amazed at the bold outburst as were the other two, but Abdul, looking out over the desolation about us, continued to voice his thoughts, oblivious to what I or any others thought of them.

"The Koran promises punishment for cruelty, even cruelty to the cruel. Every man in Sinkiang will do well to say five *Nemaz* a day if he hopes to escape *Davsakh*."

6

DAYBREAK of the day that would take us to Khotan, we rode through green fields and under blossoming trees over a broad smooth highway of packed earth. Ma Ki Fu explained that it had been constructed by the Tungans, to accommodate the heavy tax traffic to Khotan. Tremendous amounts of grain, produce, and wood travelled over the shaded trail. Tribute camel caravans, all loaded with wood and grain, shared the way with hundreds of little donkeys, each bearing a paltry burden of sticks.

Out of the oasis, over a brief stretch of desert, and we once more descended into a verdant settlement. Through little bazars, past the homes of both *kambagal* and *bai*. The poor sat on their thresholds and picked lice from one another and their garments. The *bai* (wealthy) rode comfortably along the highway on high-stepping mounts. Beggars lay by the roadside, crying for alms and promising to pray for the generous. Solace for their misfortune was the fact that Muslims give one fortieth of their wealth to charity.

Bazars became more frequent, and, at last, the great battlements of the Tungan city Khotan stood before us.

Towering high above the castellated battlements, and directly above the city gates, was an ancient watchtower, so vast and high that its curl-eaved roof had been built in stories.

That many armies had besieged the walls was mutely testified by the debris of broken tile littering the tower roofs, and by its cannon-splintered pillars. Countless sandstorms had robbed the eave-clinging dragons of their gilt and glaze, but neither armies nor elements had shorn them of their menacing dignity. Battered and holed as it was, the roof seemed crown—not covering.

As we rode through the gate portals a sentry commanded us to halt and examined our passports. Seeing the stamp of the Zeho and that of Ma Hsi Jung on my credentials, he snapped to attention with the Tungan salute *"Jelit,"* and as we moved on into the city a bugle blared out behind us. Every man in uniform came to attention and saluted as we passed and I began to feel like a Napoleon marching through my own *Arc de Triomphe.* Soldiers were at ramrod attention and all the Turkis respectfully at a stand as we cantered by. Several Turkis looked at me closely and voiced their conviction:

"A *Pasha* has come."

I sat a bit straighter in the saddle.

The close-packed bazar street was a riot of color with the vivid silks of the women's dress, the rich sheen of fur-brimmed velvet-crowned hats which adorned the brows of every Turki, man and woman alike. Everywhere were the khaki of soldiers' uniforms and the flags of their forces. In Turkistan, I had stepped into yesterday, but the passing of Khotan's gates had been a transition into remoter antiquity—to a world of six centuries before. Customs, clothing, language and attitude were of an ancient age. Turkis bore hunting eagles on their shoulders; soldiers, scimitars; women wore veils; children wore nothing but the dirt they accumulated in the roadway, while dogs dodged kicks and barked at one another.

As we rode past a *Yamen,* I had a glimpse of a man being punished for some misdeed. His ankles bound together had been secured to a long stick. From this hung the man, head down, while a Tungan soldier flayed the bloody soles of the fellow's feet with a handful of thin sharp rods. Beside them

123

stood an officer calling out the blows. His voice carried to my ears after the thwack of the descending rods *"seh-bay ersherh"* (four hundred and twenty). We rode on.

An hour later I was installed in comfortable quarters, and the remainder of the day was spent in grooming myself to meet General Ma Hsi Jung on the morrow.

In the midst of a special escort, I was taken to the sovereign's headquarters. We marched through twenty or more gateways, to walls within walls—a veritable labyrinth, this Asiatic citadel. At last we came to what apparently was *the* gateway. My bodyguard stepped aside, some one pulled open the iron-sheathed gates, and I passed under the archway and into a sun-lit garden. In its very center, stunted by the great walls rising on four sides, surrounded by a bridge moat, was a long one-storied casemate, the court of the greatest of Tatar chieftains.

A swart Tatar officer, impressive with bristling beard and equipment, took my arm and gestured on towards the heavy structure. Across the moat, I first passed under a vine trellis, then through the double-line guard that came to strict attention. We climbed up a flight of broad stone steps to be met at the top by a tall, if slightly bent, Tatar who greeted me with extended hand. It was Ma Hsi Jung, Padishah!

The necessary homage done with, I was seated at one end of a massive table, facing the General at the other. A table and twelve chairs were the only furniture in the room. Despite the out-of-doors warmth, the place had a tomb's chill. There was nothing to relieve the earthen drabness of the room except the two-handed scimitar adorning the wall behind the General's chair.

Tea was brought by a child soldier. Twice I attempted to speak and each time the Tatar general laughed, head thrown back, then by pantomime gave me to understand that as he spoke no dialect in my repertoire we would wait for an interpreter.

Slouched in his chair, the General contemplated his tea on the table before him. He picked up the cup in a large hand, holding it precariously in two unbelievably long fingers. Those hands would better fit the hilt of the great scimitar on the wall behind him. Twice he passed the beverage beneath his nostrils and they quivered like an animal's. His was an unusually mobile face, long and thin, with square beardless chin and high forehead topped by a heavy mane of jet-black hair.

Looking up, he caught my eyes upon him. Thin lips curled away from his teeth. Only one part of that face forgot to smile—the eyes.

Ma Hsi Jung's eyes were like none I had ever seen before. His face smiled, his whole being smiled, but his eyes fulfilled only their purpose—they watched. Light did not penetrate to their depths but was reflected from their crystal-hard surfaces. One understood how it was that this man had done all he had. He might have been in rage, or ecstasy, but those eyes and what lay behind them looked out upon the world with icy coldness. Such are the eyes of eagles riding on the shoulders of Pathan tribesmen.

The soldiers outside the door snapped to attention and another Tatar entered the room, a dumpy little man in too smart clothing, as like to the General as Sancho Panza to Don Quixote. There was a brief exchange between the two, then the little one turned to me, requesting in Turki, "Credentials, please."

For the first time since my arrival in Turkistan, the document was perused by one thoroughly familiar with the English language. From the pages of my passport, speaking in a tongue foreign to me, the little officer read every word. Ma Hsi Jung, listening attentively to the very last, at length himself took the book and, scanning the various visas, abruptly slipped it into his pocket and arose. Taking my hand in both of his, he vigorously shook it.

When I sat back in my chair, it may have been too heavily; the thing creaked ominously. I was, though previously unaware of the tension, relieved.

That night I tried to satisfy myself as to why I had been greeted with such enthusiasm; surely a man as great as Ma Hsi Jung could realize no pleasure from meeting an outlander. That he had an ulterior motive was the only logical explanation. Not endowed with clairvoyant powers, I gave up and slept, with the philosophy, What is—is: and that to be—will be.

I was aroused by an orderly. Sitting up in my bed, I demanded what he meant by waking me in the middle of the night; the sky was dark. General Ma himself had sent for me.

At breakfast, I learned that the General was in the habit of rising early and, therefore, expected all others to do so. (It was four-forty-five A.M. when we sat down to eat.) With us, at the breaking of bread, was the officer who had so closely scrutinized my passport. For the first time since we met, the man spoke in perfect, if halting, Oxfordian English:

"We have examined your credentials and have found them to be authentic." Then in a deprecating tone he added, "Both the General and I ask that you forgive our skepticism and accept the return of your passport, and this—as a token of our esteem."

My passport restored, a bit of cloth was pinned on the left breast of my shirt. Lettered in Chinese, stamped with both the Nanking star and General Ma's personal seal and bordered on one side by a series of triangular dots, that badge was a puzzle to me.

LAND WITHOUT LAUGHTER

"General Ma asks that thou wilt come with him," the interpreter again addressed me, this time in Turki.

Rising from the table we went out of the walled garden, through the high-vaulted *Yamen* and to the compound yard which faced the bazar. An escort of soldiers split as we came, half preceding us and the others following as we walked down the dawn-cool bazar street. I fell to wondering just what was happening to me. The tag on my chest meant something and it wasn't the kind hung on people before they were shot. The soldiers looked at it intently and saluted. "Well," I thought, "if they salute, it can't be too bad."

A few hundred yards down the bazar street we turned off to enter a walled, heavily constructed building. The escort remained behind. Ma Ki Fu led the way into the building.

The first glance showed the place to be an arsenal. A tremendous cannon on trucks dominated the room and, at the General's smile of assent, I went closer. A brief examination proved it to be as antiquated as it was ungainly and as inefficient as ugly. The barrel was about ten feet long and uniform in diameter from muzzle to *touch-hole*, for it was a muzzle-loading cannon! The legend on the breech told its vintage, "18—? *Mockba*." A heap of ammunition lay in the corner; iron balls approximately eight inches in diameter. Around this progenitor of cannon were a number of smaller modern breech-loading mountain guns. All but one were of Russian manufacture and the orphan boasted the name Krupp. Every one was, the General said, captured from the Russians.

Another room revealed a stock of light and heavy machine guns. The third disclosed many unbroken crates. It was in this room that the strength of the Tungans was concentrated. Every crate held a new Lewis gun, and there were hundreds of them.

Three men who had been assembling one of the guns came

to attention at our entry; they were sent back to their work. The guns' dull gleaming parts were extracted from their crates and smoothly fitted together. These guns were the only truly mobile armament that the Tungans possessed. The rifles I had seen were of a dozen different calibers, from .22 to .440. The cannon and mountain guns were of no use because of their weight and the difficulty of transporting them across the shifting dunes.

We continued into the next vault; there lay thousands of rifles, and, I am sure, the only modern and unused rifles in the whole Tungan army. Inspection revealed them to be a conglomerate of sporting and military rifles of British, German, and Russian manufacture. There were even two Savages, left behind, no doubt, by some expedition. The sporting rifles (British) had been factory-equipped with bayonet-locks and telescopic sights, a point that delighted the General no end. At the other end of the place were many revolvers, practically all wooden-holstered Lugers. Another narrow room revealed rifles in various stages of decomposition, in practically the same condition as those in general use.

My gargantuan orderly, Ma Ki Fu, preceded us with a lantern down a dark flight of stairs. Eventually, at the pitch-black bottom we turned in through a door that the General himself unlocked. The anæmic rays of Ma Ki Fu's lantern revealed a large number of hand grenades of all shapes and manufacture. There were Russian bombs that looked much like wine bottles, and others like baby rattles. Most were of local manufacture and round as the proverbial cartoon bomb, with small shielded shank and dynamite fuse.

I wondered at the intellect of him who had planned this place. There were thousands of bombs and grenades, and every one alive. Ma pointed to another heavy door and explained, through our interpreter, that beyond it lay gunpowder and high explosives. The place in which we now stood was, as nearly as I could calculate, in the very center of Khotan proper, and beneath the bazar. Ma Ki Fu leaned against a supporting timber, lantern in hand. He was unimpressed by the fact that one spark from his smoky lantern could blow the city of Khotan to Hell.

Mad as seemed this storing of hundreds of tons of explosive beneath the bazar, there was no alternative. To make a cache in the mountains would necessitate sending the bulk of the bandit army to guard it. Ma Hsi Jung could spare no men. His only salvation was the maintenance of a highly mobile force capable of attacking and smashing any force sent against him. He must keep both men and munitions at the very hub of operations—Khotan.

Later, above ground, much to my relief, we marched back to Ma's *Yamen*. People again looked at the tag on my chest, soldiers to salute, civilians to stand in respectful silence. I began to wonder just what that bit of muslin said that made me so important. Safely installed in the *Yamen*, I asked my toothbrush-faced interpreter just what the gadget meant.

"That thou art Sho-E Ju Yi, a Tungan officer," was the reply.

Silently I weighed Ma's generosity and wondered what would happen when and if the northern Bolsheviki government discovered my Tungan alliance.

General Ma is a prophet with honor in his own country. While Khotan resounds with fabulous legends about him, the facts are no less colorful than the fables.

As, for instance, the incident of the Bolshevik General who lost his head.

He came from the north, that General, with seven hundred men and orders in his pocket to bring back bandit Ma, dead or alive. The seven hundred were annihilated by the Tungans and their leader, together with his instructions, was brought to Khotan.

General Ma with his own hand took the papers from the captured Bolshevik. He read them. He smiled in that cold, cruel way of his, at the humor of the situation. There was no time wasted. With one stroke of his scimitar Ma decapitated the prisoner, deftly catching the falling head by an ear.

An hour later the head of the Red General was on its way back to Moscowa, Ma Hsi Jung's seal stamped in red upon the forehead. Its bearer was a Bolshevik whose ears had been cut off.

My host had then implied that the incident might be a lesson to unfriendly neighbors.

For modern savagery, consider the fall of Yengi Hissar, a beautiful little city and fortress near Kashgar on the Yarkand road.

The Tungans, in retreat from Urumchi, had taken Kashgar and were garrisoned there, systematically looting the country before moving on toward Khotan, their ultimate destination. Arriving at the gates of Yengi Hissar, Ma Hsi Jung found them closed and the battlements manned by seven hundred armed men. Two Tungan mediators who were sent in to negotiate for the city's immediate surrender were returned, their heads hurled from the wall's crest to come to a bumping halt at the General's feet.

Roaring with rage, Ma Hsi Jung commanded the city laid siege. Days later, when the walls were breached, the Emir who dared to withstand his might was beheaded by Ma's own sword. Those who remained of the original defenders were herded into a large serai and there forced to kneel while from dawn to dark a band of executioners labored. Not a man was spared.

As a final fillip to the proceedings, Ma decreed that the

Emir's head be taken to the *Mesh* (parade) ground. There, with the army divided into two competitive forces, the Emir's head was tossed in to be used as a football—until it wore out. And this occurred in A.D. 1933.

Late one afternoon, while General Ma, our interpreter, and I were having tea, a courier was ushered into the room. He handed his message to Ma and then departed. The preoccupied General stuffed the bit of paper into his pocket. Then, thinking the better of it, removed and read the dispatch. His face darkened. He crumpled and threw the message from him disgustedly.

"If thou desirest to see how the Tungan makes war," he said, turning to me, "go thou with the expedition which now rides to capture two hundred deserters. They flee north, toward Tan-Jung."

Our conversation was held through an interpreter and, jumping at the chance to see such operations, I thanked both for the privilege.

"Thou wilt go as one of the officers," General Ma said in answer to my acceptance. "Discharge thy *Chan'tu* servant; Ma Ki Fu will go with thee instead." Abdul-the-meek was immediately paid off. While I prepared for the ensuing journey he tearfully took leave and en route, as I later discovered, swiped a blanket and my one spoon. In that instance crime paid, for I never saw him again.

Mounted, and on our way out of the city, Ma Ki Fu beside me in Abdul's place, I found myself, instead of "one of the officers," *the* officer in command of the thirty-five-man contingent sent to round up the renegades. Just before we departed, I had asked the General how thirty-five men could be a match for two hundred.

"If two hundred are such cowards as to desert, thirty-five

who are not afraid should be able to bring them back!"

In such convictions lay much of the power of this strange man who stored high explosives in metal cans beneath the bazar and expected the impossible from his people.

My first move as senior officer was to elevate the next in rank, a fellow about my age, to the command. I explained my action was due to my ignorance of the country, of Tungan field tactics, and of their language. (Not more than one Tungan in ten understood the Turki tongue.) He refused to accept my office, but agreed to handle the men in my stead.

We held to a canter until dark when we reached a little corral, changed our mounts for fresh, and departed at a fast pace which we held for hours.

We had two submachine guns besides our rifles. Even I, though in ranking position, had been issued a rifle. The rifles were of the best the Tungan forces boasted. Mine and Sho-Sho Ju Yi Lu's were Wesley-Richards fitted with telescopic sights. Ma Ki Fu carried a Mauser, and the rest had the usual motley assortment. The two hundred, we had been told, carried a rifle per man, four machine guns, and ample ammunition. It seemed that the General had been a bit vague as to *how* we were to stop the renegade army.

The night was broken by hour runs and half-hour canters. Most amazing was the fact that the horses held up under the killing pace and only one accident marred our midnight chase. While we were moving swiftly through broken country, half dunes, half rock, one horse fell with its rider and strained a tendon. Since the rider's face was badly torn, he was ordered to turn about and make the corral as best he could with his injured mount.

The eastern sky had just begun to herald the approaching dawn when Lu pointed out a lumpy ridge.

LAND WITHOUT LAUGHTER

"They must pass that on their way north and we can stop them there, our men spread along the heights."

We moved ahead and I wondered just how long it would be before we did find our men and then, what? Ma Ki Fu rode alongside me. He touched my arm and pointed towards the heads of our horses. Their ears were standing straight up, listening!

That last thing they heard and the first we could detect was a far-away whinny. Then the ridge we had intended to occupy came to life. Right in front of us a machine gun broke into a stuttering chant and all along the dark slope rifles began to crack. I was suddenly shovelling up desert sand with my chin and the rifle slung across my shoulders whacked against the back of my skull. My mount had been struck by the first bullets.

I made a dash for a clump of tamarisk that had gathered about it a great mound of sand, finding there several who had been even swifter than I in hunting shelter. Ma Ki Fu, Lu, and three others lay at its base and there were a few welcoming jests as to where I had left my horse. Seeking more favorable concealment, one after the other we ran toward a higher dune a hundred feet away. The firing from the deserters was ineffectual, for we were in a dark hollow between dunes and by the time they were able to see our stooped, running figures, we had gained the shelter sought. All of us but Ma Ki Fu. He had disappeared absolutely. Lu pessimistically insisted that he had seen Ma Ki Fu fall.

Foolishly, I ran back in the open to look for him, and I found him still in the shadow of the broken tamarisk. He asked if I had gone mad with the rest. Then I saw where he had been. A bag lay beside him, and in it were the grenades that had been tied behind Lu's saddle. On top of the bag, to keep it out of the sand, lay a submachine gun. He took the heavier

133

gun and ammunition and I the sack of bombs. We reached the
dune untouched by the fusillade directed at us, to find there
Lu lying flat on his back, his feet under him. His face, which
he held with both hands, was spurting blood. He had been hit
while sighting over the dune's crest. Pulling him around so
that his head was higher than his body, we pried his hands from
the bloody face. He had been struck in the eye, and Ma Ki Fu
pointed at a wound just over the ear. The bullet had passed
through his head. Permitting him again to clasp his face with
both hands, we pulled him a little farther down the dune, out
of harm's way; not that it much mattered.

Ma Ki Fu took up Lu's rifle, wiped it off with his sleeve,
and together we began to give an account of ourselves. From
the other side of the far dune came the staccato chuk-chuk-chuk
of the machine gun that had cut down our animals. The sound
gave Ma Ki Fu an idea and he unlimbered the little gun he
had taken from the scene of our ambush.

"Watch," he called over to where I lay.

His handiwork was cheering to see, as he laid a stream of
bullets over the crest of the opposite dune, twice disturbing
lumps that lifted themselves to slump forward again in full
view. Then, the other targets having removed themselves, we
crawled back down to Lu. He was dead. His hands were still
locked over the wound. As we sat beside him, seven of our men
came over the top of another hill beneath us. Of the seven,
one was being supported by his companions. As they came to
a panting halt beside us, I saw that he had been shot in the leg
just above the ankle. One of the men told what had happened
immediately on our being ambushed.

"We saw thee fall, and the rest of us turned our horses and
ran back of the great dune. Only eighteen of us escaped. I don't
know what happened to the others, but their horses were lying
with thine in the gully."

LAND WITHOUT LAUGHTER

Ma Ki Fu admitted, "I found three when I went back, but all were dead."

The wounded one didn't remember being hit, but swore as he told of dismounting with the others and having his leg go out from under him.

Firing continued on the far side of the dunes. Evidently others of our party were alive, too. We had rifles and went once more to the dune's crest to use them, even the wounded one joining us. The sun's glowing orb raised itself above the edge of the world, and made for effective shooting with the telescope-fitted rifle, which had been ineffective in the semi-dark of the early dawn. Just as excellent targets were presenting themselves for Ma Ki Fu's and my high velocity rifles, some one began jerking at my heel. I turned. It was Ma Ki Fu motioning that I should follow. He slithered down the sandy dune-side with me behind him. We passed Lu, who lay as he had died, hands bunched over eyes. We continued down through a draw between our dune and the one behind it, over a smaller dune that was screened by the one we left, then in a dog trot we followed a roundabout route that put us on what proved to be the deserters' right flank. Crawling cautiously up behind some higher rocks, we looked out over the position they occupied. There lay a group of men fanned out over the full circumference of the dune. Ma Ki Fu's two machine-gun casualties lay on top of the ridge and three others, obviously wounded, lay side by side in the dune's hollow. We saw for the first time why the others had not continued in their flight.

After our ambush had failed, they had either to cross over a higher dune that backed the one behind which they hid, or descend into the open and circle it. Either maneuver would put them under our fire. From where we hunched, it was two hundred feet to the nearest of their men. A good two thirds were exposed to our fire. But disconcerting, to say the least, was the fact that we, too, were perfect targets, and the others had already spotted us. Sand began to kick up before us under the impact of their bullets. Ma stood up full height, completely exposed to their fire. His arm whipped back, then forward, and the black gyrating blob of a grenade soared over the rim of the far dune.

We hunched down to escape the whining bullets sent in our direction and waited for the detonation. Waited, and just as Ma began to curse the *bomba*, it cracked and the air was rent with its soaring, whistling particles. A cloud of dust and sand puffed over the rim of the far dune. We waited to see its effect; it apparently had none.

On the opposite side of our enemy, some one else threw a grenade. The thing was so slow in detonating that the renegades were able to escape by running from it, then throwing themselves to the ground. It went off as had ours. It duplicated the dust cloud, and the untouched deserters swarmed back to their previous positions. However, our compatriots' bomb had more far-reaching effect than had ours, for a moment later a pack of horses stampeded from behind the dune and fled out over the rolling country. Immediately following them came a pack of horses with men hunched low over their backs. A dozen animals fell kicking, at the chatter of the submachine gun from behind the dune we had left a few moments before. Several of the dismounted riders tried to scramble up the slope they had to cross to escape us. All collapsed under the relentless fire our men poured on them.

We were later to learn that fully 135 escaped, and that of the 181 that had originally deserted,[1] only 29 remained behind the dune to do combat, and they were dismounted. Theirs had been the first riderless horses to stampede.

[1]For it was later determined that 181 and not 200 soldiers deserted.

LAND WITHOUT LAUGHTER

Those left behind were desperate and their aim improved accordingly. Ma Ki Fu and I were forced to vacate our position when they opened fire with a machine gun with the evident intention of knocking the hill, behind which we hid, to pieces bit by bit. I remember thinking what excellent story material the action was providing and that I might have to tell it through a Ouiji board.

Back at our old location, we found the others as we had left them, except for one who had lost a patch of scalp an inch wide and three long, and in its place acquired a fine headache. All of us crouched beside Lu as the enemy started to level the surrounding countryside with their machine guns.

"They are all frightened and don't know at what they shoot," Ma Ki Fu remarked. "It will not be long before the guns jam and they surrender."

Exactly that came to pass in less than an hour, when all firing suddenly ceased. Ma Ki Fu became doubly cautious. He threw a grenade across the intervening space and it burst, leaving a dent on top of the dune. Some one yelled and cursed us in Tungani. Ma Ki Fu called back, demanding surrender. A handkerchief went up on a rifle barrel and cautiously one of the other party came over the crest of the far hill. Ma Ki Fu recognized the man and called him to us. Once in the shadow of our protecting dune, the newcomer cursed us thoroughly, for we had thrown a bomb at our own people. Our men explained that the unmounted deserters had surrendered to them half an hour before when their burnt-out machine guns refused further duty.

We tramped over the dune's crest, down to the level separating us from the others, then over the second of the dunes.

We had fared luckily; the deserters had suffered horribly. Now, as Ma Ki Fu and I counted heads, we found that only four of our party had been killed and two wounded. Of the deserters, there were in the dune's hollow seven dead and five more on the hillside where they had fallen when trying to escape. One of our men climbed to the top of the hill and called back to us that there were three more lying on its far side. The machine gun had done its work. On top of the dune's curling edge lay the two that had first fallen to Ma Ki Fu's marksmanship. Seventeen dead in all. And of the twenty-nine prisoners, there were three wounded, one in the jaw, another in the nose, the third had lost a few fingers, and every last one had in his eyes the shadow of abject fear. Four of the lot stood to one side; theirs was the greatest crime. *Veteran* Tungans!

A young Tungan who had been next in command to Lu asked what was to be done with the prisoners. I told Ma Ki Fu to do whatever was customary. He ordered that they be taken back to Khotan with the exception of the four veterans. They were to be shot. There was none of the usual formality of such affairs. Immediately on receipt of the order, the officer took from its case his Luger, cocked it, and pulled the trigger. The first two of the four slumped to the ground and the remaining two each chose a different course: one charging for the spitting Luger and the other running away. Both lost the race.

Just then one of our men came up with a bunch of escaped horses. Ma Ki Fu and I mounted, as did those who had lost their animals in the first few moments of the fight. The others regained their horses, which were concealed behind some dunes a few hundred yards away. At last, all of our contingent mounted, the machine guns loaded on the extra horses, we parted company, seven of our men to haze the walking prisoners back toward Khotan, and we twenty-four to turn our horses' heads in the general direction the escaped deserters had taken.

7

NORTH we travelled as the sun rose high in the heavens and brought full realization that we were trespassing on the earthly domain of Satan: the Taklamakan Desert. Mirages formed about us and the tops of hills floated on mirror lakes. Never were there less than twelve whirlwinds of gigantic proportions traipsing over the horizon and leaving their hourglass reflections in the mirage. Midday found the fierce heat robbing us of any energy we had previously possessed. The sun, blazing in a cloudless sky, seemed intent upon reducing the earth to a cinder. Littering the desert floor, countless ink-black rocks glistened.

We had had no sleep since leaving Khotan the day before and we lolled in the saddles of the tired, stumbling horses. Ma Ki Fu was the first to break the silence, pointing his heavily muscled, sweat-glistening arm at a dark blob floating on the mirage directly ahead.

"A dead horse," he said. "They are running their horses in this heat. It will be easy to catch them. By nightfall not one will have a mount to ride!"

He turned to me then and asked disgustedly, all the while wiping the sweat from his musclebound, bare chest: "Does thy Amerikaluk soldier have to bake like this when he pursues deserters?"

I rolled a heavy tongue around in a leather-walled mouth, swallowed a couple of times to tune up shrivelled vocal cords, and replied:

LAND WITHOUT LAUGHTER

"This is nothing. Why, in America——"

And all the while I wondered if any other brand of soldier except Tungan would not change, under such adverse conditions, from pursuer to deserter. The last water we had tasted had been at the corral the night before, and I could literally feel myself shrivel as the sun drew my life's moisture to make clouds.

As we drew nearer the dead horse, Ma Ki Fu slung his rifle from its place on his back and motioned, without speaking, that I should do likewise. All communication in our band had changed from that of the tongue to pantomime. Our mouths were too dry for comfortable or distinguishable speech. At Ma Ki Fu's gesture the band broke up and we approached the dead horse fanwise. Something moved behind it! Every man levelled his rifle. Then, as a blob raised itself, head and shoulders, above the carcass, we all fired. It sank back out of sight and we kicked our weary mounts into a shambling trot and, once we reached the horse, a not pleasant sight met our eyes. He who had lain behind the horse was riddled through and through. In his hand was a rifle on whose barrel was tied a dirty silken handkerchief. Ma Ki Fu, seeing how the sight affected me, spoke in a thick voice.

"It matters not. We could not have left him here, nor sent him back."

We settled once more to the ride, leaving the young fellow as he had fallen, face down in the hot desert sand.

Toward evening we came on several more dead horses, one with his rider beside him, a suicide. The others were without riders. Just as the sun sank behind the hills, and the first chill breezes of the night made us once more bind our clothing tight around us, the horses picked up to a trot and began eagerly to sniff at the breeze. Water was near. The horses moved right to the hole and, dropping to their knees, stretched their heads

140

down the hole. One by one they snorted and regained their feet without even mouthing the water. We, who had dismounted, pushed the horses away from the hole and knelt beside it to determine what was wrong. Ma Ki Fu sniffed and disgustedly spat into the water.

"Befouled! A latrine for those bastards that got here before us."

As we mounted again one of the Tungan soldiers spoke bitterly, and as he did, waved a long knife. Ma Ki Fu translated:

"He says that if he catches those *tongus* (swine) that polluted the well, he will take both their manhood and eyes, then free them to seek their way to water with stones filling their eye-sockets, and no use for life if they find it."

Two hours farther on our way Ma Ki Fu led us off the trail and along a narrow rocky ledge to another water hole, this one full of clean unpolluted water. The others had not found it. We fed the horses from the woven hair-bags of grain slung behind each saddle; drank our fill of the brackish water, and, in the cold of the desert night, ate the stale onion-bread we had carried from Khotan.

Four hours later we continued on our way, this time with ready cocked rifles. Dawn slew the stars and brought the first puffs of warm air that warned of the heat to come. The changeless desolation of the unbounded sea of dunes exhausted the vision so that most of us rode with half-closed eyes.

The sun was half way to its zenith when we topped an undulating dune to see three men working over a foundered horse.

So intent were they on bringing the exhausted animal to its feet that our presence was not noticed until one sat down with a bullet from a telescopic-sighted Wesley Richards in his neck.

LAND WITHOUT LAUGHTER

The remaining two, panic-stricken, swung on their mounts and started off. Another shot broke one horse's shoulder and the unhorsed one ran after the other, begging to be taken on with him. However, the one who was still mounted whipped his horse over another rise in the ground and was lost to view.

Left behind, the other ran back to the cover his horse afforded and prepared to go out fighting. The man was far away, at least four hundred yards (not a distance to be seriously considered under ordinary conditions, but in the desert equal to thousands of rifle-range yards); a tiny speck just jet against the glaring sand. Waves of heat distorted vision between us and him. It seemed an impossible target but Ma Ki Fu thought otherwise.

His rifle rose, snuggled to his shoulder, his cheek caressing the stock, hawk-eyes peering through the telescope sight.

"In the name of the Merciful, the Compassionate!"[1] He breathed the words softly so as not to disturb his aim. It appears the gods of all men are on the side of the strong.

As Ma Ki Fu squeezed the trigger the black figure of the man behind the body of the horse straightened up in that spasmodic instant of death, and then lurched down upon the sand, like a dead dark beetle.

Ma Ki Fu stroked an imaginary beard with his free hand, something very near a grin wrinkling the corners of his eyes.

"God is great!" he remarked devoutly. And he patted the rifle with affection after wiping a dust speck from the miraculous sight.

By midday, we passed two more exhausted horses which the deserters had left lying in the trail resignedly awaiting death. Ma Ki Fu voiced his conclusions:

"They leave their horses to die without shooting them, and ride double. Theirs is panic; we shall soon meet them."

[1] This is a fair example of Tungan humor.

142

LAND WITHOUT LAUGHTER

Another day was drawing to a close and the sun, an orange ball, hung just above the shimmering western horizon. We were about to give up the chase and return when one of the men, who rode a little ahead of our cavalcade, whooped and waved to Ma Ki Fu and me. All of us quirted our jaded mounts up beside him and strained our eyes in the direction indicated. There at the foot of some wind-worn bluffs were two squat yurts and a corral full of horses, mounts of those we had been pursuing. Even as we watched, they began to ride out of the camp in a northerly direction.

"They have escaped us, but we can still stop some if we leave our horses here and wait," Ma Ki Fu pointed to the rapidly setting sun, "for it to go. Then we can creep up and trap those in the yurts."

The horses were left in one man's care and the rest of us, stiff from long hours in the saddle, went forward on foot. The terrain was broken and slashed into thousands of wrinkles that provided excellent concealment for our little band of bush-whackers, and we were within three hundred yards of the two yurts when we gathered in a little arroyo.

"What now?" the men asked of me.

I told them to fan out in a semicircle about the yurts and under no circumstances to occupy the enemy's position and fight each other, as had happened two days before.

As the men departed I asked Ma Ki Fu, who had acted as interpreter, if my orders had been correct. Ma Ki Fu slapped his bare chest and swore that, "There was nothing else to tell the men." Then he added, with a sly grin, "For what thou did'st not say, I did."

We crawled to another ledge a bit closer to the yurts, and, as we watched, men came out of them, looked over our heads and in the direction from whence we came. As they spoke, a strange tongue was carried to our ears by the night breezes— *Russian!*

143

Suddenly one of them shouted in an excited voice, and they leaped for the yurts and cover. Our men had been seen. Seven horses that were tied together became frightened, and, straining back at the rope feed-line, pulled the stakes holding it and went at a stumbling run off across the hummocks. A man ran out of the yurt with evident intention of pursuing them, but a rifle cracked and he abruptly fell to his knees. Rising, he made for the yurt only to have another shot stretch him out before it. Then every rifle cut loose, pouring round after round into the flimsy felt-walled yurts. Our heavy fire continued for fully five minutes and then ceased at the lack of response from the yurts.

I started to rise but Ma Ki Fu jerked me back with an angry Tungani expletive. Angry at his rough handling, which had sent me grubbing in the rocky bottom of the cleft, I started once more for the open, cursing him as I went. It was then that a machine gun chattered from inside one yurt and swept three others as careless as myself from the edge of the earthen hump and sent me leaping back to cover behind it.

Just behind me came the whirling, singing bits of rock dislodged by the stream of ricocheting bullets. For a moment the air was full of warbling hissing things. Then as suddenly as it had begun, the gun silenced and both of us sat back and pursed our lips in surprise. Certainly he who lay behind the machine gun in the yurt had almost proven his immortality by surviving the shots we had thrown into his hiding-place.

Ma Ki Fu dumped the grenades out of the sack he carried; he was in the act of picking one from the lot when the air around us was shredded by the wasplike buzz of shot. Ma Ki Fu had two grenades in his hands as he threw himself, with me, face down in the gully. Some one was on our flank. Ma Ki Fu whispered to me that he was hit and I looked at the arm indicated and saw four black oozing holes—shotgun wounds. The accursed thing blasted away again and once more the earth near our heads spurted up as the shot spattered against it. The one whom we had to thank for the poor marksmanship was hidden except for the black barrel of his gun which protruded from between two mounds of rocks that had been piled on each side of it. He was above and behind us, about two hundred feet away. At the third shot, which missed as had its fellows, Ma Ki Fu got to his knees and hurled a grenade at the black barrel and the one who lay behind it.

The moment the grenade left his hand, the machine gun spoke again and knocked Ma Ki Fu on top of me. Behind us the shotgun and its owner vanished and a fine mist settled on the surrounding rocks, but Ma Ki Fu, stung by the bullets, grabbed two more grenades and started for the yurt. He was again knocked off his feet, but he rose and once more started forward. Four times he went down on his face, but still struggled on. Given courage by his example, the rest of us came out in the open and fired as fast as we could work the bolt of our rifles.

Ma Ki Fu threw another bomb but, injured as he was, it went too far to one side. Down again and unable to get to his feet, he sat as does a child, feet straight before him, and threw his second grenade. The thing lighted right on top of the gunner's yurt, rolled off, and burst, blowing to shreds the flimsy shelter and those in it. Reaching Ma Ki Fu, I knelt beside him while the others ran past and on toward the one remaining yurt. Ma Ki Fu gasped a moment, looked down at his red streaming body, then at me, and in a voice surprisingly full, said,

"My destiny is fulfilled. My blood is all gone. My veins are empty. I die." And, lying over on his side, he did.

Running over to the yurt, I found the others had captured four badly wounded Russians and already executed one. At sight of me the other Russians pointed to my occidental face, then their own, and begged that I stop the wild Tungans. It was of no use; the soldiers would have shot me if I had interfered. Little did the Russians know how luckily they fared by being shot.

Even as I gazed at the corpses of men who but a few minutes before had been so very alive, the darkness came sweeping down from skies already jet.[1] Beady-eyed and nervous the night hovered an instant, then, with a flirt and flutter, settled. It was as though a vulture stealthily returned to an interrupted meal.

Once the horses were rounded up we started back toward Khotan, riding silently as we thought of the four dead we left behind: valiant Tungans stretched out shoulder to shoulder under the ragged felts and boulders.

Returned to Khotan, I went with my one remaining officer, a scrawny turkey-necked fellow, to the *Yamen* and my quarters. I had no more than decently gotten to sleep, dirt and all, when some one nudged me and I roused cursing the indiscreet disturber. To my consternation I discovered he was none other than Ma Hsi Jung. The General laughed goodnaturedly at my embarrassment, and, shaking hands, seated himself on the bed at my side. Ma Hsi Jung told me through the medium of his aide-de-camp interpreter, that the ringleaders of the deserters had been executed when they were returned to Khotan. And, most amazing of all, that three hundred men had been sent after us as reinforcements, though we never saw them.

Later I learned that this body of men, anxious to overtake us, took a false short cut instead of following our trail. Missing

[1] A phenomenon I again witnessed near the Etsin Gol. Apparently it is brought about by layers of dust suspended in mid-air. Light refracting, these dust strata effectively blot out all light. As a consequence, daylight descends in horizontal layers—keeping pace with the setting sun. At the instant of the sun's plunge beneath the horizon, earth—and sky—are left in absolute darkness, save for the light of a heaven filled with stars.

146

us, they arrived at the scene of Ma Ki Fu's death the day after we departed, where they met a small troop of Bolsheviki soldiers sent to relieve those men we had annihilated at the battle of the yurts. In the ensuing conflict the Bolshevikis were reported killed to the last man.

General Ma explained that it gave him a great deal of pleasure that the American had seen the conditions under which the Tungan had always been forced to fight. The pleasure was all his.

With the dawn I was rudely awakened by the heavy hand of a soldier. Rising with a groan, I wearily demanded of the orderly just what next was to be inflicted upon me. He, in lieu of reply, tendered me a note written in a beautiful but extravagant Persian hand. One of the writer's idiosyncrasies was his neglecting to dot the characters; a very grave mistake in my instance. With that lack, as well as the lovely chaos of interwoven words, I could make neither head nor tail of the message's import. Just as I was about to resume my interrupted rest my eye fell on the signature: Ughlug Beg![1]

Rousing with a start, I called back the retreating orderly. "Did the bearer wait? He did? Then bring him in." At first glance I chortled with delight; it was Kuen. Embracing him with both arms, I pressed first against his left, then right, side; Turkistani greeting among close friends. But upon releasing my welcome guest I saw that he smiled in a quizzical, embarrassed manner. It was not Kuen! The stranger laughed at my embarrassment, aware that I had mistaken him for his brother.

While we breakfasted Tokhtamish explained his presence. Ughlug Beg, his father, had been commanded to come to

[1]This name is commonly spelled *Ulug*; however, in this instance it was spelled with the $\dot{g}$ (or *gh*). I assume that this is the antiquated form.

Khotan. There was a matter of a beaten tax collector and un-paid taxes to be explained to Ma Hsi Jung. The note contained salutations and a request that I, out of friendship for his son Kuen, assure the Tungan General that Ughlug Beg was an honest man. Kuen had obviously returned home and told his father of me. Certainly the old man had been generous, for as I spoke with Tokhtamish I wore a splendid silken coat: a gift from Ughlug Beg.

This, it seems, is as good a time as any to go into detail regarding the Turkoman chieftain. Ever since my days in Ladakh the man's name had been one to conjure with. Such preposterous tales were told of Ughlug Beg that I had thought him but a fictional character very like America's Paul Bunyan. Upon meeting Kuen, Tokhta, and Muhammad, sons of this impossible character, I had pieced together, bit by bit, the old man's history.

Born in the desert—the Starvation Steppes of Russian Turkis-tan—southwest of Lake Balkash, he had followed in the foot-steps of his brigand father. In his youth a terrible warrior, he had, at the head of his clan, massacred and driven away all Russians within raiding distance. Then, without opposition, he had established a small monarchy; setting himself up as its head. For thirty-two years he had ruled, beginning his reign at seventeen years of age. As one tale went: "A fierce warrior in his childhood, he became a wicked bigot in his years of power and authority. Compassionate when he chose to be, Ughlug Beg was so mighty that he could be cruel yet name the cruelty *justice* and have it so recognized throughout his reign of influence."

In his fiftieth year the Russian Government had sent an expedition against him. Outnumbered, Ughlug Beg had led his band of outlaws in a smashing thrust, out of the trap. With his entire clan: men, women, and children—of whom most

148

were his progeny—he fled. Crossing the Pamirs, he had continued on towards the east until finding a land to his liking. This proved to be a lost valley somewhere south of Tikilik Tagh, which itself is several days south of Khotan and close to the Tibetan frontier. Dispossessing the few Kirghiz who objected, he had established his rule in the mountains.

Ughlug Beg's children's first memories were of hunger and plenty; of obeisance before a majestic and terrible figure who took wives as often as childbirth killed them; a creature who was one month demon, defying the laws of God and man, slaying his enemies, burdening the wombs of his women, and filling his stomach with *kumiss* (the fermented mare's milk)—his brain with its intoxicating vapors; the next month leading wives and offspring away from their dwellings and into the wilderness. As fierce in his repentance as he had been furious in the deeds he repented, Ughlug Beg for weeks forced his family to endure his penance. They had lived in caves, starved, and prayed. They had looked on when he commanded God to declare him a Prophet and reveal the appropriate visions. As the month turned so had he become less and less pious, until, in anticlimax, he had reviled an unresponsive God, daring Almighty wrath to strike him dead. His wives had clung to him, their children to them, both screaming in terror at such words; for some inexplicable reason unwilling to be widowed or orphaned of such a man.

Having defeated his God, Ughlug Beg had gone back to the habitations of men, consumed more *kumiss*, filled more wombs, frightened his allies, murdered his foes, brought back their daughters as wives—who loved him—become pious, then sacrilegious, and by the unflagging vigor of his loins gradually built up a clan of his own blood about him!

With the years his temper had cooled, but not his capacity for begetting offspring; who now numbered—by the conservative count of Tokhtamish—one hundred seventy-three! Of grandchildren: two hundred eleven. Great and great-great-grandchildren? Ullah alone kept count!

Such a man, now ninety-seven years old, I was to meet.

Mounted, riding out of the city to meet the old man's cavalcade, I asked Tokhtamish how his father travelled. Surprised at the question, he replied:

"He rides a horse or camel as would thou or I, brother. How else?"

An hour's canter brought us within sight of the approaching caravan. Riding two and three abreast, laughing and jesting, a motley array of fur-capped, bewhiskered sons and grandsons preceded the main group by about a mile. All were clad in heavy outer coats; open now in the lowland heat. Underneath this were lighter jackets bound around by broad sashes. From below this to halfway between knee and ankle hung yellow gold-stitched leathern breeches. Their boots were of better leather than the kind ordinarily sold in the bazar; they were not pieced, but made of whole leather; the heels were about three inches high and ironshod. Each man carried a rifle, some of which were modern carbines, others muzzle-loading matchlocks! In greeting us they wildly discharged these weapons with utter disregard as to which way the gun was pointed. As a result beards and eyebrows were singed away and many a farmer's wife in the surrounding field was nearly made a widow.

Together we reined up to wait for the camels that constituted the caravan proper. Arriving with the first of these, riding in ease between the beast's humps, came the patriarch: Ughlug Beg. A gold-embossed *kindjal* (dagger) hung suspended from his Paisley girdle and the butt of a smaller knife protruded from a boot top. The *old* man I had expected to meet was not a part of this Turkoman. His beard was white, but it seemed a product of dignity, not age. His face, long and aquiline, was no more creased than his sons'; and what wrinkles there were were about his squinting eyes and on the cheeks, where they gathered in the grimace's effort.

Tokhtamish spurred up to his father's side, announced my presence, then called me to him. Ughlug Beg took my two hands in his, voiced the salaam, passed his hands over his beard— as did I—accepted my gift of a pair of binoculars without ever looking at them, and rode on. I was nettled at such treatment, but the others assured me that it was the way of their father.

"You," they said, "he loves most dearly for your kindness to our brother Kuen."

Back in the *Yamen* with Ma Hsi Jung, I told of our meeting. The General laughed as I told of my treatment; however, he grew grave when I mentioned that all the family bore fire-arms. At the taking of Khotan, Ma had passed an edict that all civilians must surrender firearms within a month or suffer imprisonment, perhaps death. Quickly he summoned an orderly, rapped out orders in staccato Tungani, then explained at leisure: Tungan under-officers were not to arrest, or confiscate the arms of any of Ughlug Beg's party. Ma, it seemed, respected the old man as much as I. Certainly he made great concessions on his behalf; even to suspending laws.

At dusk the General summoned me from my quarters. Together, a few soldiers preceding and following, we went out of the *Yamen* courtyard. As we strolled leisurely through the dustless bazar streets—wet down by the shopkeepers and smelling richly of the centuries that had trod them—the young Tungan explained the occasion of our walk. We were going to visit the old Turkoman. The King humbly visited the tax evader instead of having the culprit dragged into his presence! Despite Ma Hsi Jung's disdain of convention, he was a respecter of tradition.

151

LAND WITHOUT LAUGHTER

As we turned into the *serai* where the household of Ughlug Beg was bivouacked, Ma commanded our accompanying guard to wait at the gates. The *serai* compound, unusually large, was filled with yurts. Mountain folk, this family preferred raising their felt igloos to living under a roof.

A regiment of sons came out of their dwellings to bow respectfully. Two led the way to the yurt of their father. The leaded felt flap that served as door was lifted aside and we entered. After us came a dozen or more of the others.

The old chieftain was just preparing to say his prayers and as a consequence all of us did likewise. Devotions completed, Ughlug Beg, with tremendous dignity, bade the General and me be seated. Kneeling, I carefully drew in my robes and settled back on my heels, respectfully covering my hands. Ma Hsi Jung, clad in uniform tunic, in kneeling ripped his tight breeches. Back of Ughlug Beg's veiled eyes I think I glimpsed a twinkle. Close by the old man's side played several naked children: two infant sons and two daughters of perhaps six years. These were the offspring of a ninety-seven-year-old man; their young mother, who looked on from the shadow behind her master, was obviously pregnant! Behind the General and me stood other children: gray-bearded sons and daughters barren with age.

Now that candlelight took the place of the midday's glaring sun, Ughlug Beg's eyes were fully opened. At our first meeting I had thought I detected a bit of the Mongol cast in his features. Instead it had been the protective squint acquired by years under blazing skies.

Ma, wearying of the preconversation ritual, downed his tea in a gulp, then addressed the Turkoman chieftain. One of the other man's sons spoke Tungani, and it was he who played the part of interpreter.

"Why is it," Ma demanded, "that thou hast defied the law:

kept thy weapons, assaulted my tax collector, and paid not thy taxes? Answer!"

With the utmost calm Ughlug Beg listened as his son translated. Then with equal deliberation he replied:

"Concerning the weapons: my people live far from the paths of thy soldiers. They hunt for food—so, we keep our weapons.

"Thy tax collectors are corrupt. We pay our taxes. They take the money, go away, and return again the next month to tax our herds again; they will not remember the money already paid. The *Book of Wisdom and Logic* reads thus:

" 'He who soweth the seed of treachery shall behold his fields to sprout in the form of the whirlwind, mature as a tempest, and at the harvesting he shall reap the blizzard; and no more bitter bread will be known than from the grain of such growing!' The tax collector was corrupt and unjust. We chastised him."

Ma Hsi Jung made no further comment; instead, he called for a pen and paper. He wrote two separate notes on a sheet, affixed his seal to each, then ripped the paper in two: one half he handed Ughlug Beg. The Turkoman held it close to the candle flame; unable to read the Chinese script he handed it to another who could. He read aloud:

"The bearer of this will be paid from the mint the sum which is due him; he will name it.

"The seal of Muhammad Hsi Jung." Ma handed him the other half of the divided sheet.

"The tax collector who patrols the mountains south of Khotan will immediately be arrested and held for execution.

"The seal of Muhammad Hsi Jung."

His mien softened, the Turkoman chieftain consoled the General:

"Thou art a Padishah and a Padishah's bed is not different

from the torturer's table. For a pillow thou hast yesterday; for cover thou hast treason—and a leaden cover it is. The woman in thy bed is tomorrow; her foul breath makes thee forget her sex and dread the next lying with her.

"And above thy head, smiting thy ears with two fiery hammers, is a sorcerer—destiny. Thou art an unfortunate, more to be pitied than a starving beggar; thou art Padishah!"

Together as we had come, Ma and I withdrew. Ughlug Beg arose and followed us out. In leaving he humbly bowed to Ma. Me, he embraced, first on one side, then the other; then he soundly kissed me full on the lips. Strangest of all I was not embarrassed, but was pleased that he should so consider me. Before releasing me the old man whispered in my ear:

"Console him, thy Padishah; he is a good man, but betrayed so terribly. And of thyself: my home is thine. My valley waits for thee, and no *Adam* hath more right to walk in it than thou hast."

Ah—but this tale is not ended. Two days later, after the old Turkoman had with his tribe gone back to his mountain fastnesses, the tax collector was brought before Ma. He was accused, but swore innocence. An orderly was sent to the mint to determine how much Ughlug Beg had taken to cover taxes falsely extorted from his people. A *quarter of a million seer* in paper had been taken! That, it was learned, had been sold for gold bullion in the bazar. Turning again to the thoroughly frightened tax collector, Ma threatened him with worse than death unless he immediately confessed. Still he maintained his innocence. A Koran was found and handed him. Would he take an oath with that in his hand? He would; and did.

Afterwards, the tax collector having gone free, the General turned to me. There was a lifting at the corners of his mouth; he burst into laughter. He had neglected to put the Koran into Ughlug Beg's hand. The treasury was minus two hundred fifty thousand *seer!*

154

8

But few days elapsed before tumult again became a part of my existence. I suggest you share this experience. Whether or not you are aware of the fact, hand-to-hand combat has a technique all its own. To those who fight today as our ancestors fought in primitive warfare the experience is not brutal but exhilarating.

So it was at Kizil Kurgan. Kizil Kurgan (the Scarlet Castle), hidden in the Kunlun foothills, has twice in the past hundred and fifty years been occupied. Originally it was an outpost of the realm of Emir Timur, Tamerlane. A maze of sand-choked irrigation canals interlace the sterile landscape, testifying to the verdure the place once knew. At the disintegration of Timur's empire the *basmatchi* (raiders) occupied the citadel. They subsisted wholly on plunder and tribute exacted from passing caravans.

The Scarlet Castle had been deserted for more than a century when one day a courier, sent from the Tungan garrison at Keriya, whipped his lathered horse through Khotan's gates. Once in his sovereign's presence he told of the reoccupation of the Scarlet Castle. A Bolshevik-Chinese garrison had taken over the ruin and were repairing the weather-worn battlements.

As Scarlet Castle is only two hundred miles south and east of Khotan, its reoccupation put the enemy on the right flank of the Tungan dominion. The place would be of great strategic worth in any offensive against Khotan. Again, it could be of importance as a contact point between Red agents, Mongols, and Tibetans.

LAND WITHOUT LAUGHTER

Three hours after his arrival the courier rode again. He bore an order from Ma Hsi Jung to his commandant in Keriya: Kizil Kurgan was to be destroyed! After him came two hundred mounted soldiers; with the garrison at Keriya they would be enough to storm the walls of the Scarlet Castle.

It was night.

"In life's short span man doth but three things which are true:

"*War* and *Pray* and *Die*—all else is false.

"*War* is not an abomination, but a function of life—as birth.

"*Prayer* is worthless unless it, too, becomes a function of life. For it is truly said that the seventh and foulest of Hells is reserved for the hypocrite.

"*Death* is compensation for both: it is the deserved rest for him who hath lived life well, and to another the pleasing belch after a tasteless meal."

Trying to be brave, a young recruit again and again repeated the proverb. More concerned with the aching of their near-frozen feet than with the impending battle were the veterans.

Mud bricks from a fallen wall piled as a bulwark before him, the *Ming-bashi* (Commandant of a thousand) with his aides-de-camp planned the attack. Gushing from the hot barrel of a machine gun on the battlements above, tracers swam through the dark to splatter against the valley's rock-strewn floor and *tzin-n* heavenward. Ignoring the pyrotechnics, the young chieftain glanced at the moon; the pale orb was still too high.

It was in the thickest dark before the dawn, the moon lost behind the horizon. Hurriedly the veteran warriors pushed the unreliable recruits before them. A long rope was taken up. For the recruits to lag back against that rope meant to die beneath the scimitars of those bearing it. The youngsters held in their hands ladders, steel grapnels, and hooks for scaling the wall.

Amateurs at war bound their clothes more closely about them. Ignoring the cold, veterans stripped off coats and jackets, some even their shirts. A wound heals more quickly if dirty shreds of cloth are not festering in it. Hands were being forever wiped on the seat of breeches, for despite the chill palms sweated strangely. Avoiding the patches of snow not yet melted by the spring sun, some men rubbed their palms against the earth; that made for a better grip on weapons.

There is a studied nonchalance about those for the first time under fire, a brooding impatience among veterans. Then, as the time for the attack draws near, the mind begins to pick at some one thing with monotonous persistence: *Death is compensation for both: it is the deserved rest for him who hath lived life well, and to another the pleasing belch after a tasteless meal.*

The firing from the wall grows fiercer. "*Compensation—pleasing belch. . . .*" The palms moist and gummy are wiped on the buttocks.

Suddenly the drums begin: *but-brrrum-brrrum.* Only the recruits start forward. The others stand fast, those with rifles covering the ladder bearers, firing round after round up at the parapet, pausing only to spit on fingers blistered by red-hot rifle barrels. The others wipe their hands and weigh their blades. The thunder of the kettledrums drives every one a little mad and those on the walls, caught in the hysteria, needlessly expose themselves.

The ladders have been placed. The drums sound the charge. *You* start forward, the kettledrums shredding your very bowels. You can't climb with the knife in your hand so you slip it once more into its sheath; the hilt protrudes over your right shoulder.

Those on the ladder above are already locked in combat with the enemy. A machine gun, firing from point-blank range, rakes the ladders and men fall, suddenly to become grotesque sprawling corpses in the moat, dimly outlined against the dirty snow. The drums throb and throb. With head-splitting detonation grenades silence the machine gun. Ridding yourself of the dead weight which slumped down upon your arms, its bulk on your face, you start upward again. Some one behind has been hit; he screams, then beseeches you to hurry.

Without warning your head clears the wall's crest. A shadow shouts and strikes at you. Automatically cringing, you escape and the weapon strikes the earthen wall, grating as only a steel blade on brick can.

Your hand grasps the scimitar hilt beside your shoulder; obliquely swinging the blade, amazed at how light it feels (it weighs more than seven pounds) you hold it over your head to fend off blows. Then, stiff-armed, strike straight down, careful to let the blade slide as well as chop. For the next man chop sideways; missing, crouch and with a full flat swing strike his ankles. Then the same routine over again.

A savage screaming apparition rises before you. He holds in an outstretched hand a revolver and the thing crashes out again and again as your blade comes down . . . careful to let it slide as well as chop. Head full of hissing, howling sounds, eyes glare-struck from the pistol's flame, you hurl yourself towards a figure standing with its back to you. A pike is in his hands. Desperately he stabs at those on a ladder. One blow and he crashes down on the attacker's heads, ricocheting into the dry moat. Others join you. Your throat is parched from mouth-breathing. Close it.

Down from the walls you run through the narrow streets, twice crashing to the ground as you stumble over unseen hazards, human debris. The enemy garrison was bivouacked in the roofless shells of age-old dwellings. Here will be the few who fled the battle at the walls.

LAND WITHOUT LAUGHTER

Finding a doorway, you rush through it, shouting. A blanched, frightened face stares back at you from the darkness. Outside is the crash of a grenade and its fragments snarl through the streets. The drums are pulsing madly. Before you is an armed man. He clubs at you with a rifle. At your swift pivot the weapon thuds against the wall. You feint, needlessly. The other makes no further effort to defend himself. Your blade is over your head, then it descends as you tug fiercely at its hilt. And with that last blow the hysteria of combat abruptly deserts you. Outside there are shouts of direction, for aid, of fright. A man darts towards your doorway, then, spying you, he turns and flees, his companions with him. After them bound others roaring with victory. There are a few brief sounds of conflict. A man calls "Ullah-Ullah-Ullah"—then hushes, an instant later, with one great last breath: "*Anna* (Mother)."

As a band of blood-drenched men come running around the edge of a broken wall, fright puts a salt taste in your mouth, almost an electric shock. Then you identify them as your own kind. A frightened horse dashes out of a stable, its hooves pounding the hard earth. Wild soldiers, their eyes seeing in all motion an enemy, shoot at the beast. It stumbles, screams and falls, intestines tangled in its hind legs.

You step back within the doorway. Head bathed in the sickening gray light that spills over the threshold, the man who last fell beneath your weapon sprawls at your feet. He was very young. The air is cold and you shiver. The *kang* is your seat, you are tired. The boy, his head cleft half in two, is beyond fatigue. . . . His mother is somewhere waiting. So is the mother of him who uttered her name with his last breath. Both had great plans for their sons. Both will weep when they learn. God damn him who lies before you, why didn't he fight? Instead, he just stood there, his eyes staring out of the dark, almost saying, "Here is my head, split it." Well, why not?

LAND WITHOUT LAUGHTER

Everything humans do is foul. Every gesture and motive is selfish, every thought designing and unclean. As long as you remember that you can keep on killing. Forget all kindness others have shown you, step once again through the door, hope that all the enemy are not yet dead. That is war! A war combining the Dark Ages' with today's enlightened murder methods, a war unheralded, which rocks hidden Central Asia as in the terrible years of Genghis Khan.

Today Kizil Kurgan is once more deserted. A few broken poplars stand amid a welter of fallen fire-smudged masonry, and a lone pomegranate feebly spires to life, growing more horizontal than upright. There is only one whole structure in the ruins; an ancient *mazar*; the domed tomb of a saint. Winter, summer, wind, wars, and time have destroyed all else.

The Kirghiz, mountain people and herders, superstitiously avoid the spot. They say it is the dwelling place of *djinns*, those beings of the middle world. That such beliefs trouble them is for them unfortunate, for there is an abundance of fuel in Kizil Kurgan; a rarity in the Himalayas' granite foothills. Besides firewood, other fuel, camel dung, also goes to waste. The little round balls burn with great heat so long as they are moderately fresh, but those in Kizil Kurgan are beginning to whiten and distintegrate.

9

One day General Ma Hsi Jung took me to the mint and I watched as the great wooden type was banged down on sheets of crude, reed-pulp paper. Only in Khotan or in the fifteenth century could such methods exist. Every bit of machinery was man-powered. One man swabbed pigment over the block as it was swung back, preparatory to thumping down, pile-driver fashion, and crudely stamping out more of the dubious currency.

"We have hundreds of camel-loads of gold here in Khotan, and the rivers to the east are full of it," the General assured me. "There is more wealth in Khotan than all *Tan Jung*[1] and the balance of Sinkiang possess!"

Back in the *Yamen*, I was led down a series of stairs that led us far beneath the surface of the ground. In the descent we passed seven massive iron-sheathed timber doors. The entrance to the passageway was in the quarters of General Ma's own bodyguard, and in the room next to his own, to make it doubly secure. Down the timbered, earth-sounding passageway we went, one man preceding us with a lantern and another following. I thought of Ma Ki Fu, who had borne a lantern when we visited the powder rooms and who now lay out in the Taklamakan, beside those whom he had slain.

Counterweights were moved and the last door swung clear of its deep-seated frame. Now we stepped through the opening and into a heavily timbered vault. There lay the bulk of the Tungan wealth—loot and tribute. Slabs of yellow metal were

[1] Tan Jung—The Northern Government.

161

stacked against the walls; two of the rectangular, two-inch-thick plates would be all a horse could carry. Bags of gold coin were stacked farther down the narrow place. They proved, on examination, to be ten-rouble gold pieces on which was a likeness of Tsar Nikoli. Also in the vault on timber shelves were lumps of molded silver, coarse, porous and shaped like two teacups that had been, side by side, partially fused to one another.[1] Chests of such silver extended for some yards. Then came bags of coin: the *Ak tenga*, a thick and heavy piece of silver —with dragons and Chinese characters stamped on its faces; highly valued in this land of inflated, worthless currency. Still beyond the dirty skin sacks of coin, were stacked a wealth of silver plates, *choguns* (Turki teapots), and quantities of every sort of utensils, all of precious metals, piled in careless confusion.

Bad air in the subterranean chamber became overpowering as we retreated up the long winding flights of stairs to the surface. Again, comfortably established in General Ma's quarters, I sat back, drank tea until I was waterlogged, and listened to the young General's boasts.

"The General says," began our interpreter, "that all the wealth lying beneath us is meant only to purchase war materials. He says that thou art to bring many *fiji* (airplanes) here to Khotan and then he will take all of Sinkiang. First, Kashgar; then north to Urumchi, and when he is ruler of all of Sinkiang, he will conquer Kansu and Tibet. And then the balance of Asia!"

I looked at the amazing young fellow who planned the capture of a continent as nonchalantly as if he spoke of his preference in women.

"General Ma says that he will give thee credentials when thou departest. These thou art to present to a man who will seek thee out in Urumchi. Or, if such a meeting is too danger-

[1]The Chinese tael.

ous, thou wilt go on—alone—to the coast, to Shanghai, there to join this man. Then, together, you will go to America, purchase that which is needed, and return."

It was as simple as that to the twenty-four-year-old warrior opposite me. He informed me of my impending departure by subtly promising to furnish me with Tungan credentials. Willingly or otherwise, I was to execute his commands.

By listening, careful not to question, I learned much of what Ma Hsi Jung planned. . . . His operatives were stationed at strategic points across the whole of Asia, from Ansi in Kansu to the Holy Land. . . . There was a wireless station in the castle by which the General kept contact with those men. . . .

"*Jehad!*" The *Holy War* was what he planned. First the *Jehad* against Soviet Russia—thousands of miles of Russian frontier would be besieged! . . . With his main force he would lead a spearhead into Siberia; over Semipalatinsk, then Novo-Sibirsk and Tomsk to the Trans-Siberian Railway. While the bulk of the Russian army would be occupied with the millions of Muslim fighting men besieging their frontiers, other governments would probably take advantage of the moment to throw an army into the field. Ten of every hundred men in Siberia and Russian Turkistan could be *relied* upon to revolt against the Soviet régime. . . . Then, God willing, Ma Hsi Jung would march into the Kremlin!

Fantastic. That's what I said. The Tatar merely laughed.

"Six years ago I, Ma Hsi Jung, came to Sinkiang. Less than five hundred men were with me. Not half of those bore rifles, only swords. . . . We came in the winter. It was so cold that many of my men gave feet and hands, even lives, to the weather. . . . The men of Sinkiang greeted us and fought at our side so long as we won battles. Then came the time that destiny decreed we lose. Those who had begged us to aid them in their war deserted us. Few, very few, remained; we were beaten again, and again. . . . The Russ brought the *fiji* and bombed and gassed us; we were lost."

As he recounted the tale of the wars, Ma Hsi Jung, for the first and only time I knew him, betrayed his inner passions. Rising in his chair, face suffused with bitter emotion as he told of battles, with his clenched fist banging the table top as he told of defeat, he thundered:

"But I, I, Ma—once more found men to follow me, and once more won my battles. . . . I defeated armies that had declared *me* bandit. I took all the wealth their cities held until today they issue money with apologies for its worthlessness printed on its face. My money," he took from a pocket one of the paper bills of his manufacture and flourished it, "my money bears only the seal of 'Ma Hsi Jung' yet they in the north give ten pieces of theirs for one of mine!"

With an easy smile he leaned back in his chair.

"I am waiting here for two things only."

"Yes?" I queried.

"For the day when I have one hundred thousand mounted troops. That day I shall take the first of the Chinese-Soviet cities in the north, Kashgar. And, second, I wait for the *fools* in occidental countries to make war!"

"How is that to affect thee?"

An orderly filled our empty cups with tea. Watching his reflection in the steaming beverage, Ma Hsi Jung smiled indulgently.

"Thy people have learned too much about war," he replied finally. "They will fight so furiously as to annihilate one another. *Then I will come.*" Emphasizing the words, he looked me in the eye, continuing with deadly earnestness: "My few men and knives will be enough. India and Russia will be open to me and Europe will be nothing but a wasteland. . . . All Muhammadins know that when the time is right a *Padishah* will proclaim himself and lead them to a new and victorious conquest of the world!"

Withdrawing, suddenly I realized the source of the General's strength and power. Men who raise themselves from nothing to kingship must have more than an orator's larynx. That and a sense of the dramatic are essentials, but one thing is greater: Logic. Ma Hsi Jung had not only the faculty of thinking and speaking *logic*—a talent which has immortalized more than one knave as Prophet—but the gift of living it. Life can never vanquish him and death is his companion. There is a Tatar adage, written no doubt by some fool more pleased with the sound of his mighty words than their stark fact: "He who lives by logic can never perish. Logic is basic. Man can become no greater—or less."

As I was being escorted back to my quarters by the General's interpreter I asked the man how long he had served under the young Tatar.

"Since the beginning of the war. And I will serve until his flag flies over all Asia."

"Thou thinkest it possible?" I questioned.

"Possible and probable. Did not Genghis Khan conquer Asia? Did not Alexander conquer most of the known world?"

Amazed at the other's assurance, I remarked:

"In those times men fought with swords and it was the survival of the fittest."

The little officer flicked a bit of dust off his highly polished boots, then soberly countered:

"Thy kind will war upon a country until as a country it no longer exists; then another will war on them and on and on until there are but a handful of victorious peoples. Then those remaining will each fear the other's might; contention will arise, wars within wars. Countries will, when they no longer have others to war upon, feud within their own borders. When the time comes we shall have little opposition. . . . It is written. Kismet!"

Before I could protest, the other continued:

"Thou thinkest it impossible. Thy kind think many things impossible. Thy kind think that *only* those things that they with their eyes see, or hands create, are real. . . . It is written in the Holy Koran: 'Faith, Miracles, and Destiny are of divine birth, thus beyond and above the mind and machinations of man.' "

It was on the eve of my departure from Khotan that I went for a stroll on the crest of the city walls. The evening prayers had been said and now the city prepared for the approaching night. As I looked out upon the surrounding countryside my attention was attracted by a commotion at the west gate. With a group of soldiers who likewise were attracted, I looked down upon the disturbance. The awkward angle of vision from my elevated position did not reveal the cause of the large gathering below. Curious, I went down from the walls, by authority of the tag on my breast bluffing my way past two gate-keepers. (All cities in Turkistan close their gates at sunset, not to be reopened until daybreak.)

Having made my exit by a different gate, I walked back to the scene of action. Providently, as was later proved, I removed the tag which identified me as a Tungan officer. In dress I was no different from a wealthy Turki merchant. Approaching the rear of the mob unnoticed, I found myself unable to discover what held their interest. Shouldering my way to a point of better vantage, I saw! A number of human heads were nailed to the gates! Two torches set in niches in the grottolike portals cast an unsteady light over the scene. Surging, fading, swelling, dripping to the ground with the oil overflow, the yellow flames drew reflections from the bloody gates and the eyes of the living. Men gazed as though mesmerized at the ugly masses of flesh and beard they had known as "friend."

Borne on the restive night wind came the fluctuating wail of a wife who mourned a husband never to return. Sound and scene, both had a hypnotic effect; the crowd about me stood very quietly.

All was still until a tall noseless man interposed himself between gates and mourners; it was my caravan man, Tokhta! Stretching forth his arms in anguish, not benediction, he cried:

"Mussulmans! Hear me!" Bitterly he railed after a cautious, fleeing few.

"You, Futteh Jung; you, Soliman, Hadjim, Eyoob, Mahmood Jan—all of you. Run like the craven dogs you are. Think ye that by running escape can be made from the *Shaitan* Ma Hsi Jung who murdered your brothers; ha? Think ye that? Fools!"

Tokhta threw open his fur greatcoat and, arms akimbo, feet firmly planted, roared with unfelt mirth of a cruel metallic timbre. I glanced apprehensively at the parapet above and noticed that others did likewise. Tokhta kept on, oblivious or contemptuous of danger. He shrieked his disgust at the crowd. Then he ceased and with lowered head contemplated his audience. The greasy black fur of his coat shone in the torch-light and the flames cast strange shadows over his noseless visage. Evil of countenance, grim of demeanor, his shadowy figure seemed something escaped from the pit. His shadow on the gates was batlike; now tremendous, now pigmy, it heightened the illusion. No genius of stage effects could with all his props achieve as much as did Tokhta the Turkoman anarchist with two oil torches, the night, and natural talent.

"Idiots!" He uttered the word softly; it angrily attacked the ears of his farthest listener. Those in close range of the

gesticulating figure started back in actual alarm at the tone of
the words which by their urgency forced a way past his frozen
lips.

"Blind imbeciles! Not until your knives split his heart and
his head is skewered like those— Not until then will you have
escaped Ma Hsi Jung! Recall the proverb:

" 'Flight is for sheep when wolves come down from the
hills.

" 'Ullah breathed life into Adam, and whispered into his
ear:

" ' "Adam! Sons of Adam! Man can be sheep—or wolf—as
he wills!" ' "

Though I was well to the rear of the gathering, I felt the
press as many started back. Such speech was treason. True or
false: treason. This was the same offense (as I later discovered)
for which the heads on the gates had fallen.

Rising in pitch, Tokhta's orating voice continued:

"It is not from the same womb as I, nor a father, nor cousin,
nor friend whose head adorns a Tungan gate.

"Ye: lecherous sons of fifteen fathers and a sick mule—flee—
flee; I will speak for the dead!"

I was almost thrown down and trampled by the panicky rush
to flee the gate clearing. Recovering my balance, I too fled,
coming to a halt several hundred feet away—conveniently concealed by the dark. Tokhta still stood in the archway. Alto-
gether deserted, he angrily shouted after the swiftly retreating
footsteps of his vanished audience:

"Cowards, weaklings, women. I, a lone man, can drive a
hundred of ye to flight."

He did not know what peril hung over his head.

"Was it I who dreamt of awakening cowards?

"To fill the wombs of women—to bruise yourselves on saddle
pommels—that and naught else do ye do to prove your sex!"

LAND WITHOUT LAUGHTER

Having advanced far out into the deserted clearing, Tokhta stopped in his tracks; still reviling us. For a moment he continued, then fell silent, paralyzed by a strange new knowledge. Slowly, apprehensively, he turned to survey the walls. Deserted by his listeners, he seemed suddenly tiny beside the battlements. From each break of the indented parapet showed the barrel of a rifle and behind it the shadowy silhouette of a soldier. Now he knew why we so precipitately had fled.

At the same instant that the men were ordered to fire, Tokhta made for the walls. To attempt to escape in the same direction we had taken would have been suicide. Huddled in the shadow at the wall's base, Tokhta apparently contemplated his escape. Cool head; I never would have used my wits with such rapidity. But then, Tokhta had made a career of anarchy and I hadn't.

Before the riflemen could locate him, Tokhta sprinted for the sunken gateway. Gaining it, he seized the still burning torches from their stations and hurled them, one after the other, far out into the clearing. One spilled its fire in mid-air; the other burned fitfully upon the ground. In a few seconds its oil dissipated into the sandy earth and, with a few spasmodic bursts of life, expired.

Unaccustomed to the new dark, both riflemen and I were blinded. The cavalry which dashed through the opened gates did not find a single victim in the night.

Hesitating immediately to return to the gates by which I had left the city, I waited several hours.

At four-forty-five the following dawn I breakfasted with the General.

We sat down to a meal of sweet *boza,* steamed balls of unsalted dough filled with a gelatinous mass of chopped nuts, raisins and dissolved sugar. In turn they were followed by juicy meat-filled *boza.* But the excellence of the meal was over-

169

shadowed by the portent of our conversation. Passing them over the table, Ma gave me a packet of papers—credentials to be presented to the operative I would meet either in Urumchi or Shanghai. And among these more dangerous documents was a diplomatic passport accrediting me to represent the General in other countries. I was now a *citizen*, if that be the word, of Turkistan.

An hour later, packing finished, Song Soldier carried my saddlebags out and loaded them on the waiting horses. I went back through the *Yamen* to take leave of Ma Hsi Jung.

"Thou art to forget Khotan, and never," he warned, "let any know of thy connection with us if it be thy intent to leave Sinkiang as thou camest, with breath in thy lungs and blood in thy veins. Those in the north do not love the Tungan!"

Taking from his pocket a little bronze tag on which were inscribed Chinese and Turki characters, he extended it to me:

"For thy service on the desert."

Bowing, I thanked the General. Instead of acknowledging my obeisance, he thrust into my hand a piece of paper literally covered with lines of black Chinese characters, and red seals of every size and description, from angling lines likened unto Buddha's intestines to perfect squares crammed with characters: a citation.

Fraternally taking my hand in his, my General walked with me to the *Yamen* courtyard. Ma's adjutant, our interpreter, took Song Soldier's place at the head of my mount. In the saddle, I took the reins from him and, saluting, took leave of Ma Hsi Jung.

Riding side by side Song Soldier and I made for the west gate: scene of turmoil the evening before. Approaching, I noticed that another crowd had gathered. Our horses shied at passing through the gates. Whips overcame their whims.

Outside of the walls, I drew up to watch as a Tungan officer

LAND WITHOUT LAUGHTER

cursed his men to greater efforts. They were scrubbing the gates. The heads had been removed from their spikes and lay in a rude heap out of the workers' way. A veil of flies and dust hung over them.

Spying the tag on my breast the Tungan in charge came over to stand at my stirrup. In reply to my query: why did he scrub the gates? he ordered the soldiers to one side.

Distinct, defying water and brush, lines of verse stood out in bold red from the pitted black iron. Divided now by the panels, they read:

"Revolution is an edifice built of many bricks.

"Each brick is an injustice.

"Blood is mortar.

"Each wall is a mountain of sorrow.

"The foundation is most important.

"Alone, it must sustain the structure.

"Martyrdom is the excellent foundation!"

As I read, the Tungan glowered at the onlooking Turkis. Averting their eyes they hurried away, casting sidelong glances of approval towards the gate's message. I will wager that there was not a man or child in the city but knew the verse by rote before dusk.

I demanded of the Tungan at my stirrup:

"Who dared to write such treason?"

"During the night," he explained, "some rascal of a Turki attempted to cause trouble. He tried to rouse the people to revolt. We frightened him away, but before the night was done he returned. Undetected, he wrote those evil words."

Ai! Tokhta. You wicked Turkoman scalawag. You are as bad as your scalawag father: Ughlug Beg. It is men like you who have given rise to the new name for Turkistan: Dominion of Confusion. Nights about the caravan fire you used to tell of your fights and escapes from the "Shaitan Bolshevik." Now you

dub him who fights the Bolshevik: "Shaitan Ma Hsi Jung."
Tokhta, the world will be a better place when you and your
kind breathe no more. But it will be a damn sight duller too;
I'm glad I knew you.

Beyond the bazar, Song Soldier and I gave our wing-heeled
mounts their heads, the five-Tungan escort that had joined us
at the city gates thundering along behind us. Horses were
changed at a little corral twenty miles on our way whence,
superbly mounted, we proceeded at a dead run.

Depressions in the land were already filled with purple night
when we rode into the salt-marsh battlefield that, only a few
days before, Ma Ki Fu had crossed with Song Soldier and
myself. By midnight we were at Zanguay; at dawn we again
took fresh horses and continued the mad pace. A hurtling ride
over the desert took us to a little oasis; horses were once
more changed and on again.

Three dawns after leaving Khotan, Song Soldier and I rode
out of Cholok and across the barren rolling desert towards the
day's destination, Kargalik. In an hour the sun beat down as
though it would fuse the sterile, rocky earth. Song Soldier
slouched in the saddle of his wilting, plodding mount and sang
some age-old Tungani song in a high-pitched violinlike voice.
The intricate pattern of the music, its rocketlike ascent to the
very heights, then the delicate variations in pitch gradually
bringing the song back to our sphere, were strange and pleasing. Ceasing on a major chord, the melody hung in the still
air; suspended with the dust risen at the horses' heels.

Nearing an oasis we began to meet little *ishek* (burro) caravans, bearing huge bundles of homespun uniforms to Khotan.
Topping a rise in the ground, we looked out over a long line
of *potai* towers, ancient edifices of crumbling mud erected by
a forgotten ruler. Originally they had been constructed to lead

the way across the wind-driven desert sands. Arranged as they were, every two miles apart, they had served as lookouts. From their fifty-foot heights the ancients had been able to see far over the low rolling desert and sight hostile armies. From Kargalik to Khotan and back again, we had followed these towers.

Thirty-two miles and eleven hours from Cholok we dismounted before the Zeho's *Yamen* and, while waiting for his excellency, I took from my pocket the bit of stamped cloth. When at last we were ushered into the apparently overjoyed General's presence it was pinned on my breast. Song Soldier presented our credentials and once more Zeho went into an ecstasy of obsequious homage, swearing that he had always thought the Amerikaluk to be of high birth. I refused his offer of his own quarters, for I had had enough of the swine and felt that if Song Soldier should witness the Zeho further humbling himself, it would go hard with him when I departed.

That night I shared the sincere hospitality of Muhammad Khan, British Aksakal to Kargalik. On his questioning, I told of the brutality of the Tungan and of how *poorly* I had been treated. The Tungan episode was to be forgotten for the present.

It was in the Khan's home that I found Ali Muhammad Khan, the little Afghan who boasted a magnificent moustache and doubtful parentage, he who had come with Abdul and me when we fled the weakening caravan.

Ali told me all that had taken place since my leaving him in Kukiar. He had come on slowly to Kargalik, left my luggage with the Khan in whose home we now stayed; then had gone on to Yarkand and delivered the jaded animals to the partner of the Ladakh merchant from whom I had leased them. The caravan had arrived days after his arrival and it, too, left my belongings here at the Aksakal's home and continued on to

Teriff Shah Hadji in Yarkand. Of the forty-four animals that left Ladakh, twenty-nine still lived.

Ali delightedly found himself the possessor of a new job, as my servant in Song Soldier's stead. Song Soldier would necessarily be forced to return when we reached the Bolsheviki border on the morrow.

When once more we started on our way the sun was high. Before we reached the little bazar of Posgam, it had but an hour longer to shine on Turkistan. Song Soldier and I parted in the *Yamen* of the Turki Administrator of Posgam; so far he could come and no farther. The Yarkand Deria, a mile farther down the road, was the dividing line between Tungan and Soviet-Chinese territory. Song Soldier saluted; we shook hands and he was gone.

The Turki Aksakal of Posgam asked if I wished to remain in his city throughout the night, but choosing only to await Ali who followed with the luggage, I ordered another horse saddled preparatory to an immediate departure. Half an hour found the road still void of any Ali, so in company with a two-man escort furnished by the Aksakal, I went on to Yarkand. It was late in the evening when we at last reached the big bazar; and I was led to the home of the British Aksakal, Abdul Hamid Khan Bahadur.

The Amerikaluk welcomed that night to the Khan Bahadur's home was, indeed, different in appearance from any other *sahib* ever to visit Yarkand: clad in dust-covered, sweat-stained Turki clothing from the fur hat on his head to the scuffed Turki boots on his feet. Even worse was the fact that when the *sahib* spoke, it was in Turki, not English, and before speaking in his own native tongue he was forced to halt a moment and throw a mental switch. Even then the English that came forth was garbled with the language of the people with whom he had eaten, slept, walked, loved, and lived for many months.

Book Three

"Confusion on Confusion heaped"

1

Days passed rapidly in the Khan Bahadur's comfortable home and I gradually began to assume the proper foreigner's appearance under the ministrations of a skilful tailor. The transformation was complete when a fine pair of soft, black Russian riding-boots was found to take the place of the Turki *mesa's*[1] that had carried me over rough country, and looked it. That I was indeed a changed man was testified by the fact that Turkis no longer greeted me with, "The peace of *Ullah* be upon thee," but watched my passing with curious, hostile stares. They thought me one with the Bolsheviki in the city.

Bursting with generosity, I gave Ali Muhammad Khan full two hundred *seer* (forty-five cents[2]) and told him to have a *Tamashah* with it. Finally deciding that the best form of a "spree" was a new wife, Ali sought one out and took her, a girl in her early teens, home to his other wife and five children. The children got out at his command, but his jealous wife raved until Ali felt himself justified in locking her in another part of his house.

Children and wife dispensed with, he and his new bride made *Tamashah* for three days. Then, tiring of the girl, he divorced

[1]A kind of boot that has a detachable outer foot, removed when entering any human abode.

[2]The reader will note that the rate of exchange varies throughout my story: each Turkistani city has its own currency. Each city discounts all currency of foreign issue, even though the "foreign" moneys are valid at their point of issue, perhaps a day's ride away.

her. Two words, *"Eutch Talak,"* had served the purpose.
Giving the girl one hundred and fifty *seer* for services rendered,
he sent her back to her family.

"But my wife was still angry, so I made *Tamashah* with her
and gave her the last of my money. Ah!" he exclaimed, "there
was much pleasure in those two hundred *seer*."

It had been my intention to spend only four days in Yarkand
but the tailor decreed otherwise and my date of departure was
set forward. On the fifth day word came from Kargalik that all
British trade caravans had been ordered stopped and returned
whence they came. The *Yamen* substantiated the order; it had
come from Urumchi.[1] The *ukase* prohibiting British merchan-
dise was the final step in consolidating absolute Soviet trade
monopoly in Sinkiang. (The Soviet monopoly might turn back
caravans originating in British-Indian territory, but Tungan
General Ma Hsi Jung had no objection to their entering his
territory, nor to the stores of Kynoch (British) ammunition that
found its way into his arsenals.)

Morning of the sixth day found me installed in what I came
to know as a torture device, and which went by the name of
mapa, a two-wheeled, springless horse cart. The bed of the
cart was only twenty-odd inches wide and approximately three
feet long. A kennel-like canopy of blue homespun was rounded
over a wooden frame which served as both walls and roof. Soon
enough I realized it had been a mistake to accept the Khan
Bahadur's suggestion that I go on to Kashgar by cart.

The lone horse pulling the contraption jounced along between shafts that stuck straight out from, and were a part of,
the cart's frame. The shafts were so short that it necessitated
harnessing the horse very close to the cart's bed; so close, in

[1]Urumchi: The seat of the Sinkiang government and the city from whence
Shing Dupen, the Governor, ruled all Sinkiang north of Tungan territory.

178

fact, that the animal's tail was forever coming up into my lap, where Ali, who sat on a little shelf beside the driver, would retrieve it. The cart's wheels were greater than six feet in diameter and studded with iron cleats that imparted, even in the smoothest of country, a tooth-clicking, vibratory motion. I tired of looking at three of everything, so shut my eyes to await patiently the *plop* that would signify my brains' tearing away from the skull pan. The horse was festooned with dozens of clattering brass bells, each the size of a walnut; with them hammering at my eardrums, I gradually sank into a coma that was broken only when I clambered out to walk.

Five days after leaving Yarkand, Kashgar was reached. The walls of the Yengi Shahr (New City) loopholed, truncated, and scarred from the armies and years they had withstood, were passed and we jounced on toward the battlements of Kashgar proper.

Ali hopped down from his perch beside the driver and strode along beside the confounded cart, calling out to acquaintances along the road. Irascible, I called to the driver to hurry his horse a bit; I wanted to reach the dwelling of the *Parang* (British) Consul before dark. Grudgingly, he complied. The animal, lame since the day before, when a sharp rock had set itself into his hoof, shuffled along, and at the touch of the whip struck into a bouncing trot. Up and down the beast did go with vigor, but forward not one iota more swiftly than before. We drew nearer the city and the smooth, shaded roadway became lined with the 'dobe Turki homes.

Heavy-jowled, pot-bellied merchants wended their way down the highway on beautiful sleek mounts. Patient, long-suffering *ishek* plodded along, dodging the larger beasts of burden. One, the size of a Great Dane, bore on its haunches two hundred pounds of sleepy Turki, booted feet dragging,

179

further impeding the little animal. Dogs came out to bark, and ran yelping from the stones Ali chucked at them. Children pointed sticks at us and threw Ali's stones back at him. A black droshky swept past, the driver high in the box urging on to greater speed the perfectly matched pair of geldings in the strange Russian harness—one between the belled, arched shafts, the other to the side and free of shafts. The carriage's occupant, a young Russian, was clad in the height of fashion: whipcord breeches, leather coat, and boots that I anxiously compared with my own mirror-polished footgear.

We passed the heavy iron gates of Kashgar's walls, and its sentries. We were in the city; a veritable metropolis compared with those cities behind me—Kargalik, Khotan, and Yarkand.

Women were as plentiful as in Yarkand, many unveiled, and Ali pointed them out as *jilop* (whores). A bevy sat before an open bazar-oven all clad in flame-red gowns. One stroked an instrument of some weird Turki design and odd melodious tone.

I questioned, "*Jilop?*"

Ali confirmed my suspicions with approval. The *sahib* was learning.

"All women without veils are without shame," he explained.

The teeming bazar streets were thronged with humanity: merchants, craftsmen, laborers, and children. Over all towered great poplars. The sight of great trees impressed me, for I had long been without them.

"Effendi, this is the place of the *Parang* Consul," as the accursed *mapa* came to a stop.

Several Indian *chaprasis salaamed* as I walked through the gate. A *sahib* had come. I stumbled over a pebble in the path, voiced a hearty curse, and carelessly returned the *salaam*. Mine was a typical British colonial entrance. In India, the Britisher must first give vent to a healthy "God damn" and a scowl before he acknowledges any courtesy. Who was I to set a precedent? The tradition was upheld.

LAND WITHOUT LAUGHTER

Still playing the part, I asked one of the men to take me to the "Consul *Sahib*" and followed him up the gravelled drive. Lawns, tennis courts, polo ponies tethered to saplings, testified to the fact that one of His Britannic Majesty's servants had made this his abode. Following the *chaprasi* into a low building, an office, I was introduced to the Khan Sahib, a fat little Afghan who bore an amazing likeness to a walrus. He greeted me in perfect English. Violently bowing in welcome, then readjusting his fez, he called another *chaprasi* who dashed in, and, after getting his orders in trip-hammer Hindustani, stampeded out again. The excited Khan Sahib found a chair somewhere and urged that I seat myself, all the while apologizing for something incomprehensible to me.

"Yes! Yes!" he exuberantly exclaimed. "News of you reached us a month ago! Some one brought word of your coming into the bazar of Kargalik from the south, and a dispatch came from the Resident in Kashmir."

The *chaprasi* came back into the room, still travelling at the pace set at his exit, but blowing a bit.

"The Consul is ready, *Sahib*," he said, addressing me.

Rising, I bade good-day to the little Khan Sahib and left him perspiring and bowing before his desk. I followed the *chaprasi* by the flurry he made in passing, for there was no keeping up with the fellow; now and again the glimpse of a heel would assure me that I was still on the trail.

At last I mounted the steps of what was a typical colonial home; the porch the full length of the house, a rambling structure. A screen door was opened, and I was ushered into the cool of the Consul's home. A moment and the Consul himself appeared. He was large and cool, with the essence of good liquor about him, appearing as should an emissary of H. R. H. and the Viceroy of India. I, in travel-stained riding breeches, on my head a Kazakh cap, the curling black wool now gray with journey's dust, made a poor picture in comparison.

LAND WITHOUT LAUGHTER

We retired to a sort of sun-room. A "boy" of about fifty summers poured half an inch of some green liquid into two glasses and filled them with a siphon. Later, while drinking it, the Consul broached the subject of my being in Turkistan, remarking on the good fortune that had been my lot thus far. I kept silent, waiting. Some comment about my illegal departure from India was surely forthcoming. Aware of my expectancy, he wasted no time.

"We are in Turkistan; there is nothing I can do about your being here. We might as well be congenial!"

The crisis reached, and passed, the conversation followed a lighter vein. We sat there in the great room, on chintz-covered overstuffed chairs, drank the civilized liver-destroying concoction, and while we talked I noted the wallpaper, the French windows, and the garden without. Only the British could attempt and achieve such an establishment; a home, large and well appointed, transported from the colonies to Central Asia.

"You intend going on from here?" the Consul queried.

"I do. To Urumchi, and, if possible, return."[1]

Advice was given and absorbed, and at our parting I was invited to luncheon on the morrow and placed in the custody of the Khan Sahib, who acted as guide to the *serai* of one Rakaram, an Indian merchant, "where," the Consul had promised, "appropriate living quarters can be found."

The Consul's Victoria carriage, the Khan Sahib, and I swept

[1]The Tungans had warned me against informing the British Consul of my true plans. They said that he often gave information to the Soviet:—in that manner hoping to reconcile the Russian powers-that-be to his presence in Turkistan. If this were so, it would be best that the Soviet officials did not know my true plans: pushing on toward the China coast from Urumchi. If, as the Tungans alleged, the Russians often arrested and held persons en route to China—in order to prevent word of Soviet penetration into Turkistan from reaching the outside world—I would best hold my own counsel until the moment of flight from Bolshevik territory.

to a stop before the *serai*. A great rotund Hindu, Rakaram, greeted us, and I was shown a room that had a bed with springs. A woven rug covered the floor. There was a chest of drawers, a mirror, and tapestry-hung walls. Even the windows were hung with some frilly stuff. Rakaram called and another Hindu appeared and with him came bowls of confections. Ali arrived with the cart driver, who fretted about, anxious to be paid off. Rakaram, *Rakobai* as the Turkis knew him, bade me a jovial good afternoon and went prancing off, leaning back a bit to counterbalance his vast stomach. I was in Kashgar and apparently at the end of the difficult part of my journey. A spring bed—ah!

Daily I visited the *Yamen*, trying to get an audience with Shin Jin Jung, the territorial administrator. To me, he was always out. After five days of persistent onslaught he capitulated and I was ushered into the presence. A little yellow-skinned, European-dressed, bespectacled Chinese greeted me. Shaking his hand, I felt a colossus beside the other's frail figure, and held the hand gently that it might not come off. The man's energetic bearing soon, however, belied any thoughts I had entertained as to his sinking out of sight behind the dandruff-flecked collar of his blue serge suit.

We exchanged niceties solely because they were part of the country's etiquette. Ours was a beautiful budding enmity that later flowered to leave me much the worse for wear. In carefully couched words, I sued for permission to proceed to Urumchi, to myself cursing the requirement that all persons travelling between cities must first procure a *yule hut* ("Road Letter").

"Your application will receive my personal attention and recommendation," Shin Jin Jung promised, "but, of course, you understand it will be some days before I get a wireless reply from Urumchi."

183

LAND WITHOUT LAUGHTER

During the passing days, I devoted myself almost exclusively to the interests of science. Previous to this I had never been able to carry on any consistent research. (And, though I little realized it at the time, this was destined to be my final effort along such lines; my existence was to become a maelstrom of intrigue, confusion, and complications ere many days passed.) Now I indulged in a veritable orgy of skull measuring and like efforts. In six sixteen-hour days I measured, with the aid of three assistants who fell to the task with as much vigor as bewilderment, one hundred thirty-one persons; of these ninety-odd were males, the balance outraged, talkative females.

At length, after compiling my records, I found that many types and races I had segregated into specific classes were by several of my contemporaries otherwise listed. Investigation proved that this was due to differences in the locale where the measurements were taken. Most scientists had visited those peoples dwelling in the more easily accessible North, while I enjoyed a virgin field (comparatively speaking) amid the least contaminated of all the races of Turkistan.

Insofar as society was concerned, I satisfied my gregarious instincts by gossiping with the always hospitable Turkis—and, more venally, visiting the Swedish missionaries. They had such delicious food, and one was invariably invited to dine.

The Turkistanis, however, occupied most of my time. Daily I visited the homes of a few who seemed unusually well informed and even more anxious to learn of the countries beyond the Gobi and the Himalayas. Once I was asked if I had ever in my journey met a Turki, one Abdul Kadir Effendi? Thinking back, I remembered the little caravan I had met in distant Sonemarg-Kashmir. I told of meeting the man; the Turkis looked one to the other and then the oldest voiced a fervent "*Kodia Shukrea*" (Thanks unto God).

184

LAND WITHOUT LAUGHTER

"Ahmad Kamal Effendi, it is best you avoid mention of that man again," my white-turbaned, bearded host advised. "The *Yengi Hookemet* (new administration) will think you a friend of his. They hate him! He fled Sinkiang because he was a man of wealth and intelligence, and the *Yengi Hookemet* is beginning to take both money and lives. Kadir Effendi saw the end of his Sinkiang when the Bolsheviki won the *inkalab* (revolution).

"The *Hookemet* learned that he was about to leave and sent soldiers to stop him, but *Ullah* smiled upon him and he escaped, though he left behind all that he possessed—his land, his children, his wife. But you have seen him and he is safe, *Ulhamdu lillah* (God be praised). It is best you go back whence you came before you, too, become an enemy of this Bolsheviki *Hookemet*."

On the following day, while I was in the midst of compiling my notes, Ali came to me.

"The *secretar* of the Shin Jin Jung is here to see thee, Effendi."

A card, Chinese characters on its white face, was presented and its owner ushered into the room. The *secretar* was as schooled in the art of prolonging the issue as his illustrious master, and his English, which had greatly assisted when first I saw the Shin Jin Jung, was polished enough to make me regret my lapses into Turki. We congratulated each other on first one point, then another, until finally my guest came to the subject of his visit.

Pointing out of the window towards a hulk of a fellow, a Turki, who sat on a porchlike *kang*[1] with Ali, he said:

"My superior, Shin Jin Jung, extends his regrets that an answer to your application has not as yet arrived, and asks

[1]"Kang"—All homes in Turkistan boast a *kang*; nothing more than a platform of wood or earth, it is used as seat, table, and bed.

that you accept the services of that *Chan'tu*, to make your prolonged stay more convenient."

His recitation at an end, the young Chinese backed hastily towards the door and out of the *serai*. He had evidently been told to get away before I could refuse the courtesy. And that he did. I took one more look at the shifty-eyed hulk of a fellow sent me, and composed a note to Shin Jin Jung thanking him for the courtesy, but assuring him that I had no use for any servant other than the one already in my employ. Slipping the note in an envelope, I called in my unwelcome acquisition and bade him take the note at once to the *Yamen*. Insolently deliberate in his manner, the Turki departed.

Immediately Ali came trotting in.

"He is not a *kismetchi* (a worker) but one of the Ghi Pu."[1]

Grabbing my coat, I made for the home of a friend, Turda Akhun, and put the situation before him. He agreed with Ali.

"Leave this country," he cautioned. "These Russ dogs are mad."

Back to the *serai* I went, Ali tagging along at my heels. There I found the man I had sent to the *Yamen*. He was occupying my chair, having boldly let himself in. Rushing the rascal out of the room by the nape of his neck and the seat of his breeches, I told him to deliver the note to the *Yamen*.

"I did take the letter, Effendi, and was given this one for thee."

A paper was extended me and, as I took it, a slow sly grin spread slowly over the man's face. At first glance I saw that the note carried the signature and seal of Shin Jin Jung himself. It read:

"It behooves me to explain at greater length the reasons why the man I have sent will do better to remain in your employ. Primarily, of course, there is the consideration of this

[1]"Ghi Pu"—(O.G.P.U.): Soviet Intelligence as designated by the Turki.

*office that all visiting foreigners be kept safe from any unpleas-
antness and inconvenience. Therefore, it was both as a courtesy
and obligation that the services of the man, Musa Akhun, were
extended you. There are at the present time several bands of
lawless men in the city of Kashgar, and the man sent you is
meant to be bodyguard as well as servant. This office is certain
that it will be conducive both to your and this Administration's
peace of mind to have the bodyguard, Musa Akhun, at your
side at all times. If ever it is in our power to make your stay
more enjoyable, please notify us and ours is your convenience.*
(Signed) *Shin Jin Jung."*

I gave up trying to dispose of Musa Akhun and, again
reading the note, picked out the one line that was already
familiar, "there are at the present time several bands of lawless
men in the city. . . ."

This seemed the stock excuse for limiting one's activities in
Sinkiang; first to use these stock tactics had been the Tungans.
I thought of the story told me by an official in the city. A
European had been locked up for four months in Urumchi
prison without any charge, for none was needed. The imprisoned German missionary had been told day after day that
he was being kept in a prison cell for safety and to protect
him from vicious Turkis.

There was not a fraction of truth in Shin Jin Jung's fiction.
There were no lawless Turkis in the bazar, and mine was,
in any case, double immunity, for I was a Muslim, too.

For two full days I stood the heel-treading, snooping presence of Musa, then fired him outright.

"Thou had'st better learn how to protect thyself from me
before protecting me from others!" I blazed at him.

Not a full hour lapsed before a beardless Tadjik,[1] clad in the

[1]See Glossary: Races of Turkistan.

187

height of Russian fashion, presented himself before my door and told Ali that he was Kasim Jan, the *secretar* of Shin Jin Jung. Anxious to meet this new secretary, I called from where I sat, inviting him to "come in."

Kasim Jan, after *salaams*, explained his mission. The Shin Jin Jung insisted that the *mehman* (guest) retain the bodyguard! Angry that the Administrator should insist, I told Kasim that I wanted no part of either the knavish snooping Musa or Shin Jin Jung. More than half the world had I circumvented without the need for a bodyguard, and I absolutely refused to keep the man in my employ.

Kasim, nettled, replied heatedly:

"The man is not in thy employ, but in that of the *Hookemet*. Thou can'st not discharge him. He must stay with thee."

Enraged at the fellow's arrogance, I made for him, Ali with me, but Kasim had evidently heard the proverb about discretion and valor, and making a quick bow, made an even faster exit. At the Tadjik's hasty departure, Musa, who had been lurking in the *serai* entrance, awaiting, no doubt, the call that would signify his reinstatement, followed the fleeing Kasim, surprise written on his features. Kasim said something to him and instead of taking flight with the *secretar*, Musa took a post just outside the *serai*. I was to be watched!

Turki friends of mine, who before had been glad to see me, shunned me now, so obvious was the fact I was being shadowed. They all had a fear of being entangled with the *Shaitan Hookemet* (Satan's Administration), now considering me one of its marked men. Even Rakobai, the Hindu *serai* owner, appeared harassed.

I resolved to catch him who was forever in pursuit of me. The fox would for a change chase the hounds. Taking Ali into my confidence, I explained what I was about.

Up one street and down another, aimlessly making a com-

plete circle, went the two of us, following, as Ali called it,
a *sarong yule* (crazy road). We repeated the manœuver several
times and at last, in the very center of the bazar, we stepped
quickly into one of the deep doorways that lined the pinched,
warped street. A moment later Musa came by on the double-
quick, not seeing us. Then we strolled leisurely about until
once more he found us, when we were off again. This time,
we declared, we would seize the culprit. But Musa, seeming
to sense that all was not as it should be, made a wide circuit
of our hiding place behind the crumbling edge of a half-fallen
wall. Then, spying us at the same instant that we saw him,
he gave a startled gasp and made off at his best pace. Letting
him go despite irrepressible Ali's eagerness to chase him, I
turned back to the *serai*. I was satisfied we were through with
Musa. He would never dare follow us now that he had discovered that even he was not immune to being watched.

I again visited the *Yamen* and asked the definitely uncomfortable Shin Jin Jung when permission would be given to
continue on my way. I explained that I didn't give a damn
whether or not it was to Urumchi. I swore that I was perfectly
willing to leave Sinkiang by way of Anjanistan and Bokhara
or even return by the road whence I came, my only object
being to get out of a country under the administration of such
as he. I was disgusted with the way I had been treated while
in his territory. Even the Tungans, the bandits, were more
gracious and courteous than those who condemned them. The
insult was ignored and the little Chinese stood bowing before
me. His very bows, the dry slithering sound of his hands rubbing one against the other, antagonized me. Throwing caution
to the winds, I ranted on, hoping either to shame or provoke
him into action.

I commented, indiscreetly, on the incident of Musa's follow-

189

ing me; how I had been treated as a criminal, when in truth I was absolutely innocent. Why, I questioned, should any one wish to stay in a country whose ruler had the intellect and manners of the king-dog of a pack? A ruler certain to fall before the first willing to adopt Chinese tactics. I assured him that insofar as I was concerned, he could put away his fears; I was a *man,* not a *Chinese.*

The abuse I heaped on Shin Jin Jung's head had cost him considerable face in the eyes of his council and bodyguard about us. Though it was a great temptation to lapse from generalities to short definite phrases, I forbore the pleasure; such action would take from me the face gained, and restore to the Chinese his.

Instead of exploding beneath my barrage of insults, the Chinese's reply was suave, almost penitent.

"I am indeed undone that you have been inconvenienced by the, it is true, apparently incompetent way in which your application has been handled, but such is not the case," he purred. "An answer to your application should arrive within the next two days. The water in the Karashahr and Aksu rivers was very high and may have caused the delay, but that difficulty is, I am positive, no longer existent."

The man's implacable calm nettled me. Impulsively, I retorted:

"Sinkiang has not only strange rulers, but even stranger wireless, eh? Wireless that runs along the ground and is stopped by high rivers!"

My words struck home and the Chinese's face, for the first time, changed.

"Shin Jin Jung, you were, I am told, a school teacher," I finished. "It is said in my country that teachers are men among children and children among men!"

The thin, spectacled Chinese came to his feet, oriental face

190

darkening. Contemptuously sizing him up from the tips of his broad square-toed oxfords, over his pinched Russian-suited figure, to the top of his uncovered, black-thatched head, I continued:

"Shin Jin Jung, a man does not attempt to obtain assistance from a dog. It is best you forget my request; others can tend my wants."

Leaving him, I was escorted to the *Yamen* gates by the bodyguard that had haunted the premises during our conversation.

Ali Muhammad Khan came to meet me from where he had been sitting with several comely members of the fairer sex.

"*Jilops*, forty *seer*. They asked what thou did'st when thou soughtest a woman?" he grinned.

"And thou said'st——?"

"I said thou did'st the same as every man since *Adam Ali Salaam;* thou foundest one!"

We went back through the streets, past the Masjid, the *Hum*[1] *serai*, *Utek*[2] bazar, *Pitchok*[3] bazar, to Rakobai's *serai* and my quarters. Ali, as usual, set out to find my favorite *Kunjut nun* (sesame bread) while I worked on my notes and awaited his return. As I wrote, a knock came on the door. Kasim Jan, Shin Jin Jung's *secretar*, entered at my request. I threw the fellow out of poise by bluntly asking what he came for. Stuttering, he lamely replied:

"Just want to see if the *Mehman* Amerikaluk is well and if there is anything he desires."

Knowing that whatever was said would speedily find its way back to the *Yamen*, I took Kasim into my confidence. I told him that I was going to the Russian Consul to ask for permission to leave Sinkiang via Russian-Turkistan. Believing himself in my confidence, Kasim tried, successfully, to draw

[1] Homespun cloth.   [2] Boot.   [3] Knife.

me out and then went back to the *Yamen* with a wealth of erroneous information.

That same afternoon I visited the Russian Consul, a rather pleasant fellow of average height, dark complexion, Tatar by birth and Abdur Rahman by name. His secretary, a tiny hunchback speaking perfect English, acted as interpreter.

Riding back to the *serai* in the droshky, I mulled over the afternoon's conversation: it was the Russian Consul who ruled Kashgar! My hopes for Soviet permission to cross Turkistan to the west were doomed to failure. The Consul would not give me permission to leave Sinkiang. He had said that though it was the longest way I would do much better to travel on towards Urumchi. He claimed that it was the easiest route, for it entailed no crossing of dangerous passes as did the Anjan (a province in Russian Turkistan) trail, which was, according to the Russ Consul, "at this time closed."

"At the foot of the mountain there is a guard who stops all travellers and turns them back if they attempt to cross while there is still snow on the Pass."

As I departed, Consul Abdur Rahman had promised that he would speak to those in the *Yamen* and secure the necessary visas for my continued journey to Urumchi.

2

AT THE *serai,* I asked Ali if he was willing to leave Sinkiang. To which the little rogue—half Afghan by a careless Kabli prostitute, half Heaven-knows-what by many reckless fathers—cracked a grin that spread the whole width of his homely hook-nosed face.

"I knew it!"

Drawing me back in the room away from the windows, he spoke with a lowered voice.

"I know a man who will give us the use of his horses for a sum. It is best we use horses; the feet of the *tuga* (camel) wear out in the mountains and the tiny *ishek* is lost if we must ford rivers. Of horses, we shall need twelve, for some will surely die. I know. We shall have to travel across the mountains where there are no trails. To buy the horses would be mad. To pay a bit, *keira kash,* costs little and then the loss is another's. I have a friend, a Kirghiz, who knows the mountains as I know the face in the mirror, and he will guide us. . . ."

The details were left in Ali's capable hands and I completed the copying of my journals, destroying indiscreet passages by using the pages as fuel for the samovar. In the same manner I destroyed various papers of Tungan origin which might prove difficult to account for should they fall into other hands. Photographs and somatological data I kept; God knows they had been difficult enough to obtain.

That evening I went to the British Consulate and told the Consul of my encounter with Shin Jin Jung. He seemed to approve the course I had taken.

193

"They say it's the only way to handle these Chinese—to lose one's temper, to speak one's mind, and then get one's way."

Returning to the *serai* on foot, Ali nudged me:

"We are being followed by the sons of Musa Akhun—*d-dongesiki*."

I looked back and saw two little boys obviously trailing us. Again we started off on the same *sarong yule* that had trapped the boys' father, Musa. We hurried through a press of people by the Hum *serai*, out of the thronged streets to the nearly deserted *Chogun* bazar, and then dodged behind a wall to wait. The two came trotting along, batting a blunt wooden spindle before them with the stick each carried. The spindle came to a spinning stop just before the doorway in which we stood. This time, however, the two ignored their game and looked anxiously down the street to ascertain whither we had gone; then they passed before us. Ali grabbed one, I the other. Their faces blanched. The one I held was too frightened to struggle; Ali subdued his with a few hard slaps. Both boys secured, and shaken until their teeth rattled, we questioned them.

"Why have you followed us about the bazar?"

The more frightened of the two was the one in Ali's hands, and it was he who replied:

"Our bellies are empty."

Before he could complete what he was about to say, the one in my hands found his tongue and boldly spoke up.

"Who is it that accuses us of following them? Are not the streets free?"

Ali decided that both needed a good beating and knocked their heads together with a resounding crack and warned them "never again to let yourselves be seen on the same street as either the *sahib* or myself!"

On release, both darted away with not a look back, obviously bent on telling the *Yamen* and their father what had happened. Ali looked after them, sadly shaking his head.

"If the head of a house beats the drum, who can blame the children for dancing?"

With the evening Musa himself put in appearance, angry enough at our manhandling his sons to throw caution to the winds and probably play into our hands. I sat back in my chair listening. There was not long to wait.

". . . the boys are free. Thine was not the right to touch them. They were told to follow thee by Shin Jin Ju——"

His voice suddenly fell away and Musa stopped in the midst of what he had been saying. His eyes grew large with terror and he stared over my shoulder.

"Stop him, Effendi. Stop him!" he screamed.

It was Ali, long caravan knife in hand, eyes narrowed, and mouthing curses. I bid Musa get out or I would let Ali at him. Musa got. With his exit, I asked Ali why he was so damnably violent.

"I am thy man. Thou hast much face, much power. Others, even the *Hookemet*, are afraid of thee. Thine is a strength that comes from here." He touched his head. "I, too, must be as thou; but to those so meager in brain as not to understand thy strength, I show them mine." Ali sliced the air with one great flourish of the knife. Then, in a confidential tone, "Thou, Effendi, could'st not threaten to do violence to such worthless people. That would take from thee thy face, but," he meditated, "thou could'st kill Shin Jin Jung with face. . . . The others I myself will dispose of and my face gains much!"

It all was a bit complicated, but I let it go at that. Ali had struck at my vanity, explaining how much face I had and how it must be, at all costs, preserved. God knows, I was later to wish I had taken his advice, not been amused by it.

Ali helped me out of my boots; plucked the lamp's uneven,

sputtering wick and bade me good night. But instead of taking his usual place just inside the threshold, he shuffled about the room.

I demanded, "What is it thou desirest, eh?"

The little rogue swaggered a few paces towards the door, then turned and sheepishly replied:

"Ahmad Kamal, Effendi, I, in a moment of weakness, sent all of the money thou gavest me to my wife and I am left without a single *seer*."

Unsympathetic, I asked, "Well?"

"Effendi, a beautiful female awaits me and I have not a *seer*, while her price is forty!"

Remembering the allure of the women I had seen him with, to refuse the request seemed too heartless, so I parted with forty *seer* and ten more for *maroshnia* (ice cream). At the door, Ali halted. He wanted to show his gratitude.

"There is a *kambagal zemindar* (poor farmer) who has a very beautiful female child, a virgin, that he will gladly sell thee for four thousand five hundred *seer*; less, with a bit more bargaining."

To my query as to whether or not the one awaiting him would become impatient, Ali started once more for the door, *tsk-tsking* as he went. At the threshold he tried again:

"Four thousand five hundred *seer*, a virgin and thirteen years old—a very good age!"

Once more he bade me good night and this time departed. I blew down the lamp's chimney, singed my eyebrows, and went to sleep.

With the dawn came not only Ali, wakefulness and food, but the *Yamen* darling, Kasim Jan, and with him another Tadjik. Kasim greeted me and solicitously asked about my health. I was introduced to the other, Ibrahim by name, and then Kasim unfolded a note from Shin Jin Jung, which after due preparation he read aloud.

"It is by order of Shin Jin Jung that Ibrahim Maklov be appointed to the service of the American guest now residing in Kashgar. He will serve in the capacity of servant, which duty he is to perform to the best of his ability until such time as he is recalled by the Yamen."

I heard Kasim out and, thanking him for the consideration, wrote a note to Shin Jin Jung. Kasim took it, amazement written over his features, *salaamed* and hastily departed.

It was all very obvious. Musa could not be forced into my service because of past difficulties, so this new pasty-faced fellow had been given the task of reporting my moves to the *Yamen*. I resolved to make such an ass of Ibrahim that he would of his own volition leave my service. He stood before me and seemed as pleased as Kasim had been surprised at my docile acceptance of his services.

"What did those in the *Yamen* say thy duties would be?" I asked.

Taking the liberty of seating himself, Ibrahim began:

"I was told to do only as thou desirest, Effendi. I am thy servant."

His first words proved his was a technique foreign to that of the aggressive Musa. Bidding him wait, I went out and called Ali from where he hunched beneath the window listening to all that was said in the room. I told him to find his friend and arrange for transportation; we should need six horses.

"We will fly like the eagles, except we fly in the night, eh, Effendi?" Ali grinned.

The runt of a fellow mirthfully roared and, hitching up his trousers, which were really a pair I had discarded and were a foot too long, he made for the bazar. I turned back into the *serai,* and, grabbing my coat, started out in Ali's footsteps, calling over my shoulder to Ibrahim; he was to seat himself outside my door and permit no others to enter. Hurrying through the bazar, I made for Chinni Baugh, the British Consular grounds.

In due order, I was ushered into the Consul's home, greeted by both the Consul and his wife, and treated to the customary sublimate-of-something to drink. At length, the incident of the morning and the arrival of the new man, Ibrahim, was related. The Consul listened.

"I can't say that I'm in sympathy with you, for I've been followed and watched ever since I first took this post. It's really quite customary in this country."

I voiced the intention of leaving Kashgar without securing the consent of the local Administration. The Consul warned of the inadvisability of such an act, relating the case of a Czechoslovakian who had left Kashgar bound for Urumchi. Having wearied of waiting for permission, he had gone ahead, only to be stopped in Aksu, arrested, and taken all the way back to Yarkand as a prisoner.

Unable to get any useful information or maps of the western mountains, I bade the Consul good-day and went back into the bazar and to the *Tilla serai,* the money market of Kashgar, where one could purchase almost any kind of currency: English pound notes, Chinese moneys, ancient Turki coins, and even American bank-notes—minted in Moscow, they were sold by Kashgar's Russian Bank! I wanted to convert my silver and paper into gold bullion. The metal would be easier to carry in the mountains and was the lightest medium of exchange in this country of valueless currency.

On my return I turned up the bazar street and just before I reached the *serai* gates a burly fellow bumped into me;

pinioning my arms to my sides with ease, he hustled me through a narrow fork off the travelled street. Protesting, I was carried along by the very strength of the fellow; it was not until I got a glimpse of my assailant that I gave up struggling and hurried along at his side. It was Song Soldier!

The Tungan was such a different man in the dress of a Chinese laborer it took me some minutes to grow accustomed to him. When we at last came to a deserted street, it was Song Soldier that did all the talking.

"I have been in Kashgar for eight days and have watched thee! These Bolsheviki follow thee everywhere and their agent is in thy service!"

"All this I know," I replied.

"Those men on the *Masjid* steps are watching thee!" he added. "Be careful. If thou must, return to Khotan!"

Song Soldier struck me lightly on the arm by way of farewell and was gone.

On the street from whence the Tungan had abducted me, I walked past the *Masjid* and into the *serai*. One glance had told me all I need know. On the *Masjid's* last step sat a beggar. By day he made of those steps a bench from which to beseech alms of the passerby, and by night a bed. Above him were two others lounging in the warm dust-laden sunlight. These two men I had seen time and again in the *Yamen* grounds, part of Shin Jin Jung's bodyguard. Then they had been in uniform but were now dressed as poor peasant farmers.

Lost in speculation, I opened the door and stepped into my room without looking up. A startled ejaculation aroused me. Ibrahim, the Tadjik, sat at my table-desk madly grabbing together the papers spread over it and crumpling them into his pockets.

Cursing the fellow, I was on him before he could fully rise

out of the chair and one knuckle-skinning blow knocked him to the floor. Before he could rise, I got hold of the papers in his pockets and compared them with my papers on the table. The swine had been laboriously copying my notes, word for word. His clumsy, botched replica of my all but illegible hand would have been beyond any one to decipher; especially since he had copied from right to left. It looked like the written language of an extinct species of gorilla.

I contemplated kicking the prostrate knave around the room until he wore out. Apparently tuning in on my wave length, Ibrahim got my thoughts and hastily removed himself from the floor. Standing before me, one hand pressed to a rising lump on his cheekbone, he made no attempt to escape as I seized the bosom of his shirt front and pushed him to the corner. But once with his back to the wall, he started at me, ratlike. Tomec's Mongol knife came out from beneath my coat and he changed his mind and, grimacing with fright, backed away. After cursing the Tatar in the Turki tongue as thoroughly as possible, and as well as I knew how in Russian, I roared at him: "Get out!"

He got, but not quite fast enough to escape the booted foot aimed at the appropriate sector of his anatomy.

3

ALI returned from the bazar.

"It is done," he announced. "Thou hast but to say when we go."

But after he heard what Ibrahim had been up to and the beating I had given him, Ali became, contrary to my expectations, dead serious.

"It is best we leave quickly; thou knowest too much. No longer can Shin Jin Jung keep face. Twice he has sent men; twice thou hast found them out. It is bad, Effendi."

The time had come to take definite action.

"Tomorrow, when half the night has spent itself."

Ali nodded. *"Makhol."*

While the little Afghan went into the bazar, I drew the saddlebags from beneath the bed where they had lain since our arrival. A few moments later Ali returned with a few pieces of bread.

"Bread?"

The wiry little fellow shrugged his shoulders.

"They followed. I went for bread. Tonight I will go again but by a different way. Then I will not have to buy bread!"

The next day was spent in making preparations for our fly-by-night departure. Food, clothing, and the journey's requisites were packed into the saddlebags. At dusk Ali went into the bazar and, seeing that he was free of pursuers, made for the home of the horse owner. Immediately after Ali's exit, Kasim Jan presented himself and, without a word about the other

Tadjik, said that I was to come to the *Yamen* immediately. Word had come from Urumchi; permission had been given for the continuation of my journey. As we hustled into the bazar Kasim refused to commit himself, evading my questions with a shrug of the shoulders.

"Shin Jin Jung will tell thee all. I know nothing more than I have already told."

We hurried through the great *Yamen* gates and into the garden surrounding the offices of Shin Jin Jung. The Chinese Administrator awaited me, and with him was Ma See Jung,[1] the Turki Cavalry General in command of all Turki troops in Kashgar. It was a royal greeting that was given me. This prelude to deceit accomplished, Shin Jin Jung addressed me, the little Chinese secretary interpreting.

"Just one hour ago the telegram arrived. I will read it to you:

" '*The American is to be issued visas to facilitate his leaving Kashgar at the earliest possible time. The authorities will place every convenience at his disposal. The visa issued is to be valid only on the road north, from Kashgar to Urumchi.* Signed *(Military Administrator to Sinkiang), Shing Dupen.*' "

The Chinese continued:

"You will be given transportation in one of our trucks and the best seat is to be yours, that in the cabinka."

Later, after much tea drinking, I left the *Yamen* and walked back through the dark and deserted bazar streets. The impossible had been realized. I was to be permitted to continue on my way. But the visas stipulated I was not to take with me a servant nor were firearms permissible. I was to travel in a military conveyance. Odd, damned odd, such restrictions, es-

[1]Ma *See* Jung—not to be confused with the Tungan General Ma *Hsi* Jung.

pecially inasmuch as I was a foreigner. In the *serai*, I told Ali of all that had transpired. He heard me out, then haltingly, as though weighing his every word, he said:

"Ahmad Kamal, Effendi, these are a bad people with whom thou dealest." A pause, then speculatively, "Thou art to leave me behind; thou art forbade the solace of a *tapanchi* (revolver) and art to go in a *Hookemet auftomachine*."

He looked at me from the corner of his eye, and taking my two hands, pressed them tight together at the wrists.

"Would it not be better to send thee in chains?"

The two of us sat in the tiny room, speculating.

"Thou art not to go any place other than Urumchi?"

"None other."

"Then, by Ullah, we will run away; the horses will be ready in an hour."

Calling him back from the door, I explained:

"Ali, this is the best way; thou art a Turki and thou knowest full well we are watched. It is best I go this way, then these *Keti haramzada* will see that all is well and we will both escape harm."

Another day and I made my way to the Tilla *serai*, then to the abode of a merchant who had in the past put himself in my debt. Ali was stationed at the gates. He was to ascertain whether we were being followed and if so, to lead our pursuers astray.

I was received and taken to a lone isolated room, a story above the ground. The room was occupied by my friend's wife and one half of it was screened from the other by a hanging rug. It was behind this partition she stayed whenever I visited her master. A window looked out over the city's roofs and down into its gardens. Women could be seen in plenty, for this was their world—the roofs and tiny walled gardens that

protected them from all but the eyes of their own sex and of
their husbands. Here, and in the home, were the only places
they could remove the eternal veil. Each of the wealthier merchants' roofs was surmounted by a parapet that extended all
the way around it, isolating those on his roof from alien eyes:
aged, infirm, youth, beauty, children. Each roof, each garden
was identical; the couch, the canopy, the vivid rug-paved floors,
women spinning and weaving. Some combed one another's
tresses, long and black, and in the sunlight blue-green as a
blackbird's throat.

The canopies of dull blue, the rugs red and rainbow-shot,
the women clad in brilliantly dyed silken gowns, all made a
vivid picture. Above flew a great flock of tumbler pigeons in
swooping, soaring circles. A falcon streaked over the housetops
and the pigeons vanished, all but one impaled on the hunter's
sharp talons.

I turned to my grinning host who, despite his illustrious
white beard, no doubt spent much of his time at this same
window meditating on the beauty of others' wives. I related
the happenings of the past week and asked his advice. Weighing
the problems in his mind for some moments, he at last spoke:

"To go in the *Hookemet* truck is bad; it is better thou
travelest in the truck of Nesserdin Hadji. In six days he departs
for Urumchi. Go thou with him; I will arrange it."

At my thanks the old Turki laughed disparagingly.

"Thou, Ahmad Kamal, art my brother. Thou hast come
from a land as near Paradise as any on earth. Here is nothing
but lies, filth, *Keti tongus* and *Russ kaffir* (Chinese swine and
Russ infidels). I help thee out of a country that is dead; a
country that stinks of its own decomposition. Thou art a Mussulman; thou hatest the Russ. Enough!

"I have a daughter of sixteen years and it is time she married.
She is as beautiful of mind as of face and figure and would
make a good wife for thee, Effendi!"

LAND WITHOUT LAUGHTER

I gave many reasons for my unsuitability.

"Thou knowest nothing of Turki women," he countered. "She can travel with thee as easily as a man, and the tongues thou knowest not, she will teach thee." He named on the fingers of his hand the languages she could read, write, and speak: "Russ, *Keti*, Tadjik, Uighur, a very little *Parang*, thy own tongue, Effendi."

As he extolled the girl's virtues, stifled sounds came from behind the rug curtain where I suspected she of whom we spoke was secreted with her mother.

"What next will come of the *Hookemet* difficulties and what would the girl do in a country far from her people, where none but myself speak her tongue?" I questioned.

"By my Faith," he snorted. "She would make a good and fruitful wife. She would bear thee many sons!"

To my query as to what the girl herself thought of the arrangement, he replied:

"Thou hast a fair skin and hair; thy eyes are lighter than ours and thou art clean and wealthy. She will be satisfied."

His unwavering enthusiasm to make me a son-in-law alarmed me and I made an excuse for an immediate departure. Further talk of marrying the girl I had never seen was postponed to a future date.

I went to another Turki—Hazeritt Hadji—and asked him to make arrangements for my departing on Nesserdin Hadji's truck. I had resolved to stay away from the marrying man. With the promise that I would be notified as soon as the bargain had been struck, I went back to the *serai*.

Later in the day, Ali hustled a little wizened water carrier into the room by the scruff of his neck.

"I caught this sneaking about outside!"

Sidling up to me, the crooked little man explained his presence:

"A message, Effendi, from Hazeritt Hadji."

LAND WITHOUT LAUGHTER

He presented a note and left with one last scornful look at Ali. The bargain for transportation had been struck. The *keira* was nine thousand *seer* Ha Piu (Kashgar paper currency).

Ten minutes later a thin pimply-faced boy of some eighteen years appeared and identified himself as Nesserdin Hadji. Seated in the proffered chair, he spoke to me in excellent English.

"You are the American, Ahmad Kamal. I am Nesserdin Hadji *Bai*. It is with me that you will go to Urumchi; you will ride in the *cabinka* with Vasili, the chauffeur. Is that satisfactory?"

It was, I assured him, and asked where he had learned to speak English.

"In the Hindustan. I lived there three years."

We talked a while longer and I extracted as much information from the young Turki as was possible. At parting, he promised that we should leave Kashgar in four days and that he would once more call before departure.

Two days slipped past without an incident to mar or mark their passing. Ali muttered in his beard, disconsolate at being left behind. One morning, while I breakfasted and listened to Ali bemoan his lot, a uniformed Chinese came into the *serai* to see me. He was a pompous little officer minus a chin, with heavy rolls of flesh folding over his stiff military collar, thick petulant lips, tiny slits of eyes and a nose that was at once flat and bulbous. At sight of me he snapped his heels together, bowed, and, with surprising directness, got to the business at hand.

"The truck in which thou shalt journey to Urumchi departs at the midday."

"One minute," I stopped him, "it is not on the *Hookemet* truck that I go to Urumchi, and it is three days more before I leave."

"No," he snapped, "Shin Jin Jung says thou art to leave today with this truck. Those are my orders!"

His dictatorial attitude antagonized me.

"I stay here three days more and when I do leave, it will be with the truck of Nesserdin Hadji, not that of the *Hookemet!* Those are my intentions!" I snapped.

My little Chinaman forgot to click his heels together as he turned to the bazar.

"First-rate, Effendi, thy words are strongest." Ali Muhammad Khan grinned.

An hour later I was drawn to the window by a commotion outside. Two determined fellows, one of whom I recognized as Kasim, insisted upon seeing the Amerikaluk, while Ali, equally determined and twice as fierce, refused them. Seeing me at the window the two pressed forward. I dismissed Ali and listened; Kasim addressed me.

"A man was sent to prepare thee for departure this afternoon; it is on this truck that thou art to go."

I stood in the doorway, keeping the two outside and on their feet as servants, instead of messengers from the *Yamen.*

"Go thou back and tell Shin Jin Jung that for twenty-four days he has kept me waiting here in Kashgar and always he refused to permit my going. Now, he expects me to be ready to start in a matter of hours. It cannot be done. I do not go today. Not until I am ready, and then in the truck of Nesserdin Hadji. Not that of the *Hookemet!*"

Kasim opened his mouth to speak, thought better of it and, followed by the other, left the *serai.*

On the following day Ali and I went for a walk out past the city wall and over the bridge spanning the boiling mud torrent, the Kashgar *Deria* (river).

Strolling through a beautiful garden village, my attention was caught by sounds of festivities. Interested, I peered over the heads of a large crowd. The object of their interest, and mine, was a dervish clad in a brilliant silken robe. While he harangued the populace, a child assistant, who knelt on a felt beside him, gathered the coins tossed to him. Every time a bit of money was offered, the speaker joyously raised his voice to a thunderous pitch.

Ali was as interested as I, and he rudely pushed a way through the protesting crowd. Following him, I took a coin from my pocket. Spying me, the dervish abruptly ceased his tale and, prodding the boy with his staff, pointed to me. Taking my hand, the little fellow led me to the very front of the other disgruntled listeners, there presenting an alms bowl, a blackened half-gourd, and begged that I fill it. Frugal Ali attempted to push it away, but I gave the little chap a handful of the cheap Kashgar *pul* (money).

Eyes starting from their heads, the two—boy and man— knelt to count their new wealth; meanwhile the crowd, nettled at my interruption, impatiently urged them to continue with whatever they had been doing.

In a dither of gratitude, the jubilant dervish took from beneath his flea-specked robes a bundle of sticks, deftly juggling them. About us, the people angrily stamped their feet, sending up great clouds of loose choking dust. All insisted that he tell them a tale—the same tale he had discontinued on my arrival. Convinced that whatever he had been saying must have been exceptionally interesting to hold such an audience, I too insisted that he tell the story. Abruptly he let his sticks rain down about the felts at his feet, where the boy gathered and bound them together. Shouting at the top of his lungs, he called to his listeners, saying:

"Then I start at the beginning of my story—a *musaphir* listens."

The others complained, but, unshaken, he began again. His

bellowing voice—nearly bursting my eardrums—soon silenced the opposition, and the tale began. It is retold here almost exactly as we heard it that day, except that I have shortened it and eliminated much that was too lewd for Western literary appetites.

"THE DOG THAT WAS: TAOTAI"

"Yah—Taotai.

"Yah—He who is remembered only with hate and curses.

"Yah—The dog born of Shaitan's seed and from a snake's womb.

"Yah—Taotai.

"For long years the narrow bazar streets had lain in the gloom and shadow of the fortress walls. To the tribesmen the height of those walls and the chill of their shadow was power personified. To the camel drivers from Lhasa, Badakshan, the Hindustan, and Samarkand, they were amazing. The foreigners, halting their caravans to gaze, would speak in awe of the towering battlements—then ejaculate: 'Yah Ullah! The work of Djinns.'

"Naked children, playing about the feet of the two-humped camels, often mimicked the strangers, much to the amusement of their elders. When these children became adults they, as their fathers before them, testified 'Not the work of Djinns, but that of Shaitan.'

"Had it not been for the man who dwelt within those massive walls, none would have cursed them. The gloom would have become shade; the chill, succor from the desert sun.

"Taotai, many years before, had come to murder the peace and tranquillity of the people of Kashgar. Mounting the throne, he declared himself *Padishah* and replaced the people's white wing of happiness with the darkened sky of sorrow. Generosity was beheaded and in its stead avarice ruled. Justice became a memory, a memory as remote as a forgotten dream of one's infancy, a dream dreamt at a mother's breast and forgotten before one awoke. And with justice a memory, cruelty became *Padishah.*

"Yah—Taotai.

"Yah—He who is remembered only with hate and curses.

"Yah—the whore-born bastard son of a thousand leprous fathers.

"Yah—Taotai.

"The great room had from its beginning been calculated to awe all who there trod. Six hundred *guezz* high, two hundred *guezz* broad and nine hundred *guezz* long, it bestowed upon all strangers an overwhelming sense of their inconsequence.

"Mounted high above petitioners' heads, intended to intimidate, supported on two massive blocks of flawless green jade, was the throne.

"His belly prohibiting his moving without assistance, Taotai lived on the throne; never did he leave the throne. Dropsy and forty wives having robbed him of all mastery over his bladder and bowels, provision had been made for their weakness. The seat of the throne was pierced and under the aperture rested a flowered porcelain bowl. The physician was always at hand, forever tapping the dropsy-filled belly and limbs.

"Gluttony had swollen Taotai's body until its bulging folds overflowed the throne; had made necessary the vomitorium at his elbow.

"Ever at his side, opposite the vomitorium, was a swan-necked pitcher of pomegranate juice. The juice of the pomegranate invigorates the flagging glands of senility. Taotai maintained an orchard of the trees on his castle grounds.

"Further insuring the perpetuation of his stallion loins, Taotai kept near at hand a gold and lacquer box from which he frequently sampled and on which was scribed 'Chuan Ku Kai.' It had been brought Taotai by a caravan sent many thousands of *li* to the east and across the Gobi for that sole purpose. In Beging, from whence the box had been fetched, were apothecaries skilled in the brewing of wondrous aphrodisiacs. 'Chuan Ku Kai' was the foremost of these specialists.

"Taotai was not, in truth, a man at all. He was a *thing* of cruelty, madness, deceit, stench, and hate; he was afterbirth matured, soulless and foul!

"Yah—Taotai.

"Yah—Dog who is remembered only with hate and curses.

"Yah—Miscarriage of a swine.

"Yah—Taotai.

"The son of Taotai's chamberlain, a pallid unclean Ketai, often boasted in the bazar: 'Oh, I have no need of a wife or concubine; Taotai's wives are sufficient. They, with the characteristic baseness of females, clamor for my favor.' Evilly grinning at the foulness of his tongue, the Ketai would say, 'Taotai's mountainous belly envelops his groin, and a female's charms—at all times difficult to attain—are inaccessible to him. Taotai has acquired a love for boys!'

"One day the Ketai disappeared and though there was much conjecture as to what had become of him, he was never seen again.

"One day a great and just warrior came to the realm of Taotai, and killed a swine—Taotai.

"Yah. But Taotai was not wholly without virtue. On the first day of each year he would bestow alms upon the poor.

"Yah—On the second day of each year the weaponed tax collectors would again go forth.

"Yah—Taotai.

"Yah—Dog that is today in the Hades created for his kind.

"Yah—Dog born of Shaitan's seed and from a snake's womb.

"Yah—Dog forever damned.
"Yah—Taotai."

As Ali and I departed, I asked if what the story-teller had said was true.

"Yes," he replied, "except that Taotai was thin, not fat; and that he had no castle so great as that one in the story."

"Then why did he tell of the Taotai's girth and his castle?"

"Because," answered Ali, "Taotai is dead and we can do him no bodily harm. The only, and greatest, harm we can do him is to his memory. Anyhow, it was true, before Taotai's time."

"Who then was *Padishah?*" I questioned. Ali shrugged his shoulders.

"I do not know."

"Then why sayest thou there was such a *Padishah?*"

"There will be such a *Padishah* if there hasn't already been one!" Ali insisted.

"How dost thou know?" I persisted.

"Because every untruth of today was a truth in yesterday's thousands of years. And every untruth of yesterday will be a truth in tomorrow's eternity," retorted Ali.

Back at the *serai,* we found the old water carrier awaiting us with a message:

"Nesserdin Hadji hath been taken to the *Yamen.*"

Ali shrugged and cautioned with a Turki proverb:

"Wait. Never listen to the rider who comes warning of the rising river unless the belly of his horse is wet. Flee to save thyself and he will loot thy house."

The proverb fitted the occasion and the old man was thanked, given a few *seer* and let go on his way. That night, I gave myself over to the task of trying to find a common denominator with which I could appraise the series of strange coincidences that had formed to thwart my every move.

LAND WITHOUT LAUGHTER

"Forget it, Effendi," Sage-Ali counselled to me from his bed in the corner. "Both new and old mud is easy to cross; it is only mud that is neither new nor old that holds one. Our mud is about to harden. Who ever heard of mud staying wet so long a time?"

After such advice Ali ceased, but only for a moment, then he sat up in his blankets, hurling a barrage of blasphemy into the darkness. Proof that his true fears and thoughts were not reflected by his trite proverbs. This fact became even more evident after I consoled him, saying:

"Perhaps these Russ are not so much a product of *Shaitan* as we think them. Perhaps they mean no harm to us, and do only that which they believe to be right!"

"Yah!" Ali mocked my words. "There once went into the wilderness a hunter. And his arrows slew many antelope. Each time an arrow went forth, the bowstring struck the archer's wrist. He killed many antelope: they covered the plains as rocks pave a river bed. Then he stood over a great mound he made of them. He wept at the pain in his bow-whipped wrist.

"From the distance, two unharmed antelope watched the hunter. One said:

" 'No harm can come to us from such a man; see how he weeps over our dead brothers. He knows pity.' Then said the other antelope:

" 'Look not upon his sorrow, but upon the bleeding bodies of our dead. Witness what his works have wrought!' "

The next day found Nesserdin Hadji at large. He disproved the rumor of his arrest. He had been seen entering the *Yamen*, where he had gone to secure the credentials necessary to leave Kashgar. The papers had been issued him and the date of our departure was set three days hence.

4

THERE were tears on Ali's ugly face that my gift of *Tamasha* money could not staunch. He had escorted me from our dwelling to the *serai*-garage; now, unhappy and wordless, he stood beside me. Several times we had begun our farewells, but unsuccessfully. When least I expected it Ali took my hand in his, kissed it, and strode away without looking back. In a few seconds he was lost in the bazar throng.

As I write this he's probably smuggling hashish into India; fighting the British on the Northwestern Frontier; or, perhaps, he's enjoying a new wife while his faithful (?) standby makes his home thunder with her pounding on locked doors. He is, without a shadow of a doubt, a worthless little cut-throat. Worse than that, he's a Shia (heretic sect of Muslims), but whatever he now does I'll take an oath he's doing it thoroughly, and justifying every knavish trick with some apt adage. If I never meet him on this earth, some time after I've passed over, or fallen off, the bridge to paradise, I'll meet Ali, who will in either instance greet me with a chuckle, and say:

"Ah, Effendi, share my eighty thousand servants and—my wives. There are some I haven't touched yet. *Whi Jan*, who would ever have thought that I would know such *Tamasha!*"

Or, after a warm greeting, he'll whisper:

"There is a trail that passes over the mountains to the south." Then, showing me a knife moulded out of molten lava while his overseer wasn't looking:

"Tonight we will fly, thou and I—after I put this blade between the ribs of the *Keti haramzada* that rules this place. I will gain much face by slaying Shaitan" (Shin Jin Jung).

My luggage was stowed away in the truck which, with the luggage of twenty-seven others, was filled to the very top of the side boards. On top of all this perched the twenty-seven men, women, and one child, a motley mass of Turkis, all struggling for a place to cling. Crowds gathered about the truck, a roaring, rattling Zeiss-5 of Soviet Russian manufacture. Hundreds lined the narrow bazar streets to see the marvel; children ran screaming back and forth before the palpitating *konka*.

At length, great length, we got under way, whereupon some one fell off the top with the scream of a lost soul. Nesserdin Hadji poked his head in through the open window and cried to the young Russian chauffeur:

"Vasili! Aiii! Vasili! Shtop! Aiii, shtop! A man has fallen; he is dead!"

Vasili cut the switch and cursed fervently.

"Dead? Hah, never did a dead one howl like that."

We all got out of the truck. The mob once more engulfed it and, better to see what had happened, I climbed to the cab's top. I glimpsed a form being picked from the bazar street by a multitude of hands from which it immediately detached itself and clambered back upon the mountainous load; a bit dusty and dishevelled but none the worse for wear. Vasili crawled back into the cab. One of our two mechanics cranked, and we once more rumbled off. We managed to stop and stall at every turn in the bazar street. We knocked down Turkis that were so overwhelmed by sight of this fire-breathing instrument of the devil that they dashed blindly before the careening thing to escape it. Then there was the time Vasili drove too close to a projecting wall-timber and cleaned the truck-top of its burden of writhing place-hunters, and left them, to the last one, piled in the bazar street. However, the indestructibles lost no time in extricating themselves from the pile of humanity and dashed back to the truck, which by this time the apopleptic Vasili had succeeded in stopping.

Eventually we drew up before the *Yamen* for another inspection of passports. My nemesis, Shin Jin Jung, acted, with the assistance of his twelve-man bodyguard, as interrogator. At my proffered passport he smiled, waved it away and instead shook my hand. I was wished a pleasant journey. Nesserdin Hadji came to my side, whispering, unhappily:

"Ahmad Kamal, Effendi: soldiers are being sent with us."

He nodded toward a big, heavy, beardless Kazakh; with him were two others with rifles. Nesserdin Hadji nodded again toward a Chinese in uniform, a foppish fellow, dispatch case and revolver swung from his belt. Most amazing of all was the fool's hair, so long that it could not be crammed under his cap, but stuck out at the sides like a shirt from a broken suitcase. At that moment he chose to strut past us exuding an almost overwhelming reek of cheap perfume. Inspection was brought to a close with a little speech by Shin Jin Jung.

"There are to be no knives, revolvers or firearms carried by any civilians during the journey, nor is any one to carry messages from one bazar to another. Any person caught transporting any written material other than in an official capacity, or carrying *nisha* (hashish) will be put in prison."

The Administrator looked directly at me and repeated himself, but modified a part of it.

"There are to be *no* knives, revolvers or firearms carried by any civilians. If any possess firearms, they may keep them providing they immediately identify themselves and receive," he continued to look at me and fluttered a bit of paper taken from his pocket, "a permit."

None stepped forward and I turned away, ignoring the

216

warning and aware of the comforting pressure of Tomec's knife couched in the small of my back. Every one climbed back on the *konka* upon dismissal by Shin Jin Jung. The perfumed soldier seated himself on top of the load just beside the cab, his feet swinging against the window frame on my door. Rumbling out of Kashgar we stampeded some horses and ran down a dog; at last coming to a shuddering *shtop* in Yengi Shahr, the New City.

Nesserdin Hadji disappeared; more red tape. Some *Ju Jung* had to be consulted before we could continue. It was by this time one o'clock; we had mounted the *konka* at eight o'clock, five hours before, and had travelled only five miles.

"If we travel with such haste all the way to Urumchi," a dour-visaged Turki on top of the load remarked, "all of my children will have grandchildren, and theirs will be white-bearded offspring, before I return!"

Young Nesserdin Hadji had no more than gone when the Kazakh who had joined our lot at the *Yamen* told all the others who had as destination any bazar between Kashgar and Urumchi to get down. Half a dozen began bickering and fighting. Un-interested, I went into an *Osh Khana* (food-house café) and proceeded to fill up on *muntu*. When at last there was no longer place for another of the meat-filled dough balls, I drank tea to fill up the cracks, and, paying the bill, went back into the bazar.

The truck's human cargo was in an uproar. Those evicted now stood in the dust by the roadside, berating Nesserdin Hadji, who had by this time returned. Months before, he had agreed to take them to their destinations and now he had let this newcomer unseat them. Nesserdin Hadji seemed perplexed, and not a little discomfited by the remarks of the outraged passengers. Turning to the big emissary of Shin Jin Jung, Nesserdin Hadji queried:

LAND WITHOUT LAUGHTER

"Why is it, Hadji Akhun? Why?"

Silencing him, the big fellow ordered, "Give them their money and ask no more questions!"

By way of comment, I asked Nesserdin Hadji who owned the truck—the newcomer or himself? Another Turki took it up.

"Yah, Nesserdin Hadji, what are thou, a woman? Any man comes and thou sleepest at the bottom, eh!" Hadji Akhun put an end to the comments with:

"Yah, *Ullah*, I am of the *Hookemet!* I say go back. Go back, understand? I say——"

I silenced him with, "Thou sayest too much."

My understudy, one of the evicted, cried:

"When thou, Nesserdin Hadji, returnest after a trip with that fellow," pointing to Hadji Akhun, "thou shalt be big with child!"

Vasili, disgusted, clashed the gears and we lurched forward, actually, I hoped, on our way to Urumchi. Out of the village, we went over myriad little bridges that collapsed just as we passed over them. At last in open territory, the road unfolded itself before us, a thin clay strip bounded on each side by steep slopes, glassy in the now driving rain. The road had been selected because it was high above the surrounding salt marshes, but naturally with no consideration for automobile tires and slithering mud. I half stood, feet jammed against the floorboards, hands grasping the window ledge with all their strength, and teeth clenched until the balled jaw-muscles ached. We swirled along the wet road, broadsiding, starting down the steep clay slope only to recover and snap around as Vasili hauled at the wheel. The cargo of rain-drenched lost souls crowded in the back rent the air with their panic-stricken howls:

"*Yah, Ullah! Yah, Khoda! Yah, Towa!*" (Oh, God! Oh, God! Oh, Repentance!)

Late that night we drove into a dark *serai,* and into an old well. Half the truck disappeared with a lurch that threw all the unfortunates out on the ground. Some one started to count heads and called out in the darkness:

"Are all there?" to which the practical Vasili answered:

"What matters it? We couldn't locate lost ones in this dark. Let's eat."

In the next four days, we were in turn baked and drenched, sunk in either mud or sand. Every time the rattling vehicle would stop in sand or mud or just in a fit of temperament, the whole pack of human cargo would unravel, clamber down from precarious perches and forthwith spread out fanlike over the surrounding desert in perfect skirmishing order. The technique was invariable. Then, at last, failing to find either hillock or bush to hide behind, each individual would assume the attitude customary to all peoples in all climes.

Vasili glanced out over the circle of crouching humans.

"Looks like a siege, eh?"

The truck extricated, we would, after warning the preoccupied humans with a blast of the horn, start forward a few yards. Thinking themselves about to be deserted, our human cargo would rise and dash back to their lofty perches, all the while gathering themselves together.

Afternoon of the seventh day of June saw us nearing Aksu, whereupon our conveyance gave a gasping, choking sigh and rolled to a stop. Vasili looked first at me, then kicked the speedometer's face in. He gave himself over to thorough, hearty Russian adjectives. Our dishevelled load gathered about the cab in which we sat.

"Why have we stopped here? Why do we not start again? Why——?"

With a glare Vasili silenced them. He pointed a stubby, grease-grimed forefinger at the percolating motor.

"Spoiled. It is spoiled, broken!"

He got out of the cab and threw up the hood to delve into the mechanism.

"The *trombulator* (distributor)."

He came up, the thing in his hand.

"No good."

A tall Kirghiz shouldered his way through those grouped about the two of us, and I recognized him as one I had come to know the night before when he, seeing my first-aid kit, had sidled up, and with a sneaky grin, asked:

"Effendi, hast thou that medicine which makes a man once more young? That which holds in one drop the power to make one desirable in all women's eyes?"

I had assured him that I carried no such medicine, but should he break his leg, I would be glad to fix him up. My answer had offended him, especially in that I spoke loudly enough to inform the others of the content of our conversation. All the women had, since that time, laughed whenever he stalked by. Like the others, I had come to know him by the alias, *Kara Kulpuk* (black hat), because of his heavy black headgear. *Kara Kulpuk* now addressed Vasili, thrusting a long thin finger into his face.

"Thou must get me to Aksu this day. Did not Nesserdin Hadji promise that four days would find us in Aksu?"

Irate Vasili would have struck the fellow, had not Hadji Akhun spoken.

"The *konka* is broken, but it is only two *potai* to the bazar. It is better we all walk. The *konka* will come later."

All but Vasili, the two mechanics, Nesserdin Hadji and I, started down the road. Hadji Akhun approached me.

"Effendi, surely thou wilt not wait here in this heat?"

Chiefly because he was so anxious that I go, I decided to remain with the truck.

LAND WITHOUT LAUGHTER

Vasili snickered at the other's departing back. "He is a very extraordinary fellow," he explained. "Walk indeed. He perhaps can walk on water. There is yet a river to cross, before Aksu."

Hours later, the trouble remedied, we once more rumbled forward, eventually coming to the banks of a large river. Our passengers waited for us at its side, as did a ramshackle flatboat.

"It was on this spot that we turned over and lost a *konka* a week ago," the boatman remarked in midstream. We looked at the swift milk-white water, removed our boots and coats, and waited for the sudden plunge and long swim.

It was late in the afternoon when we at last rolled into the Aksu bazar and trembled to a voluntary stop, almost our first. Immediately the truck was surrounded by the curious. There were more Chinese than in Kashgar; Russians were everywhere, their fair complexions and blond hair in contrast to the dark Turkis and Chinese. The Russians, for the most part in Cossack uniform, all seemed to take me for one of their kind, and I was several times called upon to return the greeting, "*Drasdi.*" The hammer-and-sickle flag hung before several shops, and beneath the flag the inscription, "Sov-Sinkiang" (*Soviet Dominion*).

The bazar itself was composed of the typical mud-walled streets and houses. The doors were heavily bound with red-rusted iron straps and padlocks. All of the buildings were pierced by loopholes which had been used in turn by both defending Russians and attacking Tungans in the course of the siege two years before.

A Kirghiz lounged by the roadside, before him a wooden tray of sunflower and watermelon seeds. Purchasing a handful, I climbed back into the cab to crack and eat them, when some Bolsheviki officers jerked open the cab door and asked who I was.

"Amerikansky," I replied. Satisfied, they turned away.

Some officious fellow returned, who, after greeting me, asked:

"*Par Russky goveril?*"

I shook my head in the negative.

He departed, apparently disgusted at my ignorance. Nesserdin Hadji reappeared, with him two officers, one Russian, one Turki. The Russian was a tall bony fellow, on his face a perpetual wry grimace. The Turki was short, squat and heavily built, and as slovenly in his uniform as the Russian was immaculate.

Vasili materialized from the crowd and took his driver's seat while the Turki and Russian seated themselves on the two front fenders.

"They are to show us to the *serai*, the garage in the new city," Vasili explained.

After bumping through narrow, gorgelike roads for half an hour, we wound once again into a broad street, this time of a Chinese bazar. We were told to turn into a *serai*. One look at it and Vasili threw up his hands and prepared to back out. The place was disgustingly filthy. Surrounding the compound was a ramshackle jumble of buildings. A shrivelled hag sat on a broken step nursing a child of perhaps eight months. At the clash of gears, the brat dropped the flat rubbery breast and turned to watch us. The perfumed Chinese soldier who joined us at the Kashgar *Yamen* jumped down from his seat when Vasili started to back from the *serai*, and, in his high-pitched effeminate voice, screamed to us to *shtop*. The two officers on the fenders joined him.

"No, by Ullah, not in that *Ketai* pigpen do we stay!" growled Vasili.

The sour-visaged Russian gained the running board. "*Shtop,*" he commanded imperatively. We *shtopped*.

"You are to stay here. Those are orders from the *Ju Jung*. This is the place where all *auftomobiles shtop*."

Vasili gave up, and to the curses of those on top of the load, we once more lurched forward to the *serai's* center.

Nesserdin Hadji, Kichik Akhun, Hashim Akhun, and I sat on the steps of one of the filthy hovels, all cursing the Amban who had decreed such accommodations for us. Disgusted, I strode out of the *serai*. A fat Turki hailed me in the bazar.

"Effendi—Aiii—Effendi!"

I recognized him as one of the cargo as he jounced up to me, his big belly and glistening rotund cheeks jiggling with each hurried step.

"Effendi," laying his hand on my arm, "thou perhaps hast seen me before?"

Assuring him that I had, I asked what it was he wished. Puffing with the unaccustomed exertion, he wiped the beaded perspiration from his face.

"Both thou and I are *musaphir*, travellers, and without kin or home; I thought we might walk together and make *tamasha*. There are *baughs* (tea gardens) and many, many places." Impressed with the jovial attitude of my acquaintance, I told him to lead on; we would make *tamasha*.

In the next hour I learned much of my talkative companion. His seventh wife was seventeen years old and by name, Nisa Han. His name was Muhammad Imin Akhun Ibn Azizoff, and his age fifty-two; he was a *sodager* (merchant) and going now to Urumchi to visit his only living relative, his sister, Tuda Han.

Then Muhammad Imin turned to me. Who was I? What was I? What was my business? Was I wealthy? A *Bai*? Married? Children? Imin kept up a steady stream of conversation, and when I ignored a question he, not in the least daunted, would answer it to his own satisfaction and ask another. Under his guidance we at length found ourselves at the tea garden, tables and chairs grouped beneath a little jungle of fig and willow trees; in the garden's center was a fifty-foot clearing.

"The place of the *tance*." Snapping his fingers, the big fellow executed a few steps.

Imin confided in me, indiscreet as are all Turkis. The *Hookemet* was foul. If only, he swore, he was, as I, a citizen of another country, he would leave this Sinkiang.

"Bolsheviki and Tungan alike, all are bandits, murderers, and Godless *kaffirs*."

He told me of the *inkalob* (revolution).

"The Tungan killed my one brother and a sister. It was during the pillage of Kashgar that they forced their way into my brother's home and, seizing him and his family, they demanded his gold." Imin shook his heavy-jowled head from side to side as he recalled the tragedy.

"My brother had done the same as every other Turki; he had hidden his gold a little here, a little there, and a little more somewhere else. When they demanded his money he took them to one of the caches and gave all it contained to them, but they knew the habit of the Turki and told him to show them where the rest was hidden. He told them he had none, but they clubbed and bound him and again asked for his gold and threatened to violate both his wife and sister before his very eyes unless he gave more gold.

"Then," continued the now serious Imin, "he made the mistake that cost him both gold and life; he took them into the garden where he had buried all the rest of his money, and gave it to them and begged that they go and leave him in peace. Instead, the devils took him back into the house, again bound him and demanded that he tell the hiding place of the rest of his gold. He swore he had given all, but they thought he lied as he had before, and before his eyes they raped his wife, his

224

sister, and his daughter, and killed all four of them before they left to torment some one else. The sons-of-swine!"

Imin laughed unpleasantly, recalling another tale of the horrors of the past.

"Many Tungans died in Kashgar and all because of their greed. Our women are brave and true to God and their people. Many a Turki woman put a knife between the ribs of those looting, raping devils. Tatluk Han was a very brave girl: a virgin before they came and killed all of her family, sparing her only because she was pleasing to look upon and a female. She took revenge for what they did to her and hers. Every day she beckoned to soldiers in the streets, and when they came she took them into the house and while in their embrace stabbed them in the side. Twelve dead were hidden in her house when she was discovered and shot."

I asked Imin how he had escaped.

"I had more sense and greater fear than my brother. I left Kashgar and went, with my wife, far back into the mountains before ever the Tungan army came. It was not until they had left Kashgar that I returned.

"But those Tungans are more to be desired than these that rule us now," he continued. "*Shaitan* take them! Those bandit devils at least fight in the sun like men; these others, the *haramzada* Bolsheviki—pah!" he spat.

"Khodja Niaz Hadji,[1] a fool; for four years he fought against the Bolsheviki *Keti*, and then because he was afraid they would kill him he crept to Urumchi and took that which was given him, riches and a title. He gave up all that for which so many of us died, that he might live. Those Bolsheviki, they had the wisdom of *Shaitan*. A Turki was made Fu Ju Shi, a few of his friends put in the *Yamen*, given a handful of gold, a handsome coat and fine boots, and all the other Turki fools, like myself,

[1]Second in Administrative Power. (Sinkiang.)

say, 'Ah, we did win the war. See, our Khodja Niaz is the same as *Padishah!*' Then we put down our *miltok* (rifle) and *kilich* (sword) and as fast as we laid them down, the Russ picked them up. We could no longer shoot, or strike with a sword; our spiked cannon rusted in the fields, its balls beside it. We went back to the *zemin* (earth) to till the fields, sow and reap and suffer more than before. Before, those of us that had wealth could pay a bit of it to the thieving *Hookemet* and take what was left to the Hindustan and live comfortably. Now, a bit of paper lies in the hand of the *Dupen*. On it *'palanchi* has this much, *palanichi* ["so and so"] has that much,' and no one named on that list can breathe freely. He is taxed beyond endurance; his animals and lands are sold when he can no longer meet the amount asked of him. Once a man is reduced to *kambagal* at least he can beg in the streets, or take a *ketmen* and dig in the fields. Khodja Niaz Hadji cannot even leave Urumchi unless it is to Russia he goes. Those Soviet are afraid he might once again gather his men and with them finish what he started five years ago."

Imin turned again to me, brightening.

"Ahmad Kamal, Effendi, now is the time for pleasure. The sun yet shines and tomorrow it may not."

We straggled down a warm roadway. The cliff of the mesa above freed little stones from its sides and they came hurtling down into the roadway, making wobbly little paths in the loose dust. A smiling boy ran out of a poplar-shaded cottage.

"It is mulberries you desire, perhaps curds?" he called.

Ever-famished Imin glanced from me to the boy.

"Is not the size of my stomach sign enough that I want food!"

The sky, the red hills, the atmosphere itself, were drenched in a silver-shot sunset as we departed that cottage, filled to

bursting. We trudged back to the tea garden and seated ourselves beneath the fig boughs. Tea was brought in a squat
samovar.

Somewhere in the distance, in the direction of the bazar, the
swift roll of drums could be heard punctuated by the boom of
a larger kettle-drum. Our host explained that it was his musicians approaching.

"They first parade through the bazar, then come here."

They arrived just at sunset. Three with drums seated
themselves on the ground before the clearing while a dozen
others with various instruments grouped in a semicircle about
them. The setting was entrancing. Great red bluffs, glowing in
the last rays of the sinking sun, formed a background, while
the verdant foliage about us rustled in an evening breeze.
Turkis filtered into the garden, gradually filling the benches.
Tea began to flow freely, keeping a dozen waiters busy filling
the glasses. The mouth-watering aroma of *shashlik* wafted
through the garden from the 'dobe-walled oven over which
the spitted morsels of lamb sputtered and dripped. The dusk
became alive with voices and laughter. Curiously, not a single
woman sat at the crowded tables or lurked in the trees' shadows.

"Are there never women at this place?" I asked Imin.

"Never. Is this not a Mussulman country? The women are
all in the houses of their husbands or families!"

After a prelude of discords the music became melodious.
High, wavering, and beautiful in its fluctuating rhythm, it was
the music of Turkistan and a dozen centuries. Two men danced
out into the clearing and then two more. If not so beautifully
executed, their dance would have been incongruous. Tiny mincing steps, quick, accurate movements of the heel and toe, two
men on each side facing one another; with quick stamping steps
they moved toward one another, and then away, again and
again, always in perfect unison. The last time I had seen such

dancing had been in Tungan territory with Ma Ki Fu and Song Soldier; there our dancers had been prostitutes.

The four big fellows performing were as graceful as women themselves, and their toil-muscled arms were nearly as sinuous; nothing was forgotten, not even the wrist and finger movements. Those dancing were, by day, laborers, merchants, and caravan men. At the dance's close, lamps were hung in the boughs, their light augmented by the glowing *paparos*, the long Russian cigarette, smoked by nearly every one there.

The music burst into a rollicking Cossack dance. A Tatar, clad, as was every one here, in boots, tight-fitting skirl-skirted corduroy coat, and fur cap, swept into the clearing and began the leaping, whirling dance. Around and around the clearing he went, finally ending with a prodigious bound.

Muhammad Imin spoke into my ear:

"There are two in uniform watching us."

I recognized one as the perfumed Chinese; the other was Russian and strange to me. With a pretended mirth I did not feel, I suggested we leave, and as we walked back to the *serai*, the uniformed two followed us. I told Imin of the trouble experienced in Kashgar, and that being followed no longer worried me.

"It seems as natural in Sinkiang as does sand in a desert."

"It is the *Ghi Pu*, eh?" Imin whispered.

"I don't know."

"It is. They follow every one of wealth or importance in Kashgar!"

To his evident relief we gained the *serai*, got our bedding and lay down beside the truck to sleep.

The second day in Aksu was like the first. Jolly Imin and I went from garden to garden, sampling fruit and in the evening going as before to the *baugh*. We had been uncomfortable the

whole day, so persistent had those following us been. Returning to the *serai* late that evening, we mulled over the day's
events. Imin was worried at the attention bestowed on us by
a new acquaintance, one Turt Akhun. The beardless stranger
had first introduced himself earlier that day. He had insisted
upon being host at a meal in the bazar tea house. "He wished,"
he assured us, "the Amerikaluk to carry away with him pleasant
memories."

"Ahmad Kamal," Imin voiced his thoughts to me, "many
Turkis would go without beards but for the fact that they
would be classed as Bolsheviki. When one of my people is man
enough to grow a beard and shaves it, one thing is sure: his
friends are either Russ or he is in the *Yamen*, the *Hookemet*.
If he is a *kaffir*-Bolsheviki he is no good. Anyhow, that fellow's
eyes are too small!"

We sought the reason why benzine had been withheld from
our party by the *Yamen*. Ever since our arrival, Nesserdin
Hadji had been put off whenever he spoke to the Amban about
purchasing fuel. Imin sighed:

"Effendi, the dust-laden air of the desert is easier to breathe
than that of this," he coughed and spat, "*kaffir*-Bolsheviki bazar."

It was dark when we turned in through the *serai* gates, and
before us blazed a battery of flashlight beams exploring the
truck and some bundles beside it. One was held full on us, and
I waved it away. Some one laughed and another beam was insolently turned in our faces. As we approached, Imin whispered a single word.

"*Hookemet.*"

Beside the truck, I discovered the nocturnal visitors were
soldiers, Chinese in Russian uniforms. A dozen or more were
about. The luggage of every one on the truck lay on the ground,
mine and Imin's to one side. Anxiously, I examined saddlebags to be sure they had not been tampered with. While I bent

over them a tall Chinese introduced himself. He had been sent from the *Yamen* to look through the contents of my bags.

I refused outright, damned if I would open the bags in the dark dirty *serai*. If he wanted to look through their contents, he could do so on the morrow. He tried to explain. I remained adamant. Nettled, he went to Nesserdin Hadji; the two returned, pushing and stumbling their way through the crowd gathered about me. Nesserdin Hadji seemed nervous and besought, speaking in English:

"Please let him look through your things. I have been promised benzine and we can leave in the morning, but first this must be done."

Baffled, I unlocked one bag to have a dozen soldiers reach in and pull out the contents. Each piece was thoroughly examined; every seam of my various garments was carefully explored. They were definitely searching for something. Satisfied that what he sought was not in this first bag, the big Chinese asked that I open the second. Angry, and cautious, I refused, pointing to the contents of the bags, lying at my feet in the dust where the soldiers had thrown them.

"Go thou to Hell! And if thou seekest to see the rest of my belongings come back tomorrow, but with an apology."

"I sorrow, but we are told to investigate."

Ignoring his protest, I crammed back in the bags what lay on the ground. Seeing that I had no intention of co-operating, the Chinese said he must take my passport to the *Yamen* for examination. He again met with refusal. He could see everything on the morrow. Tonight: "Nothing!"

Pondering my words he opened his mouth to speak, thought better of it, and bidding me good-by with an exasperated wave of the hand, left the *serai*. With him went his soldiers, all decked out in Sam Browne belts, shoulder straps, doodads, swords, and revolvers. One, I noticed, had a dispatch case on each hip, beneath each case swung a holstered revolver, and most ludicrous of all was the shoulder-holster which he wore on top of his tunic. Protruding from the holster was the tiny black butt of a .25 automatic.

Nesserdin Hadji spoke to me.

"Something is wrong. All this was not done without reason!"

He drew me aside and Imin followed. At Nesserdin Hadji's questioning look, I approved Imin's presence.

"Ahmad Kamal," he began, "I am worried. It is not true that there is no benzine in Aksu. I have found that there is. For some reason, we are being kept here." He threw a nervous glance about us, then continued: "I am afraid that it is me they watch. My father, Myodin Jan Bai Hadji, left this country before these Bolsheviki took it. I, too, was in the Hindustan with him, and, fool," he spat the word, "I returned. This new *Hookemet* hates the *bai*—the rich. Ever since I returned they have spied upon me. I cannot go beyond Yarkand to the south, nor can I take my mother even that far. These new rulers fear I will run away to the Hindustan. I am afraid—afraid they watch me."

"They watch not thee but Ahmad Kamal here," Imin snorted. "Whose saddlebags did they want opened? His, and mine because I have walked and talked with him. They came here and only one man's road letter did they want to see—only one. It is him and me they watch, not thee."

"I will offer thanks unto God when once more we are on our way," Nesserdin Hadji sighed.

We lay in our blankets looking up at the stars. It had been hours since we lay down to sleep. A stranger came into the *serai*, and his rattling of the gates disturbed all of us. Imin turned restlessly in his blankets. Some one gave voice to an angry "Who? Why?"

LAND WITHOUT LAUGHTER

The stranger approached and Nesserdin Hadji asked what he wanted.

"The Amerikaluk, where is he?"

"On top the *konka* and asleep. Every one was, until thou camest. Is it not the hour for sleep?" Imin grumpily added.

The other took no offense and laughingly replied:

"Rise, Imin, thou hast every night in the year for sleep. This night we three, the Amerikaluk, thee, and I shall make *tamasha*."

I recognized the fellow's voice, that of the beardless one, Turt Akhun, whom Imin had so disliked when first we met.

Imin snorted at the fellow's reply: "Thou art either mad or, *Ullah* forbid, drunk."

Others that had been disturbed by Turt's noisy entry made remarks in sympathy with Imin's. Calling down from the truck top where I had made my bed atop the load, I asked, "What is it thou seekest, Turt Akhun?"

Hearing my voice, he climbed up beside me.

"Ahmad Kamal, thou once said'st thou should'st like to see a real Turki *teatra* with real Turki *artistes*. Tonight thou mayest see it."

I turned a deaf ear. I did not care to go. I was tired and on the morrow, *Inshallah*, we would go on to Urumchi. It was best I slept this night. After bidding me a courteous "Abide in peace," the beardless one departed.

The truck rocked as some one climbed up on its far side. A roll of blankets appeared, followed by the head, shoulders, and leg of Muhammad Imin. He flopped in with one great effort, rose and spread his blankets, then lay down, head close to mine.

"Effendi?"

"Huh?"

"Do people make *tamasha* this late at night in thy country, or in the Hindustan?"

LAND WITHOUT LAUGHTER

"Just that."

"Not in Sinkiang," he replied. "The bazar is now deserted; the *teatra* closed hours ago. Why, every woman that is able hath by this time conceived a son and both she and her husband sleep soundly, exhausted by the effort. That *kaffir* Turt Akhun was here for no good."

All night long I dreamed a dream wherein figured a beardless eight-legged spider named Turt Akhun. With the spider, I went into the bazar and attended a play that was performed without actors, and in an empty darkened playhouse.

5

NEXT midday found us back at the *serai*, stomachs full of a generous farmer's fruit and *atchuk soot* (sour milk), and feeling slightly indisposed. Addressing a pair of feet protruding from beneath the truck, we queried:

"When do we leave?"

"God alone possesses such knowledge," Vasili testily replied.

The voice was laden with emotion. An ominous clanking from beneath the truck discouraged conversation. In the shadow of the *serai* gateway Imin and I vacantly watched the little swirls of dust that rose at the heels of a string of donkeys mincing along the bazar street. Imin nodded toward a Chinese who sat drowsing in a narrow doorway down the street. It was the same who had followed us since our arrival in Aksu, this time dressed in the clothes of a laborer.

"It matters not," I shrugged. "They are mad, these Chinese."

"Just that, Effendi," Imin agreed.

Later we went off to the *hummum*, where we suffered ourselves to be cooked and rubbed to a state of clean exhaustion. That done, we headed back to the bazar only to run into the beardless one, Turt Akhun, who immediately inflicted himself upon us. The fellow's infectious good will overcame our distrust and, being at a loss for something to do, at his suggestion we went again to the tea garden.

After a time Imin, still nervous from the happenings of the previous evening, suggested we leave for the *serai*. Turt Akhun

234

laughed, a laugh that alarmed me; it was mirthless and too knowing. I insisted we leave, saying that I needed a hat and wanted to get back to the bazar before the shops closed. Turt came with us, declaring he would assist in finding one should the bazar be closed.

Turt took us back a different way from the one we had followed before.

"Effendi, come with me by this road; it is little used and I promise many delightful visions shall unfold before thine eyes. And should the bazar be closed on our return, I will take thee to the home of a friend, a merchant, who has many hats—the best in Aksu."

The road was in many places higher than the walls that bounded it, permitting us to look down into the enclosed dwellings and gardens where, it seemed, the city's entire feminine population was gathered on that humid summer evening. The secluded ladies scorned flight, preferring to remain conveniently unaware of our presence. Had they deigned to notice us, they would have been compelled to dash away into hiding; instead, ignoring our presence as though we were part of the surrounding scenery, they revealed their charms to our not unappreciative gaze.

I somehow found it easy to delay on our erstwhile anxious return to the bazar, and it was not until the setting sun drenched the land in molten glow that I realized darkness was upon us. Imin, noticing my impatience, started off beside me, ignoring the cajoling Turt Akhun.

"You are not sons of Adam," he laughed. "No warmth or blood flows through your hearts. Waugh! You hasten to such a dirty *serai*, when such sights are to be seen!"

Imin glanced over his shoulder and then nudged me. The Chinese who had dogged our steps for the past two days was there and with him several others, soldiers. One I recognized as the tall Chinese who had been so insistent on seeing the contents of my bags. Imin and I went down the road at an increasing pace and I damned the avalanche that had robbed me of my automatic in far-off Ladakh.

When at last we reached the bazar, an hour's darkness had closed over Turkistan and the bazar was locked and deserted. Shops presented only their boarded-up exteriors. Turt Akhun suggested we come to his *serai;* he would send to his merchant friend for the hats.

The bench tilted back, our backs against the earthen *serai* wall, we watched and waited as the tea in our untouched cups grew cold and an even thicker quiet spread over the city. Still no hats came.

Strangely ill at ease, I arose to leave, but Turt anxiously asked that I wait a little while longer; his man, he said, must surely come soon. The very anxiety in his voice seemed out of place, but just then the man for whom we waited came trotting into the *serai.* Under his arm there was a bundle, the hats. Reluctantly we resumed our seats as strings that bound the package were broken. I glanced at the hat handed me; even in the dark its inferior quality was evident. Imin fingered the goods.

"These are not what thou seekest. Not one is of worth!"

Turt Akhun picked one up and threw it to the ground near the servant that knelt beside the bundle. He told the fellow to take them away.

"I am sorry such as these came," he said to me. "My friend knew not that they were intended for an Amerikaluk *musaphir* or he would have sent much better."

He suggested we go with him to the merchant's home.

We walked through the yet warm, dusty bazar, our footsteps hushed by the blanket of dust that at each step eddied upward to hang in the still air. The dim light of the oil lamps that stood, as in all Turki homes, over the hearth, cast thin ribbons of light across the street from the cracks of doors. Dogs barked behind heavy doors that led into tiny gardens. At last we came to a great wooden *serai* gate. Turt Akhun stepped forward and knocked.

The gate opened wide enough for one to pass. Turt Akhun respectfully stepped back that I might pass first. He voiced one word:

"Guest."

I stepped through the gateway, Imin after me. The one who opened the door, bowed to me. His face, I recollected, was familiar. Turt joined me and we walked together, Muhammad Imin just behind with him who had closed and chained shut the gate. Glancing back to see if Imin followed, I had a swift vision of uniformed figures running silently, hunched almost double, toward the arched gateway, where they stopped in its shadow.

"It is here, this way, Effendi," Turt gestured toward a ramp that led down to a level lower than ground level. "After thee, Ahmad Kamal." His voice, nervous and tight, seemed about to crack. He kept sucking in breath and nervously clamping his teeth on his lower lip.

I started down the ramp and in that instant a chill crawled down my spine, and a thin prickling drew my scalp until it seemed too tight for the skull beneath it. At the bottom Turt Akhun opened a door that led off the ramp into a sort of cellar. The yellow light of a smoky kerosene lamp spilled out through the open door and lit up Turt Akhun's face. He was a man transformed! His depraved mouth twitched. His eyes narrowed evilly. Not until that moment did I realize that I was trapped! Those men running in the *serai* darkness were to cover my one retreat.

I started back, drawing my knife as I did so. I turned, something struck me a violent blow in the back. Spinning through the open door, I landed on my hands and knees in what a lightning-swift glance revealed to be a narrow, dead-ended corridor that ran parallel with the ramp outside. There were black iron doors, all barred and hung with heavy padlocks. Bedlam broke loose. Roused by my involuntary shout of alarm, some one flung his body again and again at one of the doors. Another laughed maniacally:

"Is that thou, God?"

Jumping to my feet, I gathered myself together and drove against the door with the strength of desperation. My shoulder struck the door and it burst at the upper hinge and latch. Falling outward, it felled two men who had been braced against it, who were at once reinforced by uniformed Chinese who closed in, driving me back against the corridor wall. There I stopped, because I could retreat no farther. Tomec's knife, bloody now, was clasped in my hand; I had baptized it sometime during the mêlée.

The two soldiers closest me levelled their revolvers at my face. A Turki behind them stuck a rifle over their shoulders, the muzzle a foot from my mouth. Light from the lamp overhead caught the foresight and laid a beady spark on it. I watched the skin on the Chinese forefinger grow taut, whitening as it crooked over the trigger, and wondered if it would be possible to see the flash or feel the impact. For some reason, I suddenly thought of Nikolai, Tsar of Russia. This is what he had faced. . . . What a damnable shame that my new coat should be so ruined, blood and holes!

Suddenly the tension was broken. A Russian officer came from behind, pushing the soldiers out of his way, striking up the rifle, and downing the revolvers pointed at me.

"This Amerikansky is to be taken alive——"

Standing before me, his gun replacing those lowered by the

others, he warned: "Must I break thine arm to get that knife?"

The knife was dropped. He slipped past me to open one of the many iron doors, then gestured with the gun in his hand that I should enter the black cell. As I hung back the others forced me in by their sheer weight of numbers. The door slammed, the bolt clattered into place, then again lifted as Muhammad Imin was thrust in and then Turt Akhun.

Imin was so shaken that it was all he could do to retain his feet. The violence of his trembling unnerved me. I explored the cell by running my hands over the walls, tapping with the knuckles. They were sound. There was no other entrance or exit than that we had been forced through. Extending my arms, I found that they reached, elbows crooked, from wall to wall. The cell was less than six feet square and devoid of any furniture except for a large earthen jar in one corner.

With palsied fingers Turt Akhun lit a cigarette. I grabbed one from his box, anxious to acquire some of the nonchalance they were supposed to bestow; he jerked away from me with a startled grunt. The door rattled open and a Russian called in to us:

"Turt Akhun!"

Without answering, Turt slipped through the open door and it slammed shut once again.

"Why is it, Ahmad Kamal?" Imin asked. "Why is it?"

"God alone knows the answer, and not I," was my only reply. Why? This was the conundrum that was to plague me for the next eight or ten days. Had my captors learned of my affiliation with the Tungan forces? If so, I was surely destined to be executed as a spy. The Bolshevik North was at war with the Tungan South, and for a member of either faction to be caught outside his own borders—and out of uniform—was to face death as a spy.

"Ahmad Kamal, that fellow at the gate, that Turki, did'st

thou not recognize him? He was one of those who met us when we arrived in Aksu, the ugly little one. At the gate he put a gun to my back and said not to call out a warning to thee who had already passed!" Frantic words tumbled out of Imin's mouth, one upon the other.

Again the door rattled. Silencing him with my hand over his mouth, I demanded he give me his matches, and as an afterthought, added:

"Tell the *Parang* Consul, Imin."

The door opened, and as I had thought, Imin was called out of the cell; when once more the door clanged shut, I was alone.

For perhaps ten minutes I stood in the hot, stinking, windowless dungeon. Stinging weals on my legs forewarned me that the hole was alive with vermin. How long had it been since the greedy insects last fed?

Once more the bolt clattered, and as the door swung open I stepped forward. But instead of calling me out, one of the two Chinese in the doorway struck out with a rifle's muzzle. Doubling over, I was struck again. . . . I awoke to find myself stripped and in the process of being thoroughly searched —ears, nostrils, and mouth were probed into. Some one ran his fingers through my hair while another tried to make me see the humor of the situation by scratching over the bottoms of my feet and in between each toe. After a while they departed.

Perhaps an hour later a Chinese threw my clothes back into the cell. The lining of both breeches and coat was slit in several places. Donning the clothing, I found a handkerchief, which had by some mischance been returned. Ripping it into halves, I immediately bound one half around each cuff of my shirt-sleeves to keep out the vermin that had already made of my lower body a burning, itching mass. Buttoning tight the breeches, I pulled on my boots and, spreading the coat over a filthy flea-filled mat that covered the dirt floor, I lay down to sleep. And sleep I did.

I roused only to brush the fleas off my coat. The damnable things, with their confounded *tik-tiking*, would crawl into my nostrils and ears, even leaping to their doom in my mouth as I cursed them.

Sometime during the night, I became conscious of a scratching near my head; raising up on an elbow, I felt of the wall and found a hole about two inches in diameter. Exploring it with my fingers, I suddenly jerked my hand clear as a sharp instrument of some sort pricked my knuckles. A voice came through the hole as if from a great distance.

"Who art thou?"

My head closer to the hole when next the query was repeated, a hot breath came through the aperture to touch my ear. Placing my lips to the hole, I whispered a reply:

"Amerikaluk! I have just been brought here! Who art thou?"

The voice from beyond the wall gave a desperate chuckle.

"Amerikaluk? What is that?"

"The same as *Parang*, as *Englis*. Who art thou?"

"*Parang*, eh? *Yah, Ullah*, what in Ullah's name art thou doing in Sinkiang?"

"*Tamasha!*"

At the word, the voice laughed mirthlessly.

"*Tamasha!* For pleasure, eh! How dost thou find this *tamasha?*"

"I am Abdur Rahim," a wild note crept into the voice. "I have lain here eight months! Two hundred and forty-four days! Eight months!"

He repeated himself, as though the time elapsed seemed bewildering beyond belief.

"Alone I have lain here, alone. I am but seventeen years old, and I know not why they keep me; they have never told." Sobs choked his voice and it cried aloud:

"God, is there a God?" At the sound of the guard's running feet, he, beyond the wall, cried out insanely:

"Ah, I hear Him; God cometh!"

The guard hammered on the other's door with a piece of metal, cursing the boy vehemently.

"Listen! God reviles those who cry unto Him, listen!"

From farther down the corridor, muffled by the walls, came a hysterical plea:

"Some one kill that mad one. Five times a day I say *nemaz*. All through the night I recite from the Holy Koran and then that one, the mad one, drives from this place all hope of good. *Shaitan* has possessed him."

The guard again hammered on the door and, walking down the corridor, gave each iron door a blow and promised that unless all stayed quiet throughout the night no food would be forthcoming on the morrow. Abdur Rahim lapsed into sobs. I decided against sleep and wondered how long it would be before I was like him. One of the prisoners began to recite the Koran and the steady drone of his voice throughout the long night made me envious—if only I knew it as well as he, that I might thus fill in the hours instead of thinking.

Hours after his outburst, Abdur Rahim called me back to the hole in the wall with a sibilant whisper. Reluctantly I answered. We talked until the rattling of keys warned of the approaching turnkey. One by one, the cells were visited. The tiny slot that centered my door swung open, a grinning Chinese face framed in the aperture. A hand passed through the slot, in it a bowl. Taking it, I waited the ladle that followed. The bowl was filled with some thick green mess. Taking deliberate aim, I promptly returned the bowl's contents into that apishly grinning Chinese face. Dripping with the green stuff, the face disappeared. The little door snapped shut. Returning to the hole in the wall, I told the boy what had happened and for the first time he laughed in actual mirth. Then suddenly he stopped, and asked what I expected they would do to me.

Hurrying down the corridor, booted feet stopped at my cell, the lock unsnapped, the bolt clattered free and the door swung open. The Russian who the previous evening had manoeuvered me into the cell stood before me.

"Why did'st thou throw thy food in the guard's face?" he asked.

"Such food is for swine, not men. He who gives me such food must be a swine. To him it rightfully belonged, and who doth contend that a pig cares whether food is thrown on his head or at his feet?"

Amused, he genially chuckled: "What wilt thou eat?"

Half an hour later the food I named was brought me.

Encouraged, I hammered on the door until the turnkey answered and I told him I wanted again to speak with the Russian. In due course he came and I requested removal to other quarters.

"Amerikansky dog! Foreign *espion!* Who art thou to ask favors? Thou should'st be thankful that thou art not yet shot, agenta!"

Stopping him before he could slam shut the peep-door, I asked if I might have paper and pencil. It was given me and the little slot was left open that I might have light to write by.

Diligently, I scribbled away. Letters to friends; letters to the different administrative heads in Aksu. I thought up every reason why I should be released or at least taken to other quarters. According to the letters, I was afflicted with a weak heart, with asthma, with every conceivable disease from athlete's foot to hardening of the arteries. I was in imminent danger of sinking into a coma from which I would probably never recover. I hinted at what American authorities would do when it was discovered that one of their countrymen had died of neglect in a Bolsheviki prison. At last the paper ran out; at my request for more the turnkey slammed the peep-hole door on my fingers.

Left in permanent darkness, I was aghast to realize that I actually felt ill; I wondered if my prophecies were about to come true. That night—it must have been night because the food came in too short an interval for an entire night to have passed—hearing the little door open, I went forward and took the food given me. With the door again shut, I was blinded in the new darkness, after the kerosene lamp's glow. Brushing the wall with the bowl, I dropped it. No matter, food was not desired. I sat down on the vermin-crawling floor, scratching the itching weals of insect bites and became vaguely aware that it was the stench emanating from the bucket in the corner that offended my nostrils. I reached over and stretched its foul cloth-covering more securely into place.

Sometime later the cell door once again swung open and two Russians came in. One, I remember, had a fine white goatee and a ridiculously thin head, a Jew. Both stood looking at me, for I had not risen. It didn't seem worth the effort.

The bearded one called some one in Chinese; a cloth was thrown over my head and with a man on each arm, I was carried out of the cell and from the company of seventeen-year-old Abdur Rahim. Up the ramp we went, the heavy odor of a summer night rich and fragrant in my lungs. Steel-shod boot heels clacked against brick steps as we entered another building. After laying me on a real bed, a soldier removed the cloth from my eyes. The Russian Jew with the thin head cursed a Chinese and asked why he had not been told of the Amerikansky *cholavek's* (fellow's) condition.

My body burned under the fiery stuff the Russian swabbed over me; at last I slept.

That same night Muhammad Imin with Nesserdin Hadji and the two mechanics, all four of them, had been crammed into the foul little cell which was too small for even me. Muhammad Imin told me the entire story when once again we met in Urumchi Prison:

"They took me out of thy cell; out into the air again. While six *Ketai* soldiers pointed their guns at my belly and back, I was marched across the *serai* that was not a *serai*, but a prison. They took me into the office of that dog's breed, *tongus*, the *Ketai* who wanted to search thy bags. He struck me in the face and laughed when I flinched.

"Then a beardless Kazakh entered, the tall Russ with him, and they pushed me into a chair. The Russ shoved a lamp across the table towards me until the heat of it singed my beard. The tall Kazakh stood behind me and pushed my head forward over the chimney until my beard again scorched and sent such smoke into my nostrils as to make me taste the foul odor for three days. I was still coughing at my beard's smoke when the Russ came to me and slapped my face and asked me if I had ever seen you, the Amerikaluk. I knew what they wanted me to say and, Ahmad Kamal, I was frightened, but not so frightened as to lose my wits. I answered,

" 'Never have I seen him!' The Russ nodded.

" 'Thou hast not seen him tonight?'

" 'Never!'

"Then the Russ put a paper before me and asked that I read its contents before I signed. On it I read:

" 'I know not what has become of the Amerikaluk. I did not speak with him the evening he went away. I swear never to speak of him again!'

"Ahmad Kamal, I lost no time in signing that bit of paper and even while I signed I schemed of telling every son of Adam I saw, once out of that accursed place. That Russ picked up the paper, looked at it and threw it on the table, then he took his *tapanchi* from its holster and poked it into my belly; laughing at my prayer, he said:

" 'Uighur, if thou lovest life thou wilt remember this paper whenever thy tongue is tempted to waggle.'

"Then a Turki like myself took me to the great gate and told me to go back to the *serai* and stay there until Nesserdin Hadji's *konka* left for Urumchi. Effendi, not one full breath did I take until I was in the *serai* and its gates locked behind me.

"By *Ullah*, Nesserdin Hadji knew by my actions that all was not as it should be. He stirred in his blankets as I laid mine on top of the *konka* where thou and I had slept the night before. Gathering his from the ground, he brought them up and laid them beside mine, whispering in my ear:

" 'Where is Ahmad Kamal?'

"I told him I could not yet speak, but he *knew*. He rolled closer to me and asked,

" 'Muhammad Imin, they have taken him, eh?'

"I nodded, 'Just that.'

"Then Kara Kulpuk, the devil who asked thee for medicine that would give him many children, came over the side of the *konka*. Nesserdin Hadji touched me on the arm and, leaving his blankets, went over the side. I followed, leaving *Shaitan* Kara Kulpuk to himself.

"Both of us climbed into the *cabinka* and then I told him

246

everything, of Turt Akhun, of the prison, and of thee who lay in it. Boy that he is, Nesserdin Hadji cried and while he cried he told me a tale of wickedness unbounded. That same day he had overheard Kara Kulpuk, Hadji Akhun, the stinking womanlike *Ketai* soldier, and the two soldiers that Hadji Akhun brought with him, and all were speaking of thee and me. They said thou wert an *agenta*, I thy servant; of Nesserdin Hadji they said little except that they had seen him speak to thee many times and in thine own Amerikaluk tongue.

"Kara Kulpuk, Hadji Akhun, and the perfumed one had been sent with the *konka* by Shin Jin Jung; they were to watch thee until thou wert captured in Aksu! Fearful of being caught, Nesserdin Hadji went quickly away from where he had lain under the truck. He knew now why there had been no benzine for our *konka* when there were forty barrels in the *Yamen!* He told me that we would know in one day whether or not the *Hookemet* was satisfied with thee or wanted the rest of us, too. If there was benzine, we would know that thou wert enough. If not? Nesserdin Hadji was undone with fear that night, and he no more than I. We sat there, never sleeping but always talking, as though there would never be a morrow.

"Thrice some one came into the *serai* and turned the beam of a flashlight on those asleep on the ground. I knew it was I for whom they searched! They had been sent from the *Yamen* to see what I did. At last the beam was turned on the *cabinka*; Nesserdin Hadji and I were seen. Cursing the day he had returned to Turkistan, the boy talked on. He told of how he had tried to leave Sinkiang, two months before, but the *Yamen* had refused him a road-letter. But he swore that if ever he could get out of the trouble we were now in he would escape this thrice-accursed land of the Bolsheviki, *Ketai*, and *Kaffir*. Go he would, even though he had to leave his mother and fortune behind.

LAND WITHOUT LAUGHTER

"Dawn found us still sitting there. Each had told the other his life secrets; it was as though we were about to die. The sky lightened and we left our seats to walk around and around the *serai*; those on the ground awoke, cleansed themselves, and left the *serai*, bound for the *masjid* to say their prayers. That morning I neglected mine, and Nesserdin Hadji his, for we stayed in the *serai*, our minds on other things. When the sun was high we, too, went to the bazar *Osh Khana* for our morning meal. Turt Akhun stood before it and saw me at the same instant as I him. He fled. I pointed him out to Nesserdin Hadji and we together damned the Mussulman that would betray his own kind.

"Hastily we ate and returned to the *serai*. For the next three days it was so. We remained in the *serai* from the dawn to the dawn. No benzine came; we waited.

"Then at dusk of the third day a note was brought Nesserdin Hadji. Before opening it, he looked at me; he was frightened; we read it together, and knew that we were doomed. Nesserdin Hadji and I were to come to the *Yamen* immediately. I, to have my road-letter once more examined; Neserdin Hadji to receipt for benzine that now awaited him. Hadji Akhun had signed the note.

"Afraid of what might happen, I told Nesserdin Hadji not to go. Tomorrow would be time enough. Then that *haramzada* —that son of fifteen fathers and a sick mule—Kara Kulpuk, came to us, took the note from Nesserdin Hadji's hand, read it and insisted we go. He said that we had been too long in Aksu. It was time we were on our way.

" 'Why hesitate while benzine is thine to take? Go quickly and we can leave Aksu in the morning.'

"Nesserdin Hadji had no stomach for the task, but taking Kichik Akhun, the mechanic, with him—I had refused to go— he went out of the *serai*.

"Half the night passed; he did not return, nor did I sleep, though I lay in my blankets. Then the lot of us were aroused by a banging on the *serai* gates. That swine, Kara Kulpuk, arose from where he lay and opened the gates.

"The same man who delivered Nesserdin Hadji's note delivered one to me. When he went away again I lay down without opening it. Kara Kulpuk called to me and asked:

" 'What does it say, Imin?'

"I told him I had not such eyes as to read by starlight, and Kara Kulpuk went to the door of the *serai ban's* (concierge's) dwelling, hammered on it until the old man woke and answered. Kara Kulpuk took the lamp from the old man's hand and brought it to me.

" 'Here,' he said, 'is light by which to read the note.'

"I asked him what business it was of his. It was mine alone. I might never read it!

" 'Oh!' He threw up his hands, spilling the lamp's oil. 'It may be from Nesserdin Hadji. It may be important.'

"There was no use in my refusing to read it, that I knew; despairing, I opened it and read:

" *'Muhammad Imin, thou wilt come to the Yamen at once; Hashim Akhun with thee. This is very important.'*

"Hadji Akhun had written it.

"Destroying the note, I lay back in my blankets. Hashim Akhun sat in his bed; he had risen as Kara Kulpuk read the note over my shoulder. Hashim Akhun was as frightened as I. He, too, knew of your arrest; both he and Kichik Akhun had been told. That *shorwicha*, that *kizungesiki*, Kara Kulpuk, called upon *Ullah* to witness my ignoring a message that was, he said, 'without a doubt, most important.' It was no use waiting. The *Hookemet* wanted me, and much as I might delay, it would eventually have me.

"I pulled my boots on and we two, Hashim and I, went out

of the *serai* into the deserted street. We walked past the *Osh Khana* towards the *Yamen*. Ten soldiers came, led by the same tall *Ketai*. Five took Hashim and five me and all held guns to our bodies. They took us through the dark streets; the bazar was silent as the inside of a thousand-year-old tomb. Not even a breeze stirred. We came to the same great gate through which thou and I had passed before; we were pushed through it. Fear plunged into my heart like a dagger of ice and my stomach was cold and heavy.

"They forced us into the same cellar where I had left thee. They opened the same cell door and we were driven in by the muzzles of their guns, to find ourselves with Nesserdin Hadji and Kichik Akhun.

"The boy Hadji grasped my coat and drew me down to where he lay on the floor.

" 'Will they kill us, Muhammad Imin?' he asked.

"I knew not and asked him where thou had'st gone.

"His tongue was paralyzed with fright and he made no answer; only lay there and shivered in the heat and stench.

"Kichik Akhun knelt in the corner, praying. Hashim sat on the floor, his back to the wall, and plucked to pieces the mat between his legs. I sat down. Fleas ran over me, so I stood up again. My hand brushed the wall; it was marked. Hashim had a match which had not been discovered in the hasty search of us. It was thy name on the wall, 'Ahmad Kamal.' I could not read it but it was not Russ nor *Ketai*, and Nesserdin Hadji at last said it was *Englis*. Three marks were beneath it and Nesserdin Hadji said thou had'st lain in the cell for three days, leaving the place that same day. Nesserdin Hadji swore, mad as he was with fear, that thou had'st purchased thy freedom with ours!

"The *Ketai* came again. The door was opened; they called for me. As I went out, I remembered what the Russ had said,

'Thou shalt die.' But it was not to be executed that I went, for they merely took me down the corridor and pushed me into another cell. There were two men in that cell, who had been there nine full months, and never in all those months had they bathed or stirred. Both were bound to the floor with chains.

"For the next three or four days I lay with them in stench and heat. When I went out it was once more to behold thee, in the *Hookemet konka*."

That was the story that Muhammad Imin told me in Urumchi Prison.

6

Awaking from my stupor, I was greeted by sunlight, and, accustoming my eyes to it, looked out of a great window with bars. A Russ soldier sat beside my bed, playing solitaire. At my request for a drink of water, he put down his cards without comment and went for it. The room was clean, whitewashed and large. On the floor was a rug and the furnishings consisted of two chairs and a long heavy table. In the wall was a cylindrical Russian oven that rose to the very ceiling twelve feet above. Best of all, I could see out of the window, if only to study the pebbles imbedded in the wall rising before it. Then, too, it was only the surroundings that the wall obscured, not the sky above or the birds that flew across it.

Two days later, once more on my feet, convalescent from the case of insect-bite poisoning and well into a case of dysentery, I reached the conclusion that it was about time I was either released or shot. If it were true that these mad Russians believed me an *agenta*, a spy, it was time the myth was exploded. But the thought was disconcerting.

"If they had found the *Tungan* credentials in the saddlebags——?"

I hoped that some one, any one, had stolen the bags before my captors had been able to examine their contents. Deep in such unhappy speculations, I did not notice the white-bearded Russian's entrance until he spoke. Roused, I unbelievingly asked that he repeat himself.

LAND WITHOUT LAUGHTER

"Thou shalt depart on the morrow; for Urumchi."

A heavy hand roused me and a weasel-faced Chinese told me to get my clothes on.

"Thou goest to Urumchi," he announced.

It was not yet morning, for when I looked out of the window the moon was yet high. Despite being a bit wobbly from the ravages of dysentery, I leaped into my clothing. But all the while I wondered why this was to be a night departure.

The thin Russian whom I had first seen when we entered Aksu now came into the room and, directing two Chinese to stand guard, told me to follow him. We walked across a paved yard towards a waiting, canopied truck—not Nesserdin Hadji's! The two Chinese who had been following boosted me over the truck's backboard and others inside pushed the canopy aside and hauled at my coat sleeves until I fell in, over some drums of gasoline. The Russian climbed into the truck after me. Thrashing around, I asked him just what the hell was going on and got, as an answer, a gun in the ribs.

"Keep quiet!"

Somehow that didn't impress one as how a man being released from prison should be treated. Sitting down, I bumped into another human, and eyes becoming accustomed to the dark, I saw him to be Muhammad Imin. As we started to speak, the Russian warned:

"*Erazgowr na nada.*" (Speech is not permitted.)

Looking past Imin, I saw Hashim Akhun, Nesserdin Hadji, and Kichik Akhun.

Nesserdin Hadji crouched in the corner, shivering. Being warm enough myself, I offered him my coat despite the angry remarks of several Chinese soldiers sitting opposite us. At my approach, the boy went into a very frenzy of shaking, ignoring the proffered coat. Muhammad Imin whispered:

253

LAND WITHOUT LAUGHTER

"He is not cold, but undone with fear."

Kichik Akhun sat beside Nesserdin Hadji, his head bobbing to and fro as he repeated again and again the prayer: *"La illaha il Ullah—la illaha il Ullah."*

Seventeen-year-old Hashim Akhun stared at the truck's canopied top, one eye bathed in an errant beam of moonlight which found entry through a tiny hole in the tarpaulin. His lips moved, but his prayers, unlike the others, were silent. Muhammad Imin sat repeating the words: "We die; we die!"

Some crawling thing ran over my neck and I understood. They had just come from the dungeon, held as I had been. The stinging bite on my neck was from a flea.

A lantern, set in the middle of the floor, weakly illuminated the truck's interior. There were four Chinese beside the Russian, all with rifles on their knees, muzzles towards us.

With a clashing of gears we started forward. One of the Chinese viciously struck Kichik Akhun on the head with his rifle barrel. He slumped to the bed of the truck, while the Russian warned the rest of us to lie flat. We were not to see, or be seen by any one in the bazar.

Clear of the bazar, we were permitted to rise again and I picked up the flapping canopy and looked out over a rolling moonlit desert. Imin pulled the canopy farther up and the nervous Russian told us to drop it. Ignoring him, I held it open, and, narrowly watching me, Imin did likewise. His nerves getting the better of him, the Russian reached over and jerked it out of our hands.

For half an hour we rode along, the truck in turn bumping sharply over rocks, or riding with a heavy sliding motion as it struck off the cart road into the soft desert sand. Within it we wondered if this was to be our last ride. My fears were not lightened by the others' actions. All but Hashim had despondent, fear-stricken countenances. Hashim, instead, was

254

thoughtfully contemplating the inside of an empty bucket. Imin nodded towards it and voiced his gruesome conviction.

"They will use it to pour the gasoline over our bodies; not an ash will remain!"

A strange sensation had seized the pit of my stomach, and it did seem a damnable shame that the feet of some swine of a Chinese would probably walk around in my boots before long. Chancing the wrath of the soldiers, I threw up the fluttering flap and looked out. We were approaching a body of men. There were many lanterns, and horses stamped about, some one swung a lantern, and we came to a halt in a Muslim graveyard. Hundreds of arched, domed tombs, bathed in pale moonlight, loomed about us. A great tomb had a large black hole broken into the side nearest us. Imin looked and shuddered.

"That is where they will throw our corpses."

The flap was again torn from my hands. A Russian I had never seen before greeted him who had come with us from the prison. Together they departed. A third Russian called:

"Nesserdin Hadji."

The boy rose from his seat and abruptly sat down again with a rather dumbfounded expression; he laughed oddly, then choked:

"I cannot walk!"

The soldiers impatiently seized him by the shoulders and dragged him out of the truck. As he disappeared over the backboard, Nesserdin Hadji threw one last, unbelieving glance in our direction. He had stopped trembling.

We four avoided one another's eyes and tensed forward in our seats, straining for a sound.

Then there was a clattering of chains, the sharp smash of steel on steel. Hashim Akhun gave a great exhalation and sat back.

"Chains—we live!" He spoke aloud.

LAND WITHOUT LAUGHTER

The hammering ceased and Nesserdin Hadji once more appeared, giggling like a schoolgirl. His ankles were chained together and encircled by heavy bands of iron. Hashim Akhun was next called; and returned in chains and overwhelmed with joy. Kichik Akhun, still unconscious from the blow on the head, blood dripping from a torn ear, was limply dragged out and chained like the rest.

Imin was not called; he needed no chains. He was too fat to run and made an admirable target. The Ju Jung in charge of our transport also spared me the indignity, for which consideration he was to be imprisoned on our arrival in Urumchi.

That night we drove off the cart road, halted, and made camp. For the first time, I had an opportunity to examine my bags. They had not been opened! Urumchi authorities had obviously ordered that all be left intact until they themselves could examine the contents.

Knowing the bags must be opened if my life was to be saved, I approached the little Buddha-faced Ju Jung. I pointed to the moon, the stars, and to the deep grass in which we were camped. From underfoot, I picked a bit of damp sand, and again pointing to the moon, held up seven fingers, then ten; it would be seven to ten days' journey to Urumchi. The little officer sat on a rock before the simmering bucket of tea and as he watched my pantomime, fed sticks to the flames beneath the bucket. I drew closer, he shifted the revolver to the other side of his body. He misunderstood.

Calling Kichik Akhun, who by this time had regained consciousness and was despondently holding his aching head, I asked that he explain our dire need of more clothing. The two spoke for some minutes, and the Chinese turned to give me a searching glance, then smiled. We had won. He turned towards the truck and we followed.

LAND WITHOUT LAUGHTER

Ju Jung took the keys of our bags from his pocket and tossed them to me. Snapping free the lock, I passed them on to Nesserdin Hadji and he in turn to the others. Ju Jung, who had stood over me as I opened my bags, followed the keys to the next to use them. Pulling my coat from the saddlebag, I felt of the inside pocket—it was there. The coat on, I laced the saddlebags shut under the watchful eyes of the Chinese, who had by that time returned. The lock was snapped, I straightened up to receive an approving glance from the little officer. I was a good prisoner. Nothing had been done that had not met with his approval.

Late that night I lay awake listening to that bit of paper digesting with the bread and tea. My worries were over now. On to Urumchi and release!

Hashim groaned and rolled over in his sleep; the chains clanked. Somewhere in the distance a dog barked, and, silently, I thanked Ma Hsi Jung for giving me edible credentials.

Days passed. We travelled steadily, stopping only when the truck needed repair. Dozens of opportunities for escape presented themselves. One night the truck sank deeply into the desert sand and both the driver and Ju Jung went off to find a *zemindar*. Horses would be needed to extricate us. The four Chinese soldiers left to watch over us stalked around and around the truck for a while. At last growing tired, they took their fur coats out of the truck and lay down upon them. One after the other fell into snoring sleep. Imin nudged me.

"Now, we could run away?" Then, answering himself, "But not I. Where would I run, a big fat fellow like me?"

Stealthily, I slipped over the backboard; if one of the sleeping guards awoke there were reasons I could give for being abroad. Didn't I have dysentery? Sand muffled my steps and, walking around the truck, I took stock of the sleeping soldiers.

257

LAND WITHOUT LAUGHTER

One lay beside a sunken wheel, his rifle and bandoleer of cartridges, which had proven uncomfortable to lie upon, at his side, an arm's length from him. A cold wind blew a fine veil of hissing sand before it and carried to me the sound of camel bells. A caravan was passing out there in the desert. There was a chance . . . but what was the use? I had done no wrong. Anyway, none that could be found out! Why steal the rifle and run away with the caravan when all of my difficulties would come to an end when I reached Urumchi?

Perhaps an hour later the voices of the returning chauffeur and Ju Jung were carried to me on the same wind that had told of a caravan.

We had been forced to drop the side flap which was always elevated when travelling over the desert. Back against the jolting sideboards, we listened to the sounds of Toksun bazar. Dogs came out to bark and children to run behind in the dust, laughing and screaming as the truck pulled into a *serai* and stopped. Ju Jung could be heard driving the curious children out of the yard and at last the *serai* gates banged shut and we were permitted to leave our cramped seats. All five of us prisoners, together, and free of eavesdropping soldiers, sat in a circle in a tiny *serai* room. The door we left open. No one could hide behind an open door. Nesserdin Hadji listened without comment as I related all that had taken place since my arrest.

"Yes," he whispered, "thou art right on all points but two. We were not taken because of any wrongdoing on our part, but because *we knew* they had thee. The *Hookemet* was afraid we would go back to Kashgar and tell the English Consul that one of his kind had been imprisoned. Thou sayest they think thee a *Tungan* spy? Thou art mistaken. They think——"

A foot crunched on some pebbles in the doorway. Ju Jung

entered the room carrying melons and bread. Another Chinese followed with a bucket of tea.

The tea finished, we sat about on the mud *kang* that serves as table, bed, and seat to the people of Turkistan. Nesserdin requested a box of matches of the Ju Jung, and proceeded to show him a few tricks. He laid them in little frames, each piled on top of the other, a fanciful custom of the country. If, when the matches were exhausted, every frame was complete, the wish was granted. The officer laughed as Nesserdin Hadji exhausted the matches and one frame lacked completion.

Then Nesserdin Hadji began again, this time in a different pattern. English words began to form, and the others sat back with knowing looks. Nesserdin Hadji and I had resumed our interrupted conversation, talking with matches.

"*Not Tungan,*" spelled the thin splinters of wood. Then, "*They asked me in Aksu. They think British or Jap——*"

The little Chinese, seeing with what intensity Nesserdin Hadji spelled and I watched, swiftly drew his hand over the match sentence, pocketing the lot. Stepping back with a puckish grin, he brutally struck Nesserdin Hadji across the face, and wagged a fat forefinger at the two of us. From that moment on we were continually under surveillance.

With the coming of day, we were again loaded into the truck and once more on our way. The Dawan Chen was crossed and at the pass's summit we saw what remained of the Tungan earthworks. On that spot, two years before, the Tungan forces had met their Waterloo under a rain of bombs and clouds of gas spread by Bolsheviki aircraft. Now I, a confidant of Tungan General Ma Hsi Jung, was crossing it to meet (though little was it realized at the time) my Waterloo. Out of the mountains, we descended to a verdant thriving countryside. Fields were just sprouting, and lowing cattle grazed on fresh spring grasses.

259

LAND WITHOUT LAUGHTER

Again we went into the sandy desolation of desert. The sun sank out of sight replaced by the cold light of stars. About two hours after sundown, we topped a range of rolling sandy hills and looked down upon the electric-lighted city of Urumchi. To us prisoners those lights meant freedom. Muhammad Imin and the two boys, Kichik and Hashim Akhun, drew the wrath of the guards by leaning far out of the truck in an effort better to see the *electricit*. None of them had ever seen electric lights before and I was almost as enthusiastic, for my last sight of an electric-lighted city had been in India, seven months before.

Once in the city, a tap on the shoulder made me take my eye from a hole in the canvas. It was Ju Jung. I was made to exchange my outside seat for that of the leg-ironed Nesserdin Hadji. Kneeling, I peered through another rent in the canvas front. A great embattlemented wall was approached; a gate.

Ju Jung clambered out of the truck and presented credentials to a sentry who came from the wall's shadow to stand in the beam of our headlights. In a few minutes the black iron-sheathed gates swung wide. Twice more the performance was duplicated and only a short distance after passing through the third gate, we came to a dead stop.

The canopy was thrown open and a strange Chinese face intruded. Ju Jung ordered us out of the truck and, leaving us standing in the roadway, the vehicle roared away. All about us stood Chinese with drawn Lugers. A Russian, a big pot-bellied fellow, gave a command in Chinese and three of the soldiers put away their guns.

With one on each arm and the third prodding from behind, I was started towards a great dark building. Angered at the treatment, I threw their hands off me. The act caused a great furor, and a rattled Chinese struck at me with his rifle barrel. I dodged the wicked blow and, before the Chinese could aim another, a Russian seized his weapon, stopping him. Muhammad Imin passed and after him the three in chains. Then, with the bulk of the soldiers behind, I followed. Every one held his Luger on me and I came to the conclusion that it must be a desperate fellow indeed who rated such an escort.

Squeezing through a two-foot-wide, three-foot-high iron door, and into the chill of the inner prison, I regretted not listening that night to the wind-blown counsel of the camel bells. A second iron door, a counterpart of the first, was clanged shut behind me. The damp, stone floor and mouldy, mildewed walls of the prison corridor echoed the sound of our booted feet. A door was opened on either side the corridor and I was made to enter the one on the left; a swift, fleeting glance over the shoulder revealed my four companions flattened against the wall of the opposite room with several Chinese soldiers standing before them.

The door of my cell opened before I could take a look at my surroundings. Two Chinese and the same Russian who had been in the yard at our arrival entered the room. The door was again slammed, and locked. One of the Chinese snatched the hat from my head while another pulled the coat off my back; the Russian commanded I strip. That done, and standing before them, *au naturel*, the search that I thought finished began over again. My hair was combed with a fine-toothed circular comb until I began to wonder if it wouldn't be less painful to be scalped. Nostrils, ears, and mouth were again explored. The temptation to masticate the finger exploring my oral cavity was suppressed at sight of the blackjack swinging at the Russian's wrist. My each toe was examined and the bottoms of my feet scraped while, naked back against the icy stone floor, I cursed the day my Turkistan journey had been conceived. I was made to stand again, only to have a bucket of cold water poured over my head. The unholy three looked my wet body over intently, but all that happened was that I turned a violent blue, panted with shock, and amazed even myself with the size and quantity of goose-pimples that literally leaped into being. Eventually, my clothes were returned by the inquisitors, except the boots.

Dressed, I was again herded into the corridor. Once more, Chinese and Lugers formed an escort. The door through which the others had passed was closed. Little did I realize that I had seen Nesserdin Hadji and the two boys for the last time. I was led through a labyrinth of corridors, across a compound and into another building even colder than the first. Forbidding padlocked doors and the intimate animal sounds that came from behind them sickened me with memories of Aksu. Far at the back of a corridor was an open cell door; a moment later that door slammed shut behind me. Sitting down on the narrow bench which was anchored in the wall at both ends, and which was half covered by a torn, lumpy quilt that stank of mould and unwashed bodies, I wondered, What next? Some one in the vaultlike prison was reciting the Koran, another belched; acoustics were excellent!

The next week was spent in hibernation, wakefulness coming only when the turnkey would open the peephole and bang on the door to determine whether the Amerikaluk was dead or asleep. Mealtimes my bowl was filled with a mess less palatable even than that I had plastered on the Aksu turnkey's head. One sip, and the bowl would be emptied in the same corner that the previous occupant had used. Then, back to sleep.

The time came when I could sleep no longer. Eternal cold and darkness began to annoy me as it never had when sleep provided respite. One virtue of the cold was that it eliminated fleas, but lice abounded and soon a weal of red circled my body under the close-fitting trouser band. Wherever my body was in any way constricted it was consumed by the gray-backed, red-stomached lice. The ease with which they could be located and mashed between thumbnails made up in some measure for the misery they caused. At least they were better than fleas, whose leaping tactics made them all but impossible to catch in darkness.

A day and a night passed and still I was unable to sleep; even louse-cracking became uninteresting. Tired of these pursuits and anxious to avoid the soul-destroying thoughts of a prisoner, I took to hammering on the door. This brought out the guards, and the door shivered to its very iron core from the pummelling it received; on the one side from me, on the other from the shushing guards. Wearying of merely kicking the door, we would break the monotony by cursing one another. But the guards eventually tired of the pursuit, probably because I could think of so many more adjectives than they. My fellow prisoners helped by remembering unflattering terms that escaped me.

That evening I had visitors. An officer, Chinese, magnificently bespangled with straps, badges, and decorations, came into my cell; democratically sitting down beside me, he explained that I must not hammer on the door.

"On the morrow," he promised, "the Kapitan will come here and thou mayst speak with him."

To my complaint about the quarters and vermin the amazing fellow, throwing his arm over my shoulder, replied:

"Thou wilt grow used to them; lice are of no importance, and as to thy dwelling, it is the best in this *Gundahana.*"

Unable to cope with such an intellect, I gave up. We finally parted after H. R. H. shook hands with me half a dozen times, bowed deeply and said that he was indeed pleased to meet a *"Megwi"* (American).

As the door was once more secured and the Chinese, with his bodyguard, tramped out of the place, I ruminated over the social contacts one could make in prison. Meanwhile, ripping a button from my shirt, I proceeded to make a frieze of marching figures around the whitewashed cell. The monotony of both mind and wall was relieved by the array of horses and men that gradually took shape under the scratching button.

Every day at the sun's waning the guard slammed shut the barred window at the corridor's end, fearful that the evening's warm breezes might find their way into the dark prison, and the heavy gloom of the cells would turn to blackness. It was no longer any use to try to draw. So, returning the button to my pocket, I would sit down on the bench, shake the fallen white-wash and mould out of my quilt, put it under me, and listen to the cells around mine come to life.

I listened to the fellow next to me scratching as he added another line to the wealth that adorned his walls, each line a lost day. My cell walls and probably his, too, contained, in addition to such countless *day-marks*, obscene drawings of the feminine figure, all sketched by men too long out of the sun, too long with themselves.

He across the corridor, sitting in a cell too short to lie full length and so narrow that, back against one wall, he could brace his feet against the other, would softly sing of sunlit places. His voice gradually mounted as the melody parted the walls and carried him out to the sunshine of memory. The song would abruptly cease as the outraged guard hammered on the door: "Silence!"

My mural completed, I sat down to inspect the work and to await the coming of food, so that it could be poured in the corner. Eventually, my door was opened. Something was wrong, for it was not yet my turn; there were eight more to be fed before myself. This time, however, it was not to feed me that I was being visited.

LAND WITHOUT LAUGHTER

The little peephole did not open, but the door itself. I was called from the cell, marched out of the prison building and into the sunlit compound that I had passed through on the night of arrival. The touch of the sun put a warmth into my veins, a heat that had been lacking since the ill-omened eve of June the ninth, when first I had seen a cell. Across the compound and into the cold prison again, still in company with my guards, I was marched to the room where the well-remembered search had taken place.

Pushing me down on a bench, my escort departed and two others immediately entered. One was a squat heavy Kazakh, neck lying in a fold over his tunic collar, protruding eyes giving him a carplike, goitery expression which was not relieved by either his shaven head or the weird way in which the cheeks swelled on a level with his mouth. After him came a big, shock-headed Russian with the typical florid, pug-nosed peasant face; he was heavy as the shorter Kazakh, but more powerfully built. Both were dressed in uniform tunics, whipcord breeches, and black Russian boots. The Kazakh threw a briefcase on the table and sat down opposite me with never a look in my direction. He ransacked the briefcase, spreading papers over the table. Then he called a guard and asked that tea and three glasses be brought. Having completed all preparations, he turned his eyes on me, smiled, and asked:

"Thou speakst the *Uighur* tongue?"

At my nod of assent, he replied pleasedly:

"Enough. All will be well."

Taking the cue, I queried:

"Then thou hast discovered all this is a mistake: I am to go free?"

For a moment my words were ignored. The Kazakh poured tea, three glasses, one of which was handed the Russian, the second to me; the third he noisily sipped before answering.

265

"There was no mistake, and as to thy going free," he sipped again at his tea, "that is in thy hands. Should'st thou escape, thou can'st go free; if not, thou hast roof and food until thou art a white-beard."

He laughed uproariously at his humor, but the Russian maintained a serious mien. Abruptly, and with a rapid change of demeanor, the little toad pushed a sheet of paper before me. It was a page from my journals.

"This is thine!" he angrily stated, and dumping from the bulging case the complete journal and all of the pictures I had taken, he accused: "These, too, are thine!"

As calmly as possible under the circumstances, I replied that they were. Coming to the table, the Russian deliberately took a sheet of plain paper and laid it before me. He availed himself of the Kazakh's pen.

"*Saiti Hadji,* thy pen." It was thrust into my hand and then the Russian directed:

"Write a complete confession."

"My confession of what?"

Saiti Hadji pounded the table and mockingly repeated my words:

"Of what? Thou knowest!" He bellowed so loudly that a guard stuck his head in the room. Saiti Hadji, his face lit with especially simulated wrath, roared on: "We know thou art a spy; we know thou art *Englis!*"

At the word, my fears were allayed; it was obvious that this mad Bolsheviki government had arrested me in the mistaken notion that I was a British agent. It struck me as so funny that I actually laughed at them.

"You are insane, both of you, and your *Hookemet* as well. Behold my passport; it's American—not British."

Saiti Hadji reached across the table and struck me on the side of the face. Even before I thought, my fist caught him on the mouth. Stumbling back over the bench, he fell to the floor, striking his head against the flagstones with a resonant thump.

While the Kazakh called upon the devil and the Russian called the guard, I addressed both with a few appropriate epithets. The door burst open and two Chinese came in to take my arms and lead me out of the place. I was hurried across the compound. This time I was taken to a different cell block from that I had formerly occupied, and pushed into a cell.

7

MY NEW cell was the largest of my increasing prison experience and evidently intended for more than one occupant. Standing on the *kang*, I was able to look out of a heavily barred window, and, by craning my neck, to see the sky. Blue it was, as I had never dreamt the sky could be. Standing there, trembling a little with the weakness of dysentery, I was grateful that at least there was air in this cell, even warmth. Ten minutes later, I was cursing that same warmth. The cell was alive with fleas. I slid my finger along a crack in the hard mud floor and tiny wet streaks revealed the mashed bodies of hundreds of vermin.

The next morning, still alive despite the ravages of the leaping legions, which throughout the night did their best to empty my veins, a plan formulated. I resolved to refuse all food until my release. That, I hoped, would alarm my captors. They would scarcely dare to let an *American* die in their prison.

At mealtime the peephole in the cell door opened. The guard beat his tin water ladle against the door, attempting to rouse me. I told him to go away and not return until he came to turn me out of the God-damn place. The door snapped shut. All that day the guard ignored my cell when he brought the other prisoners food and water. The next day passed and I began to wonder whether self-starvation was not just what the Russians wanted.

The third day of my fast had dawned and waned when I was attracted by a whispered conference just outside my door.

It was opened and a soldier bade me come out. Together we went back across the compound to the very room that had already been the setting for two acts. Saiti Hadji was seated at the table. He waved me to the seat I had occupied at our former meeting.

"Thou do'st not eat. Why not?"

Reasons were given, but Saiti Hadji countered:

"Thy case is being investigated. Thy papers and pictures have been sent to Moscowa for examination and thou can'st not be freed until a decision is returned. If thou must starve thyself to death, there is nothing I can do about it, but if thou art willing to eat, I will send to the bazar for whatever kind of food thou desirest—at thine own expense."

Rising, I told Saiti Hadji that I wanted to be taken back to the cell.

"No food, eh?" he grinned.

I was taken to a still different cell. Muhammad Imin rushed to greet me. The erstwhile rotund, happy fellow had changed; now his cheeks were sallow, his jowls fallen and flabby. His jolly countenance had gone into mourning. We stood back and surveyed each other.

"*Yah Ullah!*" Imin exclaimed. "What has happened to thee, Effendi?"

"And to thee, Muhammad Imin?"

He laughed bitterly.

"I have lain here for eleven days and done nothing but think, and too much thinking is bad for any man." Imin took my arm and pulled me over to the *kang*. "We can't stand on the floor, Ahmad Kamal. The fleas will consume us."

We sat on the *kang's* edge; brushed our legs free of the vermin and then pulled them up, away from the flea-ridden floor. Together we laughed at the strange knowledge of fleas and their ways we had acquired. Imin began to speak, stopped

269

to catch and smash to a bloody pulp a flea that had chosen that moment to run across his leg. Then he began once more, describing all that had transpired since our arrest in Aksu. He did not know what had happened to the others. Immediately after being searched, he had been brought to the cell he now occupied. Far into the night, we talked. I became Father-Confessor to him and he to me. The man had brooded so much over trivialities as to have made gigantic distracting horrors of them.

"Ahmad Kamal," he swore, "if thou had'st not come, I would have gone mad. Every wrong I had done in my lifetime came back to torment me."

Minor wrongs done others had pyramided themselves in the unstable, conjuring mind of one in solitary confinement, until they had been magnified into cardinal sins.

"Effendi," he continued, "many times when I was home in Kashgar, I would return to my wife, after a day in the bazar, and I would curse, and even beat her if she were slow at preparing my food, or, souring at my angry words, would threaten to sleep with another."

He burst into tears as he told of one occasion.

"I beat her three times one day," he mourned. "Once in the morning because she, who is so young—a mere seventeen—let her face be seen by another; a second time, when I came home in the evening, and only because I found the sash of another hidden in a corner." Great tears rolled down his cheeks. "She swore it was that of her brother and yet I beat her. Then, once again I beat her when she could not tell me whence came the money she had hidden in her bosom. I have been a wicked man."

Muhammad Imin told me of his divorce, when he was "inspired by *Shaitan*." Nisa Han, his "innocent" spouse, had angered him to such an extent he had uttered the words:

"Thou art trebly divorced."

270

LAND WITHOUT LAUGHTER

Immediately upon voicing these words Imin had regretted them. In his rage he had shouted the *final* divorce. Had he declared the less definite "Thou art divorced!" he could have reclaimed his wife at any time within the three lunar months that Muslim law insists a divorced woman remain single. (Until delivery, if pregnant.)

Having declared the irrevocable, *treble* divorce, he was forbidden by law from again marrying the girl—until she had again married, consummated the union, and in turn been divorced!

Locking his wife in the inner apartments, Imin had rushed from his home to seek out an old friend. This chap had a son not yet reached puberty; with the boy in hand, Imin had returned home. An Emam had been sent for to officiate at the incipient marriage ceremony.

By law the girl must remain single several months before again wedding; just as she must again observe a like delay in the event of a subsequent separation. Transgressing upon this phase of the law, Imin looked on as Nisa Han was married to an eleven-year-old boy. The Emam was then paid and sent on his way. Then came the more serious *consummation* of the marriage! By this time having consoled his put-upon ex-spouse, Imin had assisted her—and the boy—to disrobe. (The boy, however, had been previously blindfolded.) The bridal night is known throughout the East as the "Night of the Entrance." In this instance the event was abbreviated to a split-second entrance, upon which Imin had led the blindfolded husband away from his wife, just, in truth, as he had superintended their coming together. At Imin's dictation the child-groom had solemnly declared himself thrice divorced from his bride of but a few moments. With a not inconsiderable gift of money the boy had returned to the home of his father; en route, as per previous arrangement, sending another Emam to the dwelling of Imin, who was forthwith reunited with his wife!

LAND WITHOUT LAUGHTER

Throughout the night he continued to extol the virtues of his bride, thirty years younger than himself. Prophetically he announced his belief that he would never leave Urumchi prison alive; this, he said, would be his retribution for a lifetime's evil works.

The fifth day of my fast, I was once more taken before my Saiti Hadji. With him was the Bo Wan Ju, head of the secret police of Urumchi. It was promised that I would be given clean quarters and, within a week, released. All this, if only I promised to eat.

A week later Muhammad Imin and I were moved to another cell, whose two beds did not at all appeal to Imin, for whom a *kang* was more comfortable.

"The accursed beds have neither warmth nor softness," he swore, "and their loose boards bite one during the night."

We had no covers and were forced to lie on the slats themselves, continually being pinched or pin-cushioned by the rough, splinter-filled framework, which crawled with bedbugs. One thing made the cell a veritable heaven and that was the large window before which we sat throughout the long days and nights. Tea and bread from the bazar were given us twice a day.

Saiti Hadji began to adopt his old tactics of denouncing me as a spy and Muhammad Imin as my aide-de-camp. Weeks passed and we were cross-examined daily; but now I was charged with being a *Japanese agenta*. It appears I was no longer British.

Muhammad Imin and I began to wear upon each other. The days passed and the feeling gradually mounted until there was actual hate in our hearts. We had not bathed since before our arrest—more than a month and a half—and though I didn't like the odor emanating from my own person, I preferred it in every way to that of Imin. We sat cross-legged before the window, rubbing the dirt from our bodies and thinking up venomous remarks with which to antagonize each other.

The two of us were becoming like mad dogs in a cage, harassed not only by our growing dislike for each other, but by the thrusts of our captors who were doing their best to frame a charge of espionage for me and an execution for both of us. I took to writing notes again but they accomplished no more than those before them. Saiti Hadji, with the Russian, Soklov, began to put on the pressure. Full written confessions were given me to sign; confessions that named every missionary and foreigner in Central Asia as my accomplice in intrigue. As each confession was given me, I would crumple and tear the thing to bits. The situation had reached a climax, when one day Saiti Hadji sent for me.

"Thinkest thou that thou can'st escape this charge because thou art of Amerika? *Amerika* means *nothing* here!" he threatened. "Amerikaluk, we have two others in this prison who have refused to confess. Both are of countries as great as thine and yet they lie here, *Von* for three years and the other even longer!"

(A German by the name of Von Hannekan disappeared in Sinkiang in December, 1933. He was reported killed by Kirghiz; Saiti Hadji's slip of the tongue gave the first definite clue as to his probable whereabouts. Days afterward, musing over the name, *Von,* I asked a Chinese turnkey if there were a *Dugwi* (German) in the prison. His reply was in the affirmative. In his thick Chinese tongue he tried to name the man, but the *na-chi-nik* of the prison heard the guard fraternizing with me, a prisoner in solitary confinement, and called him away to a beating before I got the information.)

Back in the cell, I told Imin what had been said.

"It is better we die than to lie in this grave and slowly rot," he declared. "Ahmad Kamal, once thou and I laughed together and now we can no longer speak to one another without cursing. We no longer sleep. Daytimes I hate thee because thy eternal pacing makes my brain reel; the thump of thine heels is to me as though thou, with each step, struckest me. By night thou hatest me because my prayers do unto thee what thy footsteps did to me. Twice thou hast struck me and every day thou art quicker to anger. I see myself doing the same things as a caged monkey. I sit here, hunched before the window. Day and night my face is turned to the sky; the night is a thousand years in length and when I pray, thou risest and revilest me."

Imin pillowed his face in his hands, continuing in a sobbing voice:

"I stop and pray in here," he held his hand over his breast, "until I would almost burst; then once more words force themselves to my lips, and thou, mad with rage, strikest me. Another week and we shall be tearing at each other's throats with our teeth. We sit here, and when food is brought, each of us grabs for the largest bread; we explore our clothing for lice, rub the filth from our bodies in black rolls. We smell and act like animals. *Ullah* never meant such things for men. Let us, before we live like animals, die like men."

Imin's face lit with fanatical zeal.

"Would it not be better to die trying to escape than forever to wait for these *kaffir* Russ to free us!"

Digging out of the place was impossible. The turnkey came into our cell every day and examined the walls and floor. Only one part of the cell escaped his scrutiny, the barred window; that, he thought, was too strong for us to break through. The bars of half-inch iron rod were sunk into sills of heavy timber. This was the only possible way out and we began to work at it. Not an hour after I began, a turnkey saw me standing in the window and asked what I was doing. It was explained by Imin.

"He is doing *gymnastics*."

Daily, the Chinese guards would come to the edge of the roof that bordered the four-walled court that our lone cell faced, lingering there to throw jibes at the mad, sweating Amerikaluk and his forever-praying companion.

Saiti Hadji, sneering, asked what I was doing, "day by day straining at the bars of the window?"

My reply that I wished "to stay in condition for the day of my release" was met with laughter.

"Thou need'st not be in condition to go to Hell. Thou would'st do better to lie quietly and grow soft as a woman; a firing squad's bullets care not for a little muscle!"

The cross-examination to which Imin and I were subjected was as ingenious as Saiti Hadji could make it. He would pit one of us against the other, knowing that the close contact under which we existed was not conducive to brotherly love. Imin was promised freedom if he would sign a confession involving me. He refused; was promised death beside me, and returned to the cell.

Early one morning, the door, with a clattering and banging of the chains fastening it, swung open. Chinese soldiers took my arms and hurried me to another part of the prison. After two or three hours of waiting, I was returned to the cell to find Imin gone. The little pack of playing cards that we had made from old cigarette cartons marked with the tips of burnt matches were gone with him. I was alone.

In a few moments Saiti sent for me. Once again I was seated in the little room; tea was brought as before, but this time the Russian-Soklov poured. As before, a glass was offered me, but as I reached forward to take it, Saiti's hand flashed forward, the contents of the glass was dashed into my face and before I could reach the Kazakh, the guards seized me. Saiti Hadji laughed as I shook the hot stuff from my eyes.

"Thou art ready to confess now, eh?"

As I cursed him the contents of a second glass was flung into my face. Soklov laid a paper on the table.

"Sign this and thou wilt be molested no longer. Refuse, and we have just begun."

That night, my face still smarting from the hot tea and open-handed blows of Soklov, I planned my escape. I would flee the prison and in some Turki-Jilop's home secure a complete outfit of woman's clothing. With a veil over my face I might escape. Not even the *Hookemet* would dare to unveil Urumchi's Muhammadin women in an effort to find even as dangerous a spy as I was supposed to be.

The moon had not yet mounted the heavens and my cell was enveloped in an almost suffocating darkness. My hands tested each bar of the window, all solidly imbedded, all except one—the one on which I had concentrated my efforts during the weeks of *gymnastics*. Seizing the loose bar in both hands, I jammed my feet against two other bars, and strained back. Memories of the indignities I had suffered at Bolsheviki hands lent me strength. The cords in the back of my neck began to ache and the muscles of my back to sting; with a great effort I put all the strain on my legs. Imperceptibly at first, then gradually easing, the iron rod bent back. The hole was big enough for me to squeeze through, and out of the cell I went.

Abraded toes and fingers painfully searching for holds in the rough brick, I climbed the chimneylike well-wall that led to the prison roof. Try as I might to control it, my heart pounded like a mad thing, threatening to dislodge me from my precarious hold. My legs took to giving spasmodic jerks, each jerk costing me a bit of skin from the tips of my toes.

LAND WITHOUT LAUGHTER

"Relax! Relax!" I kept repeating to myself, knowing that the nervous panic that I suppressed would destroy me if it found a breach in my will.

At the top of the wall, just under the eaves, I gave a short lunge backward; my fingers struck and caught the roof's edge. An elbow over the eaves, then a knee, and I was up. Prostrate and panting, I lay on the roof top. A breeze brushed over me, rustling my hair; the first breath of air that I had known since entering the prison. Despite the agonizing weakness of dysentery that swept over me in waves, I felt new strength flow through my body. Ahead of me, approximately seventy feet away, was the crest of the prison wall. All was as I had planned. Now for a dash to its edge, then to drop over the side—to freedom.

Rising, I started forward. The beginning of the sprint seemed as in a dream, my body dropping forward so slowly and my legs weighted as by waist-deep water. The illusion was heightened by the sudden appearance of a sentry blackly silhouetted against an inky sky. He saw me. His startled gasp was plainly audible and he leaped back, fumbling with the wooden Luger case at his hip. Some one else cried out in the dark and a Luger spat from the shadow of the wall ahead. Its staccato burst was forgotten as another broke loose behind me.[1]

Now the wind sang in my ears. All at once I seemed to have stepped over a void; I plunged forward and down for what seemed to be an eternity. Is this, I wondered, what it is to be shot? With an impact that dashed the breath out of me, I struck flat on my back. Momentarily paralyzed, I lay on a cinder heap. Breath and strength returning, I regained my feet and flexed both arms and legs; no broken bones.

Feeling my way around the dark hole, I found it to be exactly like the well-court from which I had escaped!

[1] I later learned that one of the two guards firing at me shot the other in the face; he died about a week later.

LAND WITHOUT LAUGHTER

Above me, figures loomed against the sky as the excited, chattering guards peered down into the darkness. Voices came from behind my imprisoning walls. A rusty lock cracked and squeaked and, an instant later, a door was thrown open; a flashlight beam struck me full in the eyes. Half-blinded by the glare, I looked into the muzzles of Lugers. The escape had failed.

In chains, a ponderous four-inch iron collar, wrist-irons and shackles, I spent the remainder of the night in an airless closet; all the while despondently wondering how I could escape in my new raiment.

Somewhere near by another prisoner could be heard in prayer. Hour after hour he persisted, droning forth *Sura* after *Sura* of the Koran. Lines, pages, chapters, then books, of the narcotic which is prayer. Once I grew angry at the never-ceasing fall and rise of his voice and shouted into the darkness:

"In God's name! Why not come to an end? Let there be peace and quiet!"

The prayer stilled, then a voice spoke out of the darkness:

"This is the night of Friday.[1] Tonight the fires of *Davsakh* are quieted. This is the holy night. Tonight Ullah may hear my prayer." The Arabic sing-song chant began again.

Removing me from the little cell before dawn, my captors loaded me into a canopied horse-drawn cart and took me to another prison. This was the seventh cell it was my bad fortune to occupy.

With the coming of day I found that the new cell was the best, cleanest, and *strongest* of all those I had heretofore oc-

[1] Jumma, or Friday, is to the Muslim what Sunday is to the Christian. Unlike the Occidental world, in Muslim countries the night precedes the day, *i.e.*, Thursday night in Europe is the night of Friday in Islamic countries. On this night it is believed that the fires which torture the damned are extinguished and the unfortunates given respite until the following eve.

cupied. It was about twelve feet long and five wide. Eight feet of its length were taken up by a raised wooden *kang* that extended the width of the cell. The ceiling was fully twenty-five feet above me and pierced at both ends and the center by six-inch peepholes; even while I looked, one of them opened. A thin stream of yellow dust cascaded down and an eye fixed itself in the aperture; we contemplated each other. The little trap snapped shut and I was left to try, without success, to find a position comfortable to one so bedecked in hardware.

That day I refused food and on the next my irons were removed. The third day brought Saiti Hadji, Soklov, and a Kirghiz. They ordered me brought from the cell to another well-guarded office and there my hosts subjected me to a steady stream of invectives. I learned among other things that a guiltless person would never have tried to escape! Then the Kirghiz, whom I had never before had the doubtful pleasure of meeting, thrust his ugly face into mine and, speaking faultless English, told me that all of my journals had been *decoded* and that definite proof of my being a Japanese spy had been found.

Then Soklov put before me a confession written in Chinese, demanding I sign it. At my refusal another was substituted, this time in Turki. Then came a third in Russian and finally a fourth in English. Like all those previously tendered, the confession involved numerous European consular officials and missionaries. All were supposed to be associated with me in obtaining military and trade secrets of the Sinkiang Government. To sign the confession would be to sign my own death warrant. Ripping it in halves I consigned the thing to the devil and finished its destruction with my feet.

The three, Kazakh, Russian, and Kirghiz, escorted me back to the cell and bade me farewell. This peaceful behavior perplexed me, for I had expected an outburst. Later, the Chinese turnkey opened the cell door and after entrusting the gun to a waiting guard, entered and gave me a dozen or more sheets of writing paper.

"It is to write letters to thy family and others!" he solemnly informed me in poor Turki.

An hour of lip-chewing toil demonstrated that I could not compose the touching, heroic epistles which those about to die are supposed to write. The middle of a sentence would find me staring into space. The melody of a flute caught my ear. Every sound took on new significance, the footfall of the guard, the melodious, pulsating trill of a wireless transmitter as it hurled impulse after impulse over the heads of free men. The setting sun threw an anemic rod of shimmering light through the corridor window and past the barred aperture over my cell door. The sunbeam swiftly mounted the wall as its parent used the horizon-bound mountains for leverage. Multitudes of flies came from dark corners and made for the bar of light and climbed the wall with it. A veritable army of the little things marched in drill formation, line after line, for the width of the beam, blue-green lights flashing from their armor-sheathed backs and helmeted heads.

Such things I saw and doubted that they would ever be mine to see again. I had concentrated on the letters when my door was opened and Saiti Hadji came in.

"Thou art willing to sign the confession now?"

I told him to get out.

"Enough!" he replied, leaving the cell. "At the half-night thy life is completed!"

I was left alone with the letters. I remembered Hashim Akhun and how, the night we left Aksu, he had found the bottom of a bucket so interesting. The hair on the back of his hand, the way the fingers had spread from his palm, all had intrigued him. He had believed himself near death and found such things of great interest.

The turnkey's pace was as steady as ever. Nothing had changed except that I was to *exit* at midnight. Hours passed and the letters lay untouched but for a few abortive starts. The obscene pictures on the wall offended me. I obliterated them. As time wore on the guard's footfalls seemed louder. It was a relief each time they passed the cell door.

I sat rehearsing what I should do at the last moment, when my thoughts were interrupted by the crunch of booted feet on the gravel outside; feet that quickly mounted the stone steps and hurried down the corridor. My door was opened with the usual prelude of squeaks and clatters as locks and bars were drawn. Two men entered the cell, one the Kirghiz, the other a uniformed Bolsheviki soldier. Handcuffed, my arms pinioned behind me, we started from the cell, each of the others with arms crooked into mine. We went out of the building and down steps, then across the shadowy outer compound. The moon was high and full and about it cirrus clouds lay in feathered wisps.

Other soldiers joined the two with me and we walked towards a dark building. The drone of airplane motors filled the air and we slowed to watch twelve shadows glide across the moonlit sky. Then we hurried on and through a narrow door into a room so dark that we lost all sense of direction, and our balance as well. We went down a flight of narrow stairs. One soldier lost footing and bumped to the bottom on the base of his spine, thereby considerably restoring my spirits. At the bottom was a cellar; soldiers stood about, waiting, and polluting the already foul air with cigarette smoke.

Detaching himself from the rest, Saiti Hadji came to me. His head looked puny, perched on its great fat neck, that spread out to meet his sloping shoulders.

LAND WITHOUT LAUGHTER

I wished that I had free hands and a stick that I might knock off his froglike, protruding eyes.

"We part now, eh, Amerikaluk?" he mocked. "Thou thoughtest thou could'st come sneaking through Sinkiang without the *Ghi Pu* stopping thee, *Amerikaluk!*"

Soklov pushed between Saiti Hadji and me and asked in his deep voice: "Thou wilt now sign a confession?"

The two had made me angry enough to trust my voice and I reviled both to the best of my ability, the while thinking that it seemed improper to die with such words in one's mouth.

Some soldier pushed me towards the wall, but not before my well-aimed heel connected with Saiti Hadji's kneecap. At his grunt of pain I wished my foot had been shod instead of bare; my stockings had long since been worn out on cell floors.

The wall had been used for the same purpose before. The conical hollows in the plaster could have been caused by one thing only—bullets. Black stains on the earthen floor were further evidence. My wrists were lashed to an iron ring on that execution wall. A lantern was placed at each side and another before me.

Saiti Hadji gave a command. The soldiers—a polyglot outfit of mixed Russian, Chinese, and Turkis—came to attention. Layers of blue cigarette smoke floated about the cellar and I wished what was about to happen could have taken place under the sky. In rapid succession the squad presented arms and came to firing position, then the rifles were dropped, bolts clattered back. Each man took a single round from a clip and pushed it into his rifle's snout. The bolts were jammed home. Soklov asked again if I would sign the confession and, at my refusal, ripped a page from a little notebook and pinned it to my shirt.

Once more the squad came to *aim* and, filling my lungs, I

282

waited. Somehow I wanted plenty of air in my lungs. At length I was forced to exhale, but then only again to fill my lungs and wonder at how long it took these fellows to shoot. With the muzzle of every rifle on me, it needed only some one to say *boo* and all would have been over without expenditure of a single bullet.

I came up for air; opened my eyes. Saiti Hadji and Soklov were before me. The soldiers stood at attention. Soklov unfastened my wrists. Vaguely, I wished that he hadn't. I wanted to sit down and there was no place but the floor. The big Russian waved a confession before my eyes.

"Sign this and go back to thy cell," he ordered.

I refused. In that instant he pushed me angrily against the wall. The commands came fast. Then, at the very climax and as swiftly as they had been put through their paces, the soldiers were dismissed. Two took me back to the cell and after they left, I lay back, feeling somehow cheated!

I slept until the next night without awakening once.

8

D<small>AYS</small> <small>LATER</small> I was again escorted to the interrogating office. The same three, as always, were there to greet me, and to explain that the time had come for my confession! However, my lesson had been learned on the preceding nights: so long as my signature was kept off that paper, I was safe. This time I laughed at the three. Saiti Hadji gestured that I take a seat beside him and then spoke in a deliberately secretive tone, a sense of evil exuding from him with his whispered words.

"Thou hast no alternative but to confess. Thou hast been treated well up to this very minute, but if thou dost not respond to kind treatment, we shall be forced to do otherwise. We can *make* thee talk!"

While he spoke *Shaitan* Hadji had pinched the flesh of his wrist with a little punch. The sinister tool left a little line of white depressions in its path. Soklov then summoned the guard.

"Think for half an hour, then we will see thee again," Saiti Hadji called softly as I was escorted from the room.

Damning both of them, I was thrust into my cell. Half an hour, then they would try to force a confession. That leather punch was designed to be used on me! There was an alternative, I must prove myself unafraid. Taking the flesh of my wrist between my teeth I bit. It was no use, the skin was unbelievably tough. I tried again, catching the flesh between the incisors. By grinding them back and forth the skin was pierced, the teeth met. I repeated the action; there was no especial pain, only a vicious twinge at the initial pressure, then numbness.

I was returned to the room. Again Soklov asked that I sign. At my refusal, the Russian blandly drew my right hand across the table. Saiti Hadji exclaimed at the two bitten gashes and the blood which dripped from my finger tips. After the leather punch scored three times (it was at least sharper than my teeth) Soklov called a halt to the proceedings.

"*Shtop!* It is useless. The Amerikansky has no feeling."

He turned angrily on Saiti Hadji.

"For thee he would confess— Pah!" With that he made an angry rush for the exit.

Two days later the Kirghiz came to my cell and asked why I did not eat, and at my reply that if I ate I would lie in the cell forever, he replied:

"No. Thou art to depart day after tomorrow; thou art to go free. Thou wilt leave Sinkiang." And, laughing, he added, "That, perhaps, is reason enough to eat!"

Two days later he again came to my cell and explained that Shing Dupen, the Chinese-Bolshevik ruler of Northern Sinkiang, had been very busy and unable to affix his signature to the necessary documents to free me, but that I would surely go free on the morrow. For twenty-five days I was promised *tomorrow*—and always the morrow came and went and I gained nothing but more day-marks on the wall. On the twenty-fifth day steps did come to the door. It was opened, but instead of my being led out, another was thrust in with me—a trembling pasty-faced fellow, shaggy with prison-grown hair and beard.

The door closed and we were left alone. This new scarecrow stumbled over to me. He seemed to have forgotten how to walk, and leaning his body forward teetered along on his toes. Both face and body were emaciated, only two items of his anatomy having size—his eyes and belly. The eyes, sunken and round as fish eyes, were so heavily glazed they seemed the orbs of a corpse. The stomach protruded from his skeletal frame like that of an eight-months-pregnant woman.

This poor caricature of a man fumbled to a seat beside me. I asked the fellow—and not too kindly—who he was and whence he came, for it was obvious he was no Turki. Looking up, he wet his fever-cracked lips with a flick of the tongue; then, before he could speak, fell to shaking as though with an ague. I repeated the question more slowly.

"Who art thou?"

The poor devil kept wetting his lips, then stammered in a whisper that was scarcely audible:

"Hamid! I—I—am from Uzbegistan. I am Uzbeg."

After that effort he was again overcome by a spell of shaking that gradually subsided. While trying to speak, he was seized by a racking cough that left a pink froth on the edge of his lips. Consumption! The very thought panicked me. Saiti Hadji had put this fellow in with me that I might contract the disease— an easy way to be rid of me. Hamid laid a cold white hand on my arm; his owl-like eyes blinked a moment before he spoke haltingly. Pointing a finger at me, he asked:

"Thou art Russ?"

I shook my head. "Amerikaluk!"

"Amerikaluk?" he repeated the word four or five times. Perplexity showed itself on his features; the great sunken eyes closed; he was thinking of something. Then it came.

"Guten Morgen."

He watched me closely to see what effect the words would have. At my reply in "Deutsch," a smile that was more a grimace spread over his dead, sunken features while the eyes kept blinking and exploring my person from head to foot. The tongue again flicked over the parched lips, and my companion began to tell his story, jerky and monosyllabic. He spoke so rapidly at times that it was difficult to follow him. For long moments he would stare vacantly into nothingness, always scratching himself.

"Amerikaluk? Amerikan! I once knew one of thy kind in Berlin. I was on *Hadj* (pilgrimage). I went out through the Hindustan—took a boat—went to Spain, France, Germany. I visited all the countries. It was in Germany I met one like thee."

In a husky whisper, the loudest voice he ever achieved while we were together, he madly insisted:

"I once saw other places than Sinkiang—Paris—Berlin—Moscowa."

Tears rolled down his sunken cheeks.

"Perhaps it would have been better if I had never seen such places. Then I would never have known what I had lost."

Another spasm of coughing shook the man, and he spat and gazed at the pink spittle for some moments before speaking.

"I went to many countries. Then to Mekka, then Stamboul, and across Turkey to Russia and Moscowa." He chuckled mirthlessly. "That proved me a fool and deserving of what these Bolsheviki do to me. My father and mother were both killed by the Bolsheviki in Uzbegistan and yet I went into the *kaffir* country. I was but a boy when I left Sinkiang, and when I returned, just a year ago, the *inkalab* (revolution) was ended. Oh, I had much face when I returned——"

He tapped the sound-absorbing prison wall with his knuckles and with a voice bitter with irony, continued.

"Dost thou understand, *much* face? I was a Hadji—I had seen much of the world—so—the *Hookemet* said to itself, 'That man hath too much wisdom. He hath a brain and he might even use it. We had better find some way to get rid of him!'

LAND WITHOUT LAUGHTER

So they put me in command of a squad of soldiers and detailed me to the placing of lights in every airplane *estanza*.

"I had been to a school outside this dark ignorant country, and I could do my work well, so the mad men that rule said to one another, 'See, he does his work well—he is dangerous—most probably a spy!' While they plotted my finish, I went on laying those little, glass-covered iron pots. I laid them straight down the center of every field; none could find fault with my work. My men liked me, even the *Ketai*, and much was accomplished. But those Bolsheviki, they were searching for some reason to finish me, and one day a letter came from a friend in Germany. They took it and declared me a spy."

He dropped his head into his hand.

"They are mad—these Bolsheviki. They brought me to this place. They locked me in a cell so dark I could not see my own hand before my eyes. Once every day they brought food —a great bowl of water and as much bread as I could eat. Thou seest," he disgustedly struck his bulging stomach, "one eats much when there is nothing to do but eat and pray."

I understood why his eyes were so dilated; he had stared into the dark too long.

"How long hast thou been here?" he asked.

I pointed to the lines on the walls. He counted them—ten marks, ten days to a line and eleven lines.[1]

"Thou hast been here even longer than I! I came on the twenty-second day of June, and thou?"

"On the ninth."

I looked at the scarecrow that addressed me, and wondered what I looked like. The shadowy reflection in the water bowl had revealed little except vague features, a heavy mane and beard. Hamid looked around the cell.

[1] I always brought the number up to date, even though moved from one cell to another.

288

LAND WITHOUT LAUGHTER

Wonder seized me as to what kind of cell he had come from. Sensing my unspoken question, Hamid explained.

"My cell was deep in the ground and black as *Davsakh*. No windows. No air. Just darkness and wet. The floor was mud, and when it rained I feared the hole would fill. The damp and cold laid hold of my lungs, so now they bring me up here to die. And they have not long to wait."

A paroxysm of coughing shook him and passed.

"Thou seest," he choked. "I am about to be given freedom by these lungs."

A night passed, a night broken many times by the racking cough of Hamid, who at the end of each seizure would sink back on the *kang*, vehemently cursing our captors. Day came again and Hamid renewed the obliterated pictures on the wall, re-tracing with a long dirty thumbnail the old outlines. Finished, he sat down again and surveyed his lewd handiwork, remarking:

"My feminine companions. Every one a virgin."

Hamid lay on the *kang*, mocking the restlessness that made me pace the narrow confines of the cell. He counselled:

"Sit back, as I, and wait. Draw some companions on the wall and revel in the way they leave one to one's own thoughts. Ahmad Kamal, thou never beheldest a mule to walk back and forth in his stall." He gave a coughing laugh. "Say to thyself, 'I am a mule,' then stand in the corner and stamp thy feet and flap thy lips."

Hamid hung his head and sticking out his lower lip splatched it against the other, from time to time throwing his head from side to side like a mule. We laughed together.

"If thou behavest like that long enough, thou wilt become interested in finding how great a noise thou can'st make by flapping thy lips together, or how far thou can'st drop thy lip. Stamp thy feet and wobble thy lips and forget the outside until some day they come and free thee. Think what a strange fellow thou wilt be—thy lips so-o-o long and thy feet tremendous from stamping."

There was something heroic about that fellow as he sat there on the *kang*, joking, while disease, eating away his lungs, brought him each moment nearer death.

With every hour of the passing days Hamid became more like a man; his eyes narrowed, his walk changed from a stumble to a stride, and he perceptibly weakened under the ravages of the cough. He admired the flaming red of my beard and scolded me for not stroking the twists out of it. We became the best of friends.

Then came the day when the cell was entered by a Russian in plain clothes. After greeting both of us effusively, he unfolded a quite impressive document and read it to us, in Russian, and very rapidly. I caught only a bit of what he read, and then disbelieved my ears. After he had gone I asked Hamid to repeat, word for word, what the Russian had said. Instead of answering at once, he sat back against the wall from which he had risen at the other's entry. He mused a moment, then, with half a smile, spoke.

"I am to be alone again."

At my urging, he elaborated.

"That paper was from Moscowa, and signed by the Dupen and Khodja Niaz Hadji as well. Thou art to be set free in Kumul and thou wilt be sent there as soon as transportation can be found. They say that thou art not to be released in Urumchi nor to be permitted to return by the road whence thou camest." He warned: "Ahmad Kamal, be sure thou dost not return in this direction and beyond the bounds of Kumul bazar, for they say that if thou art caught this side of Kumul thine will be the death of a common criminal: beheading."

LAND WITHOUT LAUGHTER

Hamid had just completed the translation when the officer in command of the prison came into the cell. The buck-toothed Chinese called another to him and presented me with a pound of roast meat and a box of jellied candies. A chit was given me to sign. Evidently sure that he had endeared himself by making me pay five times the bazar cost of both foods, he called still another soldier. Hamid laughed at the effeminate ways of the "buck-toothed bastard," addressing him time and again as *haramzada* (bastard), the import of which was lost on the unknowing Chinese.

The last of the soldiers had brought with him a coat. I smelled and recognized it as the coat that had been used to blindfold me when first I was brought to the prison in chains. It was leathern, Moscow-made. The officer presented it to me. I asked Hamid what was going on and, shrugging his shoulders, he addressed the Chinese.

The two spoke in Chinese for some minutes, the Chinese continually patting his hair and girlishly adjusting his uniform. Hamid, grinning wickedly, aped the other's every action as he translated for my benefit.

"The *tatluck* (sweet) one says that this coat is only slightly worn and he would very much like to give it to thee except that he is a mere soldier and very poor. He only asks that thou sign for the sum of 60,000 *seer*."

Hamid mimicked the other, daintily patting and tucking at his own filthy, ragged shirt.

"He assures thee that the price he asks is but a third the bazar cost; and I assure thee it is three times that."

The Chinese extended a chit. Despite the price, I signed it. The coat was mine.

When we were once more alone, Hamid took his place beneath the *Houris* and, pointing up to the lewd ladies, wryly remarked:

"Soon, they will be my only companions, and they are as silent and cold as the wall itself."

He lay back, a bit more like the man I had first seen when he had been pushed into the cell, shaking and biting his lips.

"If only I could leave this place and once more see the sun before I die. Ahmad Kamal, behold thou the sun, the clouds, feel the sun on thy skin and think of me. Then, if thou dost not forget, speak my name at *nemaz*." He raised both hands, turned his face to the dark ceiling and passed both hands over his beard. "*Ah . . . meen; Ullahu Akbar; men tookeda.*" (The end; Ullah is great; I, finished.)

The next day the door swung open and as I was called out, Hamid pressed my hand.

"We shall meet again. Say a prayer for me; may *Ullah* go with thee."

He gave me a little push. A last glance over my shoulder revealed him, head thrown back, smiling at his ladies on the wall, his only companions till he die.

The turnkey entrusted me to the care of a guard and slammed shut the cell door. Rapidly we three went down the cold corridor. We crossed the compound, and I absorbed a little of its warmth. Entering another building, the two escorted me to a great, barnlike room. I was told to sit down, and immediately changed from the seat indicated to another in the sun. Clothes were brought me, then my boots. Those boots were the most welcome of all; they seemed the personification of freedom. Shedding the filthy prison garb, the same clothing that I had been arrested in four months before, I donned new, clean clothing. A comb was given me, and for the first time in four months my hair was combed, then my beard. A bowl of water was given me. Ablutions completed, a mirror was handed me, and, after one eager glance, I almost dropped it. What I saw was of the hue of something from under a board that has long lain in a damp corner of a cellar. Laying the mirror face down, I resolved to get plenty of sun before looking at one again.

I found my boots were too large. Twice I examined them to be sure they actually were mine. My feet fairly moved about inside them. The fault was not the boots. My feet, long unused, had shrunk in the cold of the prison and it was a week before they regained their normal size.

The guards, nervous at my parading back and forth, insisted I sit down. In perhaps ten minutes the door opened to let in a little, sallow-faced fellow. The newcomer was lost in his uniform and walked bent over and with a cane. Even his belt and shoulder-straps hung loosely. He took a seat at the desk, letting himself into the chair very slowly, lifting his arm to the desk top with a nervous flirt of the shoulder. It was Saiti Hadji! This scrawny-necked, hollow-cheeked, cadaverous fellow was Saiti Hadji, the Kazakh devil that had nearly driven me, and how many others, mad with his false accusations. His goitery eyes still bulged but the man was but a shadow of him I had last seen more than a month before.

He lamely beckoned me to a seat opposite him, and his first words proved that his spirit, as well as his body, had suffered in the past month. His words were not those of the bull-like swine that I had known before.

"*Yah Ullah,* but I have been sick—malaria and *tuberculos!*" were his first words.

As he named each disease, the man rolled his head from side to side, invoking all the sympathy possible.

"This is the first day in thirty that I have left my home!" he explained.

Looking at Saiti Hadji, I wondered that we both could be of the same faith: Islam. I remembered the words of an old

Emam who had addressed me shortly after I was formally accepted into the faith.

"By the One God," he had sworn, "you have done a thing which will bring you only regrets, unless yours be a great soul."

Angry comment had drowned the sound of his next words. He patiently waited for the outraged to subside, then persisted:

"All that I have voiced is true. Entering into the edifice of Islam, you have brought down the ostracism of all the Western world upon your head. But that is the least of the tragedy; such a trial is easily survived, but there is a greater ordeal. The bitterest draught is that you have divorced yourself from one people to join others who are no better! They are, in fact, much worse, for, possessing the right religion and betraying it as they do, they not only become guilty of treachery, but deify the word.

"You will find perplexity to be your lot; you will be ashamed of the faith and people you have chosen as your own —unless yours be a great soul.

"If you have come into Islam expecting to find men abiding by the tenets of their faith, you have walked into the sea expecting to find it dry. If you have expected to find loyalty, you have entered a den of wolves expecting to find them toothless. If you anticipated knowing a people who look, each man upon the other, as a brother—the only thing elevating one man above the other being, according to the Koran, his greater veneration of God—you have put your hand into the fire, expecting to find it cool."

At these words the others again resumed their abuse of the old man, but he continued, speaking as much to them as to me:

"You may punish me for what I have uttered, but if I succeed in rousing only one man in ten thousand by such words, I shall bear my punishment as service to the cause of Islam."

LAND WITHOUT LAUGHTER

Those words of long ago still ringing in my ears, I gazed upon Saiti Hadji with all the hate and loathing the old Emam had warned that I should know. Here was a man—Saiti Hadji, a pilgrim who had visited the holy *Ka'aba* in Mekka, who by his own admission led the prayers in the *Masjid*, and alternated such holy tasks with condemning falsely to imprisonment and death people of his own faith and race. In anticlimax, the man had once sworn to me that the blood of the Prophet ran in his veins; the shame of such betrayal was greater still.

Now, luckily, I was permitted to witness the recoil of such ill works as this man had been capable of; the hate of all those he had betrayed had returned *en masse* to destroy him. I thought of those who still lay behind walls, for no reason except that this devil incarnate had sold out his own faith and people to the Bolsheviki. I knew what Muhammad Imin or Hamid Akhun would have said, and I spoke for them.

"There is a God, eh? *Shaitan Hadji!* All of that which is written in the Holy Koran is true and it has taken this long for thee, a Hadji, to discover its truth. Thou hast buried men in cells for things they never did, and now their hate puts thee into a grave. This time it is by a just decision; thou, who callest thyself a Mussulman, yet joinest the Bolsheviki in the murdering of thine own kind!"

"Thou art going out of here," he replied, "not because I so choose, but because the *Dupen* decreed it. If I had my choice thou would'st have died the day thou struckest me."

At his words, the guards drew nearer. They knew not what we said by our words, but by their tone. I laughed in his face.

"But instead of my dying, thou wilt stay, to die in my stead."

Saiti Hadji mastered himself with difficulty. He opened his briefcase and spread out papers I recognized as those taken from me at the time of my arrest—passport and miscellaneous visas.

295

"These are thine?" he asked, and at my nod threw them to me.

The passport was devoid of visas necessary to leave the country. I mentioned the fact. Saiti Hadji slammed the table top with his fist.

"They will be given thee at Kumul and thou art never to return to Sinkiang." He wagged a finger at me, "If thou dost —*finis!*"

I solemnly promised that whenever I had the desire to return I would think of *Shaitan* Hadji and that Sinkiang was his country. Then the desire would, no doubt, desert me. The little man scowled. Reaching once more into the briefcase, he drew forth a package, opened it and spilled several pieces of gold on the table top: two gold coins, each ten roubles, a bar of the stuff weighing perhaps four ounces, and a little sack of dust mixed with nuggets. Another package of silver followed, thirty of the dragon-faced *Ak Tenga*. This was followed by a bundle of *Ha Piu*, Kashgar currency.

"These are thy valuables?" he questioned. He pushed a bit of paper towards me, "Sign for them."

Thrusting my chair back from the table, I refused.

"Not yet. Where are the jade, camel bags, and other moneys?" I demanded. The Kazakh scowled.

"Thou hast nothing else. This is all."

At my protest he raised a hand.

"Insist, and thou can'st go back to thy cell while we investigate thoroughly." His eyes narrowed slyly, "It would take five or six months—perhaps longer!"

The receipt was signed. To hell with everything! I wanted only to be free, away from the sound of padlocks and keys. I reached for the money; Saiti Hadji was quicker than I, and taking the gold, said:

"Not yet hast thou paid for the food and clothing!"

296

LAND WITHOUT LAUGHTER

The gold was sent to the bazar and in its stead bundles of paper currency were returned. Saiti Hadji took a counting-board from a drawer and began to figure the amount I owed for four months of prison lodging. Saiti Hadji came to an end of bead clicking and named the sum for which I was indebted—230,000 *seer*. He began to count out the sum.

"Thirty thousand more for transportation to Kumul," he added.

I was to pay for being deported, as well as for prison board and cell!

"How much do I owe thee, Saiti Hadji, and the soldiers that arrested me?" I inquired. "You labored so!"

"This *Hookemet* takes only that which belongs to it!" he growled.

Two hundred sixty thousand *seer* was extracted from the currency on the table, and the sadly depleted remainder, approximating less than one hundred twenty-five *Yuan*, was all that was left to carry me to the coast of China. A journey across Mongolia and the Gobi desert had to be financed on less than *forty-five dollars*, gold!

That night I was taken to another cell and locked in with two gray-faced Chinese, both consumptive. We three lay upon our saddlebags, the lumpiest and most comfortable bed in months, a bed symbolic of far places, of caravans and snow-bound mountain passes, of travel and of freedom. In the dark cell a mouse came out of hiding and perched on my booted foot; a kick sent the thing hurtling against the wall, where its death squeaks soon ceased. I wished that it were Saiti Hadji.

Morning brought a tramping of feet outside the door. A key turned in the lock and the door swung open. Out in the cold compound a Mongol introduced himself as my escort to Kumul. The prison gates were thrown open and we strode out past the grinning sentries into the bazar. The solid clack of steel boot heels against the frozen ground was a free and pleasant sound after listening so long to the soft slap of naked feet on damp cell floors.

We were stared at by all in the bazar. Our gray faces, shaggy heads, and beards, marked us as did our uncertain steps. To walk so far in a straight line after months in coffin-sized cells required some concentration. A truck awaited us, a Zeiss, that roared and vibrated as badly as had that of Nesserdin Hadji. My bags stowed, I turned to exchange stares with the curious.

Urumchi bazar differed drastically from the Muslim bazars in the south. Here unveiled women, even Turki, walked in the streets. Russian girls skipped by, high-breasted, buxom and blonde; their faces pink and expressionless under blonde eyelashes. I remembered Ali Muhammad Khan's flattering "Black Eyebrows," the endearment that he had so lavishly bestowed upon all of Turki femininity.

As soldiers marched by, the Mongol picked out the different services by their uniforms.

"The gray-clad are soldiers of Khodja Niaz Hadji."

He spat on his little finger, a gesture of utmost contempt. Next approached khaki-clad Bolsheviki-Russian troops, biggish and farmerlike, their thick peasant faces knotted into martial frowns, swinging hands protruding a bit too far at the cuffs. The Mongol shook his head in disgust.

"Those Russ would better pull a plough than carry a rifle. Theirs are the brains of *zemindars* and the backs of draft animals. During the *inkalab* they decided to fight for themselves instead of the *Hookemet* and many were killed; it was very sad that any were left!"

We climbed upon the truck at sight of the three approaching chauffeurs. Half a dozen Chinese followed us, loading their belongings on top of the already heaping cargo. A young Chinese, dressed in the height of fashion, a green leather cap on his head, a coat of some checked red and white blanket material and violently blue trousers, came to the truck top. Arrogantly he surveyed us who were already seated. The green celluloid dust mask that concealed the lower half of his face caused the Mongol to fall back in his seat in mock horror.

"*Shaitan!*" he cried.

We were scorned as *Shaitan* stepped over us and began throwing our bags out of the truck, jamming his securely into the places once occupied by ours. Very, very deliberately, my Mongol rose to his feet and then, with more force than deliberation, kicked the stooped "Satan" in the face. Ignoring the cries of the outraged Chinese, we piled our things back into their rightful places and threw out the other's luggage. When at last the abused one recovered from the indignity, the spectators handed his wife over the side.

Another riot was immediately in progress, this time our rainbow-boy versus the bystanders. I asked the Mongol what had been said.

"They lifted her up, and then she told her husband that they handled her in places that only a husband should touch." The Mongol chuckled: "It is very, very complicated!"

An ancient hag came over the side of the truck, bearing in her arms a drooling toad of a child. The effort was almost too great and she all but dropped the squalling brat. Dancing with anger under jibes thrown at him by the crowd, the Chinese snatched his child from the ancient one and gave her, as reward for her efforts, a hard kick in the breast. Had it not been for the alacrity with which the Mongol caught the old woman, she would have been felled to the earth below. Recovered from the blow, the old one climbed into the truck with never a word of protest. But the Mongol took the young Chinese by the throat, cursing him.

"The *Hookemet* says we soldiers may shoot mad people and mad dogs. Thou, I think, art mad, and unless thou changest thy ways, I will blend thy blood with the colors thou wearest!"

Without warning, the truck lurched forward; a dozen or more Chinese came over the side like pirates boarding a ship; we were on our way. I would be freed in Kumul, but all the fruits of the long journey behind me were lost, for my saddlebags had been looted of all valuables—journals, pictures, jade, currency—everything!

We passed over a range of hills and out into a great plain. The road was cut time and again by trenches, mementos of the Tungan attack. We bumped along over the rutted roads past Turki carts, two-wheeled things that had wheels of such diameter as to span, in their single revolution, ruts and bumps that meant destruction to any smaller wheels. At our thunderous passing, the cart horses would stampede, their drivers clinging to the bits and cursing their beasts. One team of six animals went chasing out over the hummocked plain, the cart making tremendous leaps as it hurtled along. When last seen the wild horse team was searching the rim of the world, and the driver, wrist twisted in reins, raced after them, invoking the wrath of *Ullah* on all involved in his misfortune.

Late in the afternoon we came to a pass and the truck halted. All three chauffeurs crawled out of the cab and, standing by the roadside, in unison chanted the many reasons why we passengers should get down and climb to the summit on foot. The grade, forty-five degrees and all sand, was truly formidable. We walked. Our chauffeurs put the Zeiss in her lowest gear, and loudest bellowing, and she followed us up the grade.

Halfway up I spied strangers coming down the pass towards

us. Their faded uniforms were familiar, even at a distance; Tungans—Ma's men! I turned to see how the uniformed Mongol would accept their coming, but he merely laughed and, panting up to where I stood, elucidated:

"Deserters; they come to join the *Dupen!*"

As the others drew nearer, their disrepair was evident. Khotan, whence they had come, was hundreds of miles to the south and the deserters had come on foot. Some, to conceal their origin, had donned their long homespun underwear over their uniforms. Some wore only underwear—their uniforms having long since disintegrated. Thirty passed us with shouted greetings and more showed themselves on the summit.

I prayed that none would recognize me, but my prison pallor, beard, and Russian clothing were disguise enough. Wondering how these men had survived desertion and journey, I took a long, last look at the line of ragged soldiers. The picture they made, straggling over the desert towards a heavy, dust-haloed, setting sun, brought a verse of Omar Khayyam's to my mind:

> " 'Tis all a Checkerboard of
>   nights and days,
>   Where Destiny with Men
>   for Pieces plays:
> Hither and thither moves,
>   and mates, and slays,
> And one by one back in the
>   Closet lays."

9

FROM time to time we pulled into little bazars, took on a fresh stock of melons and started out again through narrow, walled village streets. The elevation at which we rode permitted our looking over walls into many a Turki damsel's garden boudoir. Impertinent as was the intrusion, it offended only the hags and sent the fair flying, veils forgotten, to a vantage point whence they might better see us and we them.

Night fell. The Milky Way spilt lavishly across the sky and a full Gobi moon lit frigidly the bleak desert-scape. Huddled deep in our fur coats, we tried to sleep. Months in prison cells had not given me stamina. Almost asleep, I was wakened as some one tapped my forehead. I opened one eye. It was the brilliantly clad Chinese. He tapped again and came near putting out the opened eye. What the hell did he want? Not in the least taken aback by my displeasure, he asked that I sit up and turn my head in the other direction. To my query as to his sanity, he explained that his wife was to feed the man-child and he did not want me to look upon her breasts.

Twice during the day, the girl had, without ado, opened her jacket and stuffed a surprisingly withered breast into the wailing brat's mouth. Each time the Chinese had insisted that we turn our heads away until his child's lunch was completed. My roly-poly little Mongol had refused on the grounds that he had seen much more horrible sights than either *Shaitan* or *Shaitan's* wife's breasts. Now, it was asked of me, in the cold night, to rise and about-face.

LAND WITHOUT LAUGHTER

Solemnly, I promised the Chinese that if he ever bothered me again or even so much as said a word to me, I would drop him over the side. Back into my huddle I went and hoped that the vampire—he looked such in the mask—would conveniently fall overboard.

Only ruins testified that people had once lived and thrived in this desolation. The walls of dead cities shone ghostlike in the silent desert, cities today without a single occupant, nothing standing but smoke-blackened, loophole-riddled walls. These empty shells marked the path of the advancing Tungans when Ma Hsi Jung and his comrade, Ma Chung Ying, took every city and fort on their march to Urumchi, a horde of warrior-locusts leaving in their wake desolation.

This same silent desert landscape had been scanned by the eyes of Genghis Khan and Timur the Lame, and many others as great! The hooves of their legendary legions had spurned the rocks in ages past. Those same rocks, now disintegrated into sand, swirled at our passage. Horses' skeletons, ghostly in the moonlight, were mementos of the most recent Tungan conquerors. Every hilltop was surmounted by little piles of rocks, barricades behind which the Tungans had concealed themselves while sniping at their retreating Bolsheviki enemy. Here and there the road was divided by a trench where the defenders had striven to hold back the encroaching bandit horde.

The night grew old and still and I was deep in antiquity-exploring stupor, when suddenly the front of the truck dropped with a grinding smash. We stopped. The truck's rear end rose until it stood almost vertical, then emptied itself of its contents, human and otherwise. I started out into space, riding the bounding backs of both gravity and centrifugal force, when still another force asserted itself by grasping my collar and stopping my flight abruptly. My Adam's apple was nearly cored by the jerk, but life persisted even when all exterior momentum had ceased. Turning, I found it was the Mongol I had to thank for arresting my exodus. We were the only two left in the truck. Even the bags we had lain on had followed the path of least resistance, strewing themselves on the surrounding desert.

The two of us climbed down to survey the damage. The front end of our vehicle had fallen into an old trench. The wheels hung over a void; the radiator cap was on a level with the opposite bank; the frame rested on the ground just forward of the rear wheels. My Mongol bent over a wailing bundle. It was our friend in the checkerboard overcoat. Kneeling over him was the old woman, his mother, who had been the recipient of so many blows during the brief journey. The two took turns venting anguished howls—first he, then she.

We turned our attention to the fellow on the ground. The Mongol stooped over him a moment, then, straightening, laughed.

"It is nothing. His chest is broken. Some one landed on him."

Together, we moved the complaining fellow. His mother followed, and after her, lackadaisically strolling along, the unruffled wife. The child still suckled; I wondered if it had lost its hold during the mother's astral journey.

A band of mounted Kirghiz materialized out of the surrounding desolation. Their camels' loud complaining was ignored as they were made to kneel. The Kirghiz walked round and round the wrecked truck, poked into things; took bits of broken glass as souvenirs. Then, squatting on their hunkers, they laughingly agreed that such a catastrophe would never befall horse or camel. Still making wry comments, they went humping out into the moonlight whence they had come.

Blistering midnoon the following day found us limping into

LAND WITHOUT LAUGHTER

Turfan with three broken springs, a twisted frame and minus windshield, headlights, hood, and front fenders. Our conveyance finally expired in the heart of the bazar and its occupants scattered in every direction. The injured *Shaitan* was deposited, his family with him, in a wayside tavern; Turfan was the demon's home. We others, being both hale and hungry, besieged the Turki melon merchants until the truck was literally covered with the bulbous fruit. Melons were the only thirst quenchers in the sterile desert. Once more on our way, we passed the two-hundred-year-old Turfan minaret, whose towering spire stood a monument to the might and faith of a forgotten reign and sovereign.

We passed out of the verdant oasis and into the Gobi. The remainder of the journey was without extraordinary event and despite the three misanthropes in the cab, we, at dusk the fourth day of our journey, reached Kumul. Night having descended upon the desert oasis, the city's gates were closed. Hours elapsed before my Mongol escort convinced the sentries that we should be permitted to pass.

Once in the bazar, we came to a halt before the gates of the Gung Nan Ju's *Yamen*—the compound of the Military Police Commandant. Officers and men met us and the Mongol presented his credentials. We three prisoners, the two Chinese and I, were delivered into the hands of a magnificently moustached Turki, the Commandant. The massive *Yamen* gates closed behind us and a chain clattered into place as they were secured. Free desert gales, stars in the Gobi sky, pungent breezes—all suddenly were forgotten under a flood of memories. But in an instant my fears were disproved. The Commandant addressed me as "Amerikaluk," not by epithets as in Urumchi.

At dawn I found the *Yamen* gates ajar and started through

them toward the bazar only to be halted by a call from the swarthy, sharp-eyed Commandant.

"Amerikaluk! Perhaps thou art aware that thou art in Kumul to be deported?"

I assured him that the knowledge was mine and that even were I offered the post of *Dupen*, I should still be on my way out of Sinkiang. The Turki smiled and waved me on towards the bazar. Free!

As the days passed, we became quite friendly despite the nationalistic arguments we indulged in. Daytime was spent enjoying the unstinted hospitality of Kumul's Turki population, but evenings were squandered, at the Commandant's insistence, in pointless controversy.

A week, to the very hour, had elapsed since my arrival. The Gung Nan Ju and I were conversationally embroiled. I insisted that the Turki had suffered defeat in the revolution, and my host countered, as always:

"Well, Khodja Niaz Hadji is *Padishah* of the Turki, and now we have more face than ever before. Now we hold commissions in the army." He tapped himself on the chest. "Behold me; am I not *Commandant* in Kumul and a Turki?"

Our arguments were interrupted by the hurried entry of a young Chinese soldier. He saluted and spoke rapidly in Chinese that, though unintelligible to me, brought the Turki to his feet. Leaving the room with his orderly, the Commandant threw a promise over his shoulder:

"When I return thou wilt be given proof of my authority."

The noisy roar of motor exhausts broke the silence as the compound's gates were thrown open and the yard was filled with bustling figures. Soldiers were turned out of the barracks to lug heavy cases from the trucks to the compound's center, where they gradually formed into a great mound. At last emptied, the trucks rumbled away in the night, and the gates were once more banged shut.

"A guard is to be placed over this until it leaves tomorrow," the Commandant ordered.

All lamps were extinguished and the night was once more silent. I went into the outer darkness at the Turki's call, and, following the beam of his hand torch, came up beside him and the mound of cases. Laughing at my perplexity, the Turki threw up the covering tarpaulin and enlisted my assistance in opening one of the boxes. A machine gun! On the breech was one word I recognized: *Mockba*. Twenty or more identical cases were stacked near by. The machine gun once more concealed, I followed the Turki to another part of the mound to be shown full ammunition boxes. Other boxes were thrown open to reveal dismantled submachine guns and hand grenades. In those boxes lay war materials sufficient to maintain a month's Asiatic warfare, and every box was stamped Moscow! Having shown me everything he shouldn't, and made me wish I were a spy, the Turki took me back to his office.

"What thinkest thou now, Amerikaluk! Am I not in command of this place—I, a Turki!"

I asked to whom the munitions were consigned.

"Tomorrow night they will be loaded again and taken into Kansu, where they will be loaded on the backs of camels."

"And then where will they go?"

He shrugged at my question:

"That is a military secret!"

The man amazed me; his was a most unusual sense of what were, and what were not *secrets*. There was only one answer to my question. Those munitions had come from Moscow and were meant for the Chinese Red Army.

Those of the Sin-Sui Motor Company daily promised that

they would have a truck on the morrow. Tomorrow invariably came but not the trucks. My finances steadily dropped until there was not sufficient to purchase passage to Lanchow. Bluffing did no good; Sin-Sui wanted not promises, but money. I was forced to abandon hope of swift (comparatively) automotive transportation. A Kirghiz caravan leader offered camel transport to Lanchow, and, beggar, not chooser, I was bickering over the price when a florid-faced fellow in European dress pushed past us down the bazar street. The Kirghiz, displeased at the other's imperious passage, remarked:

"He is made to leave Sinkiang because he is German, and yet he walks like a *Padishah. Pah!*"

A German! An angel, a foreigner with funds, I hoped. The Kirghiz was left talking to himself as I started after the straw, in human form, of a drowning man. Quickly, I overhauled the fellow.

"Do you speak English?"

The man's jaw dropped. To be addressed in the English tongue, in the forgotten little bazar of Kumul, was to him definitely phenomenal. He regained his speech.

"I thought you were a young Commissar, a Bolsheviki! But what are you, you sound like an American, but——?"

Kirghiz and Mongol, hill men, stopped to listen and laugh at our strange tongue and actions. The German, portly and looking exactly like a Communist-cartoon capitalist, insisted I come to the *serai* in which he lodged; a decent dinner was promised, and he seemed anxious to show the curiosity to his family. I was introduced to the Frau and seven-year-old Maedchen.

"Whence come you?"

"Urumchi!" I explained.

"No, no! It cannot be!" They were perplexed. "How was it we never heard of you?"

308

LAND WITHOUT LAUGHTER

I explained in English, and the German amazedly translated for his wife's benefit. My new-found friends asked about my financial status, and if the Chinese had taken my funds as well as my time. Funds, I explained, were the least of my worries inasmuch as I had none over which to concern myself. Assistance was immediately offered, and immediately accepted. We spent the afternoon together. The German asked as many questions as had Saiti Hadji. I became wary. It seemed certain that he was in the same position as I. He couldn't be of the *OGPU*. But if he were?

Taking leave of the German and his family, I walked back to the barracks, uncomfortably aware that I had divulged too much of my story if he were other than what he seemed.

Again in the *Yamen*, I found uproar. A soldier elucidated:

"A new commandant is coming to Kumul, a *Ketai*. The Commandant is to be relieved of his post!"

The Turki came ranting past at that very moment, berserk with rage at the thought of the usurper, a Chinese, taking his command.

In his office he unburdened himself:

"They are sending a *kizungesiki* of a *Ketai* to take my place."

I took my cue and heartily cursed the Chinese: *"Jilopsnungesiki!"*

Satisfied, he continued:

"It is true, that pig, Shing *Dupen*, is taking the Turki out of the army. Soon there will only be Russ and *Ketai* with *miltoks* in their hands, and we Turkis will be given a *ketman* and made to dig in the fields, the same as the Anjanluk!"

The Commandant was in a man-eating mood, so I sat quietly by and voiced approval as he declared, "Now is the time for a first-class war; we Turki against the pork-eating *kaffir*—the Bolsheviki!"

LAND WITHOUT LAUGHTER

For the *kaffirs* my host conceived tortures almost as diabolical as those I planned for Saiti Hadji if ever I caught the man out of Sinkiang. By describing a few appropriate tortures devised by Imin and myself, I gained the Turki's undying respect. On the following day, the Mongol who had come with me from Urumchi was issued orders to return. While he packed, I did my best to get the man to tell me what had happened to Muhammad Imin and the three boys whom I had last seen in Urumchi.

The Mongol, before, had always dismissed my questions with a wave of the hand. But this time he told. Without looking up from where he knelt lacing the saddlebags, he said all there was to be said: *"Dead! Shot!* All of them."

The guiltless Turkis had been murdered and for no reason except that they had been my *friends*. Four more men had been martyred by the Bolsheviki!

That same day the German shook my confidence by warning me against a newly arrived Russian. The newcomer was, according to the German, in the service of the *Dupen* and the *OGPU*. I couldn't quite figure things out. The Russian had *four* children, the youngest less than a year old, the oldest four. If either were of the Soviet secret service, it would seem to be the German, or better yet, myself. I was without wife or children! There was intrigue enough without imagining more.

Days passed while we waited for a truck to take us out of the damned country. Three of us, the German, Wilhelm; the Russian, Nikoli; and I, made daily trips to the offices of Sin-Sui and insisted that they furnish us with transportation across the Gobi to Kweihua, Suiyuan. Once in that city, we could take the railroad to the coast. But getting there was the immediate problem.

310

Deportation order issued at the time of the author's departure into Mongolia from Sinkiang. (See translation on following page.)

LAND WITHOUT LAUGHTER

It has now been found that the Public Safety Administration has sent to us under escort a person named Semujan Shawei (?) who has entered the pass from the eastern route. Besides retaining the Huchao issued by the Province for submission for cancellation, it is desired that the various frontier guard stations examine this document and let him pass. This is important.

Hami High Administrator: Hsuing Hsiao-yuan
(His Seal)
Commissioner of Public Safety: Yü Ch'eng-fa
(His Seal)
Garrison Commander: Yao Yueh Po Shih
(His Seal)
October 25th, 25th year of the Chinese Republic

(Stamp on the reverse side): Examined 8th
Military Police
Detachment at Suiyuan
November 3rd

On the twenty-first day after my arrival in Kumul—departure for Mongolia had definitely been set for the morrow—an orderly presented himself before me. The Commandant had ordered me brought before him. I had a premonition of impending doom, no less. That something was amiss was testified to by the newly hostile mien of my soldier escort. Always before he had been exceptionally cordial.

Standing before the desk of the Turki Commandant I realized that my fears were justified. Without looking at me he took up a telegram and read aloud:

" '*Now in Hami*' " (the Chinese name of Kumul), " '*is a Tungan agenta. Release Megwi arrest and hold for transfer to Urumchi prison.*' "

LAND WITHOUT LAUGHTER

The last sentence was garbled by the telegraphist; by that prank of destiny I was saved.

Two hours after my entrance I walked out of the Turki's office. Much as I might want to tell of all that was said and transpired within the span of those hundred and twenty minutes it cannot be done. Seizing upon the last, garbled, sentence of the order for my re-arrest, I convinced the Turki that the message verified my release. I suggested that one of the recently arrived traders was the Tungan spy. You see, I wanted only to divert suspicion from myself—the next day would see me across the border and out of danger, if only I could delude those who would return me to prison.

Leaning against a wall of the dark compound, I watched as a detachment of soldiery ran out through the gates. They were going to arrest the three newly arrived merchants, who were stopping in a *serai* a short distance down the street. The cold night air chilled my sweat-soaked shirt; I shivered. My throat was parched, so I went over to the well, lowered the bucket, and began to bring it up again. The windlass creaked abominably and rather than risk attracting further attention I went thirsty.

I was watching the heavens, picking out familiar constellations, when the footfalls of the returning guard came from the direction of the gates. Taking myself to a darker part of the compound, where a mound of cotton bales would conceal my presence, I watched.

Thrust along before the soldiers were three thoroughly cowed civilian prisoners. I recognized one as a merchant who just this day had entered the city. He had come from the south, not Urumchi; his arrest had been a mistake. For that matter, the whole filthy business was a fraud. If I was to save my neck they must bear the moment's punishment. God willing, I would be far away by the time this ruse was exposed.

LAND WITHOUT LAUGHTER

Even as I looked on, the three were stripped of all clothing. The Gung Nan Ju had by this time sent for torches and by their light he supervised the interrogation. The three, all frightened, poured out to him protestations of their innocence of any wrongdoing. Viciously he answered them with stiff open-handed blows to the face. The turban of one was knocked from his head to the ground. Sight of such treatment, which I had brought about as surely as if it were my hand that smote them, sickened me.

By torchlight the soldiers carefully examined their prisoners' every garment. The three, stark nude, dumbly shivered in the cold. A Chinese soldier discovered something. He ripped open a coat sleeve and extracted a few gold coins. Disappointed with the find, the Commandant grunted his impatience.

The search was over and the three had covered their nakedness when a Chinese suggested looking through the prisoners' boots. One of the prisoners, he who came from the south, protested. In righteous wrath he exclaimed that indignity enough had been inflicted upon him. In reply a soldier struck him in the face, felling the merchant. While he lay weeping upon the ground two Chinese pulled his boots off. Each took one and, after exploring them with their hands, held them close to their ears, crinkling the soft leather. One of the searchers exclaimed. He took hold of the boot lining, split it, ripping the interlining. The man on the ground shrieked that this, too, was but a hiding place for money. He was ignored. Intent upon his task, the soldier pulled something out of the boot: a packet of papers! Their presence had been revealed by a brittle crackle.

Half risen, the poor merchant rocked on his knees; tugging his beard, he wept aloud. The Commandant took the papers. He unfolded them with difficulty, then scrutinized one by torchlight. Several times in the next few moments he was to

314

exclaim with joy and surprise. At last he turned upon the kneeling man; the accusation he hurled came loud and bitter to my ears:

"Thou art a thieving Tungan!"

He read, " '—discover the date of the fort's evacuation and with it give this man a list of armaments stored at——

Sealed: Fu Liu Jung!' "

I recognized the last as the name of a ranking Tungan officer—we had often met in Khotan.

The three merchants thrown into the garrison's prison, the compound once again dark and deserted, I stole back to my mean quarters. Sick at heart, I lay awake for hours, unable to rid my mind's eye of the sight witnessed from behind the cotton bales. Proven guilty, certain to suffer the death penalty, the Tungan had presented a woebegone sight as he was dragged away to a cell, manacled hand and foot. Bitterest of all was the thought that *I had betrayed him*. The telegram had meant me when it ordered the arrest of the *Tungan agent*. Somehow the Urumchi Government had learned of my affiliation with the Tungan forces and in consequence had ordered my re-arrest. That they had meant the merchant and not myself was unthinkable. He had come from the south, not Urumchi, and those who sent the telegram couldn't have known of his existence. Bluffing my way out of the dilemma, I had cast suspicion on others, to divert it from myself. By some unholy coincidence one among the men I innocently named had truly been a Tungan spy! He would die.

It will be a long time before I forget the doomed man's face. He was as dumbfounded as I by this turn of fate. He had travelled alone—as a respectable merchant—no one had known of his mission; no one had known except his God!

The following morning I, with my Russian and German

companions, mounted the hurricane deck of a truck and went bumping out of Kumul.

Late in the afternoon we reached Sinkiang's last outpost, two little shacks erected near some trees on what had once been the site of a village. On the summit of a near-by hill an ancient Muslim tomb pointed its arched dome towards the paradise of all true believers. This would be our last stop in Turkistan; standing on top of the welter of goods that comprised the truck's burden, I turned to the west. Back there lay the richest that life could hold; and the most horrible. Not yet departed, already I was homesick—for Turkistan.

In the mountains the nights had been as thick with stars and sound and silence as the winter was white and the winds bitter. Often I had taken my blankets away from the caravan tent to where the animals were staked out. Listening to their grinding teeth and muffled footfalls, I had watched the skies the whole night through. Stars had fallen all about me and clouds had gathered and grown, then had come the snows. Fitfully descending, they had covered my blankets, dyed the gray rocks and even the animals' backs with their whiteness.

In the oases and desert of the lowlands the days had been as filled with light and space as the summer was alive with living things and bowed down with heat and labor. Dew had taken the place of snow and the earth and living things had contested with the dawn, each trying to drink up the moisture, like two thirsty horses at a narrow trough. But never could I tell who won, earth or sky.

I was leaving a land I loved as no other. Not for her security, there had been none; but, perhaps, for all she had revealed to me of herself—and of myself. I almost wept.

An hour later we were in Kansu; before halting we were in Mongolia; Sinkiang was but a memory. That night and those following were spent under Mongolian skies. Day by day the temperature dropped; water holes were few and far between, and all frozen solid. Nights were an ordeal, for high winds swept over the desert.

Ours was but a four-truck caravan and Wong, the Chinese caravan leader, feared attack by Red Mongols and insisted, despite our protests, that the motor caravan keep going day and night. Chauffeurs stood up wonderfully well under the grind, considering that they drove twenty-one out of the day's twenty-four hours, under conditions that would exhaust any Occidental in a few hours. We on top of the trucks huddled under a welter of quilts and blankets and yet ached from the cold, and were worn out for lack of sleep. The sixth day found us skirting the Gashun Nor on the extreme northern reaches of the Etsin Gol. More than half the Gobi had been spanned in less than a week. It took a camel caravan full three months! The day was fleeting before the gathering night when we at last halted on the banks of the Etsin Gol, beside the mid-Gobi store of gasoline. A flaming west made sparks of the fine cold sand that blew off the dunes to be carried hissing over the desert's floor.

Despairing of finding a sheltered spot, Nikoli and I set about making one with empty packing cases brought to Etsin Gol as containers for tins of petrol. Then the wind changed and blew directly into our shelter until it became untenantable. Once more we adjusted our windbreak only to have the wind, on sudden caprice, shift again. A roaring fire we had built in the shelter was fanned to unbearable intensity. At length we smothered the furnace with sand and lay down on the warmed surface to sleep until a high sun wakened us. Arising, we shook the sand out of our ears; ground what was between our teeth a bit finer, and swallowed. Our German friend strutted by, boasting:

"I have washed my face!"

317

LAND WITHOUT LAUGHTER

"Marvellous!" we admitted, grudgingly.

Nikoli the Russian returned to the shelter with a can of condensed milk and a box of Zwieback toast that he had thieved from the children's larder. Both slightly bilious after such a repast, we started in search of the German. He was found, as was his bottle of Jamaica rum. Sweet condensed milk, Zwieback, and rum can create disheartening results. Thereafter we spent the morning looking for Mongols and ducks. Ducks were plenty; Mongols few. Those we did see were a seedy, disconsolate lot, who clumped about in their turned-up-at-the-toe boots.

A hail called us back to the camp. Caravan leader Wong declared the caravan was once more ready to go. That day saw mostly dunes and an absolutely dead terrain. Gnarled and grotesque, dead tamarisk forests jutted out of the sand, withered limbs twisted in attitudes of despair. Once, evidently, there had been moisture in this land now so dry.

Sunset made the desert a cauldron of purple and gold and saw us securely stuck in shifting sand mid a jungle of rotting tamarisk. As usual, we got down and proceeded to set up housekeeping. Nikoli and I, determined to avoid being involved in the multiple woes of desert travel with women, struck out with the voiced intention of getting firewood. Before objection could be raised, we were gone. After several hours' labor we had a great circle of tree trunks piled next the camp. It was ignited; the dry wood took fire as though it were impregnated with oil. In three minutes the heat drove every one out of camp!

The German, after feasting on sand and a can of beef, took his family, with Nikoli's, back to the truck where they bedded. Both Nikoli and I decided to sleep within the circle of blazing logs. About an hour after retiring we woke to find flames over our heads and sparks burning holes in our blankets. The wind

LAND WITHOUT LAUGHTER

had changed and put us in immediate danger of cremation. After that we wandered around in the freezing wind until an empty cab was found. Crowding into it, Nikoli pushed the signal button and the camp wakened to heap imprecations on our heads. We had no more than gotten decently cramped when another horn raucously shattered the night's silences. The caravan leader was awakening the camp.

"*Quai, Quai, Tzo, Tzo.*" (Hurry, hurry. Go, go.)

Each shivering member of the party started out into the pre-dawn desert, all taking opposite directions, all searching for a spot protected from the driving wind. All failed, and returned suffering from extreme exposure. Nikoli jibed at the shivering German:

"Aha, Hitler! Don't you wish you were comfortably constipated like Roosevelt and me?" (Each of us had nicknamed the other with the name of his national *Padishah!*)

Every one resumed his lofty perch, blew on numbed fingers and made a wild grab for something solid as we lurched forward. At midday the trucks came to a halt. The caravan leader warned that we were about to enter Outer Mongolia. *Soviet territory.*

"There will be no halts until we have crossed this forty *li* of Red domain." He addressed his next words to the women, who were forever demanding that he stop. "Absolutely no halts!" Then, in an angry undertone, "Not even for childbirth!"

Once more rolling through the hills that abounded in this territory, "Hitler" repeated a tale told him by Wong of how the Red Mongols had captured one of Sin-Sui's trucks on this very spot and held it, personnel and all, for ransom. Nikoli recollected another incident in which two British adventurers had been captured and killed by Red Mongols. Then both men retold the stories in their respective tongues, for their wives' and children's peace of mind.

319

LAND WITHOUT LAUGHTER

That night the caravan halted in the midst of a Mongol settlement and we bribed one young buck to let us share the warmth of his yurt. Day by day, we gradually approached the Mongolian steppes; an abundance of wild camel dotted the browse-covered hills. One morning we awakened to find ourselves in the midst of a fertile grassland, the steppes. A band of Mongol ponies stood a moment to watch our coming, then the king-stallion trumpeted warning and led his followers out over a rolling valley at a hurtling pace. Great white monasteries loomed up in the midst of grassy plains, yurts of the devout dotting the grasslands about them. Bands of horses ran parallel to us and at a better speed than our iron mount could make. Larks sang in the fields and hawks soared over them. After the Gobi the wind-swept steppes seemed a garden, a land of plenty.

A tax collector, his only badge of authority the rifle on his back, stopped his camel to wave a welcome to us. Cultivated land began to show itself, then low, mud-walled homes. Before every dwelling was a sunbaked, grain-covered plot of ground, and over each yard hung a halo of smokelike chaff; this was the threshing time. We entered a jagged range of hills to twist through cypress-studded gorges. Above, hung eagles aroused by our noisy passing. About us soldiers sweated, building fortifications.

War was in the making. Japanese were coming down from the north. Every turn in the canyon road was commanded by a pillbox machine-gun nest, and we hoped that overzealous soldiers would not declare open season on truck-riding foreigners. But we suffered no greater inconvenience than being repeatedly stopped and forced to show our passports.

Out of the mountains, we rode across a no-man's-land of trenches and barbed wire, and into the walled city of Paoto,

320

the first bazar since Kumul, more than a thousand Gobi miles behind.

The city was typical of all others in northern China, in that it supported as many dogs as humans. The shaggy Mongol beasts prowled through the streets, while the hair coats worn by the human inhabitants testified their ultimate usefulness. The bazar was purely Chinese and filthy in keeping with its national heritage.

Our motor convoy at last rolled to a stop before a dingy little Chinese hotel. Nikoli, "Hitler," and I spent three hours removing a ten-days' growth of beard and changing into respectable clothing. "Hitler" discovered that he had developed an eleven-year yearning for bananas, and went into the bazar to purchase and consume five dollars' worth. Those that were green he liked best—at the time. Despite his agonized protests, the journey was resumed the next morning and completed late that night at Kweihua, Suiyuan. Approximately seven hundred miles northwest of Shanghai, we were close to both the Soviet Mongolian and Japanese Manchukuo frontiers.

We had crossed the Gobi. Our desert journey was at an end. More than twelve hundred miles separated me from Urumchi; over forty-seven hundred miles of bitter cold, blistering heat, anger, impatience, war, love, and torture, from Bombay.

My left thigh ached rheumatically, memento of the Zoji La. The opaque spot in one eye told of the Karakoram. The unpleasant saline shock which flooded my mouth whenever any one approached from behind was mute reminder of an ill-omened eve in Aksu. The weakness of dysentery still clung deep down inside me and the scars on my wrist itched, conjuring memories of Saiti Hadji, forsaken Hamid, and damp, dark cells infested with insects.

At Kweihua I learned that I was dead. At least, my disappearance and death in Central Asia had been reported long since. Although news correspondents showed me clippings, it was possible to convince them I was still alive—after all, they are accustomed to resurrections.

Also I discovered the probable reason for my release. A friend had become alarmed at my long silence and, months before, had sailed from the United States for China. He had intended to journey into the hinterland to find me or at least definite word of my death. Refused visas by Soviet-Chinese, he sent letters and telegrams to officials, British, Chinese, and Soviet, seeking information. At length, apparently unsuccessful, his funds exhausted, he had reluctantly abandoned hope. So he gave the newspapers full particulars of my disappearance, practically an obituary, and prepared to return to the U. S. A. But actually his efforts had not been in vain. Doubtless some of the many communications he wrote and wired fell into the censoring hands of Soviets. They had thought it an official inquiry, had made last efforts to force a confession from me, then had despaired and released me. . . . Kismet!

At seven-forty-five one dank morning, a hand was laid on my shoulder, shaking me.

"Mebbe mo' bettah you get up pletty quick, please."

I warned the Chinese porter away, but he persisted.

"Proper fashion you get up now, please. You mebbe want to get down Sanghai—mebbe—ah?"

"Mebbe," I agreed.

"Then mebbe you get up, please. This place Sanghai—eh—ah? Journey finish, eh—ah!"

But he was mistaken. Here, in Shanghai, I was supposed to meet the Tungan who would go with me to America. We were to purchase aircraft, ship them to Iraq—you see Inter-Continent has no rights there and by so doing we could purchase planes direct from certain factories without having to pay the sales commission ordinarily due the aforementioned firm. Ghazi, King of Iraq, would permit us to assemble the planes on his territory;—and there are ways of reaching Turkistan without coming into open conflict with the British. There are ways, but they are not to be written about—until it is done, God willing. Until such time——

APPENDIX

APPENDIX

June 3, 1937. The entire world seemed fulfilling the Tungan's prophecy: "Wars—and wars within wars. . . ." China in a death grapple with Japan. . . . Spain heaping the fagots of revolution about her feet . . . all Europe arming. . . . I found in an obscure corner of a periodical this United Press news item:

> In Chinese Turkistan, vaster than France and bordering Russia and India, General Ma Ho Shan launched a Moslem revolt against the Moscow-maintained régime. Striking by surprise, he besieged Kashgan, a capital fabled in the travels of Marco Polo.

Mis-spelled—both his family name "Ma Ho San" and "Kashgar," the city besieged. Ma Hsi Jung had told me: "When I have one hundred thousand mounted troops . . ." then the number had been secured. The march on Russia had begun. His next move would be to declare Jehad—Holy War! Tens of thousands of mounted warriors, a new horde, would once more make conquest of Asia.

Months passed; a message from a Muslim friend in Tibet reached me. He told of the Turkistani war. Ma Hsi Jung was consolidating his hold on a captured Kashgar, constructing earthworks. The Soviets were sending vast armies to meet him and had established themselves in Aksu, a few hundred kilometers north of Kashgar. All the Russians occupying the territory around Kashgar had been annihilated by the Tungans.

"Now," my friend wrote, "a really great clash is in the offing."

The year turned without any further word from Turkistan.

327

APPENDIX

But then Sinkiang was a country without communications; without a single railroad and with few roads that would comfortably accommodate a two-wheeled cart.

It came at last; an item all but lost amid news more comprehensible to Western eyes:

By I. N. S.—Tokyo, October 21.—Fifteen Soviet airplanes bombed a number of towns in Southwestern Sinkiang Province in Chinese Turkistan, according to unconfirmed reports reaching Tokyo today.

The towns which were attacked included Yarkand, Kargalik, Guma, and Khotan, according to the advices which said the planes co-operated with Soviet troops which occupied Kashgar, Yarkand, and Khotan.

Yinggissar, south of Kashgar, was alleged to have been wiped out. Civilian casualties were reported extremely heavy. The Kashgar area was said to have been occupied by anti-Communist Mohammedan troops since last May.

Tokyo, October 21.—UP—Reports received from 'certain quarters,' believed to be British India, said that a Soviet air force has invaded Sinkiang, west of Mongolia, and bombed cities along the Tibet border.

The report said the attack was by 15 bombing airplanes from Russia.

According to the dispatches, the Soviet forces bombed the city of Khotan, known also as Hotien, near the Tibet frontier, and British officials were considering a "protective invasion."

The report said, the "inhuman acts of Soviet air force, attacking non-combatant citizens and also bombing unprotected cities, were the most vicious ever seen.

Believing (yet not believing) General Ma destroyed, I framed a letter to the Bolshevik Governor-General of Sinkiang. In an effort to take the curse from it—a request for the return of all those of my properties confiscated at the time of my imprisonment—I also applied for permission to return to Urumchi and Soviet-controlled Chinese Turkistan, as follows:

To His Excellency
The Governor-General of Sinkiang Province (Chinese Turkistan).
Your Excellency:
Approximately one year and a half ago I passed through your terri-

tory, *i.e.*, Sinkiang. Having entered the region via the Karakoram and Hotien, I proceeded in a northerly direction with the intention of visiting Urumchi, then journeying eastward—across the Gobi to the Chinese coast. En route, passing through Kargalik, Yarkand, Yengi Hissar, and Kashgar, I at length reached Aksu. It was at this point that I came to suffer the misfortune of which I now write. Arrested on some obscure (and subsequently proved incorrect) supposition that I was a spy, I was confined in the local prison; later to be taken to Urumchi and there held until proven innocent.

While in Aksu all of my belongings were taken from me, not to be returned. Among said belongings were listed several valuable pieces of jewelry (wrought gold). Then, too, there were countless photographs of your most interesting domain; several handwritten books which comprised my travel journals, and several packages of fine silk. None of these did I ever see again. I now ask that you endeavor to find who it was that proved himself unworthy of your administration's trust by such theft. It may be that incident was brought about by some oversight in the executive offices: a thoroughly understandable happening in so busy an administration as yours. It is this latter possibility I prefer to consider.

Realizing your integrity, this party leaves the matter in your hands; certainly it shall be a pleasure to hear that you have located the missing objects—all of which are invaluable to me.

And now may I petition for permission to return to Sinkiang. I wish to carry on my studies (ethnological) which were, due to the press of circumstances, abruptly brought to a standstill on my recent trip.

May I look forward to an early reply?

Your most humble and appreciative servant.

While awaiting a reply I heard vague rumors of the return of Ma Hsi Jung to power. These were all without substantiation, and I could but hope that the answer to my carefully worded petition would inadvertently reveal the true state of affairs.

Then one morning the postman delivered into my hand a thick, heavily lettered envelope; on its face was the great seal of the Sinkiang Provincial Government.

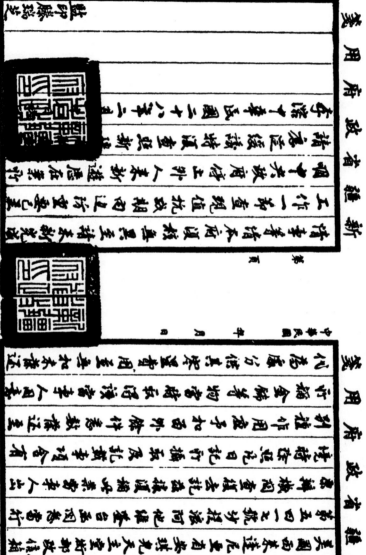

Letter bearing the Great Seal of the Sinkiang Government

APPENDIX

(A free translation of the document.)

Sinkiang Provincial Government—February 28, 1939
Sir:

Your communication duly received, and noted.

The original organ, having investigated the matter referred to, reports that when the party concerned departed from this territory, only his films and diary were detained because their contents were susceptible to other uses, but all other of his personal effects were returned to him. As to his alleged jewelry, etc., the party at the time gave his assent for their disposition to furnish him with miscellaneous expenses. They were not detained, so cannot be returned.

As to coming to Sinkiang to wind up matters, since the Central Government has banned foreign visitors to this province for the duration of this province's present war of resistance, owing to the importance of defensive measures, the application for a permit must for the time being be denied.

Please note this reply.

                Lee Yung, Chairman

Sealed by   Sinkiang Provincial Government.

T'eng Jin-tzu

So! The *war of resistance* by the Tatars yet persists. Ma Hsi Jung lives, but how many of my other friends live with him? There is one consolation: the fury of man may destroy everything that lives and breathes, but Turkistan will not— cannot—be destroyed.

I recollect Khotan's lawn: the horizon-piercing Himalayas, the flaming peaks ignited by the first rays of a benevolent sun. . . . The color dripping from the heavens whose infinite vastness was far too tiny to hold the paints of an extravagant Creator. . . . The first breath of the desert wind—firm as a virgin's breast, delectable as the lobe of her ear. . . . The melodious call of the Muzzin, urgent, music to the ears of the faithful:

APPENDIX

"Ullah is the greatest! There is no God but Ullah, and Muhammad is the Prophet of Ullah! Come to pray! Come to pray! Prayer is better than sleep!"

Ameen

GLOSSARY

Adam . . . . Man.

Adam Ali Salaam . . . Adam: the first man. (Koran.)

Agenta . . . . Agent of military secret intelligence.

Aksakal . . . . White Beard: Village Elder.

Aksham . . . . Dusk.

Aktenga . . . . Dragon-faced silver coin.

Bai . . . . Wealthy person. Capitalist.

Ban . . . . Inn Keeper. Concierge.

Basmatchi . . . . Raiders. Overthrowers.

Bash . . . . Head. Bashi: leader.

Baugh . . . . Garden.

Beisht . . . . Paradise.

Budd . . . . or Böt. Tibetan Buddhists.

Chan'tu . . . . Turbaned Head. A Muslim as designated by Tungan and Chinese.

Chapan . . . . Coat padded with cotton or raw silk, then quilted.

Chaprasi . . . . Menial, serving a member of Indian Government.

Chini . . . . Tea cup.

Chirak . . . . Lamp. An Aladdin's lamp.

Chogun . . . . Teapot made of metal.

Davsakh . . . . Hades.

Dawan . . . . Mountain pass.

Deria . . . . River.

Djinn . . . . Beings who dwell in the middle world, or that region between those of humans and angels. (Koran.)

Docandar . . . . Shopkeeper.

Dugwi . . . . A German as designated by Tungan and Chinese.

Dutar . . . . Two-stringed guitar.

Emam . . . . Elder of the Muslim faith.

Estanza . . . . Airport.

333

APPENDIX

Eutch Talak ......Third or *final* divorce.

Fiji ....Airplane. (From the Chinese.)

Ghi Pu ....O. G. P. U. Soviet secret intelligence.

Gundahana ....Prison.

Hadj ....Pilgrimage to Mekka.

Hegira ....The flight of the prophet Muhammad from Mekka. The Muslim calendar (A.D. 622) begins with the date of this event.

Hookemet ....Government. Political Administration.

Howai Jehaz ......Air armament; airplane.

Hummum ....Steam baths.

Ishek ....Donkey. A very tiny species much like the American burro.

Inkalab ....Revolution.

Inshallah ....God willing.

Jehad ....Holy War.

Jilop ....Prostitute.

Ka'aba ....Inner temple and holy stone at Mekka. Muslim holy of holies.

Kaffir ....Infidel.

Kambagal ....Beggar. Very poor person.

Kang ....A bench or divan constructed of earth or wood. On it the household eats, sleeps, and lives. Usually it extends the width of the room. Outer shoes are removed before putting foot upon it.

Kara Kash ....Black eyebrows.

Kara Kulpuk ......Black hat.

Ketai ....Chinese. An adaptation of the ancient "Cathay."

Khodja ....Pious master. Khodji'im: *My* pious master—endearing.

Kismetchi ....Worker. Laborer.

Konka ....Automobile.

Kumiss ....Fermented mares' milk.

La ....Mountain pass. (Tibetan.)

Li ....Chinese measure of land distance. Less than an American mile.

Makhol ....Right! (The exclamation).

Maroshnia ....Ice cream.

334

APPENDIX

Masjid . . . . Mosque.

Mazar . . . . Tomb.

Megwi . . . . American; as designated by Tungan and Chinese.

Mehman . . . . Guest.

Mesa . . . . Boot that has a removable outer foot to be taken off when entering any human abode.

Miltok . . . . Rifle.

Musaphir . . . . Wayfarer. One from beyond the passes.

Muzzin . . . . He who announces the time for prayer, calling from atop the minaret.

Napa . . . . Two-wheeled, covered cart.

Nemaz . . . . Muslim ritual prayer. Performed five times daily.

Nisha . . . . Hashish.

Nun . . . . Bread in any form.

Padishah . . . . Protecting King.

Palanchi . . . . "So and So."

Paparos . . . . Cigarette: Russian.

Parang . . . . Frank: Occidental. (medieval designation.)

Potai . . . . Measure of land distance. Approximating two miles.

Rakhmet . . . . Thanks.

Ramazan . . . . Muslim month of fasting.

Sarong . . . . Insane. Crazy.

Serai . . . . Compound and stables surrounded by a solid wall of living quarters. Built after the fashion of a fort.

Shamal . . . . Gale—North Wind.

Shashlik . . . . Bits of lamb skewered and barbecued.

Shorwicha . . . . Procurer. Panderer.

Sobun . . . . Soap.

Sodager . . . . Merchant.

Tamasha . . . . Spree. Any form of hilarity.

Tance . . . . Dance.

Tapanchi . . . . Side arm; revolver.

Tatluck . . . . Sweet.

Theatra . . . . Theatre.

APPENDIX

Tongus . . . . Swine.

Turam . . . . My Champion. (*Am:* my.)

Ukase . . . . Edict, proclamation.

Ullah . . . . God.

Yuan . . . . Dollar: Chinese.

Yule . . . . Road. Trail.

Yurt . . . . Hemispherical tent constructed of felts over a framework of wood.

Zemin . . . . Earth; dirt.

Zemindar . . . . Farmer.

THE RACES OF TURKISTAN

NOTE: *Only those nations mentioned in the narrative are listed.*

KIRGHIZ: (Kirghiz-Kazakh.) A mongoloid, nomadic race. Powerful and raw-boned, they are extremely fine horsemen. They are given to the breeding of the Bactrian camel and to the tending of extensive sheep flocks. (Sunni—orthodox—Muslims.)

TADJIK: Aryans descended of the pre-historic peoples who once inhabited Iran and southwestern Central Asia. They are a sedentary people, building their homes in the most inaccessible and mountainous regions. Tadjik blood is probably the purest of all Central Asia's races. Their women are certainly among the most beautiful. (Shia Muslims—heretics.)

TURKI: (Also known as Sart, Uighur, and Chan'tu.) Handsome pastoral people of Iranian-Turkic origin, supposed to be closely related to the ancient Uighur. Some bear strong monogoloid characteristics (facial); others are so definitely Aryan that, dressed after the fashion of the Occident, they would be accepted as Europeans without question. (Sunni Muslims.)

TUNGAN: Some authorities claim them to be Chinese Muhammadins. Others declare they are Chinesized descendants of the true Turkic-Uighur. I am in favor of this latter classification, for legends native to the race declare that they (the Tungan) as-

APPENDIX

sisted Genghis Khan in his conquest of China. It is very probable that during their invasion of China the Tungan suffered contamination of their relatively pure Uighur blood. They are among the fiercest of Asiatic warriors. (Sunni Muslims.)

TURKOMAN: Iranian-Turkic people; predominantly nomadic. A tall, wiry race with regular features and kingly bearing. Ages of professional brigandry have robbed them of any inclination towards a sedentary, peaceful existence. (Sunni Muslims.)

UIGHUR: A highly civilized race that inhabited Central Asia upwards of a thousand years ago. (Pre-Islamic race.)

UZBEG: A mountain people of Turkic-Uighur origin. Their tribal designation—Uz (self) Beg (Master-Chief) or "Master of Himself." True to his name, the Uzbeg is proud, wilful and generally ambitious. An Uzbeg proverb: "We bear hunger, thirst, torture, and death—but never a master." (Sunni Muslims.)

A HISTORY OF THE ARYAN TATARS

(To Those Who Would Know More)

FIRST, it behooves me to explain the designation *Tatar;* then to qualify use of the accompanying *Aryan.* To avoid any misconception primarily, it must be understood that the name Tatar (more commonly and incorrectly Tartar) cannot without an identifying prefix be bestowed upon any one people. This is best explained by reference to an ethnographical map. All Asia north of the Himalayas and west of the Volga, including all of China, Tibet, Mongolia, and Siberia, is Great Tatary. Lesser Tatary cannot be contained by even these vast boundaries, but also compasses all of the Russias, most of Poland, Hungary, and Finland: Pacific to Atlantic!

Excluding Lesser Tatary and with it China proper, for both

APPENDIX

are Tatar by conquest alone, the geographer and historian are yet confronted by a vast land and countless tribal and racial groups. That the name Tatar originally belonged to an eastern Mongolian tribe is no solution, for almost all tribes inhabiting High Asia—Mongol and otherwise—have come to be so classified. The following is a *condensed* list of so-called Tatar peoples.

MONGOLOID OR TRUE TATAR	TURKIC (ARYAN) TATAR	SEMITES AND MISC.
Samoyed	Turki-Sart-Uighur	Turkistani Arab
Tungus	Turkoman	Turkistani Jew
Kulmuk	Kirghiz-Kazakh	
Mongol	Kara Kirghiz	*Mongolized Turki*
	Kara Kulpuk	Tungan
	Kipchak	Turkic Kulmuk
	Uzbeg	Eastern Khazar
	Tadjik	
	Taranchi	*Miscellaneous*
	Bashkir	Turkistani Hindu
	Nogai	Turkistani Tibetan
		Turkistani Afghan
		Turkistani Armenian
		Turkistani Kurd
		Turkistani Persian

Lest I be thoroughly censured for so listing these various peoples, let it be understood I refer not to ethnological treatises —which in the instance of the above tribes are based as much on conjecture as fact—but to the people's own version of their descent.

The Turkic (Aryan) Tatars of the center column all claim descent (with a few fanciful innovations) from *Yapit:* Japheth. They also contend, as does Biblical history, that the Semitic races are descended of *Sem:* Shem; the Negroid races from

APPENDIX

Ham. So, donning the authority of a people's own history, I take the reader back to the debut of the Aryan Tatar in authenticated world history.

1300 B.C.	Humans in Western Europe and the British Isles live in caves, run naked through the forests, and paint their skins blue. The Trojans are at war.
JUDAISM	In Egypt a man named Moses is proselytizing to a new faith and evading a murder charge. There exists a group of city states on the lower reaches of a river named Yellow. About these cities —one day to be known as China—range the hostile "barbarians": Tatar.
1100	Tiglath Pileser I. Solomon I reigns in the height of his glory. The Tatars attack the slowly gathering Chinese Empire.
900	China steps out of legend too, driving back the Hsiung Nu: Huns (Tatars) emerge into the light of history.
BRONZE AGE 700	Bronze is introduced to the Western World. Rome is founded: 753 B.C.—and the Tatars again attack China, for the next six centuries—during which the Great Wall comes into being—keep Chinese historians busy recording attacks by the Hsiung Nu; these scholars comment on the fair skins, blue eyes, and red beards of their Aryan foe. The epithet "Hung Hosa—Red Beard" is applied to the enemy and the name becomes a part of Chinese speech for all time to come, all foreign brigands being so known. Zoroaster, the Persian author of the Zend-Avesta and the Magian faith, is born: 589 B.C.

APPENDIX

Sakya (Buddha) is born: 543 B.C.

Persian Wars
Socrates.
Aristotle.
Alexander the Macedonian (The Great) 356–
324 B.C.
Herodotus.
Constantine.

China, besieged with almost monotonous regularity
through many centuries, suddenly enjoys a greater
degree of peace-of-mind than ever before. Her enemy
no longer displays the oneness of purpose which char-
acterized his earlier warfare. Trouble, brewing on
the "barbarians' " far-western frontier, is the distracting element. Alexander is marching on Persia, Afghanistan, India, and what one day will be known
as Russian Turkistan. (This is a generalization, for
the Macedonian conquests were carried on by Alexander's successors for some years after his demise. In
the end the Macedonians conquered not only the
whole of Bactria, but all of western India, most of
Persia and Baluchistan, then defeated the "White
Huns," to occupy Kashgaria.

(Throughout the ages of conflict, Hun tribesmen
had advanced on China from the North. This because
the journey from Central Asia was made easier by
the marshes on the northern reaches of the otherwise
waterless Gobi. Legend and recent scientific explora-
tions seem to indicate that simultaneous with the
Macedonian advances a general desiccation of the
northern Gobi made the onslaught of the Tatars on
China extremely difficult. In any case, the warrior
nomads withdrew from the Chinese frontier to face
their new foe.

Interesting to the historian is the fact that immediately following the Tatar return to Central Asia
the Macedon-Asiatic Empire came abruptly to its

APPENDIX

end, destroyed by warriors who but a short while before had stormed the walls of China. Not content with Bactria, North India, and Persia, the Tatars attacked, and conquered, Asia Minor. Ever victorious, the Central Asiatics then occupied Turkey. Their tongue was the pure Oriental *Turki*, today spoken only by the inhabitants of Eastern Turkistan. As the blood of the Tatar conquerors was diluted by intermarriage with Arab, Persian, Jew, and Moor, the tongue changed. Today's Turkish language of Istanbul is no more closely related to the original tongue than is Italian to classic Latin.)

The Destruction of Carthage and Corinth: 146 B.C.

Caius Julius Cæsar.

The Tatars withdraw from Bactriana: 56 B.C.

Christ.

China, after more than a century of comparative peace under the Han Dynasty, once again hears the *twang* of the Tatar bow.

Descending *en masse* upon a dissolute, degenerate Celestial Empire, the Tatars assist the imminent fall of the Han Dynasty. The Great Chinese Wall is passed and, aided by the Celestial Empire's internal disorders, the barbarian horde with fire and sword puts the great nation on her knees. Dark Ages, which later are to visit Europe, enthrall China for four hundred years.

While China contemplates a renaissance—not to be realized until the Tang Dynasty—the Tatars eye the lands beyond the Gobi. As before, they come howling down upon the West. Their leader is Attila: known to Europe as "the Scourge of God." Before his death in 453 A.D., he waters his horses in the Danube, puts the torch to Rome, and marches triumphant to Chalons in northeastern France. There he is defeated by the

APPENDIX

ANNO DOMINI Roman Aëtius. Another horde follows Attila: the Avars, who also passed the Danube. After their conquest comes an uneventful period.

The Roman Empire comes to an end: 476 A.D.

500

Justinian (The Great), Byzantinian Emperor, rules 527–565 A.D.

600

ISLAM Muhammad the Prophet flees Mekka and the Islamic calendar begins: 622 A.D.

The Tatars resume their general offensive. Two centuries have elapsed since the Avars descended upon Europe. Warriors destroyed in the conquests had to be replaced and the "Age of Silence" has been devoted to procreation; the arrival of each generation to maturity is indicated by warlike expeditions against China, Persia, India, Northern Europe, and the Russias.

Now two tribes: Khazar and Kipchak, lead a new conquest. They enjoy a measure of success, but none of these later expeditions have the vigor of the Avars, Attila, and his antecedents.

700

The Muslim Arabs are fought to a standstill at Tours, France: 711 A.D.

Arab missionaries visit Central Asia. The pagan Tatars, at first hostile, are won over to Islam. (Only those tribes dwelling in the extreme West.) The warrior faith: Islam, supplies the requisite element to revitalize the Tatar race. The immediate reaction saves Europe any extensive depredations, for the Muslim (Turkic) Tatars attack their Mongol neighbors.

800

Charlemagne: 728–814 A.D.

Fierce fighting between the Turkic and Mongol Tatars. The Mongols seek unity among their tribes

900 in order to save themselves from the numerical superiority of their Aryan enemy.

342

APPENDIX

Islam spreads throughout the Turkic Tatar tribes and they gain in strength.

China enjoys new life under the domination of the Tatars. Her arts reveal a virility never before attained, nor in the future to be surpassed.

Crusades begin.

Genghis Khan: 1164–1227 A.D. Of this great Mongol warrior little need be told that is not already attested by the above dates. In the former he was born, in the latter he died, and between these years he unifies all the Tatar peoples—Turkic and Mongol —captures Russia, China, Northern India, Persia, Asia Minor, and all Northern Europe. Hearing of the advance of Genghis Khan's Golden Horde, St. Louis —about whom rallies the inadequate Chivalry of Europe—exclaims:

"Erigat nos, mater, celleste solatium, quia si proveniant ipsi, vel nos ipsos quos vocamus Tataros ad suas Tatareas sedes, unde exierunt, retrudemus, vel ipsi nos omnes ad coelum advehant." Loosely translated: "Heavenly Mother, let us arise, because if they come either we invoke the devils to return to their hellish pit or that they convey us to heaven." (The play is on the word *Tartaros:* the abode of the damned —a deep abyss below the infernal world. Tatar and infernal became synonymous until the original name was forgotten in favor of the epithet; thus the distortion of the pronunciation and spelling of Tatar.)

(Quoting Prichard, I authenticate my contention that the Horde was for the most part Aryan, not Mongoloid.

"Until the time of Tschingghis Khan the Mongols were confined to a comparatively small territory. If we consider the impression which they produced and the part which they performed in the history of human events, the Mongolian nation appears to have been wonderfully small, and in respect of numbers

343

APPENDIX

insignificant. Even in the armies of Tschingghis and his successors the number of Mongols was inconsiderable in comparison with that of the Turks, who, though at first unfortunate in arms against their more barbarous foes, yet in the sequel gained victories under the banners of Mongolian leaders, and formed at all times the body of those numerous armies which were said to increase like a snowball in their progress.")

Maintaining the rule of their predecessor, the successors of Genghis Khan—Ertoghrul, Hulaku and Kublai—hold sway over Asia for two generations. Ertoghrul raids the Southwest, capturing Jessin in Asia Minor. Joining with the Seljuk Turks, he then takes Turkey. (Dying in 1288 A.D., Ertoghrul leaves a son, Osman, to rule in his stead. So begins the Othman (Ottoman) Dynasty of Turkey, and that nation's expansion as a world power.)

Hulaku pushes on towards the West, capturing Baghdad in 1258 A.D., utterly destroying the Arab civilization and terminating the Abba'sid Caliphate by murdering Musta'sim, his two sons, and all relations.

In the Eastern Mongol domain Kublai Khan rules as monarch of China. But immediately following the unrelated fall of Acre, 1291 A.D., last stronghold of the Christian Crusaders, internal unrest again begins the destruction of a Tatar Asiatic Empire. Those Aryan Tatars not already Muslim adopt the faith and forthwith turn away in disgust from their Mongol allies. The Aryan Tatars engage in a series of revolts against ruling Mongols.

1300

Renaissance in Europe.

The Mongols, strength dissipated by internal wars and their adoption of effete Buddhism, once again find themselves outside the "Gates of Han." Returning to the insignificance from which their great national Genghis Khan had rescued them, the once

APPENDIX

powerful Mongols stagnate, their power at an end for all time. Sustained by Islam, the Aryan Tatars fare otherwise. Roaming to the West, they find a new leader in Bokharia:

Tamerlane: Emir Timur (The Iron Prince), 1334–1405 A.D.

Thundering down upon India, Afghanistan, Persia, Kurdistan, Baghdad, and Asia Minor, the armies of Timur achieve everything they attempt. India suffers as never before and in Baghdad the descendants of Hulaku Khan are overthrown. Damascus and Aleppo fall before the invincible Timur. Sultan Bayzid is defeated in the battle of Angora. This, unfortunately, is the last of the great military successes to be enjoyed

1400

under the banners of Timur, for in 1404 A.D., while marching on China, he dies. His western dominions —ruled in turn by Timur's son and grandson: Shah Rukh and Ulug Beg—gradually crumble away and the Timurid Dynasty comes to an end with the latter's murder in 1449 A.D.

America is visited by Columbus: 1492 A.D.

1500

1600

1700

1800

The last of their great leaders gone, the Tatar tribes break into individual units. No new leader arises to lead the Tatar nation in world conquest; instead, they are governed by tribal *Begs* or Chieftains. Warlike activities are limited to raiding Persia, Tibet, Kashmir, Badakshan, and Asiatic Russia: object —loot and slaves. The Tatars are feared as brigands and are so mentioned by the historians of the aforementioned nations.

Russia subdues the sedentary Tatars dwelling west of the Pamir Mountains: 1867 A.D. Capturing Bokhara, Russia liberates tens of thousands of slaves. The nomad tribes resist the Tsarist efforts to settle them on "reservations." Eastern (Chinese) Turkistan enjoys several revolts against Chinese rule. The whole of Central Asia is torn by periodic revolutions against

345

APPENDIX

foreign rule. In the early 1920's the Soviet regime, their doctrines having been spurned by the Tatars, massacre tens of thousands of their Muslim enemy; starving to death (according to the report of His Britannic Majesty's Consul to Turkistan) over three quarters of a million people.

Perpetual skirmishing against Russian and Chinese authority persists to the date of this writing. So ends this history of the Aryan Tatar. But one thing must be remembered: there are several millions of these people inhabiting Asiatic Russia and Chinese Central Asia. They are as virile today as in the terrible years of Genghis and Timur. Patiently, awaredly, they await—a leader.

IN CONCLUSION

This, obviously, has been but a martial history. That the dominion of confusion once knew a culture surpassing that of Europe's most glorious age is also history.

To those dwelling in the land of Golden Samarkand, Silken Bokhara, and Jade Khotan, I offer my most humble salaams.

To you who have read of the land without laughter, my respects.

AHMAD KAMAL

346

9 780595 010059